MONSTROUS HEART

MONSTROUS HEART

CLAIRE McKENNA

HARPER
Voyager

Harper*Voyager*
An imprint of HarperCollins*Publishers* Ltd.
1 London Bridge Street
London SE1 9GF

www.harpervoyagerbooks.co.uk

First published in Great Britain by HarperCollins*Publishers* 2020

1

A catalogue record for this book
is available from the British Library

ISBN 978-0-00-833712-4 (HB)
ISBN 978-0-00-833713-1 (TPB)

Set in Sabon LT Std by Palimpsest Book Production Ltd,
Falkirk, Stirlingshire

Printed and bound in Great Britain by CPI Group (UK) Ltd, Croydon CR0 4YY

MIX
Paper from
responsible sources
FSC™ C007454
www.fsc.org

This book is produced from independently certified FSC™ paper
to ensure responsible forest management.

For more information visit: www.harpercollins.co.uk/green

For Mum

Book One: Vigil

1

It was only when the Coastmaster

It was only when the Coastmaster turned to remonstrate the old man struggling to load the Siegfried's voluminous trunk that Arden Beacon seized the moment and made her escape.

She sidled behind the wheels of the automobile — a thing callously ostentatious in this wild country — and walked off with such a laboured pretence of a casual stroll that it could not be seen as anything but. With each step she feared Coastmaster Justinian's realization that she was not waiting patiently for him, but had instead slipped his leash.

A sharp turn at a bluestone wall, and then Arden was free.

Out of his sight she felt overcome with relief, and had to lean against the salt-scored stones and gulp chilly air before she felt remotely whole again.

Had it been so long since she wasn't confined like a criminal under house arrest that she didn't know quite what to do with herself? This was the first time since she'd arrived in Vigil that Mr Justinian had allowed her out of the Manse, his huge family estate that overlooked the small, coarse coastal town. The instinct to make a sudden getaway had come with such an awful slug of panic she'd almost been inclined not to move at all.

Hadn't he told her it was *dangerous*, hadn't he told her . . .?

1

But he'd spent a month telling her these things about Vigil, and her thudding heart and acid stomach were evidence enough of the contempt she held for Mr Justinian, the man who was both the Master of the Coast and her employer. He had made it clear he wanted to be more to her, still. Arden shuddered.

Still, forced to endure his hospitality, Arden had observed Mr Justinian with a calculating eye and taken his measure. She discovered that foremost her host had a predilection towards causing humiliation. It delighted him to be petty, and mean; and so she had grasped the opportunity to be well away from him while his voice still remained fixated on castigating the poor elderly porter.

'You fool, you'll break every dish in that trunk! Put some backbone into it, guy, or I'll have the Magistrate charge you with the damage . . .!'

Mr Justinian would occupied for quite a while longer. Arden straightened her jacket and skirts and looked down a street undergoing some kind of market day. Market day was trading day in this town where even the dread sea-serpent, *maris anguis*, could find itself pickled in salt and up for sale with the lumpfish. The siren song of trade brought the coastal dwellers out of their hamlets and huts, hauling with them their spoils of the sea. A row of trestle tables fronted anonymous doorways. Each table was topped with the ocean's produce laid out like a museum of grotesque curiosities. For every recognisable ichthyosaur in a zinc tub filled with ice there bobbed something ghastly and incomprehensible; fish with ten eyes, a barnacle the size of a woman's torso.

Arden set off, searching for the experience that would make her brief sojourn into freedom worthwhile, and instead found to her sinking disappointment that her host had not lied to her. Vigil was both grim and drab in appearance and utility. An oily yellow mist shrouded the slate roofs and slunk about the chimney pots, giving everything a murky air. The cold air had a burned and salty miasma, despite it having drizzled earlier. Arden startled at the tootling of foghorns as the fishing boats came into the harbour. People wore the odd uniform of the shore: salt-country linens dipped in flaxseed oil and fish-tallow, shirt-collars embellished in bleached thread, plain hogwool jumpers knitted thick and warm.

All this strangeness, but no real sense of *blood*. No impression of the power that eddied and washed through her own hot northern country like a tide of whispers, that great sympathetic connectedness with the manifestations of life. No *Sanguis*.

Blood was the great divide that separated the country of Lyonne from the wilder climes of Fiction. The talents that had once been so powerful in this land were now all but forgotten. Once upon a long time ago Arden would have found kin here, talented users of blood like herself.

Arden rubbed her hands, and felt the cut-coins beneath her soft leather fingerless gloves catch and tug from where they'd been newly sewn into her palms. Before the Seamaster's guildsman had come into her Portmaster's salty office with bad-news and orders wrapped up in a vellum scroll, she'd kept respectable employment as a lead signaller upon one of the busiest trading harbours in the world. She had been *Sanguis Ignis,* flame-keeper. Respectable.

But with a single request she had been sent south to this place where no *ignis* had been born for a hundred years. Nobody would share what she was. She would be at best a novelty come from far away. At worst . . . well. There was no bottom to that particular pit.

When Arden walked past one market table, a scarred, bearded man touted her in a foreign language. Old Fictish, the dying tongue of the shorefolk of these cold, grey southern oceans. Then he stopped, and stared.

Arden pulled her fine leather coat about her, feeling as much an outsider as she had at any time in her life. If she thought the Fictish people backwards, then they would see her as inexplicably strange, with her sun-embraced complexion, the bright colours of her clothing, and the waxed cotton of her skirt still creamy and un-stained by the oily coal that heated every rude little home here.

'Roe for sale, madam, sturgeon eggs? Would you like a taste?' he repeated in a passable Lyonnian.

'I'm not buying anything today, I'm sorry,' Arden replied, even though she didn't even know what he was trying to sell her, for the mess in front of him was as unlikely to be caviar as it was anything edible. He shrugged, unconcerned with her disinterest, as she was not quite his usual customer anyway.

There wasn't much of a town centre to be had, and soon she found herself back on the waterfront again, where six feather-footed dray horses provided the counterweight to a pulley and a load bound for an overladen cargo boat. Arden stayed to watch at the marvel of such a thing, for in Lyonne's capital city of Clay Portside a *sanguis pondus* could make a counterweight weigh whatever it had to, ten tonnes if needed, and no effort was required except a simple pulley. Just as she suspected, no blood here in the country of Fiction, no control over elemental forces, just pure labour.

From the waterfront she had her best view yet of Vigil clawing itself from the sea as a hillocky mess of factories and trade offices fronting a sheltering port. The region played host to fish-processing warehouses, one merchant hotel, and a clumping of lonely, ugly little houses with tiny windows. It had not always been so miserable and backwards, perhaps. At one stage in the recent past there had been an effort to modernize the town, for wires still occasionally strung between lamp posts, evidence of *elektrifikation*, that startling new technology. Yet on closer inspection the wires hung lax and broken, the lamps in their curlicued galleries browned out, their internal globes grey with a fine ash from where the filaments had charred away.

A shout and Andrew whirled about, expecting to have been discovered by her jailer.

Instead of Mr Justinian however, it was a rotund man with a publican's medallion about his neck, fleeing his own establishment. Vigil's lone merchant inn, the *Black Rosette*, was at three storeys high the largest building in town, ramshackle in stone base and tin cladding. The entirety of the ground floor seemed to have become a cross between a pub and charnel house, for whatever drama was going on inside the Black Rosette tavern, it caused not a few strangled shrieks and cries for mercy.

A man in an oily duffel coat staggered out of the warped saltwood doors, barking for reinforcements. In answer, to which three men ran in. An intense curiosity made Arden linger a moment. Not more than a breath later, the fight that had begun in the Black Rosette's stifling interior burst its banks and spilled out across the fish-gut cobbles of the Vigil waterfront.

Two men, caught in a savage embrace. It was a hopelessly unequal combat, for one was bearish and older, armed with twelve dangerous inches of boning knife, the other a slighter man blinded by a bloody gash across his forehead.

The boning knife darted towards the younger man's pale chest and snarled itself in the grey linen of its victim's shirt. Tied up in threads the two men fell against a table burdened with a decapitated ichthyosaur head, narrowly missing the row of serrated teeth as the scuffle took them past the carcass, and in doing so they collected Arden, inconveniently in the fight's way.

'Oh!' she cried, and struck the ground with her shoulder, felt her coat tear and a hot pain flower from her elbow.

The fall gave them all only a brief pause. The men were back at each other immediately, locked hand-over-hand around the boning blade while Arden rolled onto her back, stunned and breathless. Beside her the two brutes reached a violent stalemate over control of the knife.

Someone grunted a curse-word in Old Fictish. The older man took higher ground, rolled upon his opponent and pinned him to the cobblestones. The blade-steel blurred in the fringes of her vision before stabbing into a cobble-join inches from Arden's nose.

'Devilment!' she cried out. 'Watch yourselves!'

In that sliver of breath between his living and dying, the younger man's head turned towards Arden. She met a pair of eyes from the distance of a hand span, and all she could see was dark iris in a bloodied face, inhuman almost, and yet . . .

There was there a broken nobility that did not belong on

a monster's face . . . and a suffering too, of the kind one only saw in children, or the carvings of salvagewood saints in poor-man's churches. They were close enough to kiss. A second ago either one of them could have died from a blade through the skull.

The knife lay between them, the white bone handle splatted with blood.

An old dockworker's instinct made Arden snatch the knife out of the cobbles and toss the blade away before either man could retrieve it. Then the demonic face was gone and the brawl was back up again, this time a thankful distance away. Arden picked herself up, chest cavity twanging with pulled ligaments and crushed organs, the fine leather sleeve of her only coat torn to shreds, the skin on her elbow pebbled with rash. The men continued to heave bloody-fisted blows at each other.

How could you have missed a bar fight? Arden scolded herself as she brushed away stringy intestines and grey pebbles. She should have known that dance in three acts all too well; the gust of hot, hop-heavy wind from the flung-open tavern doors, the roil of spilled bodies and flailed fists, and the denouement where someone came close to joining the lamentable list of tavern-deceased.

The younger of the combatants had clearly grown weary of this entertainment, taking only two more hard punches to the torso before turning the fight to his advantage. An upward thrust of hip, and he upended the bearish man onto the cobblestones.

Without a word to yield or surrender, the victor took to pummelling the snarling face of the conquered until a flap of skin sheared clean off the eye socket. Blood across the stones. Blood thundering through Arden's arteries, for suddenly she could feel . . .

Sanguis? No, it was impossible. The talent was gone from here. It must be her panic, making her sense power where there was none.

Something small and wooden escaped the tangle. Not a

weapon this time. A turned black mangrove-wood handle with a screw thread of brass, such as would prime the oil in a ship's pilot-light.

The handle rolled several feet before bumping against the toe of Arden's now woefully scuffed patent leather shoe. She was loath to touch it, for the handle's owner was upright now, a demon-faced man, taller and more brutish than she had thought him at first, his pale chest working like bellows as the blood runnelled from the broken skin of his knuckles. She could not even tell the colour of his hair, for blood from his forehead now coated his scalp with a wave of sheeny black.

How quick the fight had been, how expedient, how unnaturally *silent*.

In Lyonne, police or militia would have crowded around the scene in an instant. Strangers would have pulled the two apart. Shrieks and screams. Accusals might have been shouted and another fight start elsewhere, for in the big city such emotions were as infectious as a plague.

And she would *not* have been left to stand there unassisted in a state of fish-and-cobble-tumbled mess.

The street took on the hush of a sermon. The priest of this hard message spat blood from his mouth and indifferently wiped gore from his beard. He glared about at his witnesses, challenging the other equally bestial fellows ashine in their waxed canvas and fishmongers' overalls to step forward and make their claim.

Nobody spoke. They averted their eyes from him, and went back to what they were doing in the dreary marketplace before the necessary interruption that passed as a trade discussion in this place. A few adjusted the coin they were charging for their bloodied sacks of produce, scrawling higher prices on the slates before facing them outwards again.

Arden sighed at her own hesitations, then with a groan of effort picked up the screw-thread handle, and held it out to its owner.

'I presume yours?'

His attention was upon Arden for less than a second, only long enough for them to acknowledge to each other that she was insignificant and he was grotesque. Despite the muck, she noticed his bearing at once. He was different enough from the locals that she understood why he might attract the ire of fellows naturally suspicious of differences. His body was raw-boned and spare, hewn by necessity. His bloodied beard was a lighter brown than was usual on these shores, and in danger of gingering. There was no sign of the pelt of full-torso hair which appeared to grow abundantly on the Fiction men as if in response to the bitter climate, or the barrel chest built to tackle a fully laden net of monkfish. Though his arms were unmarked, under the tatters of his clothes she spied tattoos blooming across his back and flanks, a pattern of blue fish-scale chevrons, as if he were a selkie interrupted mid-transformation, and had decided to stay on land rather than the sea.

Stayed on land for love, she thought ridiculously, then immediately berated herself, for who could love such a terrifying creature enough that he should return it in kind?

She had thought his eyes dark, but they were Fiction-blue. A common shade. Eyes that averted as he took the handle out of Arden's hands, shoved it back into his belt and returned to the tavern to resume whatever conversations had perpetuated such a disagreement.

Not even a thank-you. His victim lay bleeding on the street, forgotten.

The fight might have been silent, but that did not mean it had gone unnoticed. Mere minutes later the person Arden had been trying to avoid before the fight made his unwelcome reappearance.

He slid in behind her, exhaling a loud indignant rasp of breath in her ear. His voice followed, both sulky and wheedling. 'You saw the fight? It is the way things are settled here in Fiction, in blood and violence. The ignoble creatures of the Darkling Coast do not bargain with words, if they consent to bargain at all.'

Then there it was, the male body pressing insistently against her back, pretending support, but hoping for the other thing too. A sharp stab of irritation made Arden grimace. She pulled away from him and affected a smile of bewildered relief, as if his appearance baffled her utterly.

'Coastmaster Justinian, I'd wondered where you'd gotten to.'

'What happened? I said explicitly for you to remain close.'

'I'd thought you were following me, when I said I was going to look at the market. Then I was lost in the crowd. I didn't realize you were only instructing the old man, and not exactly helping him.'

His eyes narrowed. Peacock he might have been, but Mr Justinian was not stupid. There was hardly a crowd on a Vigil market day. Arden had evaded him. No mere accident had made her slip away while his back was turned.

'You do understand you may call me Vernon, now? We are not strangers to each other.'

His hand slithered about her waist. The flinch was instinctive. Handsome he might have been, with his coif of pomaded hair and smooth chin, his height six foot by the old measure, grey eyes the colour of an institutional slate, perhaps some hint of a tan to his skin that a distant and more noble ancestor had begrudgingly gifted.

But something in the Coastmaster's features was small and bitter. *Snivelling*. As if the world owed him more than the sizable portion he'd been given, and he resented any other soul who merely received a fraction of his advantages.

For a woman newly arrived at this town under the employ of the powerful Seamaster's Guild, Coastmaster Justinian was the only thing close to an equal associate she had. Even though she was *sanguis* and he was not, they were both of them isolated aristocrats in a way, graduated from Northern technical academies, degree-holders beholden to the great service Guilds that linked the two countries into one fraternal parliament. It made a sort of sense that they should cultivate a professional partnership.

The man's constant touching, well, that was merely a Fiction trait, was it not? Certainly, the cold weather made even bare acquaintances huddle.

'. . . now you have made a fool of yourself by running off unaccompanied.' Mr Justinian continued to scold Arden while steering her towards the row of trestles that made up the last of the marketplace stalls. 'Fortunately you must only contend with appearing slovenly in public.'

She held the sharp tongue in her head that would have corrected him, *I have seen more and bloodier dock fights than this one, and I'd prefer a hundred of them rather than one more day with you.*

These things she would have said, if her position in Vigil was not so dreadfully fraught and insecure. Though she had taken her orders dutifully, coming to Fiction had meant abandoning her secure signaller's position in Clay Portside. If she lost this one, she would be effectively over-specialized and unemployed. This was a bad position for a *sanguis* to be in.

So Arden kept her counsel, and stored the little nuisance in a mental glory box of accumulated offences.

Mr Justinian steered her back towards the main street with its row of trestles while maintaining his lecture.

'. . . the worst of the reprobates operate out of that establishment and upon these streets. See? *This* is why I have kept you in the safety of the Manse all this time, despite your obvious lack of gratitude. I have saved you from the worst outcomes that occur when men gather.'

'They rather seemed more concerned with their own arrangements,' Arden said, pulling away from him, and gladly so, for the Coastmaster's hands were never content to rest upon her middle and had the unfortunate habit of crawling up towards the undersides of her bosom or the smallest part of her back. 'My standing there was completely accidental.'

'Oh, so you think yourself lucky for having escaped their attention?' Mr Justinian said mulishly.

'I do, in fact.'

He picked at the ruined sleeve of her coat. 'Go buy a replacement for your torn coat and charge it to the Guild. Then we can leave this place. But don't wander.'

I'll wander off however I like, you insipid creature, Arden thought ferociously, her anger a physical pain that could not be soothed by her speaking the curse aloud, so remained inside her like a swallowed coal that did not cease to burn.

Arden picked in despondent indecision at the mess of fisherman's clothing with gloves too fine for a village on the edge of nowhere, until her arms smelled of fishwax and linseed oil.

She had wasted so much time shut inside Mr Justinian's decaying baronial estate, and at her first breath of liberty all she'd been allowed to see were street-fights and offal sellers. Despair – always so close and so suffocating – had fermented in her time under curfew. She had heard the domestic staff talk behind closed doors or under stairs. To them, Arden Beacon was not a professional guildswoman sent from the great ports of Clay Portside. She was merely produce fatted up for the eventuality of Mr Justinian's bed.

'A devil's curse upon you, Mr Justinian,' she said beneath her breath, tossing aside a scale-speckled pair of trousers, 'and curse you, Mr Lindsay, for—'

The bronze flash caught her by surprise, stopped at once the bleak train of her thoughts. What imagination was that, her seeing such a thing in all these stained linens and thistle-cottons?

Arden dug in deep again and disinterred her find – an odd, slightly sheened garment – out from the knot of unwashed rags.

She raised to the day a thing that in her hands made no sense.

A coat. A stout, utilitarian coat cut for a female worker of hard ocean climates. Not too long in the hem though; no loose fabric to foul a hurried journey up stone steps in a high storm. A thing rightly made of old canvas and felted wool, worn on a body until it fell to pieces.

But the fabric . . .

Arden had to rub the collar with her fingers, make certain her earlier fall was not causing her to see wonders. There was only one creature alive that could supply such a hide. Leather as bright as an idol's polished head and with a crust of luminescent cobalt-blue rings across the arms and yoke. Subtle grading to black when it hit the light just so.

She turned the coat around and her breath caught. She had not expected the fabled *kraken crucifix*, the terrifying pattern of a sea-monster's crest. By all the devils of sky and blood, you'd have found its likeness only in a Djenne prince's wardrobe in Timbuktu, not a filthy rag pile at the edge of the world, and yet here it was; hidden away with thrice-mended broadcloth trousers and sweaters that were more knots than knits.

Before Arden could inquire about the article, her benefactor already had his hand about the coat's collar.

'Let me put that aside for you,' Mr Justinian said and, without asking, slid in between her and the table, ready to yank Arden's prize away. 'This is not suitable.'

Despite her relatively short stature, and the dark, fragile air of over-breeding about her, Arden was no pushover. Growing up within the labyrinthine map of the capital city docks, one learned in the hardest of ways those streetwise traits anybody needed to survive. She saw the snatch coming in Mr Justinian's beady eyes before he made his move, and quickly secured the coat within her strong lantern-turner's hands.

'No, Mr Justinian. I wish to buy it for myself.'

'These wares are filthy. Look at them. Fish-guts and giblets. You are required to own a new coat to work the lighthouse, not cast-offs. As Coastmaster of Vigil I will have a fine plesiosaur leather coat made for you and sent from Clay Capital.'

'I am not fulfilling your list by this purchase, Coastmaster Justinian. This coat is for my –' she doubled down on her grip '– *personal* use.'

'I'm telling you, you do not *want* it!'

He yanked harder, with enough force to pull Arden off her feet had the trestle corner not caught her thigh. She wedged herself deep into the splintering wood and hung on for grim life. Her ribcage groaned from the earlier trauma, sent sharp currents of pain through her chest, but still she held on.

'No.'

'Let . . . it . . .'

'No, sir, no!'

They struggled for a while in stalemate, before he gave in with a hissed curse.

'Keep the disgusting thing if you must,' he said, tossing his end of the coat down. Arden heard the snarl under his disdainful words. 'It is only a murdered *whore's* garment anyway.'

2

A *whore* clothed herself

'A *whore* clothed herself in this rag,' he concluded with caustic passion. 'A *bitch* who lay down with an *animal* and got herself killed for it.'

His curse words spoken, and with God having not struck him from the face of the earth for saying them, Mr Justinian shoved the trestle table once for emphasis, then stalked off across the town square towards the Black Rosette.

Arden exhaled, prickling with both triumph and remorse. She had won something over Mr Justinian, but at what cost?

The jumble seller, a stout grey-haired woman with the pale vulpine features of a Fictish native, remained cheery in the face of Arden's dismissal.

'You'll get used to the muck and bother here, love. Once our Coastmaster gets a pint of rot into him, all will be back to normal.'

'I must apologize,' Arden said with forced brightness to the jumble seller. 'Ours was not a disagreement we should have made you witness to.'

'The young Baron is correct about the krakenskin, I'm afraid.' The woman shook the violet threads of ragfish intestines off a pair of trousers that looked identical to the ones she herself wore. 'The coat is a cast-off and completely unsuitable for any purpose.'

'But it's hardly used. I need a wet-coat to work the lighthouse. Only krakenskin could reliably stand all the weather that the ocean might throw at it.'

'The lighthouse? You mean Jorgen's lighthouse?' The woman shifted her now-nervous attention over Arden's shoulder. The horizon behind the town was mostly obscured by fog, but a good five or ten miles away as the crow flew the land curved into a hooked finger of stone. At the very tip of the promontory a granite tower stood erect as a broken thumb, a single grey digit topped with a weakly flashing light.

'I am Arden Beacon, Lightmistress, Associate Guildswoman and *Sanguis Ignis* from Clay Portside, the traders' city of Lyonne,' Arden recited, still unfamiliar with her official titles. She held out her gloved hand. 'I have come from Clay Portside in Lyonne to take over the lighthouse operation from my late uncle, Jorgen Beacon.'

'A sanguinem?' The woman frowned at the offered hand. 'All the way out here?'

'It's all right,' Arden said. 'Touch doesn't hurt me.'

Still cautious, the woman shook Arden's hand timidly, her eyes still on the pony-plantskin gloves, so fine compared to the ubiquitous bonefish leather of the coast. Was not the gloves she minded, but what lay *under* the gloves that gave the woman pause. The coins. The little metal spigots that were both symbol and necessity of her trade.

Arden did not take offence. The reaction would be the same in Lyonne, among the commonfolk. The woman was gentle, and released her quickly.

'Oh, I wasn't minding your hands, dear. I was surprised that Jorgen was replaced so quickly when we could have well put a distillate lamp in there and be done with all the sadness.'

'The Guild is very protective of its properties. That flame has been kept alive by *sanguis* for centuries, and they'd not likely stop now. Anyhow, what is the price of the c—'

'Now that you say it,' the woman interrupted, 'I see the resemblance to Jorgen in you, that Lyonne high breeding, so *elegant*.' She simpered a little, trying to curry favour with a rich woman from the hot North country. A rich sanguis woman, possessed of esoteric skills. 'I am Mrs Sage. My husband is both apothecary and doctor in our town centre.' Mrs Sage waved towards a rude row of wood and brick that even in Clay Portside would have been considered little more than ballast shacks. 'We were told of Lightmaster Beacon's passing, and that a blood-talented relative would soon replace him from the North, but . . . We expected a *brother*.'

'All my uncle's brothers have permanent Lightmaster positions in Clay Portside,' Arden explained, annoyed that she would now have to have this conversation, and justify her sex, again. In Lyonne there would have been no question of her capabilities – labour was labour, regardless of the source. 'I was the only one not contracted to any gazetted navigation post, and the Guild requires a sanguinem to crew their stations, so . . .' She shrugged. 'The Seamaster's Guild requested that the Portmaster of Lyonne provide someone of the talent to take his place. So here I am. Buying a coat—'

'Just like that?'

'Well, the Seamaster's Guild does have to administrate a lot of coastline. I cannot shirk a duty.'

Mrs Sage shook her head that Arden had not questioned such a direction. 'It's not right, a woman sent out to those rocks alone . . .'

'The Portmaster of Clay is also my father,' Arden said with a theatrical display of generous patience at Mrs Sage's concern, so desperate was she to conclude this sale. 'He understands more than anyone what my abilities are. He also understands that if there is not a Beacon at that lighthouse, it will go to a Lumiere or, God forbid, a Pharos, and,' she stopped to give the most forced of smiles, '*ignis* families are very competitive for those positions offered us. It would break his heart for our family to lose another lighthouse post.'

'Still. It pains me to sell you this coat, Lightmistress Beacon. I must refuse.'

Arden saw the coat sliding away in the manner of a barely glimpsed dream. She clutched it tighter.

'Then why have it for sale if you won't accept my purchase?'

Mrs Sage smoothed a sou'wester out upon its pile. Her red, chapped hands rubbed the linseedy surface of the rain hat. 'I was hoping one of the ambergris merchants from Morningvale might buy it today, and take it far away from here. Sell this garment for a profit in a city where nobody knows its source. The young Baron was correct. The woman who owned this coat is dead.'

Murdered whore. Coastmaster Justinian had delivered the words with such venom, meant to hurt with all the force of a slap. Why had it concerned a Coastmaster so much, this discard on a rag-trader's table?

'Poor girl. The wife of the brute who killed her,' Mrs Sage continued. 'When her corpse was at last recovered from the water over yonder, all that remained was her scalp of golden hair and this coat, washed up upon the harbour shore.' She tilted her chin towards Vigil's small, pebbled waterfront, lying a short way down the rotting boardwalk. 'Perhaps it was merciful, after all those months she suffered in the bed of a monster, that death should claim her so she might not suffer any more. But still, what an end. Slaughtered, and your meat used as a fisherman's bait.'

Mrs Sage sounded so resignedly matter-of-fact at such an ignominious and unlikely method of dying that Arden couldn't help but snort a laugh at her story.

The woman glared at Arden with brittle offence. 'How else do you think the fisherman calls a sea-devil up from the deep by its own volition, to harvest it for such a fine leather, eh?'

And Arden saw then, the true price of the coat would be in her providing Mrs Sage an audience for a tale, a story that by the aggressive delight in her rheumy eyes was a particularly unpleasant one.

Mrs Sage dipped in close to Arden. Her breath stank of fish chowder and dandelion root.

'These abyssal monstrosities, the kraken, the *maris anguis* and *monstrom mare*, they can only be compelled to surface by human meat. The fresher the better. They are drawn by gross desires and mutilations. There's only so much of a slaughter-man's own body he can give. A toe, a finger, a slice of tongue or a testicle, hmm?' Mrs Sage sucked her lined lips in thought, imagining the kind of man that would take a blade to himself for his profession. 'An eye, a hand, a penis most probably, for in what world would anyone fornicate in consent with such an unholy creature as a man who feeds himself in fragments to the sea?'

'I don't—'

'Yes, was him that killed his poor young wife for profit, slice by agonizing slice, and the coat made to clothe her, and remind her just what her sacrifice brought. What other worth was she to him? He had not the tool with which to *fuck*, and from that lamentable position her life was foreshortened indeed.'

Arden recoiled, taken aback by the salacious details of Mrs Sage's story. 'Ah, all right then, thank you for the, um . . . providential lesson.'

'Was no lesson. Was *caution*, Lightmistress.' Her eyes widened. 'Was *warning*.'

Having exhausted her social resilience, Arden hurriedly dug into her purse and took out every note inside it, a wad of Lyonne cotton-paper bills that were not legal tender in Fiction, but all she had. Shoved them at Mrs Sage.

'Here, here, take this money. I'll make sure I give this coat a proper new life.'

Mrs Sage smiled and made motions of pious refusal, then took the money anyway. Her tongue pushed through the gaps in her teeth. Both pity and triumph she showed, as she made her announcement.

'But you are still in the *old life*, Lightmistress. T'was for that reason I hoped you'd be male. If you are bound for the old lighthouse, then see that murderous hybrid of man and monster over there?'

Mrs Sage pointed past the grey haggle-hordes of the market plaza. Beyond the ice-baskets, one figure walked apart from the fishermen, shrugging into the same copper-black-coloured garment that Arden held in her hand. The man from the tavern fight. The demon. The victor.

Next to him, a handcart without a horse. Upon it was laden the raw, bleeding tail of a leviathan.

'See that one? *Mr Riven*, he goes by, the monster of Vigil. That, my poor dear, is your new neighbour.'

3

Oh dear

'Oh dear,' Dowager Justinian said, her thin mouth drooping further once she saw Arden Beacon on the afternoon of her market adventure. 'I didn't quite believe my son when he told me of what happened this morning. You got the Riven-wife's coat.'

Arden brushed the perpetual wet from her dress. 'Was Mr Justinian terribly upset? I rather let him go his own way afterwards.'

'I had not the chance to ask my son his full opinion,' the Dowager said. Her eyes darted evasively behind her black gossamer veil. Dead a full decade her husband had been, and yet she still wore the same silks as for a planned funeral march. 'I have been busy today.'

The Dowager was a thin, regal woman who may have once been warm in her beauty and generosity. Years on Fiction's bleak coast had turned her sallow. The jewellery which she wore upon her constant uniform of black mourning had more in common with dull chunks of quartzite than the diamonds their settings suggested.

'Well, there's not much that can be helped, you weren't to know about the histories of our town. I'll have tea brought to your room.'

'Thank you. I'd like tea.' Arden noticed a small pile of correspondence on the sideboard. 'Are there any letters from my family?'

'Not since the ones from last week. The mail is slow, here.'

There were however some postcards from some old academy friends, mostly of mountains and chalets in daisy-meadows, for the summers were hot in Clay and those who could afford to escape to alpine hostels, did. Arden read the brief messages with a combined muddle of gladness and envy, and doubted finding any similar image to encapsulate Vigil when she wrote in return. Maybe a heavy-set fisherman in gumboots, waxed overalls and a gigantic cable-knit sweater, standing by a wicker basket of headless eels.

The Dowager followed Arden up the creaking stairs of Manse Justinian. The estate house had been built on an escarpment of basalt, and by its position looked down upon the town and much of the shaggy scrub of the Fiction peninsula. The family occupied less than a quarter of its space. In her first days, Arden had found herself easily lost in entire abandoned wings, stripped of furniture and fittings. Swallows nested in the faded walls, flitted through empty corridors. A cold wind moaned through broken windows. Powdered mortar fell from the brickwork at each strong gust, and if one day the house would fall, it would not be a day far distant.

Behind Arden, the woman's black skirt hem whispered ill-gossip against the bare floorboards. By the bleach on the wood Arden suspected the stairs had worn carpet runners once, such as that found in a Bedouin tent-palace, but such valuable things rarely survived the harsh, damp climates south of Lyonne.

Besides, barony or no barony, a Coastmaster's salary could not afford to deck even a quarter of a country estate out in the manner of its Northern equivalents. The house rested on a precipice of decay, the way a family mausoleum will crumble after the last casket is interred. The men in each candle-smoked portrait lining the walls had all long since passed on. Any other images were daguerreotypes and tinplate prints, things one could obtain with half an hour of a photographer's time.

Strangely, no women's faces had been seen fit to add to the cheerless décor. The Justinian line seemed to have sprung like gods, each generation from the other's forehead without need of a woman at all. Going by the profiles she saw as she squinted in the candlelight, the line had grown a little less vital with each passing iteration, until only Mr Justinian was left at the far corner, his photographed face dilute and chinless.

A little like the blood talent that had drained from Fiction itself, Arden thought.

The Dowager did not leave when Arden laid the krakenskin coat out on her small, slender guest bed.

On first arriving at the house twenty-five days previously, Arden had asked the Dowager privately for a room with a lockable door. A request she could not make of the son.

Dowager Justinian had been surprised at Arden's wishes, for the Coastmaster's Manse was patrolled by dogs and a quartet of retired soldiers in her employ. She had granted Arden the room with its hard, narrow bed and a window little bigger than a postage stamp, despite it being hardly a fifth of the size of the guest house Mr Justinian had first expectantly offered.

Still, for three nights in a row Arden had heard footsteps on the landing, the sound of the knob being turned until the lock snapped tight in the jamb. Those nights she drew her bedclothes to her chin and clutched hard the small knife of her profession.

The night visitor never tried to defeat the lock. With entry thwarted, the footsteps would only linger for a moment before moving on.

Now in the dim light of the small room, the blue kraken-cross glowed, an entirely different kind of uninvited visitor. A sullen phosphorescence in each mottled spot, unearthly and benthic. The cut came from the head of the beast, where the fabled *kraken crucifix* graced the cranium of a bull male at full maturity, one of the few places upon that immense, strange body that could be preserved and tanned. Rarely would any one animal produce enough usable leather for half a garment, let alone the panels for a complete coat. Those pieces never even made it to Clay Capital, Lyonne's largest city. They were sold to foreign princes or corporate scions, displayed in glass cabinets and only worn during coronations or lying-in-states. A strange call had drawn Arden to this coat in the market.

A murdered whore's garment.

Arden stroked the decorative leather tooling at the jacket's sleeve. Pretty, but not stamped in deeply enough for permanency. A too-tentative hand had struck the die on these clumsy patterns. A woman's hand, she guessed, one unused to those sharp instruments that her brothers all their lives had been allowed access to. Probably sewn the leather as well, judging by the tiny, precise stitches that suited a formal dress better than a coat. A woman's labour in the threads. Places such as Fiction did not tend towards providing their sons a fully rounded education. Despite an innate skill at leather-work, Clay Portside tailors did a roaring trade in repairing breeches that clueless southernmost men could not repair themselves.

'It's such a beautiful thing,' Arden said. 'I can't imagine anyone just throwing it away, no matter how it came into their possession.'

'I can imagine the beast it once was.' The Dowager's black mourning-dress hushed against the cold hearthstones as she went to the miserly fireplace, where the embers of the night before still collected under the ash. She agitated them with an iron poker, adjusted the flue so they would have air to last them into the evening.

Arden wondered if she would see one, at least once, and if it would be as magnificent and terrifying as her books, and beautiful as the coat upon her bed. An entire mountain of copper-body, sinuous beneath the ocean, with arms as long as a steam train of twenty carriages, a pupil so large she could stumble through.

The Dowager seemed to have heard an inkling of her thoughts and said, 'By the time any specimen makes it into town, it is already cut up for processing. And thank goodness for that. They are hideous. Such arms and legs. Those cold eyes, such unholy thoughts. I've heard they grow large enough to consume a whale, or a bull plesiosaur.' She shuddered. 'A plesiosaur can grow as big as two elephants, so you can make your own decision as to exactly how much monster we are speaking of.'

'You've actually seen one, Madame Justinian? *Monstrom mare*? Or is it *mostri marino* here?'

The Dowager's poker thrust hard into the ash and disinterred a still-flaming coal.

'*Monstrom mare*,' she said. 'Once, when I was a girl in Manhattan, I saw a kraken chick washed up upon an oyster-shell beach. Very immature, just a baby really, but each leg was twenty paces long. The old Emperor Krakens never approached so close to shore, there. It is different in Fiction. The creatures are indigenous to Vigil, and in these waters they breed and die.'

A silence descended upon the small, chill room. Though she was mostly Lyonne by blood, Dowager Justinian hailed from that great country far west of the Summerland Sea, in a small village between two rivers called Manhattan, at the province's south border. Her mother tongue was Lyonne-Algonquian, that great trader's language that most spoke with some measure of fluency. However had a Vinlander ended up on this windswept Fiction coast, presiding over an immense family estate with a husband who seemingly, based on his portraits, had never aged?

Breeding and death perhaps. That was always the way.

Arden pushed aside the lace curtain at the small window, where beyond the sad patches of lawn and holly oak trees – stunted by the wind and salt – the patient expanse of Vigil's shallow bay lurked. Giants lived in that place, creatures that had endured the aeons that had made extinct their ancestors. Every dream or terror that existed in a sailor's lonely night moved and surfaced in those waters. *Here be dragons.*

And somewhere in the fog was her lighthouse, waiting for her.

She had not entirely been truthful with Mrs Sage today, when she had said the Seamaster's Guild had requested she to go to

Vigil – and that her father approved. They had merely relayed the instruction. The request came from altogether another, deeper branch of government, and one not entirely known for sincerity.

Her Portmaster father had not been pleased at the Guild orders. Had begged her not to go. But she had gone anyway, because of what had been promised. It was worth risking everything. Before she'd departed for Vigil, Portmaster Beacon had taken Arden aside. The post was an unlikely request from them, he'd cautioned her. He'd fought hard for her to receive her little signaller position after she'd matured so late and so weak in her talent. The Seamaster's Guild had been so reluctant in even that small concession. Now here she was, being offered a prime flame-keeper's position . . . in Fiction granted, but still a full-degree holder posting.

Refuse the post, Daughter. I fear you are in the sight of Lions. If you agree to go to Fiction you will be a puppet. It's not for Fire they've called you. Just give me the word, and I won't sign your release papers.

She should have taken his advice, but an odd, resentful stubbornness had made Arden disagree with her father.

And yet . . .

It's not for Fire they've called you.

The Dowager spoke then, interupting Arden's thoughts. 'The season is too early for kraken, they come in deep winter, most of the time. If the fisherfolk can bring in at least one or two small hens, it will certainly stave off the hungry months.'

'That's good,' Arden replied absently, her mind still on her father's reproach. Had he been right and her wrong? What if the Lyonne Order only wanted her to stay in this mansion for a Coastmaster who desires to have a high-bred wife?

'Yes the kraken are important to our economy, and that's why the Riven man is tolerated here, despite what he did to his wife.'

'*Suspected* to have done, I assume, given that he's still living among you.'

'Suspected.' The Dowager nodded at the coat. 'Because he can bring the giants to shore in the winter time.'

'They're worth covering up a murder?'

'Krakenskin is precious. Not just for leather.' The Dowager picked up the coat and stroked it reverently. 'Keep the skin wet, put it on the deepest burn and there will be no scar. The ground-up beak is medicinal against all sorts of tumours and growths. Kraken eye-jelly dissolves cataracts, can make the blind see. The oil is health tonic for a heart, and fuel and perfume, and is far more expensive than either jasmine, civet or ambergris.' She nodded. 'The flesh makes for a fine meal, if the fishermen butcher it early enough.' The Dowager counted the treasures off as if they were the accounts of a banker.

'I heard the monsters are worshipped as gods, here.'

'Yes. They once were. The old religion is gone now, but we still host many tourists in this Manse during Deepwater season, the winter time. There is even a masque on the longest night, where men dress up like a sea-serpent and rampage through the town until a king is crowned among them, for a day. More than one child owes their beginning to the Deepwater Night. More than one dispute finds its permanent end as well.'

'It sounds very, ah . . . primitive.'

'They love their brutalities, do our Vigil folk. And with its history, and that devotion, are you sure you want to keep that odd coat? It would fit no sea dog of course, but a good tailor could unpick the seams and marry the panels with a dress suit. I could get you an entire bonefish wardrobe for the price of the leather.'

Arden shook her head. 'I could never destroy such a beautiful thing. It would be a desecration. More to the point, this coat is equipment I need. I will be able to attend my duties at the lighthouse and relieve Mr Harris sooner, especially now that I don't have to worry about freezing to death.'

'I am surprised you are not out there already.'

Arden bundled up the coat so that it might fit into the steamer trunk she kept under the bed.

'Mr Justinian has such concern for my wellbeing, you see.'
Her irritation prickled her tongue. 'He will not sign a certificate
for the interim Lightkeeper's release until he is certain I am *ready*.
He has undertaken to prepare an extensive list of equipment.'

She didn't add that she'd never heard of a keeper charged
with such a list, full of items not so easy to obtain and that
required delivery via a postal network that worked only when
certain people felt that it should. Poultices for exotic ailments
and shipping encyclopaedias for irrelevantly distant shores.
Hot-water heaters and a strange pachyderm-fibre blanket
rather than the goat-hair one that suited just as well. Three
kinds of leather shoe, the manufacture of which could be
carried out only in Portside. An expensive coil of Mi'kmaq
coal-ether rope, for no purpose whatsoever. What was wrong
with Lyonne-laid coir?

'My son has been a Vigil Coastmaster and proxy for the
Lyonne Seamaster's Guild for quite some time too, Mx Beacon.
You have a dangerous position out there, literally between the
devil and the deep blue sea. I'm sure he knows what he is
doing.'

'I need to start my *job*, Madame Justinian. *Soon*. The chemistry of the perpetual flame requires tending by a sanguinem,
and if it goes out, the Lyonne Navy will be down here in a
flash wondering why half their marine fleet is littering the rocks
of the promontory.' She widened her eyes for emphasis. 'I can't
imagine what the Seamaster's Guild will say if they start getting
invoices for fuelling a regular lamp.'

The Dowager muttered words in a Manhattanite tongue,
gave a little hiss between her teeth. She frowned up at the dusty
lamp-covers. 'Ah, it reminds me. Best I light the house lamps
for the night. It comes quickly on these shores.'

Arden was being dismissed. The staff could very well have
lit the fifty lamps within the Manse themselves and the Dowager
could have made a promise to convince her son to hurry up
and release Arden to her lighthouse. Instead, even the black-
veiled woman seemed complicit in Arden's extended stay.

27

'I'll give you time to freshen up,' the Dowager concluded, as she lit the first lamp in Arden's room. 'Supper will be in an hour.'

Arden waited impatiently until the Dowager was gone before she opened up the flame-embossed lid of her steamer trunk. Though Mr Justinian's mother was harmless, she was just as guilty of familial designs as her son, and possibly just as curious as to what was stopping Arden from falling into Mr Justinian's arms.

Arden's trunk was her life reduced to a painted tin box, four foot by two. It contained all the certificates of her career as a signaller, ten years as a Lady of the Lights upon the Clay Portside docks. It was an odd paradox that she was both nobility and labourer in a country where there was such a deep and unfathomable division between commonblood folk and the sanguinem with their precious and valuable labours.

She paused before the trunk and studied her gloves before sliding one off. Her hands were strong as any common worker's, with calluses from the endless winding mechanisms of signal-work and canal locks.

But the new coins in her palms made her weak.

A metal disk in the centre of each inflammed hand – a silver moon stitched in between the heart and head-line. They were protective grommets for the act of blood-spilling required to keep the lighthouse fire burning.

The small fires of the signal lights she had tended before had needed far less blood. She hadn't needed the disks before now.

With a hiss of discomfort she pulled the gloves back on and shifted books and papers aside.

'Only a few months,' she said herself. 'Then you'll have everything you ever wanted.' All her shuffling of the contents of the trunk to make way for the coat ended up uncovering a small trinket-chest carved of bone. A small noise escaped Arden's throat.

'Don't open it,' she said to herself sternly. 'Don't open it, Beacon.'

But she couldn't help herself. The enchantment within was too great. Love was venomous, its toxin poisoned you forever. Arden opened the box and the past fell out.

A silver-print on paper floated onto the bedspread, no bigger than her palm. A clean-cut man in an airship officer's uniform looked out at her, his black hair grown long from a military shave, rakishly tilted cap, twinkling, good-natured eyes.

On the back, a blue-ink cursive. *Thinking of you always – Richard.*

The regret hit her hard. A bitter memory came, of a stolen kiss at the Guild Ball a year before. *I'll come back for you,* Richard Castile had said to her. *I will be a Captain at last. We will be married in the winter. Wait for me.*

She had wanted to spirit him away to her apartments that night. But Richard had been evasive, preoccupied. Danced with other women. She'd tried not to be upset. Their love was forbidden, so of course he wouldn't risk affections in public. He'd told her that he had already bought a ring for their upcoming elopement. All she had to do was wait. Fretting would only be foolish.

The cracks in their relationship, so easily ignored, could not be ignored forever.

That Guild Ball was the last time she saw him. He left before dawn on his packet-ship to Vinland. Arden didn't arrive in time to catch him, but had caught instead the girl coming out of his apartment, the one wearing Vinland pearl earrings and the rose-gold stag-brooch of the Castile family crest. Perhaps Richard had told her about Arden, for upon seeing a frantic sanguis marching in her direction the girl had blushed ferociously and ran off, dropping the silver-print in the gutter. Arden was about to call after her when she'd seen the face staring up from the cigarette butts and orange peels.

Richard's face.

Thinking of you always – dr.

The pain had been an assassin's dagger, slid between her ribs. She had always wanted a picture of him, but Richard had constantly refused. Too risky, he said. If an Order agent found an image of a common-blood man in a sanguis trousseau, then he would be demoted, if not worse. Arden was a *Beacon*, that oldest and most ancestrally fortified of sanguine genealogies. She would need to wait for Richard to catch up. Until he was a Petty Officer. Flight Lieutenant. Captain. Or the god-damned King of Lyonne, it seemed. Ten years of waiting, with no end in sight.

She snapped the opal box shut. No. He would never change his mind and she'd not lock the damn krakenskin coat away with her other failures. She would wear it, defiantly and proudly. She shared something with Mr Riven's wife, after all. She too had been betrayed by someone she loved.

Arden stood up from the steamer trunk, the photograph still in her hand. Walked woodenly to the fireplace and threw it in. The flame leapt green, the paper crisped black. His eyes, twinkling and knowing. Eyes saying, *do what you like, lantern girl. It's really because of me that you are out here.*

The eyes were the last to burn.

4

As was the custom

As was the custom in the old aristocratic families, she changed clothes for the main meal. Wore a grey linen shirt with no ruffles, a narrow dress that finished in a fishtail at the top of her boots. Bound her hair in severe knots upon her head. She headed down the bare wooden stairs towards the shabby velvets of the Justinian dining room, quite prepared to continue the argument about her new coat. Despite Mrs Sage's pronouncements and the Dowager's warning, she was feeling combative.

Mr Justinian arrived back from his Coastmaster meetings in the languid sort of mood that comes when one has had those meetings in the Black Rosette tavern over seaweed spirit cocktails, and in the presence of somebody generous with their affections.

He took off his coat – a slate-grey plesiosaur leather he could still ill afford on both a Coastmaster stipend and the dregs of a faded title. He sat at the table with a flourish. Arden huffed an understated disapproval. Mr Justinian knew what he was doing. A war of garments. His coat was an affectation that in Lyonne would have been vulgar, like something a slumlord crime boss would wear to impress the poor tenants. The tanned material had the tough grain of a shark or a ray. Less unfinished versions tended to take away a layer of skin against the poor soul unfortunate enough to brush against it.

Her fellow guests, a man and his wife from South Lyonne, glanced at the plesiosaur coat and kept their own counsel.

To pay running costs, the old Manse ran as a guest house for other important merchants and businesspeople who might wish to make profit off the Darkling Sea. Perhaps it did not make as much of a profit as was required, for to save on fuel not every lamp was lit, so instead of bright, cheery galleries, the large rooms became crepuscular, full of shadows and damp. The old tablecloths, laundered to transparency, were held together by little more than browning claret stains. The silverware would have better been called *mottled nickel with silver-plate patches*, and a century of cigar smoke now blackened the plaster ceiling roses with a dour velvet. In more than one corner, water-rot frayed the plaster walls and caused a drooping of the faded stripe wallpaper. There were not quite enough glasses to fill the display cupboards, and none of the tableware arrangements ever quite made a full set.

Altogether, a house in decline. The guests, already unsettled by the Baron's mobster coat, glanced awkwardly at Arden's fingerless gloves. She rubbed her hands. The bloodletting coins snagged in the oblique arches on the side of her palms. Twanged each time she closed her fist.

'New gloves, Madame?' the husband asked her quietly when Mr Justinian left the table in search of a better wine than the cloudy vinegar they'd been served.

He showed her his Guild pin as he spoke, a railroad degree. Though he himself was not gifted with any endowments, the Permanent Way required many sanguis disciplines, from *ferrum* to *pondus* and *vaporis*. A genteel way of telling Arden that even though he was commonblooded he was familiar and sympathetic to her kind. It had been the reason the trade guilds had originated, to unite their labours into one brotherhood, a fraternity of workers despite their wildly different means.

'I've had my coins about a month,' Arden admitted. 'I'm only now getting used to having them in my skin.' She recalled the little Guildsman who had watched with a clear, genial gaze as the nervous phlebotomist inserted the tools of her new position into her hands. *Mr Lindsay*, his name was. He had been a small, delicate fellow in the tweedy suit of a clerk, and wore a golden pin in the shape of a rose. He'd also been the one to bring the orders to her father.

For the railwayman's benefit, and because she did not want to treat them as shameful or remarkable, she rolled her gloves up slightly and showed him the silver buttons set between the heart and the head lines. Her skin was still a little tender at the edges, and she suspected would not ever truly heal.

'Why in the hands?' asked his wife. 'Isn't it dreadfully more painful to cut your hands?'

Arden nodded. 'I suspect they want us to feel pain. To remind us that power doesn't come without a cost. Hands . . . well they are symbolic in a way no other body part is.'

'I could think of one other symbolic body part,' the wife giggled, before hiccupping wine. Arden saw that in anticipation of another awkward dinner the woman had pre-emptively gotten rather drunk. 'The body part they always mention in those funny little Deepwater rituals, ha! I had that strange Mrs. Sage tell me all the stories of what goes on among those deviant brutes . . .'

The railroad man patted his wife's hand and took the glass off her, before returning to Arden and attempting conversation again.

'You must miss Clay Portside, Lightmistress. I've been there many a times, seen the air-harbours stretch out as far as the eye can see, *sanguis zephyrim* making the aerostats fly and the *pondus* who anchor them to the ground. Produce and trade from all over the world, the menagerie of animals, the babel of tongues! Of all those wonders, this place must seem like the colour has been taken from your eyes.'

She nodded, relieved at the admission. She could have never said such a thing to her hosts. 'I do miss home. One does whatever the Guild asks. Especially if you're sanguis, and there's duty involved.'

'Ah,' he said, as if she had confirmed a suspicion. 'I wondered why a grown sanguis woman should be getting such protection on her flesh when it's the preserve of children. Isn't eleven the most usual age?'

She gave them both a tight smile. 'My blood tithings never required much from me before.' She slid up her dress-sleeve to show the calluses on the back of her arm. 'A cut here would last the better part of a week, and I had no symbolic act required of me.'

'But now your work requires more blood, I see. Hence the disks to protect your skin from the knife.'

'Yes.'

'Did the Lions follow you here, Mx Beacon?' he asked.

A sudden question. His wife pretended to sip her thistledown wine, but Arden could feel her listening on with harp-string tension.

'Lions?'

In her mind she saw the little Guildsman Mr Lindsay smile. Arden took a swallow of her claret, to buy seconds and still the sudden shake of her hand.

'I don't quite know what you mean.'

'The Lyonne Order. The Eugenics Society's attack-dogs.' With his fingers the railwayman made the sign of teeth. 'Did they follow you to Fiction?'

Arden went for her claret again and found she had finished the glass. She knew exactly what he meant. Businessmen in Fiction were not at all keen on coming across Lions of the human kind. She was a sanguis invested late into her profession. Such a thing had the stink of Order activity, their skulking and investigations and sudden disappearances. One would think the powerful Eugenics Society would concern themselves only with policing sanguis folk, but they frequently expanded their purview into the citizenry as well. The guests viewed her with no small suspicion.

'No, was on instruction of the Seamaster's Guild that I take up position here,' Arden replied.

'All the way out here? In Fiction, where the blood has faded?'

'Well, the lighthouse is under the navigation chain of the Lyonne sea-road. It's still a blood light, so it needs a *sanguis ignis* to maintain the flame.'

The wife spoke next, and despite her high spirits she was not as generous with her trust. 'Why not install a petrolactose lamp in that tower? Or a natural gas, which is plentiful here. Why deal with such esoteric chemistries as yours? Whenever there are *sanguis*, there are always Lions. The blood attracts them.'

'See, it is . . .' she drifted off, and paused, for she didn't know either. 'I'm sure it's very mundane,' she capitulated. 'Keeping the trade and Guilds of our two countries aligned through the sea-road navigation chain. My family has always maintained the Vigil light. It would be a loss to lose a station from sheer neglect, even an unimportant one.'

The wife pondered, then visibly relaxed. Arden's explanation seemed sound. If her posting was just a matter of navigation, then there were no Lions about.

The husband drained his wine in one gulp.

'Ah then, let us drink to the trade Guilds, the great fraternities of Lyonne.'

They might have been at ease, but there was already an ill cast to the night. *Did the Lions follow you here?* The Order worked in the shadows and bore no oversight. They should not be meddling in the mere business of keeping a navigation road safe.

It's not for Fire they've called you, warned the father in her mind. And Arden shivered, even though the room pressed in oppressively close and far too warm.

A fourth guest joined them then, a man of middle years and a certain overbearing pomposity. His voice came before him, echoing from the foyer, a complaint about the condition of the roads, the driver who did not give him deference of title.

Mr Justinian called Arden's attention as he re-entered, guest in tow.

'Mx Beacon,' he said. 'I'd like you to meet Mr Alasdair Harrow, the Postmaster and Magistrate of Vigil.'

Despite the size of his voice, Mr Harrow was not particularly tall, had fallen into middle-aged stoutness, yet still possessed the domineering characteristics of his youth. The broad, heavy shoulders of a brawler, a pug nose, a cauliflowered ear. She thought his hair was white, but on closer examination in the gloomy light he was a faded blond.

'A shared title, Postmaster *and* Magistrate?' Arden inquired as she shook the new guest's meaty hand. She wondered that Mr Justinian should be so keen as to introduce her to this fellow when he had never presented Arden to anybody else. The day's excursion to town notwithstanding, Mr Justinian had kept Arden all to himself in the same manner as a dragon might sit jealous upon its hoard. If he could not have her for a night in his bed, then she should be walled up within brickwork isolations of his own making.

'It is difficult to find men suited to all the offices of authority,' Mr Harrow said in a barking pronouncement, not talking to Arden but rather a central place in the room where a silk arrangement of artificial flowers collected dust. 'Especially here, in this town. So, I must fulfil my duties by occupying both roles.'

And drawing a double stipend from the Coast Office, Arden added silently. She gave Mr Harrow a nod and returned to her meal, busied herself in chewing the most inoffensive slice of potted meat, so she would not have to fight for her place in the conversation.

'*Miss* Beacon here intends to take over the lighthouse operations that old Jorgen abandoned,' Mr Justinian said, dragging her back in. 'A request from the Seamaster's Guild themselves.'

Caught drinking, Mr Harrow coughed mid-swallow. 'What's that you say?'

'Jorgen Beacon. This is his niece, a Beacon scion and *sanguis ignis* from Clay Portside, sent all the way from our air-harboured capital city to bring some culture to our humble hamlet, and to keep the old promontory flame alive.'

Mr Harrow stabbed a pink cube of fish. 'I'd not allow it, if it were up to me.'

'Well, it is not up to you,' Arden said.

Mr Harrow did not respond to her. She might have been an empty chair for all that she had spoken. 'More fools in the world than there are decent ideas, Vernon,' he grumbled.

'I have my opinions too,' Mr Justinian said, flicking a look Arden's way. At least he recognized that they were speaking as if she were not there, though presumably because a woman *angry* was not a woman who would be *amenable* later. 'But the Guild was adamant she fill the position.'

'She'll be dead within the week, her corpse twice-ravished, mark my words.' Mr Harrow shoved a grape-melon in his mouth, and the juice ran down his chin. 'Give her a rifle and make sure she knows how to use it. I'll not be called out to the promontory to pick up her body like a damned fool.'

Arden stood with a crash, rattling the tableware. 'Gentlemen, I can manage my own business. I've worked harder docks than this pissant bit of rock!'

Mr Harrow started laughing, barks of laughter. 'They served her up for the slaughter Vernon. To the fucking *slaughter*. Wasn't for her blood they wanted a woman out there. The Guild pimped her to the monster on the promontory, and Riven will rape her bloody and thank them for it.'

The house staff came in at that very moment bearing plates of a flavourless broth that would never have been conscionable to serve in Portside, and in the meantime Arden fumed. The gall of these men. The unmitigated dreadfulness of their words.

A server-girl came by with nothing but cow-eyes for Mr Justinian, and spilled claret on Arden's sleeve with a smirk. Between her jealousy, Mr Harrow's gleeful predictions and Mr Justinian's knavish gloating, Arden was twisted up into a knot of frustration so painful it made her want to scream.

'Excuse me,' she said through a rage-strangled throat. 'I'm not feeling well. I need to get some air.'

She fled the crushing mood of the dining room and ran down the murky corridor, finished in what was either a large study or a small ballroom, a gloomy expanse of sapwood parquetry and mildewed corners.

Past the curtain-rags, a cold moonlight spilled across the polished floor. Arden hauled open the double doors, fell out onto the balcony where the frost clawed her face and her breath steamed. All the menace the night could give was immensely preferable to the atmosphere inside, the terrible delight of men savouring that she be in harm's way.

She sucked down salt air until the tremor in her limbs stopped and her breathing slowed. Gooseflesh sprang on her bare arms, and she welcomed that clean discomfort.

Someone stepped into the room behind her, and imagining it one of the guests who had watched on in deep disquiet at Mr Harrow's performance she said, 'I can't stand it, those uncouth—'

'Then I apologize. It was not my intent to harm.'

Arden startled. If she had gained a modicum of relief by going outside, the feeling was gone. Mr Justinian stood behind her.

Had Arden been of a more histrionic nature she might have considered throwing herself off the balcony, only this balcony was at ground level and the act probably lost much of its meaning when one landed safely on the other side.

'Perhaps I'd prefer ravishment by this Mr Riven than being subjected to your snide gossip upon my sense and my work. At least he's honest in his dreadfulness!'

Mr Justinian huffed. 'All right then. You're welcome to him, and him to you, just please come inside. These chills might not seem so much, but they can kill a man.' He tilted his head towards her. 'Or a woman.'

'One may be surprised how resilient I am.'

'But I am not quite as cold-blooded as you. Allow me to explain our trespasses inside. Please. Please.'

Mr Justinian gestured beside him. She shook her head. They were at an impasse. He threw his crumb.

'Postmaster Harrow's her father.'

'Her?'

'The woman whose coat you now own. Let me explain.'

Truth be told, the night was infernally cold, and she wanted to know about this Harrow daughter; in the same way hearing of another's misfortune made one's own life easier to bear. She stepped into the warmer surrounds of the study and closed the doors behind her. On cue, a servant ran in bearing a jug of tea, deposited the tableware and departed as silkily as a shadow.

The large, dark study had the air of a mausoleum viewing area, the books in the shelves gone dusty and unread. When she had first attempted to pass the time in this neglected library, most of the tomes were reference manuals of one permutation or another, lists of shipping indexes, dry histories. If there had been any books read for pleasure, they were sequestered elsewhere, or never existed at all.

Trapped by circumstance, Arden circled a daybed and a chez lounge as big as a small skiff before her attention was caught by a wrinkle of light in the shadows. A gallon-sized specimen jar, containing the formaldehyde-pickled coils of something aquatic and otherworldly – something octopoid somehow. She tapped the glass, experiencing equally the suffocations and convolutions of the poor beast inside.

'My ancestor kept a *Wunderkammer* before he died. A collection of oddities,' Mr Justinian said. 'If you would believe it, a *woman* gave birth to that thing. Nobody but Great-grandfather Alexander wanted that abomination in here, but we were rather forced to keep it.'

She left the pickled monster and returned to him.

'Don't change the subject, Vernon. You say Mr Riven's wife was Postmaster Harrow's daughter.'

'Yes. Mr Harrow is a man grieving.'

'I'm sure he is.'

'He is a wellspring of bitterness. He is too keenly aware what lies in wait for you upon that promontory, having seen it up close, and to someone he loved.' Mr Justinian poured himself a snifter of brandy, but did not offer the same to Arden. The liqueur left runnels upon the glass in the firelight. 'We also must talk of what happened today, else it will always fester in our minds.'

Arden exhaled. 'You were quite adamant I should not have the coat. *Murdered whore*, you said.'

'I acknowledge that.'

'Marrying a monster does not make one a harlot, Mr Justinian. If what you say is true, then it was her husband's fault that she was trapped in the marriage, not hers. You disgrace the dead by your blame. What you said today towards me was unconscionable.'

Mr Justinian stared at his shoes, affected a hangdog expression. 'It upset me to lose such a fine young lady to such a miserly end, that is all.'

'So she is *fine*, now?'

'She was beautiful, and fierce and somewhat intelligent in her own way, and did not deserve what became of her. Reduced from vibrancy to a *shade*. My guilt at not stepping up to save her, my cowardice, is constant. I chose the pejorative out of my own grief.' He glanced about, clearly hoping a voice might pipe up and rescue him, as it usually did when the servants were about. 'But Bellis made her decision to help her father by prostituting herself to Riven when there were other ways out of her predicament.'

'Bellis Harrow,' Arden said. 'So she has a name of her own, then.'

The brandy displeased Mr Justinian. He threw the liquor into the fire, causing a blue spirit to rise from the coals. It reminded Arden of her own arcane fire, starving in its glass in a far lighthouse, waiting to be fed.

Mr Justinian spoke to the fire, and not to her.

'A hundred years ago a family was procured from the

Sainted Isles. The Rivens, they were called. Or at least they received the name because they were shorefolk, sea-savages, not sophisticated enough to understand the concept of familial lineage. It didn't matter that they were brutes and inbreeds. Alexander Justinian, my great-grandfather, needed hands to process kraken-flesh and saurians in his factories upon the promontory. Who minded if the Rivens were illiterates and barely human? Thankfully they were not suited to the modicum of civilization Vigil provided and mostly remained upon the promontory, away from town. Within the span of a century the Rivens fought and sliced and incestually pared themselves down to one disgusting remnant individual.'

Mr Justinian made the sign of the krakenskin crucifix upon his chest before adding, 'Your lighthouse neighbour. T'was he that killed his family in an orgy of ritual and violence nearly twenty years ago. Slaughtered every man, woman and child on that promontory in one night. His own blood, gone.'

'I see,' Arden said. 'But if all this brutality did happen, shouldn't he have been hanged in punishment?'

'Oh, Riven was punished indeed. Charged and pleaded guilty to killing his family, sent away to the hulk prisons of Lyonne. Rotting boats on Harbinger Bay, converted to hold the worst reprobates and degenerates ever disinterred from the social sewage.

'But then some syphilitic judge had a weak-minded moment, and over a decade later returned the animal to this town. That is not the tragedy. Fifteen years of imprisonment merely sharpened the criminal's hunger, made his sexual urges tend to the obscene. Riven was ill-content in wallowing out on the promontory among his factory ruins. He came into town, forced a local girl to wife. Mr Harrow's daughter.'

'Forced?'

'Yes.'

'Now there,' Arden said tartly. 'There is the strange part.

41

The heart wants what it wants and it takes two to marry. If he wanted to marry anyone, then they would have had to at some stage *consent* to it, to *allow* it. Before witnesses.'

'Allow? Allow? You speak about request and consent upon this brutal shore?' Mr Justinian laughed with an adult's condescension towards a child. 'The woman was stolen, just as you would steal a hog or an unsupervised cure of meat. Dragged her screaming to the Sainted Isles, where illegal unions can be effected as easily as an attack in the dead of night. She came back with both eyes blackened, and never spoke for nearly a year afterwards. Not even to her father.

'Her last year alive she spent in abject horror and torment inside those factories and in his stinking bed. Escaped only once, whittled down to skin and bone and scar. Wanted an abortifacient for the monster curled in her womb, and Mr Sage gave her a tea that . . .'

'I have had experience with such a tea,' Arden snapped. 'You do not need to explain in detail what Mrs Sage already has. Continue, if you decide this salacious horror is what I must hear to make my informed decision.'

'Riven came back for Bellis that night, threatened Mr Harrow. Assaulted him, even as he tried to protect his daughter. A month later she was dead. All that was left was her coat, washed onto the beach. The Rector of our church was to make a statement to the magistrate about her death, for it was to him that she had confided. Our Rector himself went to Riven, to beg that he confess for the salvation of his holy soul. He never returned, his body was never found. Without evidence of death, the mongrel could not be charged or convicted. Two deaths within days. But let us merely agree as to who did both.'

'Circumstantial, still . . .'

'The Rector was your *cousin*, Arden Beacon. Rector John Stefan, the son of Jorgen Beacon, the Lightkeeper.'

Arden's heartbeat quickened in her chest, the rush of panic that any thought of unfair violence brought. Her cousin she remembered only vaguely, for their meetings had been so long ago, a slender, dark youth with the same soft-smoky hair as Andrew and soulful eyes. He had been her age, Stefan Beacon, ungifted in blood but touched in other ways – deeply sensitive, accepted into a religious seminary and visiting his family in the North. Arden remembered more her step-mother's exclamation. Stefan and Arden could have been brother and sister, how similar their looks!

Her cousin, murdered, along with the woman.

She needed to keep calm, for such tales were not just for her safety. Her fear was a coin that could buy Mr Justinian several more weeks of her time.

'Surely such a performance as a literal kidnapping by the bogeyman of Vigil would have risen one or two men to heroics. You say all this happened to her, and to Mr Harrow, that you yourself stood by and watched?'

'You don't understand. Riven cannot be killed. The devils of the sea keep him safe, for all that he cut off his cock and fed it to them for his protection.' In the candlelight Mr Justinian's face darkened, and pearls of sweat sprang up from his brow. 'And he makes money! Money for foreign businessmen who purchase his kraken hides and will not allow harm to come to him.'

He snatched at the mantelpiece, held himself there shaking, before the brandy decanter called to him once more. 'I am sorry. For you. For her.'

'Are we done in the telling? Is this all I must know?'

Mr Justinian nodded. 'It is what you must know.'

'Coastmaster, regardless of whatever went before you must sign my release papers. I must go to my lighthouse.'

'You need not hurry. Mr Harris can—'

'Mr Harris is not qualified to keep a lucent flame alive and the season of summer storms will be upon us. A perpetually burning flame is still vulnerable to going out, and a *sanguis ignis* needs to maintain the light.'

'You cannot yet go,' Mr Justinian insisted. 'Not so soon. Not while Riven still lives out on that accursed promontory! He will come to you in the night, come prowling with lust in his black heart!'

Arden sniffed. 'It will not be the first time I've been in situations with lustful men. Anyway, didn't you say he fed his manhood to the devils for his protection? What is he meant to do to me without it?'

He did not take her scoffing bait. 'I cannot release you! My guilt over Bellis' fate prevents me.'

Arden had one play left to her. Such a play could only be used but once, and she had to take a deep breath before she deployed it.

'If you do not sign the papers, Mr Justinian, I will have no recourse but to return to Portside with your so-called essential list. I will present such evidence to the Seamaster's Guild and there will be an investigation. They may do more than investigate me, and cast their eyes on other parts of your business. Good night to you.'

As she turned to leave, Mr Justinian grabbed her arm. His fingers dug hard into the muscle, with the clear intent of leaving an imprint of himself upon her.

'It is not safe.'

'Safer than here, perhaps.' She pulled free. 'You cannot keep me from my lighthouse.'

'All right then, damn you.'

He strode to the desk, unlocked it and pulled out a sheaf of papers from a leather binder, the certificates that completed the Guild transfer. 'I have tried to warn you of the creature who will be no further from your doorstep than the east wing of this Manse from the right. This thing I do will condemn you to danger.'

'The danger is mine to face,' Arden said. 'Otherwise what good am I as a Lightkeeper anywhere?'

He met her steady gaze with something approaching panic. His nostrils flared like a horse sensing the harness.

She held the gaze, until he broke first, picked up his heavy

44

fountain pen from the inkwell and signed both copies with such violence that Arden winced for the paper and the wood of the table beneath.

He held up the certificate. She held out her hand.

'Thank you, sir.'

Perhaps she was too subtle. The certificate never went her way.

'One condition.'

Arden frowned. 'I am not happy with conditions.'

'Allow me to court you.'

'Excuse me?'

'I am a Coastmaster with a barony to my name. You are an interim member of the Seamaster's Guild, the youngest ever. By winter you yourself would hold a full Guild degree, marry whom you wish. A good couple we would make. Our mating would be well-matched. The Eugenics Society will allow it, for we may yet breed some as yet unheard of talent.'

Unbidden, Richard Castile stepped into the halls of her mind. His smart uniform. His rakish cap. His handsome face taking her breath away with yearning. To touch him. To wrap herself up in a body that was not her own.

She shook her head firmly to rid herself of the association.

'I have no interest in eugenics or breeding. Besides, in the interest of fleeting pleasure – which I am quite forbidden to pursue openly – I barely know you.'

'Then come to know me. Allow me the chance to court you and present my case. The Society is favourable to a high lineage such as mine. You could receive a marriage dispensation at the very least. Non-breeding of course, but the operation to remove womb-horns is often quite successful.'

Arden exhaled. She shouldn't shout. Would be unprofessional, but still, the gall of the man!

'Mr . . .'

He moved to the fire, the certificate still in his hand. She saw the leaping flames, the devouring of her freedoms, the going home, the censure of the Guildmaster who might have to come out here and mediate this mess. Maybe even Mr Lindsay, whose owners even the Portmaster of Clay feared.

They would find in her favour, but the taint of being a Lightkeeper who could not handle their own business would remain. She would not keep her degree, not even the associate one. Her signal post had already been reassigned. She would be . . .

'Stop!'

'Well? What say you, Mx Beacon?' He shook the paper. 'I am a man alone in this cursed, misbegotten peninsula courtesy of my great-grandfather's sentimentality. How am I to meet any woman of my equal among these inbreds of the coast? How will my family be redeemed if I marry into worthless muck?'

She wanted to say words in their defence, for the girls of the town were quite the hardworking, straight-talking type. She was no eugenicist, but something of the stoic Vigil seaworthiness in the Justinian line might be a bit more welcome than Mr Justinian thought.

The flames leapt, hungry for paper. She let out a sigh.

'You may come to my lighthouse once a week and court me in the interests of social engagement,' Arden said through gritted teeth. 'I will need regular supplies brought to me anyhow. Your driver can make himself useful at least.'

'Yes. Very good.' Mr Justinian's smile showed his incisors.

She wondered just what shame had sent him packing back here from Clay Portside, a cur with a tail between its legs. Arden reached for the paper again. He pulled the paper away, put the certificate back in the leather binder, then returned the binder to its locked drawer.

'It is still much safer to keep items here,' he said. 'The tower structure is in poor condition. You would not want an inundation or damp to destroy your Certificate of Work. The best place for it is in the safety of the Coastmaster's office. Any high-ranking Seamaster judge would agree with me, if there were ever – as you say – an investigation.'

'Fine,' she said. 'Just make sure that I am paid on time. Certificates on fragile paper are one thing, but Djenne coins survive a sunken ship.'

With that, she swallowed her brandy-laced tea in one gulp, and stomped up the stairs to her room, and made damn sure she both locked the door and shoved a chair under the handle before retiring for the night.

5

Her uncle had left her a boat

Her uncle had left her a boat.

More correctly, Arden thought, putting her hands on her hips in unconscious imitation of her Portmaster father, he had left a boat to whomever the Guild appointed as Lightkeeper after him. No doubt the bad news would have sunk through the layers of missives and post-rumours, that Lucian Beacon's eldest child was *malorum* and dim of blood.

Such a condition reflected badly on a family who made their name in fire. The great genetic and ancestral ledgers of the Eugenics Society would be opened in the inner sanctum of the legendary Clay Library. An accusing cross scrawled in blood-red ink next to the name of *Beacon*. Their partnerships and progeny would be scrutinized for generations to come. Jorgen would have suspected that no Beacon-born would follow after him.

Perhaps he'd made peace with the passing of the baton to a Pharos man, maybe accepted that a lesser Lumiere would take up the fire he had once tended. One of the other *ignis*-gifted families, just not a Beacon. Jorgen wouldn't have ever thought little Arden here, even if he had still remembered her.

Oh, Uncle. If only I could tell you I made it. Like her cousin Stefan, Uncle Jorgen had appeared in her life only in blinks and snatches, a thin, slighter version of his four brothers, timid around adults, but with a rare patience when it came to children. She remembered his peculiarities most clearly, the shine of his nails, his moustache severely waxed at the ends, the precisely polished brass hobs in his shoes. His face was a smudge. They said that the Beacon brothers might have been handsome youths, but only Jorgen was beautiful.

She imagined he looked like her father.

An unspoken trouble had early on separated Jorgen from his Clay Portside brothers. For all that he had died only weeks ago, he had long since passed over in Arden's life. He'd stopped making his annual pilgrimages. He'd refused contact with his family. He became a memory, and then a corpse.

And yet she wondered if he would have been pleased that his niece would be the one to have *Fine Breeze*. It was not the sort of craft she had expected her dour, exiled uncle to own. Instead of the faded blues and greens of those few fishing vessels that dotted the harbour, *Fine Breeze* was as red as a polished lacquer cabinet from the Middle Country.

'Lightmaster Beacon loved that boat,' the Harbourmistress said with a sour expression, as if such an emotion were peculiar and unwelcome. Her accent was pure Lyonnian, as if she'd only come from Clay City yesterday.

Mx Modhi, the Harbourmistress of Vigil, if that was what one could call the position of watching over a miserly pier for most hours of the day, was a tall, stout woman of grandmasterly years and an ancestry that went beyond the small pale folk of Fiction. The shipyard domain she beheld and no doubt ruled, from a sturdy, leather-upholstered rocking chair in the primo position to watch all the comings and goings from the bay. She wore waxed canvas trousers, not a skirt, and her legs were as broad as ship-masts, and her arms suggested the same strength of clipper ship cross-beams. She still had in her oaken face the shades of the beauty she must have been when she was younger.

A curved pipe in her mouth bobbed as the Harbourmistress

watched Arden gingerly put a foot out to test the red boat's wallow. A city girl's apprehension made for fine entertainment.

'Don't fall in,' the Harbourmistress said. 'I'll not get out of this chair to rescue you.'

'Jorgen couldn't have had the boat built here.'

'No, she belonged to a traveller through these parts. Lost her in a game of cards – Beggar's Blight of all things. Ended up in Jorgen's hands – your uncle might have been slight, but he was fiery. Would take on a shorefolk brawler twice his size if he felt an injustice had been done.'

Arden smiled. 'Oh, he was definitely a Beacon, then. We are all about correctness and balance.' She indicated her gloves. 'But if there was fire in him, he kept it under a bushel for the most part. This boat is very unlike him.'

'Sometimes the most austere folk will have a weakness for rare and beautiful things.'

With that said, Mx Modhi nodded at Arden's blue-spotted coat and, grinning, puffed a smoke-halo from her plesiosaur-ivory pipe.

'Well, beautiful things can be useful. And utility is beautiful too.'

'And you're off to the promontory now. Our sea-washed sunset gates.'

'I am.'

'I shan't have to tell you all the local histories then. Nearly twenty years of them I've learned. No doubt every cock-eyed Billie-and-Bob has fallen over each other to breathlessly fill you in about the tale of poor Mrs Riven and her awful comeuppance.' The ivory stem clicked against her teeth as she spoke, and Arden once again was amazed at the Harbourmistress having been here for so long. She could have stepped off a Clay City boat yesterday. 'Frankly, the people in this country can be disgusting.'

Arden picked up a loose end of rope dangling from an arterial-blooded bow. As she coiled it, she asked as casually as she could, 'You've been here twenty years. Did you ever meet Mrs Riven yourself?'

'I did,' the Harbourmistress said. 'Knew her well.' She chewed on the pipe, and a long moment of appraisal followed, as she decided what to tell Arden, and what to leave out. 'Watched her as a child from this very post, coming down here among the fishing boats and yearning out towards the sea. Her father was not a marine-affiliated gentleman, but the girl . . . something was in her. The tide, perhaps. All the fishermen were besotted with their little queen, brought her whelk shells and sea-dollars, mermaid teeth on a string. She would sing them a song for a penny.'

'Sounds like a bit of a sea-sprite, then.' Arden flung the wrapped coil into the boat. 'Very romantic.'

'Oh, no romance there, not our Bellis. Cunning little thing, she was. Never missed a trick. A little gang of orphans and illegitimates used to run riot through the village then as they do now, and Bellis Harrow was their ringleader. Their tiny Genghis Khan, but certainly a benevolent one.' The chewing stopped. 'Then she grew up. Things are different for women around these parts, although one cannot say she didn't fight harder than most to keep from being crushed by the conditions of femininity.'

Arden blinked at the sudden fellow feeling, a rush of warmth to her skin. 'I know what that is like,' she said with deep sincerity. 'I've fought those battles myself. I still wear the scars on my heart.'

The Harbourmistress remained aloof, but her countenance gentled.

'You take care out there now, Lightmistress. There's more powers and prejudices in these sainted waters than you'll hear about in your city towers. Not all the monsters have twelve arms and live in the sea. Some have two legs; you can be sure of it.'

There followed from her a brief instruction on how messages would pass from lighthouse to harbour. Fiction had no reliable telegraph radio infrastructure, nor cable out to the promontory. Arden would need to use a mirror heliograph each morning on the tenth hour, and each evening on the third. Emergency messages to flash on the hour, if required, but anything less than the tower having fallen over was not an emergency, so she was not to bother Mx Modhi with it.

How different from the constant flurry of communication in the signal house! Arden agreed to every instruction the Harbourmistress made, and realized she would need to relearn the mirror code she had forgotten a decade ago.

The Harbourmistress returned to her scanning of the ocean, and Arden went to her uncle's boat, wondering if she should have asked more about her Riven neighbour. Nobody was quite telling the same story. Was it fey and vulnerable Bellis Riven, anchored in a terrible state of marital imprisonment, or was it fighting Bellis Riven, the tough little girl who could make coarse fishermen do her bidding with just a song?

Was there a true story at all?

In contrast to her father, Jorgen Beacon had not been a tall fellow, so he had made the rudder and sail adjustments to suit his height. Conveniently they suited Arden as well. *Fine Breeze* had a small cabin for sheltering in, and batten sails that were cut in a square style. The forward sail was the largest, with a smaller sail behind the rudder.

The waves were not so rough that morning, so after Arden familiarized herself with the craft, she unfurled the mainsail and put Vigil behind her.

The cold bay held as much of a sparkle as the climate would ever allow, and the promontory, as always, was barely visible in the constant mist. Yet each slosh and roll took the days of strain and worry away. Arden had not entirely grasped how tense she had held herself, until the moment she tied off the rigging and relaxed at the rudder. A brisk wind filled the canvas, and she manoeuvred *Fine Breeze* out into the open water for her first proper, clear view of Fiction's last sanguis lighthouse. Her heart skipped a beat, and Arden smiled. There it was, the sense of blood, powerful as homesickness and yearning. Her hands tingled in anticipation.

Eyes upon the promontory spotted Arden long before she made it to the pier.

As the boat danced close to the weatherworn bollards of the tiny sheltered inlet the familiar figure of another Portside guildsman appeared. Friendly Mr Harris from the nomadic Sea Guilds, a man round and bushy with his great blond beard and shipwright's shoulders that could seat both child and full-grown woman on each. He kept his hair short, a custom of the fisher-folk here. Far better to have it under a waxed woollen cap rather than getting caught in all the sea-spray, though Arden suspected hair-locks often ended in the water in superstition before a good catch. There was a parallel to the sanguis giving of blood, though anyone around here would have argued bitterly that it was not the same thing at all.

'Hoy!' he cried out, waving an arm as thick as a ham. 'Hoy, Lightmistress!'

'Hoy,' she shouted in delight. 'You have turned wild since I saw you last in Clay, Mr Harris!'

'We have merely moved up in the world, you and myself both! I'll throw a rope, let me tie you off.'

The journey of a month was ended. At last she saw her light-house up close. It stood at the end of a long, thin natural mole of basalt blocks, squat and wide rather than the tremendously high spire of the Clay Mouth. Whitewash might have daubed the granite once, but neglect had scored the paint down to bare stone, leaving only a thin crust on the lee side. Some of the glass panes in the lantern room were broken. Not much of an attempt had been made to fix the missing panes other than a ragged piece of wood hoarding, to stop the flame from blowing out. A weathercock at the very top leaned at a forlorn angle.

Desolation shrouded the tower. Mr Justinian had been telling the truth about its decay, at least.

Mr Harris lumbered to the end of the pier and tossed out a rope hitch that had to weigh as much as she did. Once she made *Fine Breeze* fast, he reached down and pulled her out with a mighty yank.

'I am glad to see a friendly face!' she said breathlessly. 'And to find the coast hasn't taken the might from you.'

'Little Ardie!' He put her back down onto the pier, his own red cheeks growing redder as he blushed furiously at forgetting his manners. 'I'm sorry, you must be properly called Madam Lightmistress now.' He took off his battered fisherman's hat and gave a quick bow.

'I'm still getting used to the name too, Gerard.'

'Ah, but you're all grown up. You'll need some meat on those bones of yours, girl. The wind would blow you away.'

Arden waved him off good-naturedly. She could not call herself slender, not from all the hard work on the wharves to fill her out. No wasp-waist for her, not if you wanted the strength to haul a Fresnel element up a hundred feet of light-house stairs.

'Don't you worry, I'm strong enough.'

'I'm sure you are.' He stood back to measure her with his eye. 'A fine coat you're wearing.'

'It's real krakenskin, before you ask, Mr Harris.'

'I noted that. How did you manage to afford such clothing? Did your father give you your inheritance early, and throw into the bargain that of the rest of the Beacon brothers?'

'Hardly,' she said fondly, even though the mention of her father made her wince with regret. 'I bought it from a rag-trader's table. Apparently, it belonged to a dead woman, as everyone is so keen to remind me.' Arden paused and added, 'The wife of a brutal murderer, apparently.'

Mr Harris' face clouded. 'Ah, you mean Mr Riven.'

'Yes. The Coastmaster of Vigil had certain other titles for him, though.'

'I think most people take care not to mention them aloud. He has a habit of appearing when people speak his name.'

Mr Harris pointed down the ridge. A mile away, three large wooden buildings crabbed the rocky beach as barnacles might cling to rock. They were as large as the workhouses back in Clay Portside, almost wharf-sized. A saltwater lichen frowsed off the grey iron roof. They had been there for a long time and suffered much the same aura of neglect as her lighthouse.

Her sharp eyes caught gulls and cormorants gathered on one corner of the compound, a congregation of devil birds drawn by the promise of a feed.

'Mr Riven lives in those buildings yonder. Does his business on the shore. Once quite an industry in the slaughter of sea-monsters here in Vigil. Serpents. Leviathans. Krakens when they could be called up. A whole family of butchers, I heard, blood-tied to the ocean, but this coast can be hungry, and the political machinations of men hungrier still, so now only one Riven remains.'

The Mr Justinian in her memory hissed, *'twas he that killed his family*.

'Blood-tied? You mean like *sanguis* talent?'

'Not quite, Ardie. Perhaps an earlier, more ah . . . *fundamental* version of the trait, eh? The talent first appeared in this country, remember. Occasionally a sanguis jumps out of the gene pool, though if they have any sense they keep quiet about it and don't let the Lions know.'

'Has Mr Riven caused you much trouble out here?'

Mr Harris shook his head. 'We've had no need for business. He goes his way, and I mine. Whether Jorgen had dealings with Mr Riven previously, that trouble lay between themselves. I would say it's hard to avoid the man if you were here any longer than a month.'

She must have made a face, for he continued, 'He won't be a problem Ardie. Come now, there's talk in town about you, but these towns would talk if a fellow wore the wrong clothes on a Sunday.'

Mr Harris had kept the tower for six weeks, not long enough to attract a maintenance stipend. There would have been next to nothing he could have done to fix the place up. The small lower floor might have had the potential for cosiness, had not the walls been so slimed with sea-damp. Anything resembling home-comforts had been knocked together from desultory driftwood scaffolding. The rude bed might have suited Mr Harris, a man used to sleeping out in the open on a wharf, but for a Guildswoman Lightmistress it seemed little better than the floor. The internal stairs were constructed – if one could consider a spiral of protrusions as crooked as a brawler's teeth a construction – from keystones in the wall. The banisters needed replacing, else Arden could foresee the very real outcome of falling to her death.

On reaching the topmost lantern house, the vastness of the promontory view struck Arden like a bell-hammer. The sea surrounded them in a smothering slab of grey, and the thunderclouds might have been the white-rimed backs of behemoths, fallen in a heavenly grave.

Behind her, the ruins scattered along the coast. Old monks and hermits had first built impractical monasteries upon this shore, hoping to win the unsophisticated inhabitants of Fiction to the church and to save their immortal souls. Perhaps the stone and glass had stood for a generation, maybe ten, but only rubble remained, slowly dissolving back into the earth.

From up high she observed the one remaining cathedral wall, one that had held a stained-glass rose window, now only a perfect empty circle of mortar and rock. The window stared out to sea with a single, sightless eye.

Old magic here, she thought. Old superstitions. The ancient saints were canny enough not to replace the cold abyssal gods of the sea-folk with the warm, dignified artifices of their own religions. She wondered if her cousin Stefan had grown into his spirituality among these old stones, if he'd felt the Almighty murmur in the drowned lands below the wind and waves and knew that he belonged to a power greater than that of his name, and blood.

Then she inspected the perpetual lamp with growing concern.

The ratio of blood was important to the chemical articulations within a sanguine lantern. A typical lamp required *fuel* to burn, the way metal required *force* to bend, force to control the weather, force to hold the vapour inside a container to give weight and mass and velocity. All things that were finite, exhaustible, subject to the grinding momentum of God's creation. What Arden had, what all sanguinem had, was a catalyst within her veins that turned mass and force in upon itself so that energy in an element (for her, fire), could be sustained and intensified beyond what should be possible.

The pain and danger of blood letting was nature's warning – lest the wielder grow too arrogant in their contortion of the natural order.

Arden remembered an Academy tutor drawing a broad circle with her finger over her heart while explaining. Sanguis blood was an alchemical ouroboros, the snake biting its own tail. *You can change the physical property of a thing. A regenerative cycle outside of time. But eventually entropy sets in. The cycle weakens. The iron remembers it is strong, and becomes hard. The flame remembers it needs to burn fuel, finds none, and extinguishes. So something must make it right. A gifting, an exchange. Blood we use, but it was not always so. In older, less enlightened days, entire bodies would be the sacrament that the cycle of labour required . . .*

Arden frowned, both piqued by the memory and the sense that something was very wrong with Jorgen's orphaned light. In the daytime, the flame should still have burned as bright as a summer's morning, but it had the cast of a midwinter afternoon. The offering funnel, through which Jorgen would have made his blood-tithe each week, was filthy. Dried blood crusted the entrance until barely a channel remained for the offering to run through.

Unthinkingly, Arden thumbed the curve of her arm. As she had shown the guest the previous night, dozens of small scars laddered there. When Arden maintained her small signal light upon the Parrot Wharf, the compact lantern's cold flame had required only a smear of blood, once a week, to stay bright. Grommets had been unnecessary in her previous life. But a lighthouse keeper needed to give so much more blood than a lamp-turning signaller did, to maintain the ratio of instruction, to make those sacrifices. The scar tissue could cause her hands permanent damage, if not for a coin to protect the skin.

Mr Harris joined her at the top of the stairs, puffing and panting. He'd never been tested for talent, but like any associate labour guildsman he had familiarity with the blood tithing of the docks. She did not have to hide the trade tools from him.

'Do you know why my uncle died, Mr Harris?'

'Heartbreak, Lightmistress. Plain and simple heartbreak.'

'Maybe the motivation, but by what mechanism? We cannot easily take our lives.'

'Not take, but certainly neglect.' Mr Harris said evasively, not quite looking at Arden. 'Anyone with implanted silver in their skin must regularly return. Return to Clay annually and have them cleaned, replaced. You think the Lyonne Order would permit their sanguineous guildsmen to live in freedom so easily?'

She tucked her hands under her arms, feigning a chill from an open window. 'It seems odd, that he should not return, or at least, find an illegal phlebotomist to take the grommets out.'

Those great shoulders of Mr Harris gave a slow shrug. 'After Stefan died – was killed, if you ask certain people – Jorgen stopped going back to Clay. No reason to, in his mind. Estranged from his family, his son lost to bad dealings. When an infection set into his hands, the Guild sent me to see what was going on. By the time I arrived, the sepsis had set in. Made him deathly ill, his blood poisoned. I could not convince him to go home. He did not last much longer after that.'

Arden moved through to Jorgen's possessions, trying to marry these crude items, this filthy degradation, with the gentle man in her memory. The knife he'd used to cut away the layer of callused skin from his decaying coins lay encrusted upon a similarly disgusting table. A whetstone nearby explained why the blade had a shapeless edge, the metal pared down paper-thin.

'Could you not have imposed upon him some *penicillium*, and some powdered kraken beak Mr Harris? Of all the places, those medicines would be most available here.'

'Oh, I tried. But it was too late, and the coins belong to the Order, the way the sanguineous do. Only Order-sanctioned phlebotomists can be relied upon to take them out. He would have had to go out to the Sainted Isles to find himself a man who could remove such invasiveness.' Mr Harris tilted his head towards the horizon, straight as a carpenter's plumb. 'People go to the Isles to die, Mx. Beacon. They don't often come back.'

'Thank you for telling me this, Gerry. I shall endeavour to have my coins removed when I finish here and return to Lyonne. A puppet string is one thing, but they shall not put a leash on me. I shall not turn into my uncle. At least . . . at least unlike him I have nobody to lose.'

The Clayman's face became so dour, he might have been dipped in shadow. He motioned her to silence. The walls could be listening. Those bodiless spirits of fate and irony in the old stones were deeply aligned to secrets. They inflicted their own bad luck.

Then quieter, 'Your cousin the Rector was a witness to all that Mr Riven did. All of it. Everything. Took the confessions of both man and wife. Knew secrets in the confessional terrible enough that he would face church censure by testifying in the magistrate's court.'

The wave-bellows echoed through the tower. Words spoken in the confession box were sacred. For a priest to bring such testimony into the open . . .

'Stefan was going to testify against Mr Riven?'

Mr Harris continued solemnly. 'He was the prosecution's only reliable witness and Mr Riven killed him. Look, Jorgen didn't take it lying down. Had it in mind that he would have Mr Riven experience the same fate. If not by an accident, then by some misfortune. He joined forces with Mr Harrow, put aside the feud the men had shared previously. Did the fellow some real damage, but only enough to rile him up, not blunt his teeth.'

'I have had the misfortune to meet Mr Harrow. Surely Mr Riven would have left this place, if he knew the townsfolk hated him so much.'

'The Rivens have populated these shores for centuries, Arden. The man would have no more left his home than call up a storm and cast the promontory into the sea. No, it has been a mighty war of subtle violence here these past few years. Jorgen succeeded in having Riven drowned once, only to have him haul himself in from the ocean as if he'd made a pact with the devil to return. The man can't be killed easily. Something in his nature.'

'I did not come here expecting duty as a foot soldier in a war.'

'Nobody ever does.' Mr Harris pointed at her coat. 'That coat on your shoulders is weighted with bad news. If he sees you in it, only the sea-devils can tell what he will do.'

She collected her resolve. A possession of the dead it might be, but the coat was *her* possession now. Salvaged, the way a shipwreck returned to shore has no owner except the one who reports it. How many times as a signalmistress and lanternkeeper in Portside had she taken up the position others would not, them fearing the dead man who had once rung the shipping bell or worked the signal stick? Accidents were common on the wharves. Every light and buoy had a ghost attached.

'No, I shall keep my coat, and if the maker wants its return, he shall do the gentlemanly thing and ask for it, with an offer of a suitable replacement. I will speak to him face to face, and we shall see if there cannot be some kind of arrangement.'

Mr Harris exhaled, nodded, knowing better than to challenge a woman whose mind was made up.

'You are your father's daughter through and through. And your poor late mother, bless her soul and curse the pirates who took her.'

Once Arden had finished her tour, she shared a lunch with Mr Harris outside the tower. Thick sourdough bread, the hard cheese that travels well, pickles and a runny syrup trying hard to be a chutney. They sat in the ruins of a rowboat that made for a rustic table, an *Owl and the Pussycat* kind of boat, as her favourite Uncle Nicolai would say. Uncle Nicolai had husbanded the great lighthouse at the Mouth, that mighty entrance to Clay Capital, the golden door to the country of Lyonne. Was to him that she had whispered her dream of keeping not just a signal flame, but the Spire at Clay's centre, the one her grandmother used to keep in the old days, before Arden had tested late, *malorum*, and dim.

No Spire for her then. A wharf-light and the associated administrations of signalling at most, but if a Beacon child might return their family's honour by winning the Spire post, it would not be Arden who would do it.

Mr Harris brought out some brown glass bottles containing a yeasty ale. She cast her attention westward, to where the first of the noon clouds had begun to build on the blank slate of the ocean. *Fine Breeze* sensed the storm before she did. The oncoming currents buffeted the boat against the pier.

'I shall move in tomorrow morning,' she said at last. 'There's no point delaying the handover any longer.'

'Very well. I'll signal for the Coastmaster's driver to collect you, first thing. Your lamphouse assistant will be here by then.'

'Male or female?'

'Female. A real stormbride of a lass, did her post out of Harbinger Bay, where the prison ships moor. A real competent sort.'

Mr Harris stood up and collected the scraps, which he threw to the motley collection of seagulls, auks and white ibis that had gathered to watch them eat. Another gust of wind warned her not to dally, and Mr Harris walked her down the cliff path to *Fine Breeze*.

'Aye, I enjoyed sharing your first day, Ardie. Those souls out there are yours to keep, now.'

He pointed at the horizon, then passed over a pair of brass spyglasses from his satchel to Arden. She peered into their eyepieces so as not to embarrass him, for her Beacon-sharp eyes had already seen what lay in the distance.

A flotilla of boats in the distance, moving in and out of encroaching fog. At least fifteen of them, and their crooked, uneven builds had not a single uniform style. Hulks and wrecks, not fit to work a canal, let alone the open water.

'They've bypassed both bays. Where are they going?'

'Sainted Isles lie out there beyond the horizon.'

'The petroleum islands? With the pumps . . . with the perpetual mechanica?' She recalled the maps in her father's Portmaster offices. A broken scatter of atolls and archipelagos surrounding three land masses in the middle of the Darkling Sea. Dashed lines where the cartographer was uncertain of the landscape. They'd seemed so lonely and far away. An exile's islands, where one went to be forgotten, and to die.

'Yes. Even the perpetual arbours and escapements or the rockblood machines need a conduit of labour to wind the springs. The Isles require hands to work. What better labourers than those folk already displaced by sanguine talents?'

Arden pretended to look through the brass again so as not to show Mr Harris her uncomfortable face. She'd seen one *sanguis pondus* replace a dozen longshoremen on a wharf. She'd seen the union riots light up Clay Portside so for a week not one ship left nor entered. 'Surely they aren't attempting an ocean journey in those vessels. Those boats don't look like they could even survive a river crossing.'

'They all of them believe there's nothing else for them in Lyonne.'

'Goodness, who would put such an idea in their heads? We can't do everything with blood.'

Mr Harris stroked his beard with sorrowful dignity. 'The idea of perpetual rockblood wells and their untapped bounty drives men to flights of madness. In Portside I hear of entire congregations afflicted with the idea . . . the dream of a place where *human* labour has real value, not sanguis labour, not machine. But the conduit of *hand* to *work* and no mystical power in between. Aye, a disease of greed and wealth grows in the minds of people who've previously known neither. Where they once sang hymns of the Holy Land and the One Who Walks the Way, they have now started to plan pilgrimages to the petroleum shores.'

Arden returned Mr Harris his brass spyglasses. 'I must not

judge. There's nothing anyone can do about them. Even the Lyonne Parliament cannot stop people from leaving. Free movement is a right enshrined by God.'

He nodded, put his spyglasses away with the finality of a man who has seen all he requires. 'Your sanguinity protects you now, Ardie, but this is the truth of it, eventually whatever privations the poorfolk suffer, the rich will suffer as well. And the rich pay sanguinem wages. *Your* wages. And keep your safety. Whatever cruel siren-song sung on those Islands will not be so easily contained there. Eventually the doctrine must make its way back to the mainland. Aye, coin or no coin, you would be safer at home.'

The wind kicked up, and they had to move again, else be tumbled from the high ground. Arden took Mr Harris' stout elbow and tried to put his troublesome words aside.

'You mustn't fret about my safety,' she said as they walked. 'The Guildsman said I'd only have to work the light until the start of winter. They'll call me back and give me my full degree.' She raised her hands. 'I'll have my coins taken out too, and there will be no leash upon me.'

He raised his eyebrows. 'All this before winter? If you leave then, you'll miss the midwinter crowning of the Deepwater King!' His excursion into dour prophecy quickly returned to jolly banter. 'It's quite a memorable festival, even in Vigil. They barely celebrate anything else.' Mr Harris grinned then, his eyes alight with mischief. Nudged her elbow. 'Could make Deepwater Bride for a day . . . and if you find yourself a suitable husband there's nothing the Order can do about it.'

She felt her cheeks grow hot. Goodness, how could she even consider tumbling into the greasy bed of a coarse Fiction man? He would make love like an animal, all grunts and snuffles, paw her bare flesh thoughtlessly, grow aroused and perhaps he would be coarse down there too . . .

Then her cheeks burned again, for it had been a year since she'd had such a dalliance after Richard Castile had left her, and she had made a firm vow. No more men, or thoughts of love.

She let go of Mr Harris' warm, strong arm and navigated the final rocky stairs down to the pier by herself.

Once there, she turned to him and jutted her chin obstinately. 'It is the ocean I shall love, not men. Besides, I'm not my uncle. I bear no ill-will or history to anyone.'

Mr Harris flicked a glance towards the old kraken-processing factories and made a disapproving grumble deep in his throat. 'Arden Beacon, I can tell you're planning to work some trader's charisma upon this neighbour of yours, but Riven is more beast than man. The monsters he battles upon the ocean, they are his brethren, not us.'

'I am not going to battle him, Mr Harris,' she said, untying *Fine Breeze*'s lashings. 'I will pay him a visit, like a civilized person. I intend to visit many on this coast by the time the storm season is upon us.'

'He may try and poke you with his harpoon rather than let you onto his property.'

'You cannot make me afraid,' Arden retorted. 'If I am to execute my functions as a proper Lightmistress, I must be at peace with all my *beloved* ocean gives me.'

'Well, you might love the ocean, but a woman with fire in her blood cannot win such love back,' Mr Harris said. 'You talk of power? In two centuries no child alive has displayed a blood-alignment for cryptobiological specimens the way the Rivens have constantly done. Aye, even the human race is closing ranks about such a damn travesty of inheritance. He is incompatible with you. He is incompatible with everybody.'

6

The tides had a certain

The tides had a certain personality in the dusk that they did not have during the day. The waters passed that stage where one would call them *frolicsome* and instead become *malicious*, and active in wanting harm.

After an hour of fighting the steadily swelling sea, the *Fine Breeze*'s bow relievedly turned towards the Vigil pier. Arden would have no trouble in securing mooring, for another boat had just left the small, rickety marina.

Within minutes she saw the shape entirely, huge and dark, an oil-powered side-paddle wheeler that didn't float upon the restless water but rather compelled it to submission. The plume of smoke had a curiously luminous blue tinge. Only one kind of oil produced such luminous particulates.

Kraken oil.

So then. Her neighbour. She adjusted her sails and continued in a straight line towards the docks. Mr Riven's giant sea-barge approached *Fine Breeze* with frightening speed. The bow wave rose on either side with the power of waves breaking against rocks.

'Sir, a sail ship heading into port on this bearing has right of way,' she muttered to the wind. If one of them didn't turn soon, they were going to collide. She wouldn't stand a chance. But the barge kept coming and if it did not turn soon, she would be crushed under the threshing wheels.

At the last moment Arden wrenched her rudder sideways. *Fine Breeze*'s sail boom swung around, and had she not had her wits about her, it would have knocked Arden off her feet and into the water.

'Come on, come on!' She cursed. 'If you old gods have any power here, give me wind!' Disturbed, the gusts roiled about her but had little success in filling the sail. And that massive vessel was so close now that she saw the hooded figure in the wheelhouse, resolutely steering his juggernaut onwards.

The chopping wheels powered closer and closer still until finally the ship bore down upon her wake, missing a collision by less than an arm span. She could have reached over and touched the black boat, so close were they. *Fine Breeze* keeled over to near-capsize in the great bow wave, the hammering engine so cacophonous in her ears it made her head ring. For an awful moment a name filled her sight. A name scored upon the black side in an unadorned script. *Saudade.*

'You monster!' Arden screamed, shaking her fist. 'You could have killed me!'

The figure in the wheelhouse did not turn back to see if she was all right. She could be in pieces, drowning, and he would have cared not one whit.

Finally her boat righted itself, the wind returned in somewhat of a constant direction, and Arden could return to the rude little harbour, shaken up but in one piece.

'How did the boat go, Lightmistress?' Harbourmistress Modhi called out as soon as she butted into the buoys lining the lone pontoon that made up the marina.

'Fine,' Arden said, still angry from her near-drowning. In rebellion against her brief imprisonment she had for a little while felt somewhat of a sympathetic warmth towards the mysterious fellow Mr Justinian had spoken so rudely about. She had not wanted the odious Coastmaster to be *right*.

'Wasn't an accident, that. He'd have seen you from a mile away.' Mx Modhi grinned and puffed victoriously on her pipe. 'I had an inkling he'd take uncomfortably to your get-up.'

Arden clutched her coat about her with defiance. One thing said for Beacons, they were known for their stubbornness. The ship moves for the signal light, not the other way around.

'I bought this salvage garment fair and square. If Mr Riven wants it back, he can be the gentleman and ask.'

The pipe smoke surrounded the Harbourmistress in wreaths of grey silk.

'He won't *ask*. He'll just *take*.' Her voice rose in timbre. 'Isn't that right, David, my boy?'

A black-haired lad ran from another pontoon pier, all gangly adolescent limbs yet to settle into adulthood, to fasten *Fine Breeze* on Arden's behalf. He was perhaps seventeen years old, and Arden noted the marks on the youth's hands, pale scars from the required testmoots he'd have taken on his eleventh birthday. Fiction children were still tested, despite sanguinity being uncommon in the south. It was not a duty shirked. A ledgered talent popping up out of nowhere could bring a sudden unexpected wealth to a poor family.

She said her thank-yous to the boy, uttered some words to draw him into a conversation, but he barely met her eye. A fine black down on his upper lip trembled. He hovered in that strange halfway world between child and man He'd be a child far longer yet at this rate under his mother's shadow.

'Don't mind my fool son,' the Harbourmistress said once David scuttled away. 'He's just out of sorts because I won't let him on board that dirty black boat. Doesn't understand I'm protecting him the way a mother should. Lord knows what perversions that fellow gets up to out there.'

'Oh, is your son friends with Mr Riven?' Arden asked, tossing her head. 'I thought him quite the hermit when not trying to run people down in his boat.'

Mx. Modhi chewed on her pipe for a weighty second before gruffly admitting, 'Guild stipend won't cover good tobacco and a proper Lyonnian education for my son. Your neighbour was the only one to give him the time of day. Fisherfolk around here don't take kindly to anyone who can't count ten generations wasting away on these shores.'

'I'll take your word for it, Harbourmistress. I haven't had much contact with the locals.'

'No, you wouldn't have, would you? Ensconced with Mr Justinian up in the Manse, I gather.'

Something in the winking way Mx Modhi spoke made Arden indignant. 'Only until I get myself ready for my lighthouse duties. And we are not *ensconced*. Our relationship is purely professional. He is a member of a professional Guild, as am I. He is bound by vow to help me set up.'

'Indeed. These things take time, do they not? And my boy David here, he's been paid already to ferry Mr Justinian to your doorstep once a week for trysts in case his car won't make it. He thinks of all possibilities, our Baron.'

Arden would wonder later why her mouth hurt. At Mx Modhi's assertion, she had clenched her jaw so hard that bright sparks of pain prickled her cheeks.

'He is Coastmaster, and Mr Justinian has to have his briefings. I would prefer them once a month, myself, but these are unfamiliar waters, and I need supplies brought to me.'

Harbourmistress Modhi sucked on her pipe, blew more smoke for her airy spirit. 'If that is the case, then I welcome the correction. Excuse my misunderstandings, there has been more than one lady here who has fancied herself the *second* Mrs Justinian, and they'll not take kindly to a stranger whisking his affections away.'

'The second?' Arden asked, although she would more prefer that she never speak his name again. 'Nobody spoke of Mr Justinian being married before.'

'Well, nearly married. So far as the priest had not blessed the union in public. They were practically at the altar.'

'What happened to her?' Arden asked, even though her deep suspicions already told her the answer. Who else could it be, to arouse such a passion in him?

'Goodness, we only just spoke of her before. Miss Bellis Harrow was her name, but she died as Bellis Riven.'

Evening fell with all the finality of a closing funeral casket. The Manse's few lights battled the darkness and in the most case failed miserably. Arden retired to the mouldering study, desperate to pass time before the morning, and her final freedom. She had quite expected another argument with Mr Justinian, but the previous day's clash had made him sulk, and there was no better sulking place than in Garfish Point, a hundred miles north, far and away from Vigil and the duties of his home.

That didn't mean he'd taken with him the constant sense of unease that haunted the mansion's main rooms. The uneasiness worked its way though the corridors like a low fog. From a proud position on the library's sideboard, the octopus-thing in the glass bell jar gave a subtle shudder, its liquid tomb sensitive to atmosphere, the barometric shifts in air pressure. Arden stopped to peer in close. Not an octopus, perhaps. No mottled hide, or suckers. Just smooth, human-like skin.

A woman gave birth to that thing.

'Oh, goodness, I'm certain our circus-find will curse you if you look at it too much,' Dowager Justinian scolded as she came in with a cup of tea. She picked up one of the large napkins and threw it over the jar. 'I have nightmares of it breaking out and crawling about the house.'

Startled, Arden stepped away. 'I wondered if it were indeed true.' She kept her voice sceptical. 'That it came from a woman.'

Dowager Justinian's lips vanished inside the disapproving line of her mouth. 'Sadly true. One of the shorefolk worked here as a domestic. They are frivolous with their affections. A child, fourteen years old when she declared herself. In the end we had to supply our own doctor to assist in the delivery.' She shuddered at the memory, twisted her wedding ring. 'The Baron was delighted. The old Baron, I mean. My late husband's grandfather, Alexander Justinian, not my son. Such things reflect badly on the House.'

'Shouldn't the Eugenics Society have been called to report the birth?' Arden asked. 'They get fussy over an extra finger . . .' She waved at the jar, not altogether concealed by the napkin. 'This would make the Society have hysterics.'

'Baron Alexander Justinian had friends high up in the Society during his life,' the Dowager sighed. 'You are right, if it were up to a reasonable person the creature and the wench both would have been investigated. But they didn't seem much to care, and the Baron did like his curios.'

'What happened to the girl? Her family?'

The older woman fiddled with her earring. The marcasite chips caught the lantern glow. 'Oh, I think they're all gone now. Nomadic folk, islanders. They come and go, and the fish are bad, lately. What are you working on?'

She showed the Dowager her map. 'Finding my way. Learning the geography of Vigil.'

According to Arden's maps, which in the last few weeks she had spent most of her time studying in lieu of actually going out to sea, the shore where the Rivens' old factory buildings clung was not particularly accessible by watercraft. The wash and tempest on the rocks made it difficult to bring a small boat close, and the remains of a pier, broken at the root, showed just how dangerous the waves could be.

However on the other side of the promontory, on a circlet helpfully named Dead Man's Bay, a divot in the cliffs provided a few natural shelters and a small pebbled beach that was spared the tumult of the ocean waves. There were more ruins here, old fortifications of a Neolithic tribal folk, made before their more enlightened current era. The map illustrated them with helpful asterisks and the word *ruins* in the key.

To access the Riven factory, she could make her way on foot through the ruins.

Dowager Justinian raised the wick on the lamp. 'It's so dim in here, Lightmistress. How on earth are you seeing?'

'Beacons are good with little light and long distances,' Arden said. 'Blood aside, they're part of our small endowments, the mark of our family.'

'The Eugenics Society must think highly of such a trait.'

'There's always someone who will. It's not just lamps and signals. There's many shipping companies who pay handsomely for the distance-skill alone.'

The Dowager squinted in the lamplight, composed a sentence carefully in her thoughts before speaking. 'My son tells me you are in your twenty-seventh year. Unless you have made a vow to God or the Sapphic orders, I'm surprised someone of your genetic value is not yet married.'

Arden pointed at the risen lamp. 'It becomes complicated when one comes from old ledgered families. The Eugenics Society must approve any union I make. For now, I am forbidden anyone until my full degree.' She closed her eyes briefly, remembering the Guildsman clerk in her father's offices. His sly winking expression. *With a full degree you could certainly choose who you would like to marry, for one thing.*

How pathetic, that Richard Castile feared discovery by Lions, when they had known about the relationship all along.

'You are of a good age,' the Dowager continued, and Arden realized at once what the Madam of the house was leading in to.

She put her fountain pen down. 'Dowager, you never told me your son was going to marry Bellis Riven.'

'Didn't I?' The Dowager's fingers dappled upon a cameo brooch at her throat. 'I could never quite keep up with Vernon's dalliances when he was a young man.'

'A proposed marriage is hardly a dalliance.'

'I suppose not.' Her eyes became hard in the lamplight, knowing that Arden had foiled an ill-considered matchmaking. 'One could never be certain if he'd only suffered a youthful fantasy. Without meaning to, Bellis could be quite the coquette.'

'My concern is,' Arden continued, 'although I have an assistant, there will be times when I'll be on the promontory alone with Miss Harrow's suspected killer nearby. I cannot have unresolved issues between him and your son making my job difficult. Mr Riven is my closest neighbour, and regardless of what he has done, or whatever rumours swirl, I may come to depend on him for assistance out there.'

A little part of her laughed at the thought of seeking assistance from someone who had tried to run her down as casually as a cur in the middle of the road. But she had committed herself to signal-keeper business, and that meant business with the other person who shared her territory.

'Miss Bellis Harrow and Vernon – I mean my son, Mr Justinian – may have made plain their intention to marry, but my son never wasted his youth on adult responsibilities.' The Dowager adjusted the wick on one lamp, for the brightness illuminated an alarming patch of swelling damp on one wall. 'By my count ten girls in all Fiction have considered themselves the next Madame Justinian. I dare not think about Lyonne. But she was the best of them, Bellis. A good, sweet-natured girl. Always had a kind word for me. They were friends from their first year. My son courted her when he still had baby-cheeks, before the city called him away.'

'So they must have been of similar age, then.'

'Yes, yes they were. Quite a few children in town were. They formed quite a cadre. Vernon and Bellis exchanged rings in promise before he left. Being a hopeful mother, I'd hoped that *meant* they would one day marry. But you see, friendships from the cradle rarely survive the storms of adulthood.'

She fiddled with the wick up on a third lamp, this one to chase away the spirits of the gathering night. The only effect was to make the shadows darker, and harshen those lights already in the room.

'Strange,' Arden said. 'With all those tales of a forced marriage to Mr Riven, it led me to believe Miss Harrow a literal child. If she shared Vernon's age she must have been in her late twenties at least. My age, then. An independent adult.'

'Age is relative, you see. Her father, Mr Harrow, is a firm

man. Very firm. Owns the general store in Vigil, and is Postmaster into the bargain. Does duties as Magistrate when we have cause to hold a criminal court. So he rather preserved his child in a state of innocence longer than most.'

'I take it he approved of the union between Mr Justinian and Bellis?'

'Of course. Not a better match could a Vigil girl make, not even the daughter of a Magistrate Postmaster. Perhaps this made Mr Harrow blind to his daughter's beauty and friendly nature, how such a thing is a flame in the night-time, and attractive to night-flying things. Bellis loved my son. What a terrible, tragic surprise that she should marry Mr Riven so very suddenly.'

'Something must have happened to have spoiled this gilded cage that Mr Harrow kept her in. People don't flee comfort lightly.'

'No they do not,' Dowager Justinian said. 'She did not flee. Mr Riven desired that he should have her. An unseemly lust overcame him upon seeing Bellis in the town one day. He is blood-bound to the wild things of the sea, you understand. No doubt his urges are similarly wild.' Her hand went to her throat, appalled at what such an indecorous affinity meant.

Arden shook her head. 'Any magistrate could have granted divorce immediately had there been any true element of non-consent or violence.'

'The economy of Vigil needs kraken—'

'Goodness, morals go beyond that!'

'Well, people tried! Once Vernon attempted to visit Bellis out on the promontory and inquire about her welfare. Mr Riven fired at him with a Middle Country musket. And then a month later the girl was dead.' Dowager Justinian heaved a breath, fiddled nervously with a lace handkerchief wedged up her dark sleeve, then went to close the curtains for the night as if the act, more suited to servant-staff, assuaged a deeper trouble of which she had yet to speak.

'Hers is a wretched tragedy, I agree,' Arden said. 'But it's more tragic that I hear everyone's voice on the matter excepting Bellis Harrow-Riven's. What was her truth? What was her reason?'

'It doesn't need a truth or reason. She is dead. I have cried enough tears.'

With her duties done, Dowager Justinian went from the study with a rustle of skirts, and left Arden in the gloom with her maps.

A storm had come upon the shoreline, whistling mournfully across the barren black cliffs of Vigil's bay. When the oil lamps burned low, Arden put away her ocean-current almanacs and headed to her bed. The embers from the fire cast orange highlights across the room, made them move with an uneven flicker. The krakenskin's thousand eye-rings watched her with abyssal coldness, wiser than any holy stone. The black ship forever bore down upon Arden in her memory.

A dead woman had worn this coat. A dead woman stolen away, as in the fairy stories, where the King of the Sea would take a fair maiden from the beach and ravish her upon his oyster-pearl bed for a thousand nights.

An innocent tale, yet Bellis Harrow's life was just that story, whisked off by a lord of the sea and ravished in a crude bed in a decaying factory-shack. For her the reality had been a story of violence and despair.

The coat, though. The puzzle piece that did not fit.

Months, it would have taken to craft such a garment, to cut and cure and fit and sew. The tremulous leather-work at the sleeves had increased in confidence at the collar and yoke. A teacher had been patient, and their student enthusiastic. The patterns were exultant and joyful. A woman in pain could not have made this garment.

Arden's Portside stubbornness returned. During her duties as lantern mistress she had seen illegal ships enter the harbour through the Parrot Wharf turning bowl, filled with the spoils of piracy and illegal gains. Her job concerned the safe passage of boats through the locks and wharves. If she had no evidence of wrongdoing, it was not for her to judge the misbegotten contents they held. That task she would leave for the sheriffs and the inspectors

She had a lighthouse to manage, and a future far from here.

Whatever the locals got up to in the meantime, that was their business alone.

7

The Vernon Justinian who went to Garfish Point

The Vernon Justinian who went to Garfish Point the day before, and the one who woke up the next morning could hardly be considered the same person. He moaned piteously through the breakfast table and collapsed on the daybed afterwards with a damp napkin over his eyes. The sound of morning rain on the windows made him whimper. The house staff were obliged to tiptoe around, for the shuffle of their feet on the worn parquetry made him yell in a manner most unbecoming to a man of his station.

Everyone from the butler to the pretty girl of the scullery found themselves bludgeoned with his wrathful tongue. The girl's darting, angry eyes found Arden, and blamed her silently for Mr Justinian's foul condition.

Only Dowager Justinian received permission to come close, to bring the opium tea laced with cannabis oil which only served to make him delirious. Within minutes of his dashing the bitter drink to the carpet, Mr Justinian fell into a daze from which he could not be roused.

Arden could not find it in herself to be very upset at the

Coastmaster's complaint. It meant she would get easy escape from the grey confines of the Manse, and an unhurried excursion through the lands she would temporarily call home. Mr Quill, the old, tweedy fellow who did double duty as groundskeeper and Justinian driver, agreed to take Arden to the lighthouse by the long-route. He too feared his employer's temper, and relievedly accepted the excuse of a road trip.

The car rattled and coughed its way along the inland lanes that led past the racelakes and the ethanol-spirit farms that brought Fiction's economy a little coin by feeding the hungry country to the north. The coastal scrub was dominated by an aromatic bush, and the air through the open window smelled of menthol as well as salt.

Through most of the morning Arden hid her gloves under her bag politely until Mr Quill told her that he was not at all troubled by her presence.

'My second cousin twice-removed went to Lyonne after he was tested, near on fifty years ago,' he said. 'I saw the coins in his hands.'

'Oh? Would I know him?'

'Would you?'

'A Fiction blood-worker quite stands out these days. They're so rare.'

Mr Quill shook his head and his mouth fell into long, sad lines. 'Lass, you were not alive when he died. Fool didn't last a week. Got roaring drunk one night. Struck his head on a low beam, fell into a Clay Portside canal.'

'Oh, that is a shame,' Arden said, and felt her hands prickle awfully. 'The city can be quite disorienting to newcomers.'

He gave a phlegmy, dismissive cough. 'Disorienting! We aren't that lumpen, or grain-pickled. I know my cousin never touched alcohol. No, it was the Eugenics Society that had him killed.'

It was such a shockingly open pronouncement that Arden wound the window down a little more and silently turned to the menthol gust and the clattering engine rather than reply. Such conversations were never had in Lyonne, where a Lion might be lurking about every corner. 'The Eugenics Society wouldn't just murder people. They're a little more subtle than that.'

The skin under his eyes had a little nervous tic.

By now the vehicle had crested an uplift in the land and they came upon a great forest of silver and rubber piping, of vessels as large as airship bladders, and tall chambers as high as her lighthouse. If Arden wanted to talk to Mr Quill more about the economies of Lyonne and blood, her thoughts were gone in an instant.

'Goodness,' Arden exclaimed. 'These are automatic rockblood refineries, are they not?'

'Yes, Sainted Isle crude rockblood, straight from the wound.'

'I've never seen one so large before.'

'You don't use petralactose in that big Clay city?'

'All the time. We get petroleum distillates transported to Lyonne, but never in the crude form.'

A giant copper distillation tank towered above the scrub, bristling with walkways and transoms. From their distance, the refinery had the appearance of a malign castle built by madmen, except no man had made this terrible feat of automatic engineering. Arden spotted a puddle of iridescent petralactose pooling at the bottom of one tank, the old edifice leaking through aged valves no living being had the knowledge to fix. It was there that she caught her first view of human figures, oily workers scuttling about the old refinery with patches and seals, trying to keep it alive the way ants might attend at the swollen belly of their great, gravid queen.

'One of them damn grey ships is at dock,' Mr Quill said, pointing. 'Can you see the godforsaken thing? Have you not in your life witnessed such a travesty of nature?'

The ship was more barge than anything, a grey vessel without windows, berthed on the far shore of the peninsula. Arden knew little about the logistical workings of the Sainted Isles, only that the grey ship was a watch-worked craft with a single purpose, obligated to ferry itself to the Islands and return with a bellyful of raw petrolactose. Compelled by old bloodworked commands, it cruised back and forth between the Island wells and the mainland refineries as thoughtless as the gears in her lantern house.

'Is that a *lich-ship*? I saw one beached at the Clay Mouth when I was a girl.'

'Really? I didn't think the lich-ships went that far north.'

She shook her head. 'Usually they don't. A storm forced one off course. The internal mechanisms were confused and it ran aground in Lyonne. The Clay Mouth swampfolk weren't impressed by their clockwork visitor.'

'What did they do?'

'Burned it. They thought it was evil.'

'Perhaps they were not wrong. What manner of sanguinity could make such a machine?'

'Ones lost to us now, thank goodness. *Ferrum perpetua, mandari, orientis* . . . the old talents. Though one would need the entire compliment to control something like *that*.' She tilted her chin towards the grey ship and its empty dock.

Mr Quill drove on, relieved to be away from the unholy automata. The copper forests faded along with the relentlessly aromatic fermented-pine smell of petroleum fractions. Some of the acrid scent clung to Arden's skin, a dreadfully bitter perfume. It made her recall the petroleum dens of Clay, where debauched scions might inhale distillations of rockblood from crystal decanters. The euphoria was brief and terrible, and long-term partakers often lost control of their faculties, became confused, and died.

Perpetua, procuro, orientis. Her intonation of the old talents to Mr Quill had made her uneasy, a feeling that carried even after the refinery was out of view. There were some sanguineous symmetries that were not inheritable, even by a Society who knew more about coaxing heritable traits out of a bloodline than any scholarly system in existence. She knew only of the old talents as one knew all general trivia, something learned to pass an Academy mid-term exam and then forgotten forever.

Out on the ocean, more boats dotted the grey slate water. More desperate, hopeful souls heading to the source of the refinery's awful contents. A land torn open and dying, like a wound. Imagine breathing that kind of air all the time, she thought with a shudder. Imagine such a place.

They stopped at a sugar-beet farm for midday refreshments, and the family were pleased to offer Arden provisions in exchange for Lyonne coin. She needed a little smear of her blood to restore antique bloodlight lanterns extinguished for over a century. They had last been lit only in those days when blood was strong in Fiction.

'These instruments are of a good design,' Arden said to her hosts, pleased at the steady glow. 'They'll not need feeding for two years, maybe three.'

And I'll be far away from here.

The children gawped at the strange, cold blue flame behind glass that had always resisted a normal fire. Their parents, as expected, were a little less enthusiastic.

Arden did not begrudge the farmers their caution around her. In Fiction, more so than in Lyonne even, there were bad stories of northern industries casting out a thousand workers after company had hired a lone bloodworker.

The one man who could replace a thousand men is dangerous to you.

How could they not be guarded against her and her talents when they see the lich-ships on the horizon, or the automatic refineries and see themselves replaced and redundant? Great powers had walked the earth in the time of their legends but it had not stopped the tide of industry. It may not have been by pure neglect that the Fiction folk had abandoned the power that ran in their veins.

The day matured and chased away the rainclouds.

Mr Quill turned the car towards the shore again, and that long, elegant spit that would lead back to her lighthouse.

Arden folded back the roof and stood up at seeing the Riven factory ruins crabbing to the rocky cliffs in a precarious embrace. She had yet to view the compound from this angle, crooked upon the old foundations of Neolithic ruins.

'Wait,' she said. 'Stop here.'

'Are you certain?' Mr Quill slowed to a crawl but did not apply the brake. 'This is the Riven ground.'

'I'm not going to waste a single night here worrying about what my neighbour might be up to,' Arden said. 'I need to speak to him. You can stay with the car.'

Mr Quill was in no way in agreement, but he pulled the vehicle over to a roadside shoulder.

'This part of the promontory is frequently covered by winter surge,' he warned her. 'It will only be you and him on the island for great stretches of time.'

'Then it is fortunate I'm only here until autumn's end.' She held up her gloves and made a face at them. 'My coins won't hold within my hands much longer than that. They'll need replacing.'

'Still. I have a powder-pistol in the trunk. It's not much but . . .'

'If I am not back on the hour, then you may commence my rescue.'

She left Mr Quill to fret in the car and gladly got out, her legs cramping and stiff from the hours bracing against the rough terrain. The road had overgrown with dandelion and salt-sedge, but under her boots she saw plaques of tar and stone, the remnants of a fairly civilized road.

Though it crossed her mind to leave the krakenskin coat with the rest of her belongings, another stubborn instinct had her wear the coat instead. Best they quarrel about this now, rather than later, when she would not have a man with a powder-pistol and a car waiting in the wings.

Now that she could make her up-close observations, Arden noted how many of the factory houses visible from the lighthouse grounds had fallen into disrepair. The environment had gnawed and savaged the metal as a shark might a corpse, reducing it to warped rust and wood splinters. Despite her coat's warmth, Arden wrapped her arms around her. An odd caul of melancholy draped over this place. Great leviathans of the deep had been processed on these shores, their meat harvested, their ambergris and oil packed into barrels, their skins tanned to leather. How odd that such an important industry be reduced to a lone man and his cart?

The squally wind tore and jostled about her. Mr Riven's black wood boat had since parked below his factory ports, louring and waiting.

I will be strong, she decided. I will be strong. So, the man had merely attempted to run her down with his boat like a coward. Let him be a coward now to her face. She had experienced worse manner of trials. A scar upon her throat remained from when a hapless dockside mutineer once took her as a hostage before taking his own life. She had worked the docks during the False Unionist war, the War of the Wharves, and the Battle of the Tea Leaves. She had seen the worst of people.

At the end of a double-rutted track, the processing compound emerged from the scrub in fits and starts of abandoned engineering, gears and old machines. If any paint had ever graced the processing bunkers and the icehouses, the sea-wind had scoured it away in a century of furious assault. Some telegraph poles leaned in the wind, their wires stripped away by time and storm.

A lone insulated cable flapped against a tilting trunk and left a dissonant image that made Arden ponder. If the Riven clan were savages fit only to play with knives, why would they have such technology as telegraphs and electricity?

She continued through the grounds, found stables for at least ten heavy horses. A printing press turning to rust, with three fonts of lead type crystallizing in their cases. The foundations of a fireplace of the massive kind that heats a great hall. Pipes and spigots, an aqueduct for grey water so it would not contaminate the small freshwater streams. Easily fifty people could have lived and worked here with the home comforts one could expect in a well-serviced Lyonnian town. And a dozen more would have been required to provide support services. The administration of an electrical and communications system by itself would have employed at least four, five trained workers.

This was no savage shore. This was an industry, ceased abruptly and without reason.

She passed a sad patch of dirt, the only thing that looked halfway cared for in recent years, and seven wooden crosses, scored and faded by storm.

Then she caught the smell of krakenhides.

A strange quirk of cryptozoology made the rot and decay of animals despised by God and embraced by the devil so different in their decomposition. The sweet smell reminded Arden of a heavy Koutoubian spice. She'd heard tell of the learned sultans of the desert kingdoms using krakenmusk to bring a garden to the senses while their eyes viewed only sand and ancient books. A Djenne mathematician might burn the oil in incense, to aid her mental acuity. Arden had smelled kraken perfume oftentimes on the collar of a sharply suited Khanate merchant as he passed by with a trolley of legal agreement documents.

But those memories belonged to her bustling trader's home, not a desolate hamlet on the coldest end of the Darkling Coast.

'Hello? Mr Riven?'

Nobody answered. The smell of the curing hides wafted stronger here. Somebody was nearby, for nobody left their catch unattended to either elements or seabirds. A ragged pair of cormorants sat on the roof of a nearby ruin, their attention longingly fixed on the source of the smell.

She walked past a pile of massive cuttlefish bones, each one as big as her torso. The tusks of a short-necked saurian made an unusual entry passage. Her meanderings took her by one of the few houses left standing, a country-style lodge decorated in the gingerbread-style that only a woman of Vigil could have appreciated.

If the lodge had made it through the disaster that claimed the rest of the compound, the years were already taking their toll. The decorative architraves and wind-icons showed the ragged edges of warp and decay. Whoever had built their home here and given the stark place such a gentle touch had long vacated it. Already the garden beds were piles of dirt, any hope of flowers long gone.

She had already made up her mind about what the lodge would look like inside. Rotted floorboards, walls leaking horse-hair insulation. A bare, stained mattress would be on the floor where a man might sleep, if he slept at all.

Beyond the house lay the vats and curing tables for kraken-skin, shining bright brass in the dull day.

Then at last she saw Mr Riven.

He had not altered since the day when she had first lain eyes upon him. If she were pressed to admit it, then he was more appalling than before. A male, shirtless figure, almost entirely encrusted in dirt, trudging up the pier. A heavy object lay floppy in his arms, a slimy thing as big as a small woman. As she watched, he dumped it upon the curing table. A coiled rope and flabby sack followed. Plesiosaur foetus with the placenta still attached, torn viciously from its mother's womb. Though they were reptilian by family, plesiosaur were warm-blooded and viviparous, same as mammals. They birthed live, had a maternal sense. Arden ached at seeing the baby's wretched limpness, would have cried out if she could.

Mr Riven was every bit the monster Mr Justinian proclaimed him. Dried plaques of blood smeared him from beard to bare belly. His body echoed the decay of his compound, flesh harrowed and scarred by sea and storm. A recent trauma had made a mutilation of his face, swelling eyes into blue puffs, his lip split, jaw disfigured under his facial hair.

She forced down her odium and approached the wicked scene.

'Excuse me, sir?'

He ignored Arden at first, too busy arranging the dead foetus lengthways on the table, more gently than one would expect given the violence he must have used to procure the poor thing. Did not glance up, and that gladdened her, for she did not have to witness his grotesque face any more than she needed to.

At last he spoke.

'What do you want?'

No asking her name, no giving of his own. No acknowledgement that she were stranger or enemy or friend. She would not have been surprised if he spoke in animal grunts.

'I am Arden Beacon from Clay Portside and now Vigil,' she said, infuriated by the tremble in her voice. Why should she be so distracted by his filthy nakedness, the way an Old Master might have painted him in a hellscape triptych, minus the trident and the pale sinner for poking?

'I am the Lighthouse—'

'I know who you are.' He fixed her then with those ferocious blue eyes, blue like the horizon that mocks the castaway sailor. 'You are Jorgen's niece, and you are not welcome here.'

'What business my uncle had with you, that was his own,' Arden said, light-headed with revulsion. 'I came to ask that whatever bad blood you two had with each other, stays in the grave. I do not intend to bother you, merely conduct my light-house business.'

'Then go conduct your business. I will not interfere, if you give me the same respect.'

She stood for a moment, strangely unfulfilled, having expected more, and less from him. Yelling and curses she could have borne. But not this quiet horror.

'Thank you.' She turned to leave, and paused. 'It has not escaped your notice, sir, that I am wearing this coat. I bought it off a jumble seller in town. I need this coat to work the flame during a storm. I want to wear it with your blessing.'

'You don't need my blessing.'

'But it is your wife's coat. That is what people tell me.'

'My wife is dead. Wear whatever you want. Just don't come back here again.'

He returned to the table, and his terrible face stared at the plesiosaur's murdered child as if it had materialized, like an awful magic trick, in front of him.

8

Mr Quill was dreadfully curious

Mr Quill was dreadfully curious, but far too polite to pry. He had seen enough to presume, from Arden rushing back to the automobile before climbing inside and taking several gulping dry sobs, to her wiping her eyes with a handkerchief and saying, 'Let's leave this place. I have seen enough.'

They drove the last mile in silence, and he watched her twist the handkerchief to knots within the tangle of her fingers.

Her composure had not quite returned by the time they reached the lighthouse, and when she saw Mr Harris she hugged him for longer than was necessary to hug a friend.

'Oof, Ardie, what is that in aid of?'

'I'm a touch vulnerable today, that's all. And dismayed by all men. Except you. And Mr Quill of course, who remains a delightful travelling companion.'

She blew her nose on her handkerchief and the tears prickled her eyes again, but every time she tried to think about something else, the poor tiny puppy-face of the foetus came back to her, a little animal that would only know the cold butcher's table and never its mother.

'And I shall refuse to eat meat ever again.'

'Ah, all right, then. Now if you have finished with your

discussions on pitiful humankind, come and meet your new assistant. She's from Lyonne originally but has since been working in—'

'Harbinger Bay. With the Lightkeeper there. Morningvale before that.'

Arden stood back cautiously as Mr Harris introduced a young, strong-boned woman as Miss Chalice Quarry, the Lightkeeper's assistant. 'Miss' and not 'Mx' of course – for she lacked the higher guild degrees for that title. Miss Quarry, pale freckled skin and auburn plaits dusted with sea-salt, had a sturdiness to her frame that made her what the signallers called a *stormbride*, for only the stoutest among them could survive the hard weather and relight an extinguished lamp or tie a giant mooring howser after it has snapped at the pier. Such folk were married to the storm, their equal. She wore a Guild-associate coin on a chain about her neck, a chunky pewter triangle.

After Mr Quill had unpacked Arden's belongings, he left with Mr Harris, and Arden, quite unexpectedly, had to share her surroundings with a stranger. This assistant would not always be in Arden's company, but she would be around enough that if they did not get along, the next few months would be miserable indeed.

They sized each other up with the wariness of fighters in a wharf-house pit-ring. Arden decided this red-haired Chalice Quarry suffered no nonsense. In their day together she had quickly made a home among the rocks and scrub of the promontory and the gruff company of Mr Harris. The arrival of an actual sanguis Lightkeeper, and a startlingly young one at that, would not have been altogether welcome.

'Um, are your hours here long, Miss Quarry?' Arden asked as politely as she could.

'Most days I will be of help,' Chalice said. 'Other days David Modhi ferries me by boat from Vigil. I have a small business in town, to keep my mind off this desolate place. Oh, and before our greetings become too long in the tooth, you shall call me Chalice and I shall call you Arden. There are no standards to uphold here except expedience.'

'Of course, Miss . . . I mean, Chalice. Mr Harris said you toured Harbinger Bay. That's a hard inlet. Are you from Clay Portside?'

'No. My hometown is Shinlock, far west of Clay Riverina. I trained in Portside for a while. T'was Mr Harris who hired me to work at Morningvale, so I did not mind joining him here when they made him an interim keeper.'

The woman picked up Arden's entire shipping trunk as casually as she might have hefted a linen basket, set it inside the tower's ground floor with an effortless grunt. 'David Modhi will come by tomorrow. We'll sail back and retrieve your boat.'

'That would be appreciated, but perhaps he could do that today.'

'Not with this place a pigsty and a squall coming. By the time we're finished here it will be almost dark.'

'Finished?'

'Cleaning, of course. Come now. Hop to it.'

A little flustered at being bossed around in her own signal post, Arden took off her coat, rolled up her sleeves, and followed Chalice's lead. They got a fire started in an iron coal-pit outside, and Chalice unearthed a large rusted kettle from a mound of rubbish. A prior attack on the lighthouse's poor condition by herself and Mr Harris had unearthed several treasures. A mercury barometer, a storm glass, a radio-electrograph that inscribed approaching objects with a needle on carbon paper. She hauled some seawater up from a blowhole, and boiled it with an oily soap.

Arden stared with dismay at the salt-encrusted remnants of a valve-telegraph, the earpiece now a home to a family of tiny spiders. A ticker tape rained a miserable confetti on the floor. She imagined composing a letter in her mind to her friends, and having to pretend everything fine and dandy, when it completely was not.

'How am I meant to report the conditions if none of the communications are working?'

Chalice hauled open a large journal, the leaves a sturdy drab green. Mr Harris' penmanship had always been atrocious, and Arden noticed he'd missed a few entries. Of Jorgen Beacon's entries, there were none.

'You'll need to make the weather observations by hand, four during the day, two at night. I will post them weekly, on a Sunday, to the Meteorological Society,' Chalice said. 'I will maintain the barometers, and we shall share the work of collecting the measurements from both bays. Any storm or adverse conditions, one of us must immediately take a boat across to Vigil and have Mr Harrow send a telegraph to the Garfish Point station.'

Arden nodded, trying to keep the dismay from her face. 'I have met Mr Harrow.'

'I can do that errand if you like,' Chalice said, kindly now. 'If you prefer to watch your light.'

At least one duty was hers alone. 'Yes, I'd feel better, staying close to my lantern.'

So, into the kettle went all Uncle Jorgen's implements of his talent. His knives and bloodletting equipment, the dishes and vials, the collectors and extractors and refiners.

They stood about the fire and watched the water bubble. The old clots floated up with the detergent.

'Well,' Arden said at last. 'This is all very rustic.'

Chalice agitated the pot with a paddle, sent some miserly soap bubbles skidding across the surface.

'We cannot waste the water here on the peninsula. There is a spring, but it is barely enough for drinking and bathing, and besides, the rain is mostly sea-spray. The streams are further down the promontory, near the pilgrim ruins. Their water must be carted by hand.' Chalice continued to stir the kettle until the blood tools lost their noxious crust.

'There,' she said after a few minutes. 'You can use them now.'

'You're familiar with bloodworking?'

Surprisingly, Chalice pointed to an old scar upon her hand. 'Went to a testmoot on my tenth birthday. Shinlock fell under the auspices of Clay Capital despite the distance between the town and the city, so of course we all had to go and get ourselves tested.'

'Did you test positive for a talent?' Arden blurted out, and instantly regretted it. Of course the woman hadn't tested positive. Children with talent were given stipends and scholarships, went to school in Clay Capital. The best of them stayed on, were utilized for their precious labour. The rest went home, often subtly neutered so they might not sully their family lines further.

To Arden's further surprise, Chalice nodded. 'Not positive, but some latencies for trace minerals. The salt of the ocean appeals to my sense of sodium chloride, but that's about it.'

'Oh, what a shame, to not have a talent.'

'Trust me darling, I wouldn't wish to be sanguine. Far too much trouble, and the Society breathing down your neck like an overly invested uncle during St Stephens dinner? Ugh, not for me.'

Over the bubbling kettle Arden admitted her own failings, of her late blooming at seventeen rather than eleven, of a half-brother with *sanguis ferro* talent. 'Between me and him, our family is not particularly healthy in the eyes of the eugenicists right now. Our ledger page is all red crosses and angry notations.'

She waited for Chalice to enquire incredulously how, with all that against her, Arden had managed such an important signal post.

To her credit, the stormbride kept her counsel and only said with genuine feeling, 'Then I hope this small sojourn to these shores works out well for you, Arden Beacon.'

'Thank you. I do hope it works out.'

'What happens once you are done here?'

'Home awaits. I'll have a full Guild membership then and dispensation to—' she faded off, worrying she might be too personal with this woman she'd only just met.

'Dispensation?' Chalice said with a chortle. 'To marry, you mean?' Her eyes sparkled wickedly.

Arden's cheeks grew hot. 'It would be nice, I suppose.'

Chalice wagged a finger at Arden. 'Then make this time quick, and marry your fellow. It will make a fitting end.'

'What do you mean, a fitting end?'

'This is the last of the blood-kept lights, and the Guild has decided to keep it no more. The light will be de-registered at your departure, and I will return to Clay and take another posting.' She picked up the triangular Guild assistant coin from about her neck and kissed it. 'God willing it be an easy one this time.'

'Oh, that's a shame,' Arden said, crestfallen. She couldn't bear thinking of her uncle's light extinguished like the beet-farmer's lanterns. A Beacon could not let a fire lapse, it was against their code.

'It's *politics* darling. The Fiction Guild folk would prefer one of their own in this tower. And since they don't lean to blood, its only fair this should be a common fire.'

Then another worrisome thought came over her, and it showed on her face long enough for Chalice to ask, 'What troubles you?'

'I think it *is* peculiar.'

'Losing a lighthouse?'

'No, that the Fiction Seamaster's Guild should wait until winter to decommission the light. it would have been better to replace the lamp now, when the days are long.'

Chalice silently stirred the pot until the tools clunked, and Arden felt bad for dumping her cares upon a stormbride whom she'd decided was quite nice after all.

'Oh, don't mind me, Chalice. I'm just glad for the opportunity. I'd never have gotten this chance in Lyonne. Maybe they're even expecting a *sanguinem ignis* from Fiction? Maybe that is the delay.'

An odd expression made Chalice's freckles wrinkle. 'Darling, there hasn't been a Fiction-born sanguinem for . . . goodness, well over a decade.'

'Who was the last?' Arden asked, wondering if she should know of a foreign-born sanguinem in the academies. The ladies of the Guild would have talked forever and a day of such a person.

Chalice seemed to pause, as if deciding whether or not to tell Arden, then pointed her chin down the promontory.

'*His* wife, for one.'

Mr Justinian's voice hissed in her mind, as it always did, as if he had infected her with a hateful memory. *Murdered whore*, he'd said.

'Bellis *Riven*? Chalice, I don't remember her being in the Clay Academies at all.'

'She never went to Clay,' Chalice continued, 'She was tested positive for sanguinity, but stayed at home.'

'And the Eugenics Society *let* her?'

'They did indeed. Looks like our over-invested Society is capable of some empathy. Bellis had a sick mother. A father with connections. You know that tale, how it goes.'

'Goodness. Well, then. I would be curious to know of her endowment, if you remember so well.'

Chalice Quarry checked for the unlikely eavesdroppers on this desolate promontory, then leaned in close.

'When the test masters applied the assessment, her blood drew powerfully to the black oil from the Islands,' Chalice replied with a fine hint of condescension sprinkled with the slightest salt of jealousy.

'Rockblood? *Sanguinem petrae*? But, Chalice, a petroleum symmetry is a golden talent!'

Chalice sat back, still as nonplussed by the fact of Bellis' result as she must have been the first time she heard it. 'Gold, and *old*! The *petrolactose* bloodline is almost extinct! Every big-city technical academy and Guild tower clamoured for her presence. She chose to stay here.'

'Chalice, come now. The Eugenics Society would not have allowed her to stay here. Much less the Lions.'

'They may not allow it, but this is Fiction, not Lyonne. There are no Lions here. Wished only to stay with her loving father, her poorly mother. Be a dutiful daughter, unlike all the other greedy little shits who run away to Lyonne at their first chance at a golden dollar and sanguis coins.' Chalice clasped her hands dramatically to her breast and affected a swoon. 'Poor Bellis. So they let her.'

'Put me in the camp of undutiful peasant then,' Arden sighed, twitching with envy. 'My father wasn't too pleased at my coming to Vigil. We had quite a row over it.'

'Quite frankly, the rockblood talent was wasted on her. What's a little innocent creature like Bellis going to do with *sanguinem petrae* anyway? Go out to the Sainted Isles and start digging around for old pipes so the prospectors can bunker them? Live with the machines? I think not.'

With that, Chalice gave the steaming kettle a kick, and they retrieved the now passably clean blood apparatus from the bowl. Arden wrapped the copper parts up into one of Dowager Justinian's towels, and they headed up – gingerly on account of the corroding staircase – to the lamp room.

Chalice watched with interest as Arden reaffixed all the bloodletting devices to the fading flame wick. When it came to Uncle Jorgen's knife, she declined the uneven blade and pulled from one of her corset-bones a small stiletto knife. It made a fine cut in the centre of the button, and the blood welled up like a cabochon ruby.

'Like stigmata,' Chalice opined, which prompted a huff from Arden.

'Coins,' she corrected.

At the touch of the blood, the white flame kicked and roared up, making both women stand back with a gasp.

'Ah, so bright!' Chalice exclaimed, her hand over her eyes. Then she put her hand in the fire and waved her fingers about so that the blue flame hissed through her fingers. 'So bright and so *cold*. I'll never get over how strange a sanguine flame is.'

Arden nodded. 'Of course it will be brighter than usual. The ratio hasn't been correct for a long time.' She wound the wick down and closed the fresnel lenses. 'My uncle suffered illness long before he came out here, I think. His blood was fading. My blood is hardly strong, either. Like I said, I came into it too late.'

'Would it have been different if you had come into your talent earlier?'

'Very much. You should have seen my Uncle Nicolai's blood-light, Chalice. You could wear welder's goggles with your eyes shut, and you would still see the flame though your eyelids. I used to love going to the Clay Mouth signal tower, helping him on my vacation days.' She stood back and sighed. 'I never thought I'd have a signal tower. It's almost a dream too good to be true.'

Chalice pressed her palms to the lens and fussed over the cold light. Arden was pleased that her stormbride had not been fearful. Hard enough to convince any commonfolk with little experience that the sanguis talents were not always dangerous, and almost never if one took the proper precautions.

Arden finished the rest of her light business, lowering the mantle so the flame burned incandescent against the knitted hood, and wound the revolving mechanica to last the night. Chalice made her final observations for the journal. They descended the spiral stairs, and Arden decided that she would like this Chalice Quarry. The woman was clearly a little older than her, past thirty years at least. Had an easy experience about her, as if she were a sturdy, trustworthy boat, unlikely to sink.

Chalice put a kettle upon the coals outside. 'You are a hard worker, and helpful,' she acknowledged Arden with grudging good humour. 'Not like Lightkeeper Pharos in my previous posting, who could barely raise a fork to his lips if he thought I could be around to do it for him!'

'I think we will make a good team,' Arden replied, shy with her new friendship. 'My light and your—'

'Well, I'm no witch, but with my chemical latencies I can make a *very* good medicinal tea. Come sit now, Lightmistress, and you may show yourself as better company than Mr Harris.'

Arden sat inside the rowboat and watched Chalice work her

botanical magicks. When the steeped brew came to her she clutched the enamel mug of tea for warmth.

The setting sun skimmed the grey sea with a scar of gold. Chalice pointed towards the horizon. A plume of luminous smoke rose against a backdrop of red sky. This time it was not a sainted flotilla, but a boat Arden knew only too well, having survived those chopping wheels the day before.

'Mr Riven's heading out to sea,' Chalice said. 'Thank the Redeemer, we won't have to think of him prowling around tonight.'

'He prowls?'

Chalice shrugged. 'Personally, I don't think he cares about us one whit. He wants to know what's happening on the promontory though. Most fishermen keep stock of their surroundings, and he does the same.'

'I came to discover what manner of man Mr Riven is this afternoon,' Arden said darkly. 'I had Mr Quill stop his car so I might make my acquaintance and beg of him not to come kill us in the night.' Arden dry-laughed without humour at her own joke, which was not amusing, was true and terrifying.

'And? Was he monstrous? Did he have giant eyes on the side of his head and the arms of a squid and a cuttlefish beak between his legs?'

Arden *tsk*ed at Chalice's bleak wit. 'A tattoo of that, perhaps. I could not look. He had his kill in his arms. A baby plesiosaur, a little helpless thing torn from its mother's body. I came upon him laying it out upon his slaughter table.'

'The devil's damnation, then. The sea will not forgive such a travesty.' Chalice studied the tea leaves skimming the top of her mug. 'Hunting plesiosaur is illegal in spawning waters. The locals say bad luck follows anyone harming an unborn pup. Once they get word of it you know there'll be misfortune upon the waters. Perhaps you could advise the Captain of the Coast, who I understand you have spent a month with . . .?'

'Ha!' Arden cried. 'And who then will Mr Riven have to blame for the accusation? The one person who saw him in the act! If Postmaster Harrow and Coastmaster Justinian could not protect a man's own daughter, what chance do I have?'

Chalice shrugged, topped up the tea, put a third mug aside for the *Old Guy* – a wharf superstition that had made its way from lighthouses and docks and to the edges of the world – before joining Arden in her rowboat throne.

'People in these parts had many envies in their hearts towards pretty little Bellis Harrow with her rockblood talent, Arden, but marrying a man who slaughters monsters, being forced into sexual slavery, neither of those was bloody one of them. Forget about what you saw in those factories. Every place needs a monster, and you won't do anybody any favours by trying to find anything redeemable in Vigil's own.'

'I wasn't trying to redeem him . . .' Arden protested, burning with that furious heat of shame because she had been, in a way, wanting to prove Mr Justinian wrong.

'You went to his doorstep, did you not? What did you think, that by your gracious, unprejudiced Clay Capital ways and your generosities and over-bred face you might tame Mr Riven the way Biblical Daniel tamed the Lions?' Chalice then softened, knowing her words harsh. 'I don't intend cruelty. Mr Riven has been implacable since the day he returned from his captivity in the worst Lyonne prison hulks the Parliament administers. Arden, you remember my posting before this one?'

'Mr Harris said it was the Harbinger Bay lighthouse.'

'Yes, and I've seen the degradations these men are put through on those floating hell-ships, what scarred abominations it creates of them. Why, the Harbinger hulks make the Sainted Isles a paradise in comparison.'

'I can't listen to the opinions of others,' Arden protested, 'I needed to confirm this for myself. Not from Mr Justinian, who has been controlling every whisper and conversation since I arrived here last month. From people I trust. From my own eyes.'

'And you found out. Congratulations, you're still alive. Now leave Mr Riven be and maybe he'll leave us.'

Dejected by the failures of the day, Arden carried the last of her belongings into the lighthouse. She rolled out a Mi'kmaq mat – repurposed from airship battens and lighter than a mattress – on the stone floor, and finished it with a cosy mammoth-wool blanket. The set-up made Chalice's eyes widen appreciatively, and Arden decided she would give the bed to the woman as a present once she left.

The appreciation did not extend to the krakenskin coat.

'I know it's hers,' Arden said after Chalice had another round of conniptions over the death-shawl of Bellis Riven so obviously on display. 'But I hadn't the heart to let it be picked apart for rags, and Mr Riven gave me his blessing.' She paused. 'Or something similar to one.'

'So who is the favourite one now? I wouldn't give you a blessing. Regardless of whose fault, it must be a dreadful thing to see again, and to remember.'

Arden thought about Mr Riven trying to run the *Breeze* down. Perhaps she was being foolish, taunting him with his wife's coat. Foolish, and cruel, and deserving of any misfortune that came in return.

9

When she'd first met

When she'd first met Mr Richard Castile they had both been young. He had just joined the Friesland Corps as an air cadet, and it was in uniform that she'd noticed him, standing near a rainbow buffet of shaved-ice sorbets. She remembered the epaulets winking gold at his shoulders, his black hair glistening in bud-lights, as beautiful as a dream. Arden had failed two testmoots by then and was unlikely to make her third, so she'd been invited to the Guild Ball only out of her father's influence. For that she was in her secret heart not at all upset. Life as a sanguinem was a roster of proscribed affection and arranged marriages and she was glad to escape such boundaries. She had made commonblood friends, and had not begrudged her old companions from her potential days, so she walked the world a popular girl without too many cares, and a curiously protected future.

Until that night.

They grew them handsome and dashing out on the north Summerland seas, and the night Arden saw Mr Castile was the moment she fell in love. Until then she had not quite known if her desires would be towards either men or women, or both, or neither, for at such an age one was little different from the other. But Mr Castile in his navy blue dress uniform and tilted sky-pilot cap could have been a character lifted out of a penny-printed chapbook. She remembered his hair black as a raven's wing, nestled under her chin after they had shared a kiss. Up close his eyes were an impish hazel, and there was a sweet curl to his full lips that would have suited a stage player of Arabian princes. Language danced easy upon his tongue, jokes and stories. Women loved him, men enjoyed his company, and then, for nearly ten years on and off, each meeting achingly brief and deeply regretful, he had been Arden's lover.

Lover. How small a word for all the importance of him.

For all that she promised to forget Richard each time he sailed away, Arden lost her senses upon each return to Clay, and maybe for the most fleeting of moments he had done the same, for there had been a time when he had spun tales of their escape by land and air and sea, away from the Guilds and the Eugenics Society and on to lands where sanguinity meant no more than a name.

But always, the sense of something between them, for each time he put off their escape for another year an invisible hand reached up and lay upon the back of her neck, said: *this man does not have the strength to fight Lions.*

Her blood was not her own. Its labour belonged to the Seamaster's Guild, and its inheritance to the Eugenics Society, and very quietly, her body to the Lyonne Order and Nomenclatures. She would always do what they told her to do.

So she had waited for Richard Castile to become strong. Not always in celibacy, for sometimes the nights grew hot, and the yearnings fierce, and there were always others with coins in their hands and regret in their words who might tangle in darkness for a few hours. Make her forget that once she loved a man, and once a man loved her back.

The months became years, and Richard could never commit to taking a chance. His fear of discovery tangled up about his affections like a choking vine. Her love ossified into a quiet despair. Their reunions were punctuated by her doubts. Until it had all become too much, and he'd flown away for good.

Tonight the winds brought back his memory. She recalled the same sharp pangs of excitement as Mr Castile made love to her, the old familiar way her heart overflowed as he shuddered and spent. The soft kisses from his sweet lips afterwards.

Arden sat up, blinking in the half-light. Her breath made steaming curlicues in the lantern's gleam.

My heart, she thought. *Why are you awake? Why are you hungering now, when you have been asleep for so long?*

Arden greeted the late morning with a stiff back, a stiff neck, and a vague ache in her lower belly, as if she had been aroused by passion in remembering her intimate moments, then left hanging in a confusing state of demi-desire.

In the manner of any good stormbride, Chalice had risen early to stoke the outside fire in the misty drizzle. The smoke from the wet logs had a slithering, seething quality, the kind witches loved.

'Pity your small combinations of minor chemical talents didn't end up with fire-lighting,' Arden said as she joined Chalice.

'Pity *sanguis ignis* coldfire gives no heat, likewise,' Chalice grumped. 'How did you fare in the night, before I took over?'

'Quietly. There were ships out there, but they never came close.'

'The same with my watch. The season is still young. Besides, you sleep well.' Chalice grinned wickedly at Arden. 'Some moaning and groaning and calling of a man's name. I hope yours was a good dream.'

Arden felt herself blushing furiously. 'I did not!'

'Maybe only a little whimper, but you were certainly stoking a mightier fire than this one.'

Her mortification must have been so great that Chalice took pity upon her and gave her knee a playful shove. 'Ease up, Lightmistress, you're hardly the first I've seen to lose their decorum when sleep comes. The air here is bracing, and the sea has the most gloomy of qualities. I know what it is like for a sanguinem, held so rigidly to task in protecting those precious genes of yours.'

'What about you, Chalice Quarry, huh? You and your latencies.'

'Huh indeed, I stick with lovers of a female persuasion and all is well.' She grinned at Arden, and then the fire gave a little skip, finally lighting the pine-cones. Chalice hurriedly threw on some kindling, and at last they had something worthy of a blaze.

Chalice put the kettle on the embers and turned back to Arden. 'What was his name, this man who drove you to remember him so all of a sudden?'

Arden could not have been more solemn if she had been a priest giving last rites. 'Richard Castile. A Frislander. Airship pilot in training. We were going to elope together. Then my talent came in late, almost to the day of our planned escape. After that, well. He didn't quite seem so keen any more.'

'Ah,' Chalice said. 'Farewell is such a sorrow.'

Arden sat on the damp log and rubbed warmth into her shins. 'I wish he had said farewell that day. He kept on orbiting like a rather uncommitted comet.'

'Taunted you with promises, did he? Swore to work towards some great application to the Society for you to marry a common-blooded man like him, but not yet? Wait, wait, wait, for the right time which never came?'

Arden stared, open-mouthed. 'How did you know?'

'Oh, you think you're the first? As soon as you said *airship*, I completely deduced what kind of philanderer he was.'

Somewhere in the smoke the flame that was desperately trying to keep hold, faded. A rain shower threatened, fat blobs of chilled water on her cheek. Arden stood to collect more dried tinder, tried to help the fire along with kindling that wasn't already sopping wet. An excuse, she decided, to talk no more about Mr Castile.

'Didn't my uncle perceive of a kitchen?' she scolded, desperate not to think of him, and irritated by the fact she needed to kneel in the rain just to have a meal going. 'Why is everything so relentlessly *difficult*?'

Her carefully constructed personality of staunchness broke down and Arden wept into her hands. Not for Richard, for she had cried those tears a year ago, or even that she was cold and sore. It was a cathartic, miserable and ugly cry, as selfish as a rich woman who has to wear a lesser golden brooch upon her breast for a party, when people outside are starving for bread.

Chalice hugged her shoulders and rubbed her back.

'There you go, dear, let it out. It's not the plesiosaur child weighing on your mind, is it? Because nature is red in tooth and claw.'

'It's not the pup. Or maybe it is. I don't know. I shouldn't have come here,' Arden said in between gasps and swallows. 'Here, this town, this place. I don't know what came over me to come.'

'But wasn't your post voluntary?' Chalice handed Arden the linen cloth she had been using to handle the hot kettle. The teacloth was damp from rain, and grubby from ash, but better than wiping her nose on her sleeve. 'The Guild never forces people to go anywhere too far from Clay City, even the sanguineous.'

Arden desperately wanted to tell Chalice about Mr Lindsay and her father's suspicions that the Guildsman clerk had really been a messenger of the Lyonne Order, then remembered how frightened the Manse's guests had been, her father, the phlebotomist that put in her coins. Even Richard Castile. All fearing the Lions. She liked her assistant too much to make the rest of their assignment a worrisome chore.

'The Seamasters offered me a full Guild degree if I came here until the start of winter. Such a title would be almost impossible to come by working a mere blood-lantern, and I'd never be permitted an independent navigation post without one.' She looked at her dirty, tear-stained napkin. 'I'm tired of being scared.'

Chalice kissed her on the cheek. 'Buck up, love. I was myself weepy when I first came to this place. The isolation, you see.

The way the waters just never let the fog go. There's ghosts in the ruins, and the sadness has soaked right through.'

'And Mr Riven down there, the beast that might one day break his chain.'

'Yes, him too. Now, if we can keep this *real* fire going, perhaps after eating we can pry through your late uncle's garbage pile. I'm sure I saw a pot-belly stove in that mess. Something remotely salvageable.'

For all the crude surrounds, Chalice managed to get a pot of porridge upon the boil, sweetened with wild honey. After Arden ate, the burden of an interrupted life lightened a little. Only a few months to go before freedom, and then the autumn testmoot, and if God and the Old Guy should both allow it by granting some sullen coastal child blood-talent, then she could go home sooner and not have to mourn being the last flame-keeper to hold this old tower's post.

The sea hissed and shushed at her mood, and the wind whispered about the lighthouse spire, and slowly she began to feel a little better. Arden reminded herself once again, and this time sternly, that it had been her childhood dream to work a lighthouse signal. So it wasn't exactly the Clay City Spire, but this was still the tallest signal in the country, which had to count for something.

True to Chalice's words, their inspection of the old lantern gears discarded behind the outhouse uncovered a rusted stove, of which its only failing was a firebox door missing a hinge. Arden repurposed some barrel hoops that would do as a gusset about the stove's belly until they could employ the services of a proper blacksmith.

They had just finished setting up the stove inside the tower, with a chimney spout through a window stopped with rags, when a distant squawk of a car horn sounded.

Arden wiped her hands on a rag. 'That not Mr Quill's automobile. The rockblood makes the engine clatter.'

The two women stepped outside. Arden's assessment was correct. It was not the Justinian Siegfried. Instead, a large black sedan that had seen better days nosed its way through the rough roads. An older-model Maybach of the kind popular in Lyonne when she was a girl, with an electrical engine that made it slink in a predatory and dangerous silence. Arden felt her hands prickle with anxiety. If strange vehicles were making their way out to the tower, it was not due to fine tidings.

The Maybach braked suddenly, its wheels leaving dark gouges in the white quartz crust. A short Fictish man in a grey damask waistcoat and a bowler hat exited the driver's seat.

Could there have been anyone less welcome at her door than Mr Justinian? Yesterday she would have said *no*, having erased the unpleasantness of Alasdair Harrow from her mind the way a body pushes out a splinter. Today however, Mr Justinian seemed as benign as a summer shower compared to the stormy presence of her visitor.

Chalice whispered out of the side of her mouth. 'What does the Postmaster Magistrate want with you?'

'It can't be good,' Arden whispered back. 'I had a dreadful dinner with him three nights ago. Best get this over with.'

Postmaster Harrow came with three others of similar pale ethnicity, two large strapping youths with ruddy pink cheeks and full yellow beards, and one sea-bitten fellow who had obviously been on the losing side of a fight.

'Mr Harrow,' she said with assumed brightness. 'What brings you here?'

Mr Harrow did not at first return Arden's greeting. He cast his judgmental gaze over the lighthouse, and his lips thinned over his gravestone teeth.

'Um, can I help you? Is this Postmaster business, sir?'

'I am Magistrate Harrow today,' he said brusquely, then grunted towards his two deputies, made them walk off around the tower grounds to scout the area. Only the sea-bitten fellow that they had brought with them remained, scowling under his drooping canvas fisherman's hat. The cant of the brim did not quite hide a purple bruise on the side of his face as big as a birthmark. Alone among them, he acknowledged Arden and Chalice with the briefest of nods.

Chalice ran after one of the large lads, scolding them for kicking over the porridge pot. Arden stayed before the door, ready to not permit entry if they tried to come in.

Fortunately they merely did a cursory if destructive patrol of the outer grounds, before returning to slouch by the electric Maybach, and smoke a sour-smelling tobacco.

Mr Harrow returned last, one of Jorgen Beacon's blood-knives in his fist.

'Yours, I presume.'

Arden took the knife back. 'Thank you,' she said grudgingly. 'I meant to throw it out, though. This tool has reached the end of its life.'

'Still, not a good thing to leave lying around outside. Not in your circumstances.'

'My circumstances were fine, up until now. Whatever is your reason for coming here?'

She may have spoken to the wind. He took off his spectacles, polished them with a cloth, then did the same to a pewter star upon his breast pocket.

'I note you have settled in well to your new abode,' Mr Harrow said. 'Not so secure, but some people have different requirements when it comes to that.'

'If you needed to do an inspection, you could have asked me for an appointment rather than barging on in.'

He put his spectacles back on his face. 'My apologies, Lightmistress, but there were chances you were already being held hostage, maybe dead.'

'Excuse me?' Chalice interjected, returning from righting the mess the deputies had made. 'Who's saying we were dead?'

Mr Harrow did not immediately recognize Chalice as a person different from any other Vigil woman in his orbit. What was one more in coastal drab? He was the sort of man that decided all women invisible, and then became startled by their speaking, as if a ghost had rapped on a spiritualist's table in the middle of dinner.

'I am Alasdair Harrow, the Postmaster and Magistrate of

Vigil. You two ladies are adjacent to my investigation of a violent act and attempted murder that happened yesterday. Thank you for speaking with me.'

He came forward and shook Arden's hand. A damp and indifferent grip. *Were you a good father to Bellis Riven?* She envisioned asking, before a deeper caution warned her to silence.

'Then sir, if this is an investigation, how may we help you?'

He stood aside. 'These fellows are Giles and Pieter Haas, brothers and peacekeeping deputies of mine.'

The two lads moved almost imperceptibly but obviously, so that their oil coats parted to reveal the long-guns they carried.

'We have come with Captain-Guide Mr Georges Cormack, who as you can see had a crime committed against him and his clients.'

'A crime, sir?'

Mr Harrow paused briefly, noting that Arden had refused to use his title yet, before he continued, 'I am investigating a theft and an assault, as a Marshal of Vigil and the Eastern Fictish Coast.' He puffed himself up, a bantam cock certain that investigating the concerns of sea dogs in far-flung coastal hamlets were equivalent to a Clay High Court.

'My livelihood,' Captain Georges Cormack barked. 'My client refuses to pay since he din' get what he wanted. I am out almost five hundred guineas! Real Djenne Bank currency, not that rubbish Lyonne rag-paper. A year's wages worth to a man here!'

'I don't quite understand how I am involved . . .' Arden started, before Mr Harrow held up his hands.

'As a witness, my dear Lightmistress, a witness.'

Chalice jumped in. 'We didn't see anything.'

'But I understand you have been to visit your *neighbour*,' Mr Harrow said. His face twisted as he enunciated the word. He could not bear to say Mr Riven's name. 'Mr Justinian's driver told me you went to converse with him at an opportune time yesterday, perhaps observed something that could assist in my inquiry.'

'But into what, exactly, sir? You haven't yet explained why you've turned up here.'

'Like I said, grievous *assault* and a *theft*. Details would only worry you, but what did you see of him when you visited him in his compound?'

Something about the four men and their half-explanations aggrieved Arden in a way that made her hackles rise. She had experienced much the same behaviour in merchants at the docks pushing her to let a ship laden with contraband through a backwater lock when they knew she could not allow them. Oh, they would not specifically *say* there were *illegal wares* aboard, but they would give the same sly half-answers to her questions.

'I saw many things in the Riven compound. But if you can narrow down your request to a specific thing, then I can say yay or nay. Otherwise, we had a deal, Mr Riven and I, to stay out of each other's business. I cannot help you Mr Harrow and you are wasting my valuable time.'

She went to move off, when Captain Cormack shouted out, 'A hunter's longboat and a plesiosaur corpse.'

'Plesiosaur?'

She exchanged a glance with Chalice, who bit her lower lip and kissed her Guild assistant triangle nervously.

'Hush,' Mr Harrow said, but the Captain had his dander up now and snapped, 'I will not hush! A longboat that wretched bastard stole from me, after he dashed a rich man called Mr Landwin into the water with an oar, assaulted another with his fists. Rich men, blood-bound men from Morningvale, who had paid me good money to hunt plesiosaur!'

'But why hunt here? These are *breeding* grounds, sir. There is no licence to hunt gravid females south of Garfish Point.'

All four men swayed in an uneasy quorum. Now they would have to tell the truth. Was not adult males the Captain's clients had been hunting.

'I issued them a local dispensation,' Mr Harrow said. 'To do some limited winnowing for the good of the species.'

'Mr Harrow, you of all people should know it is an Act of Parliament that the breeding females not be touched,' Arden said. 'A local Magistrate cannot grant such things.'

Georges Cormack came close, and he smelled of fish oil and old tallow. 'Then you saw it? Saw the bounty that my clients paid me good money to procure?'

He turned back to Mr Harrow. 'Sir Magistrate, the bastard twice interfered with us and let the quarry flee. We shot him out of his ship with a stunning cannon. A face-full of cotton ballast he took, and fell straight into the water as good as dead. A godly man would have been killed instantly. The thug rose out of the waves as the devilspawn he is and pursued us for a night. An *entire night*. He boarded just as we cut out the pup from the plesiosaur bitch.'

'You cut out a foetus,' Arden said. 'You . . .'

'T'was not a foetus. It wriggled and cried, fresh enough that we could skin the caul from it's face and have it take a breath. A thousand gold coins that runt's skin was worth to them and to me, and a thousand more for the egg case!'

Mr Harrow caught the Captain's arm before he could advance more on Arden. 'Easy now, friend. We will get your property back. Plesiosaur veal does not degrade so quickly as beef-meat.'

The Captain continued in a frenzy now, his grievances storming about him. 'And then he assaulted us again, a madman possessed by all the devils of the deep, beat this bruise upon my face and broke the arm of Mr Landwin who wants compensation for his lost property!'

Arden felt a tightness in her chest that made it hard to breathe. Hunting and fishing was a way of life on the sea, that was true, but there were laws and morals attached to procuring bounty from the ocean. This Captain had allowed a barbarism to occur on his watch, and worse than that, had people pay him for the privilege.

'I am sorry, but I cannot help you.' Her voice came out in a rasp, her tongue felt like an iron filing, her throat sand. Her fists clenched to think of the little beast squirming and crying on the bloodied deck of the longboat, a dead mother nearby. At least with Mr Riven there had been a sense of a lone sailor hunting for sustenance, but these men had done so for *sport*.

Why, if she were certain her punch carried the weight required, she would have struck the Captain herself.

'Lightmistress, you can tell us what you saw. Give your testimony to me in my capacity as Magistrate and it will go no further,' Mr Harrow said.

If he had promised this Captain a quick fix to his complaint, Mr Harrow was about to find out that he was not the only authority on this coast. Arden set her jaw and shook her head. 'If you have an issue with Mr Riven, then take it up with him.'

'He has assaulted men. The plesiosaur cow was dead already, he had no cause. Is that not enough of a reason for you to assist us in his arrest and prosecution?'

'Go home, all of you. Go home and school yourself on moral equivalence,' she said. She shook now, sick to her stomach with the sheer effort of keeping a calm countenance. 'Away with you.'

Mr Harrow's face grew as red as a fresh-harvested beet. 'This is not the end of it, *Miss* Beacon. You do yourself no favours helping that *nephilim* over yonder.'

'If he is a fallen man, then your complainants are doubly fallen. A beast has nobody to speak for them. Good day, sirs.'

Muttering to themselves, three climbed back into the Maybach. Only Mr Harrow remained, bloodless as a ghoul.

'Your safety is dependent on us, you know this? You won't be the first woman to disappear from this coast because of him.'

'You use your dead daughter as part of a threat to my life?'

His nostrils flared. 'I use her as *everything*, for she meant *everything* to me before she was taken, raped and discarded.'

Would be a wretched life, she thought, as the sole orient of existence for this man. To be on a pedestal was much the same as a prison.

She remained at the transom of her lighthouse, refusing entry and Mr Harrow returned to the sedan with failure naked on him as a burn, spun the vulcanized rubber wheels in the soft road, and left angry gouges behind.

The waves fretted along the promontory. The gulls screamed at each other.

'Sea slime,' Chalice said. 'Miscreants.' She pursed her lips. 'That Captain Cormack. Heard a few stories about him, oh yes. On the off-seasons when there are no wealthy game hunters for him to escort, he ferries poor, unlicensed folk to the Sainted Isles. If there is not enough room on the boat, or if he runs into trouble, he is known to dump his motley cargo into the ocean. Entire families, murdered by drowning.'

'I'm not at all upset about Mr Harrow,' Arden said as gamely as she could, given that her hands were still trembling. 'They'll not be the first and last men to threaten me.' A strange concern made her nod towards the factory sheds in the fog. 'Do you think they'll go to Mr Riven's now?'

'No, you could tell they were too scared. Mr Harrow would have to request the Morningvale judge to intervene on a visit, and she won't send anyone here unless they could provide a clear reason for it.'

'Such as the testimony of a former Clay Portside Lightmistress.'

'Exactly. If Mr Harrow were to ask for vexatious help too often, then the Lyonne courts might decide the region cannot manage its own affairs. Both Magistrate and Coastmaster could lose their positions.'

With that, Chalice headed off to the ratcheting log-splitter, a contraption that resembled a torture device from the oldest times.

Arden hurried after Chalice. 'Go on. Tell me. I'm an *idiot.*'

'What are you on about, Arden Beacon? If you're coming to that conclusion now, you are quite behind the times.' Chalice hefted a log into the cradle and pumped the handle with the enthusiasm of winching a garrotte.

'I was completely wrong about what I saw in the compound. I jumped to all the wrong conclusions. Mr Riven hadn't killed the plesiosaur pup. He had rescued the animal from Cormack and his hunters, and I had . . . in my rush to agree with everyone . . . *failed* to entertain that possibility!'

Chalice only gave a snort at Arden's crisis. 'Just because Mr

Cormack is a devil, it does not make Mr Riven a saint. I have known many a bad man to show kindness to animals. It is something of a perversion that they appreciate a beast for keeping its place in the scheme of things, that is, lower than low.'

'Yet, the other way is just as true. If you have no compassion for animals, hard to extend it to humankind.'

'Then consider this,' Chalice said, giving the splitter a few final hefts. 'It takes two boats to hunt plesiosaur comfortably. Far better for a lone rogue to attack a couple of milksop dandies in the company of an old man than single-handedly attempt a giant beast about to whelp. Our neighbour wasn't being compassionate. He was being expedient.'

She turned away from Arden and with a sharp kick, the log was torn asunder.

10

Mr Harrow

Mr Harrow did not return. If he'd found any other proof of the crime he had accused his former son-in-law of, the balance could not have been enough to send his men to arrest Mr Riven. Arden worried for her mail, her tenuous links with her family. It would not be unheard of for a malicious Postmaster to withhold her correspondences.

But the letters from her former life still came, albeit with some crinkled evidence of steaming and re-gluing. A riotous scrawl from her Uncle Nicolai, speaking of lighthouse matters as if she were an equal to him in his great tower at the Mouth. Her father's careful penmanship, reviews of some books he had read and promised would send in the next post. Well wishes from step-mother Nina, and her step-sister Sirena, and her half-brother Odie, who was *sanguis ferro* – his blood trammelled iron – and whose labour contract had been won at auction by Clay's largest steel-works. He quoted a tremendous sum. Arden wrote back to him cautioning that he see a financial adviser at once.

More postcards arrived from desert countries, where the sand moved like a river, and the men wore blue robes. An engagement announcement from a close friend who'd made full Guild on her eleventh birthday, and another letter mourning the end of a brief affair.

Arden read them all with detachment. For all that her name was on the envelopes, they were missives meant for another person. A Guildswoman with her own posting, one obtained honourably.

On the second week, a message came from Mx Modhi across the harbour. The Coastmaster had been called away on business for at least a month. It would be her son David who would bring supplies.

Arden greeted that particular news with relief. Since the dream of Mr Castile, she had agonized over meeting up with the young Baron and his whispered offers. Fretted that she might cast aside her good nature and say *yes*. The nights had been strange to her, aloft in the sea-facing tower while the clockwork motor ground out its constant refrain of escapement and arbour. The wild messenger pigeons in the dome, cousins to the ones Chalice kept in a roost behind the lighthouse to run the daily observations, cooed to each other in the darkness, an avian language, full of augury. The ocean breathed and retreated. The nights held Arden captive, overwhelmed her with a physical hunger of missing – *something*.

But what? Not the blind fumbling of intercourse surely, for she'd experienced enough to know it would only lead to sadness and emptiness upon the sunrise. But something. An experience deep and meaningful, an equivalent revelation about another human being.

The days passed quicker than she could mark them, for an instinct lived within Arden to find joy and purpose in things she could rely on, and in her work. The rising of the sun, the clock-chime advising the keeping of records, the morning and afternoon flash of mirrors to Mx Modhi signifying that all was well. In the afternoons a lich-ship might grind towards the horizon, and in the morning another would return. She logged them studiously in the journal, along with the records of flotillas, single boats, patchworked barges, all heading in one direction and these ones never returning.

Over those first days of her seasoning, she emptied the last of the old furniture and rubbish from the house's interior. On Chalice's first return to Vigil, she came back with buckets of whitewash paint, and for a while they slept in the upper convolutions of the tower with every window open, just to escape from the drying paint-fumes below.

Chalice made good company during her waking hours. She collected many stories of her time in Shinlock a mining town not so different from Vigil, where the fibrous asbestos from the mines would turn the air smoky-blue, and the men chewed kraken-beak pills so as not to get tumours in their lungs, though sometimes unscrupulous doctors sold squid beak instead, and they died anyway.

She gossiped too, about her Harbinger Bay assignment with the sanguinem Lightkeeper Stephen Pharos, of the rotting ships lashed together to make the floating prisons in the small bay, for the laws on the sea were different from on land, and a man could be disappeared into the prison hulks without legal recourse or trial. A prisoner had escaped once, found shelter in the lighthouse. Chalice had cared for him three days, until he had died of his injuries. He had not said much, Chalice recalled, but his ruined eyes and terrified silence spoke volumes.

In the afternoons, when Chalice slept and took her stories with her, Arden subsumed herself into her hermit's life. In between blood-letting and record-keeping she walked through the missionary ruins and down to the rocky shore. Occasionally she saw a plesiosaur pod rise their necks, swan-like, above the waves, and once found a sea-cow sunning itself on the pebbles, all glistening bulk with a sharkskin hide. Each rhomboid flipper was the size of Arden's torso.

Arden dared not come any closer, but the saurian was not at all comfortable with the added human presence, and humped back into the wave-wash with agitated hissing.

Near the sea-caves she disturbed trilobites and anemones in the rockpools. Fossicked small relics clearly discarded from the older settlements, small icons of religious protection. A pottery kraken missing most of its glazed arms. A small tooth of nephrite jade. Her favourite was a blanket-ring featuring a tiny cast iron man straddling a coiled *maris anguis* – a giant sea-serpent.

'That's the Deepwater King,' David Modhi would tell her later, when she showed him her find upon his weekly visits to the lighthouse.

The young man rubbed the crust of red oxide from the small figure's face and gazed at it. 'The King lives in a cathedral under the ocean, and all men who drown must serve Him.'

'He must be a fierce regent, if he rides a serpent like a horse.' she quipped, keeping the tone light, for she knew belief systems were inscribed deep upon Fiction hearts, and the Harbourmistress' son might take offence to mocking.

'Oh no, He's killing the serpent here, see? Bringing the meat to feed those people who keep His laws. It is His gift for those who believe and still follow His ways. He won't ever let them starve or go hungry . . .'

'Does your mother know you're familiar with such legends, young David?'

He blushed, and shook his head.

'I won't tell her,' she said. 'It can be our secret.'

David Modhi smiled, before gazing at the ring fondly. 'This will bring you luck. It reminds me of Mr Riven, don't you think?'

She smiled with kindness, for love and worship tangled pain-fully in the young. 'I wouldn't know Mr Riven well enough to say.' She paused and then said, 'Would you like to have it?' She offered the blanket-ring to him.

He shook his head again. 'The King made you find his image, so it's yours to keep Lightmistress.'

The youth looked over her other finds, then picked up the legless ceramic kraken. 'And this is the King's enemy, the Old Emperor, whom He must battle on the Last Day. The sea belongs to the Deepwater King. Everything upon the shore and under the waves.'

He leaned in close as if whispering a secret.

'And in the midwinter He takes a wife.'

'Goodness,' Arden said, laughing. 'That's quite a thing to say.'

'It's true,' he said flaming with offence. 'He's given you his ring, Lightmistress. He's seen your face.'

11

Mr Quill's car

Mr Quill's car chattered out of a fog bank the same way the
devil might greet lost travellers, appearing from nowhere while
trailing malice and shady agreements. The Siegfried's patched-up
wheels churned through the thin, sandy slip of soil that made
for the lighthouse road. The skids from Mr Harrow's arrival
in the month before still scarred the top layer of stones.

Arden, in the challenging middle portion of throwing a
seldom-laundered bedsheet up over a rusted washing line her
uncle had probably never used, watched the car's arrival with all
the sinking dread of a condemned criminal. Well, so much for
her peace. Reality had arrived over the walls of her austere
garden.

She raised her hand in greeting to Mr Quill, who did not
leave his seat. Instead the rear door of the car opened, and a
pinstriped trouser leg emerged, shining shoes, that spotted plesiosaur leather coat.

'Mr Justinian? I thought you were away on business until
next week. I'd have made an effort otherwise.' She pointed at
the sheet with arms as raw as pork skin in an icebox.

'I cut it short, after news came to me.'

'What news?'

'I was concerned for your safety,' he said. 'You left without saying farewell, and Mr Quill said you did something rather rash a few weeks ago when he first took you here.'

'I can't quite—'

'Of course, he neglected to tell me all this, so he'll get his pay-packet lightened.'

Arden sighed and looked in sympathy at Mr Quill, cowering behind the steering wheel. 'Coastmaster, please don't blame him. We were quite safe. As for yourself, you were in no fair condition that day. I needed to act in haste, to save my uncle's light.'

Mr Justinian dropped his pleasant-face for a brief moment. 'Those Garfish Point ingrates should tackle that particular blame. Will cheat a man out of honest money and sell contaminated liquor to boot.'

She returned as much of a smile as she could without it being forced. 'See? Mr Quill did excellent work. He must be rewarded, as an example, otherwise your staff might lose their sense of pride.'

'Hmm,' Mr Justinian said, unable to figure if he was being manipulated or her request genuine. In the afternoon light Mr Justinian stepped towards Arden. She had to admit his dress was impeccable. He wore an expensive cologne, touches of gold upon his eyelids, carmine on his lips. Handsome in any part of the world, and here among the 'lumpen inbreds', as he so dismissively called his Fiction counterparts, beautiful.

The only man of any worth available to her, if she were to choose that path.

'Anyhow, where is your Miss Quarry? I thought your storm-bride should be out doing the hard domestic work, not a Lightmistress.' He sniffed disapprovingly at the flapping sheets.

'She has taken the boat into Vigil,' Arden said. 'She must deliver the tide observations to the Postmaster.'

'Why do you not do it yourself? I seem to recall you had a desire to meet the good people of our town.'

She shrugged, and pushed a damp tendril of hair from her

brow. 'I like it out here. I can see why the missionaries chose to build their first church upon this site.'

'For all the good it did. The loneliness killed them, in the end.'

'Yes,' she said, then berated herself for agreeing with him.

Mr Justinian blinked, not missing that tenuous connection. 'Have you felt it, Lightmistress, the noonday demon? What the climate of the Darkling Sea does to those newcomers unused to our great melancholy sink?'

He took another step closer, and the heat from the Siegfried's internal heaters still radiated off him.

With an inward sigh, Arden suspected that Mr Justinian might not have gone away on business at all, and waited for the isolation to do its work. He would know her alone with only the waves and wind. Her defences could be breached now.

'I dare say one could get used to it. Under the right conditions.'

'There were no right conditions. Those missionaries, they were constantly at *war*, my dear. With the old religions who worshipped the kraken and the spawning monsters of our coast and the abominable King in his abyss. Built their first church they might have done, but they could not stay. More than one massacre has left behind a choir-load of bones.'

She shivered, not from cold. Ghosts perhaps. His closeness, so unwanted, but piquing her memory. Coldfire in her blood, but still, her needs had always burned hot.

He saw the shiver, and her response pleased him.

'Go on then. Clean yourself up. We shall go for a walk, you and I. A sortie of your assigned portions. I shall tell you more history, if you wish.'

Arden searched for excuses, found none. Why should a Lightmistress not patrol grounds that a Coastmaster controlled?

And walks tended to turn into much more.

'I'll meet you out here,' Arden said brusquely. 'I won't be long.'

*   *   *

She closed the driftwood door and leaned hard against it. This had to be a test, surely. What would she endure for that full Guild degree? She had invited Mr Justinian to her lighthouse, and he would be unlikely to leave without his pound of flesh. Arden knew his kind. Too much refusal would make an enemy out of him. Trapped in a cage of possible disasters, Arden lingered over Bellis Riven's krakenskin by her bed, the blue eye-marks bright in the dim light.

'Why not just once, scratch the itch, get it over and done with? It's not like he's the kind that makes a habit of it,' she said to the empty room. Squeezed her fists until her coins hurt. He had dressed well, at least. It would not be distasteful.

In Lyonne, Arden's position and her family protected her. Here, she would need to put all the morals of the North aside. Why not spend a few uncomfortable minutes with Mr Justinian and consider her duty done? The act would put a firm boundary between the woman who used to believe in love, and the one who saw it only as expedience. She would be gone before the winter and he would be forgotten.

As she had promised, Arden changed quickly. At the last minute she decided to forgo her utilitarian cotton undergarments for a particular gold silk lingerie set purchased from an old traveller-folk merchant back in the days of Richard Castile. Maybe they would make her think romantic and sensual thoughts, yes? She still remembered the old woman's shrewd sales pitch. *An old magic in these gold threads. Wear this before your beloved and he will be overwhelmed with desire.*

Not that they worked, for she'd had no chance to disrobe in front of Richard when she last wore them. The garments had most likely been fenced from a pirate haul, and were possibly not altogether made of sea-silk either. Yet for the story the old woman wove Arden had bought an overpriced courtesan's corset, cut far too low about the neck and boned such that her upper half would be forever in danger of falling out.

Such an ignominy to waste their prettiness on Mr Justinian. Quite the opposite of the krakenskin coat, which bore such a disagreeable tale. What better way to discard a memory that had also become disagreeable?

Her best dress was a blue broadcloth, warm enough against the wind but not too dowdy. She fixed her hair and stained her lips with crimson.

Mr Justinian smirked when at last he saw Arden again. His fingers and thumbs made small circles, already envisioning her skin between them.

His back is straight and his voice is well spoken, Arden thought to herself in a desperate catalogue of positive things. *He has the kind of style that serves a man well in high company. He is a Baron by blood.*

None of her silent declarations eased the antipathy that kept intruding on her desperate attempt to feel remotely interested in her companion. Instead Mr Justinian's little annoying traits amplified into ugliness. He complained most of the time he walked, and when his discussions were not negative, they were aggrandizing monologues on his own advantages over other lesser folk. The wind snickered through the scrub, blowing her dress sideways, and making her regret she had not chosen to wear a decent pair of woollen long johns instead.

They trekked along the old coastal path, following the limestone and shale pavements that led to the other side of the promontory, where the larger and more windswept cliffs of Dead Man's Bay battered the cliffside ruins.

The wind whipped up with angry little teeth and got underneath Arden's skirts, and at one stage she shivered enough for Mr Justinian to sidle close with the offer of a warm embrace, his move fouled only by the narrow path. On the old trail they could only walk in single file and not two abreast, a situation that Arden preferred, for the silky rustle of her golden lingerie made her anxious with impending unpleasantness.

A sea-spray spangled Arden's lips with salt kisses, caused Mr Justinian's hat to blow away and a careful coif of hair to droop sadly over one eye.

'Ugh, this blasted climate. I could have driven you back to

town, my dear. I know I said a *walk*, I can offer something more civilized. Such as, the promenade.'

The idea of the pair of them strolling the fishy-smelling, sad little boardwalk had even less appeal. 'No, this is nice,' Arden replied. 'I prefer the wildness.'

'Don't prefer it too much,' Mr Justinian cautioned. 'It drove your uncle mad in the end.'

'We are entirely different people, Mr Justinian. You must not worry.'

At one cliffside Arden stopped at a pile of stones that were newer-hewn than the ruins, a careful little cairn in the shape of a rotunda. A flat piece of stone at the base bore chisel marks. A crude *Bellis* pitted there. Someone had added underneath – and this with a different hand and including the Beacon family mark – *Stefan*. Her cousin, who had disappeared along with Bellis before he could testify against Mr Riven.

Mr Justinian *tsk*ed. 'Such a rude little cenotaph. She deserves better than that pile of rubble. I should have it knocked down.'

He shoved it with his foot, swept a few stones from the surface with the dismissal of clearing a table of crumbs. The cairn held fast, mostly. The sea grumbled through caverns below them, as if upset at the interference.

'Perhaps you could build her one.'

'Out of what, dear? She deserves better than rubble.'

'I saw much hidden statuary mouldering in the Manse gardens. Maybe the little mer-girl that sits at the edge of the south fountain. Put her on the promenade. Have a brass plaque made in Bellis Harrow's memory.'

Mr Justinian laughed, and did not bother to hide his ridicule. 'Arden, the Coastmaster budget would never extend so far as to encompass such fripperies as statue moving and random emplaquement.'

'What about your own money, Vernon? Doesn't Bellis deserve that?'

His laughter stopped. Arden cast her eyes over his wormsilk suit, his plesiosaur coat, the pink diamond on his index finger in a recent gaudy style. There might not have been a lot of money left, but that did not mean he couldn't liquefy old baronial assets for his own *fripperies*.

Annoyed now, he changed the subject abruptly. 'We must talk about you visiting Mr Riven.'

'I made my introductions on the first day, yes.'

'You are brave, I give you that.'

'I doubt Mr Harrow would say the same thing.'

Mr Justinian shrugged. 'His job is his job. The wretch did assault three people the day before. You could easily have been the fourth.'

'I find that unlikely.'

'Unlikely, you say?' With barely restrained glee, Mr Justinian launched into a story, told her of the corpses that might wash ashore from the Sainted Isles, bloated with seawater and lungs black with congealed rockblood. He described the white bone poking through paper skin, the scars upon their flesh that suggested shackles, or worse. Purposeful mutilations, bodies hurt beyond measure.

'. . . not long after the man returned from prison, myself and Stefan Beacon came to this very spot. We saw Mr Riven down here trying to carry away one of the bodies. A woman, I think. He ran away when he saw us. No doubt he intended to use the corpse for his own pleasures. Eventually he became tired of such easy pickings and turned his attention to the living.'

The disgusting descriptions excited him. His face flushed, his breath quickened. Vaguely nauseated now, Arden hurried on ahead, down the rough stone steps that gave access to the inlet. The steps were slippery from the sea mist, so she capitulated to take Mr Justinian's hand to help her down.

'Arden, my dear, this is hardly a beach. Come up and we might rest in the old ruins. You can have my jacket for warmth.'

She ignored the lingering squeeze his hand left upon her fingers, and concentrated on making her descent in a halfway vertical fashion. She would succumb to his invitations eventually, but the mood had not taken her quite yet.

'I'll scout around down here, first.'

Realizing she wasn't yet ready to submit, Mr Justinian resentfully followed Arden to beach level.

The rocky shelf had a sharply uninviting atmosphere where it met the waves. The monastery ruins above fell away at the eroded cliff and into a jumble of slime-shiny basalt blocks. Spars of grey shale occluded coarse yellow sand, and the remains of anchors, winches and other rust-smeared equipment littered the shoreline.

'Ah, your cousin's boat is still on the rocks.' He pointed to the sea-battered remains of a small oak and steel dinghy wedged in the granite, several winters' worth of storms melting it into the earth. 'I remember that day too well,' he added. 'No sea-sense in Stefan Beacon. Twelve years old and pretending himself a master sailor.'

'Did you know him very well before he became a Rector?'

'We were youthful friends, but adult responsibilities are what they are. Years in a seminary and he never lost the . . .' Mr Justinian picked up a sea-stone, worn smooth from the waves. '*Impulsiveness*. A certain rash wanderlust. His mother came from the Sainted Isles, and she lived with Jorgen for a time. Only a time, mind. The blood of the rock has a call on certain people. She abandoned her child to go back to the Islands, left him to live with a half-mad Lightkeeper. In the end, they both went mad together.'

'It would be a sad story, though my account is a little different.'

'Is it now? Who have you been talking to?'

Arden rolled her eyes. 'Stefan was already six years old by the time he came here. I knew his mother. She was a Lyonne *sanguinem*. Jorgen and her divorced amicably, and sometimes she visited during Festival.'

Mr Justinian's face went scarlet. 'So, my memory is rusty. It was a long time ago.'

'Which leads me to think that maybe memories can't be that reliable.'

Mr Justinian waved her away. 'Perhaps his early years are shrouded in mystery, but I can recall crystal clear when our Rector started stealing back here for trysts. When he began his affair with Bellis Riven.'

Arden shook her head, not understanding.

'Excuse me? Stefan was a priest. He had taken vows. Would only have been out of friendship that he spent time with her.'

'The idiot abandoned his vows. Oh, did you not know? He had an affair with Bellis in the last month of her life. He would meet her here in the ruins when Riven was away, hunting. He brought her medicines for her injuries, sympathies from when her treatment had been rough. Then he gave her his body, and you know where that leads.'

As much as she tried, Arden couldn't visualize Stefan Beacon having such a rash affair. He'd seemed so deliberately fey and insular whenever they'd met, even now she could not quite imagine him having an affair with any human being, much less a woman.

'Are you sure, Vernon? Or is it another bit of fishmonger gossip ill-remembered?'

'He confessed to me his sin,' Mr Justinian said. 'In confidence.'

'The local Coastmaster seems an odd choice for a holy man to reveal such a dangerous relationship to.'

'It may be gauche to say this, but I called Stefan my best friend, once. We grew together as boys. Brothers, almost. Yes.' He nodded to himself. 'Confessed to me. Wanted my blessing since Bellis and I were once engaged and the guilt weighted his brow.'

'Blessing for what, exactly?'

'To run away. Bellis' brutish husband suspected something afoot.'

Arden exhaled. 'Running away. Of course. The one idea always doomed to failure.'

'Devil curse him, that Riven.' He threw the stone at the distant horizon with an almighty heave. 'If he never existed, Bellis would still be here.'

'Mr Justinian, look out—'

A wave broke upon the rocks, so close that they were spattered with foam. Mr Justinian turned upon Arden and seized her up by her waist and pressed himself close. His wet lips caught the side of her mouth. His tongue, foiled by her clenched teeth, trailed damp upon her wincing cheek before turning wet slug-trail circles under her ear.

'Arden, don't fight me.'

She attempted to squirm away. 'Wait a minute, Vernon, this is rather sudden.'

'Why must we tease each other?' he whined. 'All these games of love are for children.' He fumbled his hand on her breast. 'Ah, your heart beats fast with passion.'

Was not passion that moved her so. Her loins could have been a desert, for all that she responded to Mr Justinian. His fingers folded over into the corset of her dress, his heavily manicured nails sharp as a scratch upon her delicate skin.

'Vernon . . .'

She froze the way a watch-escapement that has danced out of synchronicity will stop the whole clock, her prior thoughts of giving in to Mr Justinian's lusts evaporating.

I cannot go through with it. He disgusts me. In the distance of miles felt him seize the neck of her corset with a frantic grip while with the other hand yanked up her dress hem. 'It's all right if you are a virgin, it will not hurt but a prick.'

A terrible antipathy came over her as the ruffled silk tore. She had not thought this thing through, not thought how the touch of Mr Justinian upon her intimate places would cause her such distress.

She was a spring wound too tight. The escapement tore free of the tooth. 'I said *no*, Mr Justinian!'

Shoved him away with her lantern-turner's strength and with a wide, swinging blow slapped him hard across his face.

The contact sent a shockwave of pain through her elbow and shoulder, sent him spinning. She lost her foot upon the wet rock. Mr Justinian lunged for her as another wave breached the rocks and suddenly the world went cold and white, yet all she could think of was to dart away from Mr Justinian's grip.

She fell into the foamy tumult, half by accident and half – the worst and most dreadful half – by the same instinct as that of an animal that will gnaw its leg to escape a trap.

Her legs tangled up in the cotton of her skirts. The wave dragged her out with an almighty surging, sucking power, casting her perilously close to the sharpest rocks before she reached the becalmed straits of deeper water.

Reeling from both water-dumping and Mr Justinian's assault, she drifted as the waves gathered for another battering. She was gone and gone.

Don't try to make it back in. The rocks will kill you.

A jolt of anoxic raptures forced her hands and she tugged on the release-strings of her dress. With a tug, suddenly freed herself from the billowing fabric. Her head cleared the water and she gasped for air, rode over the swell as it headed back to the rock where Mr Justinian, drenched and horrified, watched his lighthouse keeper drift helplessly out to sea.

12

She swam with the surge

She swam with the surge, and the further she went from the rocks, the more the sea-rip lost its power. By now her jaws ached from her clattering teeth, and she had overshot the small stony bay by far too much of a distance to consider swimming back. Another inlet appeared, this time one sheltered from much of the waves. Gathering the last of her strength, Arden over-armed herself through the slosh, half-blind with salt water. When her boots touched gravel, she wanted to weep with joy.

The cold had numbed her completely now, and she staggered chill-drunkenly out of the foam. Her torn undergarments stuck to her in membranous translucent flesh, made her a sea-monster half in the process of shedding skin. She limped across the sand, only half-believing that she'd survived and not lost herself within the rapture of drowning.

Before Arden could fall upon the dry beach a dark shape flopped towards her, as large as a mastiff but not a dog, not a seal, a thing with a long neck and a sharp head, and a toothed reptilian mouth that let out a chatter of sharp hissing coughs.

Arden braced for impact, received none. The beast swung wide at the last moment, entered the water to her left instead.

It splashed on past in a riot of flipper and barking, before diving under a small wave. A scar on the pebbled grey back, like that left by a flensing blade . . .

'Plesiosaur,' she said to herself as if the speaking would make it seem less perplexing. 'That's the baby plesiosaur.'

She turned back to the shore. A man stood there on the sand, watching her with dumb surprise.

Only then did Arden notice the glowing blue rings of kraken-hide and the tall figure made spare and severe by the ocean's trials. Wasn't an ordinary man. She was in front of Mr Riven.

Naked, in front of Mr Riven.

Three Djennes'-worth of the gold silk she'd intended for her only love, and now her promise-night garb hung in tatters. The sight that should have greeted Mr Castile was given instead to a bearded, swollen-eyed brute. She didn't bother to cross her hands about her chest. It wouldn't make much of a difference to what he saw anyway.

'Well then,' she said to any devils that might be listening. 'This day cannot possibly get any worse.'

He did not stare, not long at any rate. The expression on his face amounted to dumbfounded shock, then to another, firmer and more decisive gaze. He dropped the bucket of fish-guts held in one hand, and shrugged out of his coat.

So, she thought with frozen, and exhausted inevitability. *This is the place where I will be ravished, and if I'm fortunate he might not finish me off with my head upon a rock.*

Mr Riven took off his woollen sweater and revealed a tattered shirt. Another chill wind gusted against her wax-cold skin. She huffed with impatience. *Get on with it so I can get back some-where warm. I'm not going to put up a fight.*

The plesiosaur child lumbered past her again. The sharp, beaky nose plunged into its bucket of disgusting meal.

Instead of disrobing completely, Mr Riven placed his sweater on a basalt spar and shrugged back into his coat. He nodded once, before leaving. In all that time he did not say a word.

Arden, stupefied by surprise and cold, merely watched him

go. She should have spoken to him, acknowledged this odd meeting, but her nakedness made her so self-conscious she could not bring herself to speak to the man. His back gave communication enough and she welcomed it.

When the fear drained away, the shivers came. She dived for the dry, warm sweater, would not have cared if the wool were filthy and crawling with maggots and prepared herself that it would be, that she would retch from the stink of unwashed flesh from this man who lay with the dead, and yet . . .

And yet . . .

A whiff of a clean, warm, masculine scent filled her senses as she tugged the knitted cables over her head. The yarn startled her with softness, but lay heavy across her shoulders, arms and bosom in a gentle embrace. Along with the smell of a young, healthy man, there came the dusky smell of kraken oil, that exotic perfume that always lingered in the air of the more important Clay Portside offices. The purled hem brushed her knees.

Relief dizzied Arden. She had expected horror and received the opposite. She might have collapsed and rolled herself up in a warm knitted cocoon if she had not heard someone calling her name.

Mr Justinian appeared, ashen, at the top of the cliffside track. 'You're all right! Oh, by the Gods! When I saw that Riven character heading for the likely deposit of your body, I was certain you'd be lost.' He stopped, realizing that from the ragged fronds of her bloomers and her waterlogged boots, she'd ended up quite naked below the knees. 'And what are you *wearing*?'

'Shut up, Vernon,' she said harshly. 'Was your fault I ended up in this mess. I told you to stop!'

'I'm sorry,' he cried. 'I'm sorry, forgive me! My desires overcame my senses, I thought they were reciprocated! I don't know what came over me!'

He crawled towards her feet, prostrating himself. Arden jumped back, not knowing how to take this sudden change in character.

'You should have asked! Presented your case, but instead you speak filth about a dead woman and her husband, then grab at me as an animal in heat!'

'I'm a goddamn fool, it's true. I was impassioned in my concern for your safety around the Riven creature!'

A font of disgust flowered in her, a sudden bloom of sympathy for her wretched, broken neighbour.

'Nothing you say about Mr Riven assists me in any way. No repetitions of my neighbour's monstrous appetites, no gloating appeals to my sanity! You relish speaking of your fiancée's ordeal with a pleasure and not a shame. You revel in her torments. In fact, I don't know who I should despise most, Mr Riven or you.'

Mr Justinian stood up, rubbed his cheek, affected an aspect of sheer misery.

'The fault is mine! I never learned how to properly romance a woman in anything other than the coarse ways of Fiction. My background has been emotional poverty and stolen, pleasureless embraces. I've never had a teacher to show me how to make love.' Mr Justinian raised his eyes hopefully to her. 'Arden Beacon, please help me become this man.'

Arden laughed, incredulous. 'Enough, Vernon. I'm not blind. The ladies of the Black Rosette have had plenty of opportunities to show you how to make bloody love. You are a disgrace to your profession, trying to use it to seduce and bully me. I won't stand for it.'

She stomped on up the beach-track stairs as best she could without toppling off them in the wind, reached the cliff-top before he did.

'Then what do you want from me?' Mr Justinian whined behind her. 'Shall I prove my newfound desire to improve myself? Do you want me celibate, and swearing off all pleasures before you will acquiesce to my devotion? Is that what it will take to win your affection?'

'Whatever you want, Vernon Justinian,' she snapped. 'Bind yourself up in thistles and itching-ivy if you must, but keep your impure thoughts to yourself. I could have died this afternoon.'

His face was furious, but he capitulated to her anger. Bowed his head. 'It is done. It is done!'

He kept his silence as they returned from their walk. Chalice had returned, and had since coaxed Mr Quill out of the car with a cup of one of her bitter teas.

'What happened to your dress?' Chalice asked, then caught sight of Mr Justinian's hangdog appearance, Arden's dishevelled rage. 'Ah,' she concluded. This required a more private interrogation.

'Come, Mr Quill,' Mr Justinian barked. 'I'm not paying you for laziness. We must be back in town before nightfall.'

The driver gave up his tea to the ashes, and quickly returned to his duties.

Once the car disappeared from sight, Chalice followed Arden inside the lighthouse.

'You cannot keep me in suspense. I return to your absence and the driver waiting, only to discover you were gallivanting with the second last person in the world I'd expect you gallivanting with.'

'And the last person being Mr Riven?'

'By God, no. I saw the expression on your face when you heard he gave a whipping to those foppish plesiosaur hunters. If I know your weaknesses yet, it would be an overwrought sense of moral justice if you gave our besmirched neighbour the portion just to say you were sorry.'

Outside with the bowl of warm water and a sponge, Arden pulled off the sweater. Chalice gasped at what she had revealed.

'Dear me, trying to make yourself a tasty morsel for Mr Justinian? By your appearance I'd wager he ravished you *both* ways.'

Arden scoffed, but had to admit she had become a sight. Getting dragged out over the rocks by the waves had knocked her bruised and bloody.

'Just be a help and get me some soap. I couldn't be worse if I tangled with Poseidon himself.'

'You need more than soap. Clean yourself off and I'll put some iodine on those cuts. Damn the devils, which man must I kill today?'

'It's not what you think. I fell into the water, on one of the shipwreck bays. Blame the rocks for my injuries.'

'*Just* them?'

'Just them.'

'All right. It is a relief. The ground around here is quite unsuitable for graves. So hard to dig and I'd rather not be breaking my back for anyone.'

Arden washed the salt out of her skin and hair, and in the fading evening light deigned to sit on a stool in her cotton nightdress while Chalice dabbed reddish balm over her cuts.

As Chalice tended to her, Arden told her stormbride about Mr Justinian's actions, the desperate swim, and the beach with Mr Riven. 'He was feeding a plesiosaur today. A juvenile.'

'I thought the man could only call kraken?' Chalice asked, mid-dab.

'Let's just say my perilous position did not allow me to ask him. But I could have sworn the creature was the same one he carried from his boat weeks ago, except it was healed and very much alive.'

Chalice shook her head, sceptical. 'Are you sure?'

'Very certain. There was a scar on its back, the exact same one.'

'An interesting talent. Truth, I couldn't tell the difference between one plesiosaur and another, myself.' She finished her dabbing, stood back and admired her handiwork. 'There you go, spotted as a leopard. Now I'll throw this old rag out.'

She had barely lifted the sweater before Arden took it out of her hands.

'I have to clean it and give it back to him.'

She hadn't managed to inspect this gifted garment of Mr Riven's until then. Unlike the immaculate coat, the uneven knots in the woollen sweater very much told a sad tale by their own selves. Songs of rending and patching at least a hundred times, pale scours from repeated washing, and threadbare where sand soap had not quite rinsed out the ichor of kraken calling. Now the sleeves from the elbows down were sticky with blood.

'Are you trying to scry the future in those woollen entrails?' Chalice commented as Arden gently laid out the sweater on the slab table and touched the fibres as one might touch a sacred object for luck. 'Because I can imagine scabies, and a furious genital itching.'

'It was clean before I bled on it. I don't want to bring it back in such a condition.'

'Just think of it as an excuse for him to change clothes for once.'

Arden tutted at Chalice's uncharitable thoughts. 'I'm just fascinated. See, its old, but the quality of the work is wonderful. You'd struggle to get similar in a Clay Capital high street.'

'I never realized the fashion tends to wearing big Fiction sweaters.'

'Chalice, you know what I mean.'

She shrugged. 'So the natives know their way around a needle.'

'Don't you think this is odd how the collar is embroidered so, with all these fun little decorations?' Arden's fingers stroked busy needlework of blue waves, black kraken-arms, a sun and moon. One read in the threads affectionate gestures, a shared memory between old friends.

'What are you trying to say, dear?' Chalice asked, droll. She dumped a load of firewood by the brazier and slapped sawdust from her hands. 'How pretty the stitches, what delight in her patterns?'

'If Bellis sewed these, she was not a woman in pain.'

'Perhaps you should offer your services as a detective to Magistrate Harrow. Devils know how useless his lumpen deputies are.'

'I don't recognize abuse, though. The sweater and the coat were both made with affection. There is love here.'

Chalice sniffed, lit up her pipe, took a long dismissive drag.

'There are *spells* here, Arden. Old Fictish magic, binding up the monster in thread so it may not harm the maker.'

Arden wanted to argue with Chalice. She saw fondness, adoration in the threads. Ill-fated, eternal, storybook love, not the brutality of the local gossips, and a twist of envy towards Bellis, small and bitter, pricked Arden's heart. She'd have made such clothes for Richard, given the chance, were it part of their culture.

Chalice sat next to Arden wrapped her arm about her waist, lay her fiery head upon Arden's shoulder. The smoke curled about them.

'I'm just glad you're alive, darling.'

'It feel so strange, though. Like I cannot trust anything I'm being told.'

The arm squeezed harder. 'Arden, the gods loved you today. Are you certain you've not got a shadow talent for enchanting wild men?'

Arden wriggled free. 'Chalice, you mustn't joke about shadow talents. They're a terrible thing for a child to be afflicted with.'

Chalice held up her hand. 'My apologies. But I can see your jealousy for Bellis Riven.'

'I am not jealous, either!'

'You are jealous. It's plain as day. You want what Bellis had, to be both *sanguis* and free of the Guild, to be blessed with such a thing as a man's tender devotion.' She shrugged. 'Even if it is Mr Riven's. And it killed her in the end.'

Much to the displeasure of Chalice Quarry and her proclamations on the dangers of lice-borne diseases, Arden washed the blood from the sleeves, and brought the sweater indoors where it might dry by the fire. It splayed out cruciform upon the washing line, a winged shadow.

In the morning's dark early hours, when her shift ended and weariness made her maudlin, she fell back into her old physical longings, walked those worlds as she hovered between waking and dream.

You are jealous.

But this time, the princes and airshipmen and dockworkers of her night-time fantasies were cast aside, and a man with swollen eyes and damaged features beheld her as she emerged from the sea, her body a gold-fronded nakedness, his expression a raw wound, and a terrible longing upon his face.

13

Something in the quality of her life

Something in the quality of her life. Something had changed. She no longer worried about her real worth on the signal tower, or her tending of a dying flame. As the weather cooled from the summer mildness Arden oriented now to the old factories down the promontory, the way a creature in pain will be drawn towards its own destruction. She had to return Mr Riven's sweater. Soon, she promised, for tardiness would raise questions.

But each hour she spent thinking about visiting Mr Riven and thanking him for the use of the garment made the act take on far more import than it should. She was not foolish enough to consider any neighbourly relationship more than casual politeness – he would never be a comrade or friend, not a Chalice Quarry or a Gerry Harris. Her imagination couldn't extend to talking with him about anything other than the best way to slaughter a thing ten times larger than yourself.

More dangerously, her isolation from any human companionship other than Chalice made her assign fictional qualities to Mr Riven that had no true bearing on his unknown character.

He had battled poachers, he was a man of moral standing.

He had nursed an orphan water-pup to health (perhaps it had not been so dead), he was patient.

He had given her a garment, was kind, he had not taken advantage, he was polite, he was this and he was that.

See, all those things make Mr Riven not at all those things that Mr Justinian accuses him of. See? See?

Afterwards, she would become angry at herself for her wool-gathering. She needed to maintain the discipline of the lighthouse, to identify and catalogue the ships that passed, the movement of air within the barometer, the variances in the tide. Her attention was required seawards, not behind her.

I must nor contrive, she told herself. *I must not.* She must not wander into a fork in the road where he had taken her upon the beach, tearing the silks from her body, doing everything the traveller woman had promised. Mr Riven existed only as a cipher for her own loneliness and worry. Arden had come here to shake herself free of a demon, not pick up another one.

Her pronouncements were only playthings for a capricious God. Her solitude made her vulnerable, to the long days of watching the coast, listening to Chalice snore and snuffle in her sleep, the low hissing roar of the wind through the sea-caves, long walks along the promontory on top of gravestones and crumbled walls.

The nights were worse, and she hid Mr Riven's sweater in a pillowcase so that Chalice might not see it unreturned. An object of veneration and suffering, to take out and press her face into the thick cables, catch a remnant of a man's scent, regardless of who it belonged to. A life not hers, but was promised, once.

She was wise enough to know the depressive condition of *acedia*, how it affected isolated Lightkeepers and signallers just as it affected monks and aesthetes. Knew how close she risked falling into that dark well-pit, and could not find any way to stop herself from sliding.

14

Wake up!

Arden startled awake, alert and in a panic. The grinding of the lens motors a level above made a sound as familiar as the whoosh of blood in a womb. Light-shadow crawled over the white-washed stone. The cold-flame burned and bright from when she had last supplied it. Devilment! How long had she been napping? To fall asleep was an unforgivable transgression in signal keeping.

'Chalice?' she asked the darkness, waiting for the returning scold of her assistant.

No reply from either the doorway or downstairs. Arden quickly checked the luminous hands of the clock against her last time-measurement. The shipwright's clock pointed to a three, the devil's number, and Arden calmed down a little. Three o'clock wasn't too bad. She had started her shift at two o'clock, already taken the half-hour measurements, noting the low pressure and high wind of a Darkling Sea storm. She could not have been subsumed by storm morphia for more than twenty minutes.

She took her pen and notated in her log book: *Atmospheric Pressure – Barometric Event?* Some exotic storm conditions caused the air pressure to plunge so suddenly that entire townships would fall into unconsciousness. The pale-skinned among them would turn blue with hypoxia. *Enchantment tempests*, the locals called such catastrophes, invoking fairy stories of princesses asleep for a hundred years, except in these ones they never woke up.

She crossed out her notation with a shake of her head. An enchantment tempest would have dimmed the beacon flame. Perpetual it might have been, it still required oxygen. The cold-fire still glowed bright.

Arden opened her glove and touched her coin to a small lantern-wick she kept for the purpose, and in the blood-light inspected her fingernails. They were bitten and split from weeks of hard work, but did not show the cyanotic darkness of a low barometric event. Something else had sapped her strength.

She replaced her notation with *Absent*, before cat-footing down the tower stairs, not wanting to wake Chalice. The bride's gentle breath stuttered, and then she too woke up. Chalice hoisted herself onto her elbow, blinked in the dim glow of the brazier, then at her own small clock.

'I'm sorry,' Arden said. 'I hoped some brew still remained in the pot.'

'Was not that soft footfall of yours that woke me.' The stormbride's eyes shone in the gloom, her distance unseeing. Arden remembered that Chalice had tested positive for chemicals and salts at a testmoot. Theirs was a shared language. 'You fell asleep.'

'Something in the weather. Can you feel it?' Arden said. 'Not a barometric event. Powerful, but distant.'

A blink again. 'Yes,' Chalice church-whispered. 'There's blood on this storm. It's almost suffocating. I can take another watch, if you want. I can't see myself going back to sleep.'

The wind whiffled at the glass of the lamphouse. 'I'd best go back up and check on the light. I wouldn't be able to sleep either.'

'I'll have the fire going. This storm's only going to get worse.'

Arden quickly slipped into her krakenskin while Chalice

changed back into her clothes. The stone staircase vibrated under her feet as gales battered the column.

The glass in the lamp room had held strong. The tower might have been left to weather, but mere squalls would not topple her. Arden remained behind the light-shade as her beam shot out into the wild night.

Blood on this storm, Chalice had said. Yes, there definitely *was* a wrinkle in the wind out there. If she were in Lyonne it would not have meant much, but in Fiction the sense filled her like the vibration from a tuning fork, struck and held.

'We'll have to run the foghorn!' Arden shouted down the tower. 'There's no visibility up here!'

'I'm on my way,' the stormbride called back, and a gust of wind came up from below as Chalice opened the driftwood door to exit.

Barely half a minute passed before Chalice came back.

'Arden!' Chalice screamed up the staircase. 'Arden, get down here!'

'What is it?' Arden tried to navigate down the staircase as best she could. 'Is it the horn?'

'There's people in the water outside,' Chalice panted. The rain had soaked her utterly. 'Down at where promontory meets the water. One of them has a flare . . .'

'For goodness' sakes, get your oil coat on,' Arden scolded. 'I'm going outside.'

She snatched up a lantern, pushed her glove aside and squeezed blood into the reservoir until her hand burned and the flame inside sprang up white as burning magnesium. The wind pounced as soon as she stepped into the night, but it could not get past the krakenskin.

She battled her way down to the promontory point. Chalice had seen true. There were people in the water, at least four of them, staggering out of the swell. The phosphor flare in the hand of their leader illuminated them in a ghastly pink.

'Hoy! This way!' she cried.

The strongest of them, an older man clad only in a sopping

waistcoat and breeches, stumbled to Arden and grabbed her shoulders as if he were still drowning. 'My family,' he said between coughs. 'The boat . . . the storm . . .' He was cold as death, and his lips blue-black in the lantern light. He was a Lyonnian, but it was not his blood she had sensed.

'A shipwreck?'

The man nodded, and ran back to help another shadowy figure who waded out of the phosphor-pink foam. A hot fork of lightning illuminated the wreckage of a prospector's boat, a spindly flat-bottomed thing lashed together from river-barges that should never have approached open water.

From the darkness a woman's voice wailed, amplified by the cliffs and rain.

'*My babies! My children!*'

A roar of horror came from the second castaway, a cry of excoriated anguish. He dived back into the surf, screaming incoherently.

Arden could not move, paralysed by empathy. Chalice ran past her and with the first survivor pulled the grieving parents out of the sea.

The woman fell to her knees and wailed. She shouted at the sky, and the dark ocean, before falling, insensible, into the sand.

'You'll all die out here,' Chalice shouted at them through the tumult. 'There's nothing you can do.'

The wind had in the space of minutes increased. Devouring the children had given the storm strength. Chalice hauled up the woman, and Arden likewise, and in a darkness crackling with sorrow and electricity they shuffled up the lighthouse entrance in the way of a blind rat king, a creature with tails snarled together in one unbreakable knot.

Then inside, to the silence.

The woman, once she was let go, fell to the floor in a puddle of seawater and spume. Arden felt nauseous from despair. At once she had seen that the soggy group were all Clay Hillsiders from the villages in the country of Lyonne, simple folk who had no sanguis endowments and no knowledge of the water except for the expanse of Clay Portside's distant Mouth. From what little she had seen of their boat, it had most likely been assembled in an aqueduct, a house-barge pulled by Clydesdale horses in summer.

Chalice, in her tough Shinlock way, went to work immediately, stoking the brazier with coal until it burned insolently against the cold. The kettle already rocked with boiling water. For the first time, Arden allowed some gratitude for Mr Justinian and his long list of equipment. On the list had been a stack of ten woollen blankets, more than she would ever need. Now, faced with these dripping strangers, the blankets became very handy. She ordered them to strip so she could hang their clothes to dry on a length of oil rope. The clothes, even after a washing in the salt, were stained and musty. The poverty of these poor folk clung to them like ship-salvager's pitch.

At a loss of something authoritarian to do, the patriarch of the family handed out dented cups of tea to the three shivering others before accepting one for himself.

'Thank you,' he said to Arden and Chalice at last. He fell into the rote of greetings. His face was waxen with the effort it took to remain stoic. 'My name is Leyland Tallwater, this is my son Gregor, his wife Helena, and her brother Sean Ironcup.' He frowned, and added in a way that Arden found disrespectful, 'Sean is a cripple. He cannot use his body properly.'

The one called Sean affected nonchalance through his shivering, but she could tell by his young face that the words cut him to the quick.

'You are Hillsiders?' Arden asked. 'From outer Clay?'

'In the lands of the plateau. We are farmers.' Leyland Tallwater bent his head to tea-mug, attempted to scry the past from the present. 'Until the land soured in the last season. My grandchildren grew sickly. I lost my younger son when we could not afford to buy him the medicine.' His face collapsed, and Arden felt sorry for him despite his crudeness, and covered his rough, cold farmer's hand with her own. She felt in him something that did not entirely sit right however. As if this journey had been his idea, and he had buffaloed the others into coming along . . .

If she thought it, she did not say it. She patted his hand again. 'My sympathies, sir. This is the worst pain a human can bear.'

'I have killed all of them. All our babies, on a folly.'

The woman, Helena Tallwater, silently watched as the patriarch spoke. In the brazier's glow her face had no expression. Her spirit had vacated her eyes. Relentless, the storm ground against the tower stones, sent deep and disquiet harmonics through the empty space of the lighthouse.

'You'd best get some rest,' Arden said. 'There's nothing we can do until first light. Maybe that will bring some good news.'

Immediately Arden regretted her thoughtless words. There was no good news in a shipwreck. There would be bodies. There would be death.

Arden excused herself. She retired to the motor-room, where her mouth might do the least damage, only to find that Chalice had claimed the space before her. She wound the clockwork with vicious yanks.

'Are you all right?' Arden asked. 'It's cold up here.'

'Can't bear being among them,' Chalice said mid-yank. 'I lost a little brother to the sea when I was a child. It destroyed my mother, made a ghost of her.'

The winder seized as tight as it would go.

'This journey was their decision,' Arden said.

'You think so? I saw your face when you patted that fellow's hand.'

Arden frowned, and Chalice waved her away. 'Forgive me. I'm in a mood, is all.'

Chalice was reliving her own tragedy. As gently as she could, Arden said, 'I remember a child pulled from the freezing waters of Clay Mouth during their coldest winter, and surviving. The sea is sometimes kinder to the young.'

'Their children are dead.' Chalice was harsh. 'Their bodies are shoring up the Sainted Island platforms amid the Sargasso strands as we speak.'

Arden took the last blanket and wrapped it about the storm-bride's shoulder and her own. She took off her damp glove and held Chalice's hand.

'Was he very young, your brother?'

'Yes.'

'I am truly sorry.'

'He lives in the halls of the Deepwater King now,' Chalice said, inexplicably, for she was not one to make a mockery of others' religion, or replace her own arid Shinlock catechisms for the old gods of the coast.

Though what was Chalice's religion? She had worked this ocean for a long time. What strange instructions had she been exposed to?

'The King will keep him well and forever,' Arden replied. 'And the children too. They belong to Him now.'

With their backs to the old dovetailed joint of the stone they huddled, and waited for the blood-soaked storm to dwindle and die.

15

A delicate pattern of daylight fell

A delicate pattern of daylight fell on her face, disturbing her through the thin veil of sleep, and Arden stirred. The previously incessant wind had stopped so suddenly, Arden's ears still rang from the absence. She would rather not have moved out from under the blanket, but a pressing urge to relieve herself put all other necessities aside. She rubbed the crook of pain out of her neck, before descending the stairway to where their rescued prospectors huddled together by the brazier.

The belly of the stove received one of their precious coal briquettes rather than a log of scrub wood. Arden quietly left the lighthouse to survey what damage had been caused outside.

The morning sun hovered low behind filmy clouds, a baleful yellow eye. A blood morning, full of portents. The sea had becalmed, but only so much that it didn't surge, merely roll as if it were the scanty covering over a gigantic resting form. Arden rubbed her damp gloves, the silver coins itching beneath the leather. Where had the blood come from, she wondered. Why was she feeling it so strongly? She'd always been burdened with a particularly powerful nose for sanguinity in others, but it never had disturbed her so much as it did this morning.

After she had paid a visit to their new outhouse, she walked around to the cliffside, and sucked in an uncomprehending breath—

Three Lyonne Hillsider children wandered down by the scanty sand of the point, dazed and lost and grey with cold, but not in the least bit drowned.

'Oh!' she cried to nobody and everybody. 'Come quick, come quick!'

Her shouts roused the prospectors, who dashed out of the door in half-dressed shambles. Arden had already made her muddy slide down the cliff-slope and was running for the children.

She reached a little girl who could be no more than four years old. Fell to her knees in front of the child, placed her hands upon the child's face, her arms, touching a miracle. Understandably clammy skin, but the girl showed no sign of chill-sickness yet. How could this be? Such a Lyonne Hillchild could not have spent the night in the ocean, on the storm, and survived it. This phenomenon was of a kind Arden had never witnessed.

The eldest girl saw Arden and walked over with a casual air. 'Excuse me, ma'am,' she asked in the polite way of Hillfolk when they come upon sanguis nobility. 'Have you seen my parents?'

'Lissa! Tomas, Deborah!' came the screams. The prospector woman ran across the cold sand and fell about with her children tangled in her arms. 'It's a miracle, a miracle! Oh, my babies!'

Arden stood back to watch the family reunion, delighted and puzzled at the same time. The children shook their heads to their mother's impassioned questions as to their survival. They didn't know how they'd bested the storm. All that had happened between the breaking up of their ship and their arrival on the beach was a blank canvas upon which no memory had been painted.

Unless . . .

Arden turned around. In the panic of finding the children she had missed seeing the boat floating at the old pier.

Not just any boat. A longboat, a hunting craft with *CORMACK* daubed on the side. Captain Georges' stolen plesiosaur boat.

And there, walking away from the commotion of the shore. A man in a wet krakenskin coat.

Arden felt her breath fall out of her, as it all suddenly made sense.

'Mr Riven?'

He turned about stiffly. It obviously hurt him to do anything more than walk upright. He wore no shirt underneath his coat save for rags. Great weeping cuts scored diagonally along the pale span of his chest.

In the weeks since their first introduction, Mr Riven's face had yet to lose all its discoloration from his battle with the game hunters. The water straggled his gingering beard into serpentine twists. He took a step towards her, and she immediately took one back, feeling by the lurch of her blood in her chest the wildness rampant beneath his bruise-mottled skin. The power had come from him.

'What do you want?'

Not a threat. Only a deep weariness, the kind that blood-loss brings.

'I wanted to say thank you,' she blurted, cotton-mouthed and quite suddenly shy. 'For rescuing the children.'

'Those fools took their children to the mouth of death.'

'But still . . .'

He made to turn away but had given so much blood to the sea. One knee failed to take his weight, and he went down onto the other as if making obeisance to an angry god.

Arden stumbled through the sand up to Mr Riven, torn between giving comfort and keeping distance. 'Are you all right?'

Not only his chest, but also one corded forearm was laid open to blade-cuts. It was a desecration of talent to bleed so profusely and openly, and she *tsk*ed in indignant concern.

'Do you even know how to use your blood endowments, sir?'

Despite the strength in his lean, raw-boned body, the clumsy cuts almost made him fragile. A creature infinitely wounded, not just physically, but spiritually too. Forgetting her concern, she reached out a hand.

He recoiled as her fingers grazed his shoulder. 'Don't touch me.' Salt-rasped, his accent falling into an odd lilting place between Fiction and Lyonne. 'Don't . . .' he said again, before staggering upright with the ungainliness of a newborn foal. 'I don't need your help.'

'Come now,' Arden scolded. 'There's only so much blood in a man before he empties himself out.' She held out her hand again. 'Do you want my support or not? Your boat is not going anywhere ever again.'

His boat – and obviously not *his* property but the longboat of Captain Cormack – had wedged high in the spar of rock at the promontory. Another improbable artefact of the rescue, along with the babes who should have been dead.

He muttered some curse word at her, something filthy learned in a prison hulk no doubt, but she had heard worse on the docks and he still leaned on her so that he might stand upright. Arden grunted in quite an unladylike way as she heaved his arm across her shoulders. Despite his clamminess, he radiated warmth where his skin met hers. Hale enough to walk.

'This way,' she said. 'And for heaven's sake, don't bleed over my dress.'

Mr Riven ate the leftover stew in starving, bestial gulps, and halfway through his second bowl fell asleep sitting upright, head thrown back against the wall, his mouth open and gurgling. For the first time she was able to look at him unconstrained. Once it dried out, his hair lightened, and had the distinct unevenness of having been chopped off with a knife blade at moments when it suited him. His nose was long and straight, aristocratic almost, and would have made him appear weak, among these people. His cheekbones high and his skin translucent, blueing where his eye sockets deepened. Long blond lashes, such as one might find on a child. A contradiction of toughness and utter vulnerability.

'So, there's the blood I sensed upon the storm.' Chalice nodded at his wounds. 'There's your Fiction sanguinem, Lightmistress.'

'It's not just a monstercalling trait,' Arden said, and the surprise she felt was a little glow of solidarity with this wild creature. 'That's proper bloodwielding he's gone and done. I never would have guessed.'

'Well, in times past, Fiction had more genetic lines of sanguine endowment than Lyonne,' Chalice said. 'The folks here were quite diverse.'

'Yes, before they thought themselves better off without blood talents.'

'Oh rats,' Chalice said. 'The lumpen out here couldn't keep a guinea in their pocket let alone talent in their blood. They lost it all in ten generations. Your fellow here's probably the last of them, along with Bellis. What a sorry pair they probably were.'

It turned out that Helena had some Hillside folk medicine about her, and she packed Mr Riven's chest wounds with spider webs procured from the rafters. Though Arden was uncertain about touching him, nursing duties required a certain intimacy. She followed Helena's lead and tugged off her neighbour's wet krakenskin coat. His breath surged warm in her ear. His ginger-blond beard tickled her neck, but did not arouse the shudders of revulsion she expected from such an encounter. There was no threat to him, only an exhaustion beyond measure.

'Webs will stop the bleeding,' Helena Tallwater instructed Arden, as the woman passed a linen bandage about the sleeping man's chest. 'A well-known cure.'

'Thank you. I don't have enough clotting powder for anything bigger than a scratch at the moment.'

'Brew up some fruit-mould tea if you have it, soak the bandage in some. It tastes terrible to drink, but the wounds are less likely to go bad under the dressings.'

'I do have some spore-powder, and the tea sounds like a good interim.'

Helena had not, however, anything to stop the deep, physical pain that came from a sanguis losing so much blood, and Mr Riven's sleep was a deep pit from which he could not be roused. Arden took the spoon and bowl from his slack hands, and tipped him sideways onto her makeshift bed, where he could sleep off the blood-loss hangover.

'Will he be all right, wife?' Gregor Tallwater asked once Helena had finished her ministrations. 'This man saved my children. I cannot leave without thanking him.'

'I cannot say,' Helena said. 'I have no experience for these sorts of people.' Her eyes swung nervously between Arden and Mr Riven's uncouth drunk-sleep. 'No offence, Lightmistress, but your kind is different from ours in body and mind.'

'Sanguine folk have a slightly different physiology, it is true,' Arden said gently. 'But there is much in us that is similar. Let him sleep off his blood intoxication, and you may thank him later.'

The patriarch of the rescued family appeared less than impressed by their saviour. Leyland Tallwater sat at a remove near the brazier, his craggy Hillfolk features not hiding his deep discomfort. In Clay he would rarely have spoken to anyone blood-bound, and only if he had known them before a testmoot, and then only as a child. Unlike in Fiction, Lyonne society stratified through the existence of sanguine talent, and in such social separations, superstitions took root. Arden had known of Hillfolk to tell their children night-creeping stories. Tales of how the sanguinem sometimes needed the blood of others to replenish their own.

Considering it took only a drop of blood to execute one's phlebotomous labour, it did not bode well to see Mr Riven so pale and lifeless. In his blood-loss frailty one could halfway believe such stories of vampiric hunger. Arden wished she hadn't been so quick to send Chalice with Sean Ironcup to Vigil earlier.

It had very much been Chalice's idea that they report the castaways to the Coastmaster at once. She'd chosen to take the Ironcup lad with her, a slim, delicate youth of perhaps twenty-two years, who had a palsy of his left side. 'Not to offend, but the more wretchedly vulnerable you people appear to the Coastmaster, the more he'll likely let you come ashore with only a warning and not a penalty,' Chalice had said. 'The Baron Justinian has a distaste for deformities. So, Master Ironcup, you come with me.'

'I'll have you know,' Sean Ironcup had said, deeply affronted, 'I can handle a boat with one hand better than most men with two. And it's *Mister* Ironcup.'

'It's true,' Helena had added. 'He's the only one of us who knows his way around a ship.'

A vegetable barge is certainly not a ship, Arden thought. From her wincing face, Chalice thought exactly the same thing. Still, it was those two who did the honours of reporting, and left Arden with six wary strangers.

'Come, children,' she said to the two eldest. 'I'll show you how I keep the lighthouse fire alive.'

'Go,' Helena urged, when they looked at their mother.

'All right then,' replied the girl. 'Come now, Tomas.'

They followed Arden up the twisting stairs to the lamp room. She showed them the disks that she kept under her gloves, and how she cut into each one in turn to feed the flame.

'How does it work,' asked the girl, Lissa. 'Your blood?'

'Well now,' Arden said, and launched into a familiar explanation. 'It is said that when God made Man, He also made angels, and demons. Demons feast on angel blood, you see. And angels are argumentative, easily offended. The angels formed a union against God for allowing such powers to exist, and there was a war in heaven. An agreement was made that He should cast them down to live with humankind. And so they do, hid in every nook and cranny of the earth. Even our blood.'

There was no response from the children, and Arden, flustered, barrelled on.

'In time, some angels rebelled and fell in love and came to mate with Men. The descendants can feed the demons not only of flame, but demons of mathematics, of memory and storm and iron and physics, make them do their bidding.'

The tale satisfied most Clay city children, but the two Hillsiders glared at her with darkly sceptical eyes. 'That is not the truth.'

'Of course it is.'

'It's not. Don't lie to us.'

Arden sighed, refastened her gloves. 'All right then. I don't believe it either. To tell you the truth, the real truth, nobody quite knows where the genetic talent comes from. There was indeed a war at some time, one that nearly destroyed the entire human race. There weren't pretend things like gods or angels involved. It was us. A war of spirit perhaps, a whispered war. And there may have been some contamination introduced into our bodies that is passed on through the family line. Men of science have speculated on many things. Morphic resonance. Machines smaller than the smallest microscope can see. Magic even, although any science advanced enough can appear like magic.'

Their mother called them from downstairs. 'Children,' she cried, 'Uncle Sean is back.'

'I don't think it's science or magic inside you,' said the boy. 'I think it is *sin*.'

Mr Riven groaned bearishly and rolled over. He had yet to fully wake, but that was to be expected. The sanguis comedown could be gruelling on those untrained in the nuances of the sacrament; Mr Riven now wallowed at the tail end of a hard bleed, where a man might flutter in and out of consciousness, the waking body quite nonplussed by the agony of the bright new day and retreating to the insensate safety of dreams.

No thank-yous for him, then. Leyland showed himself only too happy to board the recovery boat to Vigil when the Harbourmistress came. His gratitude was tempered by preconceptions and prejudices. This wild man had returned Mr Tallwater's family entire, yes, however the methods of rescue filled the Hillsider with deep dread.

Arden reluctantly left Mr Riven sleeping on her now-ruined bed, before retreating to the pier.

Mx Modhi in her usual foul temper, barked at her boy to help the children into the dinghy. 'David, lad, they've had enough trouble with the sea, they don't need it from you,' she said between furious puffs of her pipe. While she sat on the tiller of her recovery boat, the youth wrestled with the waterlogged pieces of Tallwater possessions that the afternoon swell had seen fit to deposit on the rocks.

Satisfied that her son had done his part, she returned to Arden.

'Won't be the first survivors you'll haul from the drink. Jorgen Beacon would average five a year. Bodes well that you got the whole family alive, Lightmistress. Perhaps we should rub you for luck.'

'The rescue wasn't just my doing. Mr Riven helped.'

Mx Modhi blew pipe-smoke towards the longboat. 'Best you not let that be known in these parts. Between you and me, Captain Cormack's stolen longboat got onto the rocks itself.'

She whistled over to Leyland Tallwater.

'Ma'am?' he responded.

'We'll attend the office of Postmaster Harrow and Coastmaster Justinian, fill out the papers advising of a wreck and rescue, friend. There are debts and charges attached to a rescue in these waters, and the licensing board of Clay will require contacting.'

The Hillsider jammed his hands into his pockets. 'We ain't had no papers nor funds for this journey.'

'No papers? No funds? You had your eyes on Sainted Island stars with no penny for the Old Guy, eh?' Mx Modhi cackled.

'We bring our hands, and the willingness to do hard work.'

She laughed again, before exploding into a coughing fit. 'Journeyman, your journey has ended. You don't know the Islands. They'll not accept prospectors to their shores unless you come with assets. They have all the labour they want over there.'

Leyland bristled and yanked his hands out of his pockets. 'And how would you know this, huh? Sunning yourself on a stinking little harbour?'

Gregor, perhaps sensing that his father might be drawn into a fight, stood up and announced, 'Well, that's it, then. All packed. In the boat, children. And wherever has Helena gone?'

Leyland gave a grunt and went to sit in the boat, sulking. Mx Modhi looked at him with a deep suspicion, and her tongue moved agitatedly about her ivory pipe-stem. She left the tiller on the pretence of bending to check a rope tie, but instead leaned in close to Arden's ear.

'You sure plucked a good one out of the sea, Lightmistress,' she gruffed at Arden. 'I don't like him.'

With her sharp Beacon eyes, Arden spotted the woman standing on the furthest tip of the promontory, staring out to sea.

'Wait, I'll get her,' Arden said. 'Make the children comfortable, Harbourmistress. The water can be rough, and another trip may traumatize them.'

She glanced at the boy, who only glared back, untraumatized and full of accusation.

The wind blew strong on the promontory. Helena stood there motionless, her shawl pulled back and her raw face rimed with salt and tears. Arden approached her with care.

'They are ready to go,' Arden said gently.

'You cannot see the Sainted Isles from here.'

'No, they are over the horizon. That cloud line to the southeast is only *Tempestas*, which you might know as the Tempest, the permanent storm. There is another route north, on which you would have gone, had your boat not wrecked.'

'You have been there, yourself?'

Arden shook her head. 'Sometimes I spot the ships heading out. They turn at this lighthouse. I make notations for the Navigation Council. But maybe it is best that you are going home, because despite what they say, I've never seen anyone returning from the Islands. Only the lich-ships heading for the refineries and distillation forests of Dead Man's Bay, never people.'

Helena turned to Arden then. A desperate faith in her. 'We will not go home. Leyland says we are going to the Islands, and he means it. He will buy us passage on a fishing boat, a smuggler's boat, anything that floats.' She tilted her chin at the lighthouse. 'That cut-up fellow in there seems to know his way around a craft. Perhaps Leyland will make a deal with him.'

'Think about your children, Helena. If you had made it to the Isles, what sort of life would it be for them? They say nothing lives out there, any more. They say that Hell would be a better place to go.'

'I know.' The woman returned to her constant scanning of the grey horizon. 'When I thought they had drowned, you know what I felt? *Relief.* Relief that my babies are gone, that they will suffer no more. All the way here I have had my heart pricked by the demons of anxiety and worry. I thought: now my children are dead, I can be wounded no more. But your wild fellow brought them back to me, and the torture begins anew. So then. Damn you both to that Hell over the horizon.'

She pulled up her shawl and wrapped the coarse wool around her, swept past Arden with a hiss of resentment.

Arden watched the Tallwaters leave the pier upon Mx Modhi's boat, all of them stiff-backed and nursing their secret determinations. Arden could not stop the dread gathering her bones. Chalice had gone with them, ostensibly to help, but in actuality to provide more muscle in case Mr Leyland Tallwater, in a fit of storm-addled courage, might steal the Harbourmistress' boat for another shot at the Isles.

Would not have been the first time it had happened, given the way Chalice merely stepped into the boat with nary a word.

Leaving Arden alone with—

'Heavens!' she exclaimed, and ran back into the lighthouse. 'Oh no!'

She burst through the door into the tower's lower floor. To her dismay, apart from the blood-stained sheets the bed lay empty.

'Mr Riven?' she called tremulously. Maybe he had gone home. Or at least she hoped he had.

The metal stairs creaked in the rock. A body moved about in the upper reaches of the tower.

In a fit of panic Arden reached for one of Uncle Jorgen's old butchering knives that hung from iron hooks in the walls, hefted it, then put it down with a groan.

What was she expecting? She had invited Mr Riven as a guest. He had not sought to harm her in all the times they had met.

With her heart in her mouth she climbed the stairwell.

Mr Riven stood in the engine room, peering out of one of the narrow windows. In the low light he seemed more beast than human, his back marked by scars, swirls and spirals lain in with squid-ink and broken shell, patterns that outlined each vertebra before flaring out across his hips to disappear into the waist of his canvas strides.

He did not startle when she came in. The bones of his shoulder blades moved beneath the flesh of his back as he shifted his point of view to another window.

'I've never been up here,' he said. 'Always wondered what kind of fire got the light flashing.'

'It's not really the light that flashes,' Arden said. 'The battens turn. The light is always lit.'

She heard the Tallwater boy's voice in her head. *It is sin.* She briefly closed her eyes. From this moment on she could either send Mr Riven on his way, or invite him into her life, and all the problems such people bring. His woman he had killed, his family he had murdered. The plesiosaur baby he had laid gentle upon the table when he had fought three men to save the mother, and the sweater he had given her when she was close to death and vulnerable to attack. The mottled, bearded face pressed against the glass.

She took a breath, took the dive.

'There's a better view in the lamp room. I'll bring the battens down over the coldfire, and you can discover for yourself.'

Those horizon-blue eyes on her again, almost unnaturally bright in the engine room. She unhooked the gate and went up first, let him make his own path as if he were an untamed creature she had fed but did not expect to follow.

He shadowed her at a silent, respectable distance. She heard the catch of his breath as he beheld the view from the height, the wide sea and the scrubby, desolate land in a thousand different directions.

Mr Riven walked about the lamp room. He touched the blood collection chamber. He studied the horizon maps over the windows, the semaphore codes, the shipping signals. Arden stayed by and watched him. Despite his height, he didn't strike her as a particularly threatening sort of gentleman, carrying his lean strength with a certain economy and his power under a bushel. As far as he was concerned there might have been nobody in the room other than him.

Arden had a strange, unbidden recollection from her child-hood, of her half-sister Sirena rescuing a stray dog from the streets. The mutt had shown no interest in its new surround-ings, only paced the walls of their bedroom for a day before their step-mother came upon them with exclamations of *responsibility* and *ownership*.

Nina Beacon had allowed her daughter to keep the pup on strict orders that it be fed and cared for by Sirena herself. A week later it returned to the streets, having never bonded to anyone, and fleeing the room at the first moment of freedom it got.

Maybe Mr Riven would flee, after he'd exhausted his curiosity about his old nemesis' home. Perhaps it was better if he did.

'I must excuse the slovenliness of downstairs,' Arden said nervously. 'My uncle never left it in very much of a good condi-tion. In fact, the only thing he was good at was reminding an eternal flame to keep eternal. Whichever way, this might be the last time you ever see it. The Seamaster's Guild intends to replace it with a regular light come winter time.'

Mr Riven didn't answer. Arden found herself looking skyward for a modicum of heavenly help with these taciturn men and boys.

He rubbed one of the window panes. Mx Modhi's boat was well on its way to Vigil with the other equally conversational guests. The bandage about his chest had soaked entirely black with blood. It runnelled over his abdominal muscles, stained the waistband of his waxed-canvas breeches and to Arden's dismay spattered the lamp room's finally clean floor.

'. . . which is why you should really consider getting some stitches in those deep cuts. The skin is likely to damage if you let it gape around in the open with just a rag bandage.' She pointed to her own hands. 'Even *I* required disks sewn into my skin when I was deployed to the lighthouse so I wouldn't destroy my hands.'

'I'll stitch it myself when I get back.'

His rebuff annoyed her. This was not charity. This was necessity. Was he being obnoxious out of spite?

'If you doubt my skill, I have my minor surgeon's certificate. It's a requirement of dock working. Lest I forget to remind you, Gregor Tallwater also wanted to pass on his thanks that you rescued his children, but he doesn't have a penny to his name, now. He owes you. I owe you.'

Mr Riven was not entirely incapable of reading the mood in the room. Sensing he had crossed a line of social grace, the man nodded, though from his expression he was not pleased.

'Do what you must.'

She encouraged him, dripping blood all the while, down to the engine-room, where there was space and light enough for her to do her work. Directed him to a driftwood stool and pulled her surgical case from the trunk. A blood-worker always had boiled needles nearby, pre-threaded in glass so they might be used at once. One can never tell when a knife will cut too deep.

Then, feeling somewhat awkward for the intimacy it presented, knelt between his knees and released the bandages.

She knew soon after that she needn't have worried about his reaction to her nearness. Only a moment where a brief apprehension crossed his face – not so easy to hide when their breaths were on each other and his leather-clad thighs spanned her waist – and Arden huffed, 'I won't hurt you.'

As if a light had gone out behind his eyes, Mr Riven became still and absent. Only the slight rise and fall of his chest made it certain he was alive. One could envisage her touch turning him to stone, like the curses of old. She looked over him, and wondered what hand had carved this clay, what had flensed this man so brute and lean? His skin was warm and pale under her fingers, pale russet hairs upon each pectoral and the thin, dark blond line to his belly, the dip of skin at his throat where his heartbeat raced.

He neither startled nor acknowledged her contact, nor the cold tincture across his chest, but she could feel a deep nervous tremble in the long muscles, a prey-animal finally caught. She wondered about his prison time as a child, and how he'd survived. About what the sea required of him. Shamefully, looked between his legs, to see if he had cut off his maleness to catch his sea-monsters, and was assured, with a flush of heat to her cheeks, that he had most certainly not.

Strange thoughts came to her. Had anyone ever touched him in love, and tenderness? Had Bellis? Or had all his human interactions been in cruelty and convenience? It seemed so odd, that he not react at all when she pierced the lip of one wound and drew through a thread, yet that he tremble so when she placed her hand upon his knee so she might draw closer.

'So, what is your kinship to blood then, Mr Riven?' she said, wanting to fill the silence lest it grow too deep. 'Storm caller? Searcher, *sanguis appellandi*?'

'I should have left the children in the water.'

Arden had not expected him to speak, and the Lyonnish lilt to his flat Fiction vowels caught her by surprise. His eyes were still elsewhere. She only sighed in reply, did not scold him for making such a comment, and tied off her stitches. 'Their mother said much the same thing. Oh, they'll find their way to the Isles, one way or another. You may have a visit from Leyland, pleading for transport.'

'He'll not have to go so far. Would be a score of fishermen

who would take him over for a bag of pennies. Or a night with the daughter.'

'Mr Riven, that's rather mean-minded of—'

He looked down at her, cold as the ocean. 'Why do you think he's taken the children, the family? Why has he gone to such trouble to drag such baggage, when it would have been more expedient to go to the Islands on his own? The Old Guy doesn't take anyone without payment, everyone knows that.'

Arden's face burned, realizing that in her wilful ignorance she had seen Mr Tallwater as equally innocent to the cost of prospecting. The family was even more abject than the crowd of hopefuls she had seen on the Firth crossing, when she had first come to Lyonne. No paddle-steamer cruise for them. They would find themselves on a boat of rot and driftwood, and be half-dead when they reached one corpse-pontoon shore.

'He'll sell the children?'

'You know it.'

'Then I'll have to warn Helena, and the Harbourmistress!'

Mr Riven stood awkwardly up from the stool. Winced at the stitching. 'Yes, warn the women. Warn the Coastmaster and the Magistrate. Flash it coded in this devil's light. Shout it to the wind, Lightmistress. Do what you must so that you may sleep at night. It will make no difference. You think I do not know this from experience?'

She bowed her head in surrender. 'By God in his heaven, this world is cruel.' She repacked the bandages. 'Every time I think that it tilts towards miracles, I am dismayed by the awfulness of it.'

'You're a fool if you thought any different.'

He went to go past her, and she shot out a hand to grab his arm.

'Did you kill your wife, Mr Riven? Am I the same fool for having invited you in here so you know that I spend most of my hours vulnerable, and alone?'

She shocked him with her directness. She wanted him shocked, not dismissive, not regarding her as a mere annoyance. If this man wanted to kill her, he could kill her now and be done with it. She stood up to him in defiance but *oh*, a part of her, a beaten, cast-off and love-scarred demon inside Arden imagined – in a wrench of forbidden and sordid joy – him doing to her what they whispered he did to Bellis; his rope-burned hands about her neck, her air-starved convulsions as he took her life, took without thought to Guild laws or eugenics or the portion of the blood that gave talent.

Her breath came fast and heavy. Her heart moved in her with the anxious fear of a bird caged in bone. Her body became an object of disgust and deceit, wanting an awful thing because it felt better that way. Better than the nothingness forced upon her by her duties as a Fiction lighthouse keeper, tending a lantern destined to die.

He did have some measure of sensitivity. Sensing the repellent desires in her, Mr Riven scowled and jerked back.

'No,' Mr Riven growled, harsh with reproach. 'I did not kill my wife. I love her and love her still. All these things you wish to do to save the Tallwater children, I have done for Bellis, and no difference has it made. Good day to you.'

Then he was gone, down the stairs in a rush, snatched up his coat and slammed the door as he left.

It is sin.

The terrible compulsion drained from Arden, leaving her wrung-out and weak. What demon had compelled her to such disrespect? She returned to the lamp room, pressed her cheek to the salt-crusted span of glass. In the dreary afternoon light watched Mr Riven's small, distant figure exit the lighthouse, throwing the coat over his bare torso before striding down the old coast road.

Until he came to the cenotaph of Bellis Riven and Stefan Beacon.

There he knelt by the cairn, placed a stone upon its peak, but not before he'd pressed his lips to the stone with all the tenderness of one whose beloved is before him. Arden knew him weeping then, this scraggled, tattooed man beaten by sand and storm, mourning a woman gone from him.

Oh, to be loved and missed so. Arden had experience aplenty with family and the embraces of itinerant lovers, wisps of passions. She considered them only temporary. When they left, she did not mourn them. Nor they, her. Not even Richard. She'd made her peace with the transitory and shallow nature of the love she inspired.

This, though. This made the bitter demon of Envy stir in her breast. She had invoked spells against loneliness with the garments of both this man and his wife, and she was now tied to them in primitive, hungry ways.

That. Give me the kind of love they had.

In her whirl of emotions, a more sensible self whispered in her ear.

Calm yourself, it said in the voice of an old signal instructor whose name she had forgotten. *You are tired and traumatized from the night and the rescue. This widowed husband might pay all the respects to the wife now, but acts in grief and regret never mirror the treatment of a real flesh and blood woman. Witnesses called him cruel. Bellis is still dead.*

I love her and love her still.

The tenses he used. He had not spoken of the past. No stumble of words, no excuse or explanation for a dead wife.

What truth is it? she wondered. *Who did Bellis marry, a monster or a man? Had the Justinians and the Harrows spread a twisted story as false as the one with the plesiosaur game hunters? Had Bellis just sailed off and fallen afoul of the weather, died by accident, an adulteress punished by God?*

There was nobody who could say for certain. Except him. Still shaken by the ghastliness of her body's lunge towards defilement, she watched Mr Riven place one more kiss upon the stone, then set off down the coast road in the waning afternoon sun, back to his decaying house and stained mattress, his krakenskin coat-tails snapping in the wind like bronze wings.

Book Two: The Lion

16

The invitation came

The invitation came on one of David Modhi's deliveries on the day of autumn equinox, a time when the migratory seabirds became restless from their nesting, and the fluffy chicks shed the last of their down, leaving a storm of white fluff blowing out across the sedge-grass and catching in any exposed laundry as if it were thistle seeds.

At once she saw that she had not received an onionskin letter from Lyonne, but a missive of an entirely different sort.

Arden rubbed the ivory card with its edges of gold scallop. The neat cursive hand requested that the Lightmistress of Vigil join an assortment of Guildsmen and Allied Persons for an evening at Manse Justinian.

She flipped the card back and forth, barely trusting the date, the words. Intellectually she had known it a year since the last Guild Ball, and that Fiction would have a ball just as its northern counterpart did, but it had not *felt* like a year. More like a deep geological moment, her life changed so utterly from that moment to this.

'I'm not going.'

'Say what, darling?' Chalice asked when she snatched the letter out of Arden's grasp. The delivery had come at that brief window when they were both awake, otherwise Arden would have fed the invite to the brazier's belly.

'Oh, Chalice, I'm not interested in going to a Guildmaster's Ball.'

'A *ball*? This is a surprise! It's not always the young David brings us anything except sausages and evaporated milk, now.'

Chalice read the invitation aloud in her most toffee-nosed Lyonne accent: 'The Masters of Fiction Annual Ball will be held at the Manse Justinian two weeks from now, and the combined Guilds of Fiction and Lyonne request your presence.'

'A request,' Arden repeated. 'Not an order. I don't need to go. Besides, the last one in Lyonne was such a disaster I've sworn off the things altogether.'

The stormbride gave Arden a snagging grin. 'Our servant of the flame gets to go to the Guild Ball. A real Guild Ball, not one of those piddling cattle-calls they hold in Portside. You know who will be there, don't you?'

Arden snorted. 'Mr Justinian.'

Chalice slapped Arden's hand with the paper. 'We *know* that useless heel will be creeping about his mouldering old mansion. I mean *men*! Real live men. Unmarried Lyonnian bachelors with their names in the Eugenics Society's ledgers, signed and underlined.'

At the mention of men, David Modhi swayed from one gangly foot to the other and blushed mightily.

Arden batted her away. 'I told you, I've put that idea aside, Chalice. I only have, oh, less than three months left of my time here.'

'Three months! Why, you've gone spare enough in the first two!'

'Look, I'll say I never got the invitation. Mr Modhi will dissemble for me.'

'Uhh . . .' David Modhi started.

Chalice mock-slapped her again. 'Fool! You know what I mean. You've been moping and pining about, and even Mr Riven is starting to look good.'

Arden's cheeks grew hot. Had Chalice suspected the methods

in which her mind betrayed her in the deep night? Since she had carried out the small intimate act of tending to Mr Riven's wounds, she had tried and failed not to linger upon her neighbour. Cast away the thought of that abraded, tattooed body forcing itself upon her, and inside her. A mere interaction would not have been enough, anyway.

No, when Arden invented Mr Riven with her, she experienced an inexplicable act of transference. She became Bellis Harrow, taken away to the Sainted Isles to marry the Deepwater King. In her conjurations Arden was swept away by a power stronger than she could articulate, wrapped up in her own obsessions of class betrayal and self-immolation. Had concocted a fantasy that could not possibly be true, but she wanted to be true, for it filled her with a forbidden delight.

In that miserable matrimonial year that followed their elopement, Bellis had not left her husband, though all the others in her life had clamoured to help.

Only one reason could fully explain why the two had stayed together. Bellis had loved Mr Riven back. Somehow she must have had to, to stay with him. In the dark, secret ways she must have loved her husband. Yearned for what he gave her, be it wrapped up in jealousy or sexual violence, or the brutishness of a man obsessed.

Such a terrible, fearful thing. It should have repelled Arden, but she was not repelled, only drawn towards it as if an inevitable outcome.

The King has seen your face.

Arden, bound to fire and light, could not comprehend such an affection, but wanted it for herself all the same. *Chalice is right. I am jealous, and I am glad she is dead.*

Alarmed that her vices should be so obvious to Chalice, Arden protested with a croak. 'That is so unfair, and a smite on my preferences. He appeals to me less than . . . less than Mr Justinian.'

'Come on now. It has been weeks since we rescued those miserable Tallwaters and not a day has passed when you don't

watch entirely the wrong section of coast and bite your fingernails down to rags. You still haven't brought back the jumper
to him.' Chalice's eyes narrowed. 'Don't think I haven't seen
you wadding it up and cradling it to your heart. You intend to
make a pillow for a man's head.'

'I haven't had the chance to return it! I appreciate nice woollen
things, ever since I was a child. Allow me some credit for taking
simple pleasures.'

'Empty sweaters and make-believe are not a man. What you
need is a friendly gentleman who will – without commitments
– ease the aches and pains of solitude. Must I explain that in
detail as well?'

David Modhi had not moved from his spot at the doorway
where he had delivered his message, and after a confused silence
at the back-and-forth argument of these older women, bright-
ened up. 'My mother has a good liniment for removing aches
and pains. She's been testing it on Sean Ironcup, the man we
rescued last month.'

'I'm not talking about those pains, lad,' Chalice said airily.
'Women's pains, which are never spoken aloud because we are
far too high on our perfect pedestals, aren't we? Anyhow, were
you being a sneak, David Modhi? It hasn't escaped my notice
the envelope to our Lightmistress' fairy-tale ball found itself
opened upon your delivery.'

'Mr Harrow gave it to me opened.'

'Of *course* he did,' Arden snapped. 'He opens everything of
mine.'

With a snatch she retrieved the letter from David and the
card from Chalice. 'Check the date. It came to Vigil a fortnight
ago. Let me add the corollary to all fairy-tale gatherings. I am
unprepared, I have nothing to wear. Will you be the godmother
to force me into something from Mrs Sage's rag-table then?'

'Goodness, no. But wear your waxen keeper's uniform, love,
because if you need something solid to weather a storm, you'll
be needing it on that night.'

* * *

Another letter came one day before the Master's Ball, this time a missive from the Coastmaster. Mr Justinian grandly proposed that Mr Quill would collect her upon sundown on the day of the ball, and that she would be welcome to stay in the guest room overnight. There was something else too. A package wrapped in brown paper, with a shape and give so obvious Arden knew exactly what it was.

This letter ended up finding itself shoved into the brazier's belly, and the package would have too, had Chalice, awakened by the noise of Arden's exclamation of offence, snatched it out of her hands.

'Oh Chalice, could you stop doing that? Is anything I own not sacred to you?'

'Darling, if I didn't, you'd never allow me to read anything. I am your stormbride and protector, and you are my little innocent babe who has received—'

She ripped the paper and gasped. 'A dress! Oh Arden, the most beautiful dress!'

Arden averted her head from a billow of peacock blue. 'I shan't look at it.'

'Your fairy godmother has indeed come. Did she mention a pumpkin too?'

'*She* . . . wants me to stay in his damned house on the night of the ball.'

'Well, why not? A lady can't possibly sleep on the streets, and there is no way you could pilot *Fine Breeze* home on a bellyful of wine and a half-moon night. You'd end up whisked into the Tempest in an instant.'

Arden paced the tower's base, before sitting on her bed as she did as a child in a temper, confined to her room and with nowhere else to go. 'He's still trying to seduce me in exchange for signing the damned Guild degree document. I might as well offer myself up on a plate.'

'I thought you told me he's made a vow of celibacy? On his knees, you said he was. You'll stay in Vigil overnight,' Chalice said firmly. 'You're not coming back here.'

Arden glared in mock-horror at Chalice.

Chalice *tsk*ed. 'I meant overnight *in general*, not the Manse overnight specific, sweetheart. Let me send one of my pigeons to the Black Rosette. I have an acquaintance there, Fionna La Grange, whom I used to know from my posting at Harbinger Bay.'

'A lady at the Black Rosette? Dare I suppose that my storm-bride has a lover?'

Chalice rolled her eyes, then returned the smirk, for what could she hide?

'We are intimate occasionally, yes, but friends more, having weathered historical storms of the human kind. Miss La Grange has an apartment behind the tavern. There is a chaise longue in her front room which does solid work as an emergency bed. Now, let's look at your dress.'

She led it up to the coldflame lantern. Blue silk, the colour of a summer's sky at the highest point, a shade so deep that to Arden's eyes it became almost violet. Seed-pearl fronds across the waist and under the bust, flowing in tendrils. A peplum of cormorant feathers, and the rest of the dress subtly hooped so it did not fall straight down but billowed as if caught by a stray breeze.

In the glittering lights of a Clay Capital soiree the dress would be beautiful, if one were hoping to win the attention of several suitors. But for a professional gathering in the cold recesses of Vigil? Beyond inappropriate.

'So, the Baron has sent you his message,' Chalice said. 'His enforced celibacy is over.'

'I'll refuse to wear it.'

Chalice shook her head. 'That kind of principle works well in story books, but rarely in practice. Just go, get it over and done with, Arden. Turn up to the stupid ball. Be as ungainly in that dress as if Mr Justinian had clad a bearded wharfman in spider silks, and you will never be asked to wear such things again.'

* * *

Unfortunately, when Arden put on the flowing layers of fabric the next day, they had the opposite effect to the one she hoped for. The dress wrapped her up in an illusion of pearls and iridescence, and her bare skin was so warmed with those adjacent hues that she might have been as beautiful as a spice-island princess. Each time she moved, the faceted glass beads on her shoulders caught the sunlight, cast rainbows on the opposite wall.

'Heavens, this is not me at all,' Arden said weakly as her chest threatened to fall out of the neckline of the dress. 'I'm a ham dressed for a Yuletide dinner.'

'I'm certain that is the point.'

She rubbed the fabric between her fingers and thought wistfully of the kraken coat – warm and protecting. She thought of Mr Justinian's hissed *murdered whore's garment*. This dress seemed a more likely clothing for bad decisions and unfortunate trades.

'Yes, but I would rather it not be.'

'Just make sure he signs your document first,' Chalice said. 'I have not had much use for a man, but Fionna tells me it's much easier if one is drunk.'

'Chalice!'

'All right. I take it back.'

'Now what other wicked magicks does my fairy godmother have for me? My glass slippers? My pumpkin coach that doesn't involve Mr Quill driving? A silver hatpin to prick him if Mr Justinian comes too close?'

'The slippers I cannot do. The hatpin you'll have to supply yourself. But the coach, well, let's just say there will be some mode of transport outside the Manse this evening at the stroke of midnight.'

'Make it ten o'clock,' Arden said. 'I don't intend to stick around for the sorry end of this little enchantment.'

The evening came upon Vigil with the sea-fog, and the Manse turned on its lights for the two hundred guests that descended upon the granite doorstep.

In Fiction's harsh austerity, there were very few opportunities for the few aristocrats of the country to show off. Arden quickly decided that the Guild had not been aiming low when they sent the invitations for a ball at the Manse. There were at least fifty North Fictish and South Lyonnian here of sanguis endowment, and three hundred of non-blood Grandmaster degree. She could smell the blood-endowed in the mingling crowd, taste metal on her tongue. The people wore garments that might have seemed restrained and severe were they at a Clay Capital ball, the men's dinner coats never moving from tones of gorse-brown and stone, their shirts plain and unruffled.

Dowager Justinian greeted her warmly. 'It's been a pleasure, and a long time,' she said, grasping at Arden's hands so hard that her coins twanged in discomfort. 'I had rather hoped you would visit more.'

'I am kept busy enough at the flame. The weather seems to change every hour – I do believe I spend more time running between the window and the record ledger than I do going outside.'

'It is the autumn, come hard winter, every day will be dreary. Let me take your coat.'

Arden didn't particularly want to pass over her krakenskin coat, but truth to tell, if the men were drab then the women exhibited for both, were unrestrained in their chiffons, their silks and satins. Arden's blue-sky dress didn't seem so outrageous in their company.

She handed the coat over to a wait-servant she did not recognize – one of the new young men from the coast, still gauche in unfamiliar fine clothes – and accepted a tall glass of champagne. Divested of her travelling garments, she headed for the ballroom, where she might hide in the crowd from the mansion's owner.

If she were eager to leave, the others were not. The guests had gathered with a view to eat and drink as merrily as they could, given that the other days of the year rarely provided opportunities for either. Rows of tables at either end of the room were illuminated with one hundred branching candle-sticks and piled with food expressly bought from the far ports of Lyonne and Vinland. Candied plums dripping with cinnamon paste, plates of artichokes and marinated octopus arranged in swirls, breadsticks cradling dodo-liver pâté, messenger pigeons baked in holy-land clay and stuffed with alpine pine seeds from Gaul and Lebanon. Shrimp crusted with sourdough bread-crumbs, cannabis-infused chocolates rolled in gold leaf, gelatine squares soaked in sugarcane brandy, a roasted boar still bearing a ridge of bristles, the crisped skin glistening with an oily craquelure, potatoes dusted with sumac-spice . . .

Arden had not seen such a feast since her father had brought her to a Guild event in Clay Portside. She could hardly have pictured that the Manse, with all its frowsy, hard-worn appearance and that low-lying detergent smell, could have put on such a civilized cloak and attain such a sense of opulence.

To add to the air of decadent consumption, more wine than was strictly required for a professional gathering flowed from the great demijohns of sparkling Clay Riverina *cuvée*. The waitstaff pushed glass upon glass of spritzing sweet liquor at her. She thought them innocuous and realized at her third glass that they were anything but. Her head spun. Another one would only make her intoxicated.

Yet even with the goldware and the glistening food, and the candles and the lanterns and the gas lamps turned to full, a dour cast fell about the Justinian residence, for the surroundings were bleached of contrast and colour. A desperate undercurrent flowed through the conversations, and it did not take too many minutes of eavesdropping upon small-talk for Arden to work out that they were talking of Clay Portside.

'Trouble on the docks in Lyonne,' said the one wharfmaster from Garfish Point she managed to capture in a proper conver-sation. 'Talk of commonfolk unions and other nonsense.'

Another young man, Fiction-pale, dark hair and craggy, weatherworn features, wore fingerless gloves upon his hands the same as Arden. 'I myself have narrowly escaped their acts of violence and sabotage. They attacked me at my very post, not more than two months ago. Called me a *scab*, an affront to good morals, a stealer of food from the mouths of children. Can you believe it? I'm like them, I have to work off my employment fees too. It's not as if I'm getting showered in banknotes. I'm paid just the same.' He held his fingers in such a way they suggested an encroaching paralysis. 'I was glad to get a post at Garfish Point,' he concluded. 'I only hope I can get my coins changed soon.'

Nervously, Arden touched her own gloves. He saw her action, and nodded. He wore a pin upon his lapel, the shape of a box. Had it in him, the pin suggested, to divest some mass from an object to make it more easily manoeuvrable. Perhaps not *sanguis pondus*, a manipulator of inert mass, but something adjacent. A useful skill on the wharves, though not so useful that he'd been carted off to Fiction.

'Many a commonblood family had their fortunes increased when a member tested positive for endowments,' Arden said. 'But there are jobs that require no sanguis talent at all. So even though I have these,' she held up her gloves, 'I can understand a mature worker's concern. How would you like it, sirs, to be replaced by a child thirty years your junior, purely due to an *inferred* and irrelevant skill?'

'Oh, you sound like a unionist,' the wharfmaster guffawed. Unlike his companion, the wharfmaster was physically impressive, a tall, heavy fellow of elderly years with an abundant grey beard made yellow with pipe-smoke. 'Malcontents and the like. Sanguine folk *enable* trade. The commonbloods should be happy enough with a job, and not starving in the hills or shoring up the Sainted Isles.' He nodded knowingly at Arden. 'Men chance the attention of Lions if they knock heads with industrial progress.'

Arden looked down at her near-empty wine glass, and debated another. This night would be less annoying if she saw it to the end in a drunken haze.

Before the others could ask further of her opinions, a hand came from nowhere, seized her elbow and whisked her away.

'No need to speak to them, Lightmistress. The anti-unionists drink to excess and make up stories of persecutions that are only the push and shove of a busy city.'

'Mr Justinian,' Arden said, nonplussed. 'I'm certain I could have worked that out for myself without having a sudden rescue.'

'You don't want sudden rescues, huh? I'll have to remember that.' His gaze scraped her up and down. He was quicksilver. 'See, the dress makes you attractive for a plain girl.'

So, all his promises of restraint upon the cliffside had indeed flittered away. She bit back the sharp retort on her tongue. *Concentrate on the signature for your Guild degree, Arden. Make that the goal you must endure trials to achieve.*

A pair of Morningvale Guilders passed them, smiling. They'd never been this far South before, and though he couldn't sense their veiled derision of his rotting house and his poorly chosen décor that was a shade too gauche, Mr Justinian still greeted them with such oily charisma he practically gleamed. With the practice born of a thousand false relationships, he introduced Arden to most of the room, spoke of her highly, made the subtlest insinuations that he was physically intimate with her on a regular basis.

The social gauntlet never showed an end, and Arden became a mess, internally quivering with a breathless rage, her hands balled into sweaty fists. She could reveal no outward sign of her distress, and that perhaps was the worst pain of all.

At last the great room cleared for dancing. Mr Justinian took her by waist and hand. She wanted to shy away from his touch. A death-moth's poisonous dust could be no less welcome than the scrape of his fingers. Her stomach churned. The wine spritzer bubbled into the back of her throat.

'Dance with me,' he said. 'It is the Guild Dance. They are expecting the Coastmaster and the Lightmistress of Vigil to lead the waltz.'

'I am not much of a dancer.'

'I insist. Just follow my lead.'

Halfway mortified by circumstance, she allowed him to take her out onto the floor while the string quartet played a lively Lyonnese Waltz, with its racing fiddle and steps that were complicated enough that Mr Justinian stood on her feet more than twice despite him claiming to know these moves. Arden began to suspect he was doing it on purpose.

'Yes, you are not quite so unattractive in this light.' Mr Justinian shuffled closer, until his hot breath steamed on her forehead. With a thumping shock she realized that it was not a belt buckle but the covert press of his erection into her lower stomach. His cologne had a noxiousness about it, a too-strong mix of civet and ambergris, but without the pleasing ratio of either.

I shall either faint or purge, she thought.

'I shall make love to you tonight,' Mr Justinian murmured in her ear. 'You have teased me long enough.'

She could have pulled away then. Should have, only they were waltzing in the centre of the crowd and all the Guildmasters were smiling and clapping and watching. *Devilment*, she thought again. *Devilment!* If she were to pull away and leave him obviously aroused, it would be a most embarrassing situation. Better she should let him extricate himself in relative dignity against a wall at least, before slapping him in private.

'What say you, Lightmistress? After this dance ends?'

'Is this your blackmail attempt?'

His unctuous voice in her ear. The bulge in his crotch grazed her hip as she attempted to thwart his unsophisticated flirtation. 'You will never be a true guildswoman let alone a Master degree-holder, Arden Beacon. Your blood is as weak as pisswater and you have no real endowment to speak of. I know you are not allowed Lyonne lovers because your dirty blood will despoil the line of *sanguis ignis*. I may be the only man you are allowed. Conversely, there are some who say I should not sign your Guild form because of your genetic failures. I am in a bind. I need convincing, you see.'

'May the devils *fuck* you, Mr Justinian.'

He tightened his hands on hers. Hard, and the coin beneath snagged hot against the skin.

'No, I don't think they will, tonight. But you shall certainly do so . . .'

He pressed closer, reeking of civet-glands and ammoniac soap. She despaired that in her isolation she might have once thought him passably handsome, for up close he was tiny-eyed and snivelly-chinned and stank with bitterness. She stared at an ill thread on his suit, swallowed the urge to scream.

'We were interrupted by the sea-waves, before. But the sea cannot extend so far. What say you? I can release you right now, Arden my dear. Just say the word.'

What would Chalice have advised, or any of her Clay Portside friends? Their ghosts whispered their practical advice. A cock in and of itself was a minor thing, despite the pronouncements of men who talked about their *lances* and *swords* and *weapons*.

The music slowed down to a more traditional waltz of the Vinland style, a dance slow and seductive. Others came onto the ballroom floor. Just as Mr Justinian pulled her towards the door, a plainly dressed boy ran up to them, bearing a folded parchment envelope affixed with a candlewax seal.

'Lightmistress,' the boy said, 'I have a message. It's quite urgent.'

'Get away from here,' Mr Justinian rasped. 'What kind of fool are you, boy?'

The boy ignored Mr Justinian's anger. 'It's urgent, Mistress.' The boy pulled a chain of tarnished brass from about his neck, and showed a small golden coin.

Arden could not make out the markings upon the coin's surface, but Mr Justinian may as well have been struck across the cheek with it. Instantly his awakening drained out of him as effectively as a slap.

'You little shit,' he said. 'You little disgraceful shit. Give her your message, cub, and be quick about it.'

Both the reprieve and the lingering after-effects of the wine conspired to make her dizzy again. With mounting unease Arden took the envelope and edged away from Mr Justinian. She need not have worried about him, for he stalked off, adjusting the buttons of his fly with angry yanks.

'Who sent you?' she asked the boy. He was a child from town, obviously. A gold coin could buy any sort of labour, especially a pretty gold coin on a chain. She saw it close now, and the stamping had the appearance of a flower. A rose, crossed with thorns.

'He said you were a friend of his.'

Curious to see what had occasioned this reversal of fortune, Arden tore open the envelope and read the message quickly. The penmanship was neat, but severe.

If you wish to save Mr Riven, follow the boy.

She glared at him. The youth only stared back at her with his guileless child's eyes.

'No friend of mine gave you this.'

'He is a Lyonne guildsman, Lightmistress,' the boy said. 'You are to come with me to the Orangery.'

A Lyonne Guildsman? There were many here, but none that should have had the necessity to be calling her away in the night using the name of her neighbour. A cold feeling touched her neck, a whisper of angel's caution. Arden glanced about her. Nobody watched this little drama, or appeared inquisitive about this sudden interruption of ceremonies. Mr Justinian had since retired to a place to lick his wounds, a corner conveniently adjacent to the liquor cabinet. He poured a dark splash the colour of treacle into a crystal glass as a pasty young lady sidled towards him, her tongue painting a wet, hungry trail about her lips at the thought of having the Coastmaster of Vigil all to herself.

'A Guildsman, you say? Who?'

The boy only thrust the rose-coin forward again.

A rose upon thorns, she thought. *You know this symbol. You've seen it before.*

The child only shrugged, knowing she would get nothing out of him. Arden nodded.

'I'll come with you, lad. Just let me get my coat.'

17

The night took on a different feeling

The night took on a different feeling upon the Manse's uplands than it did closer to the water. For all that Fiction bunkered in the southern chill from low latitudes, the coastal climate remained blunted by the great temperate sink of the nearby ocean.

But in the higher altitudes of the Justinian property the air sharpened, and Arden was glad to have her krakenskin coat. Still unsteady from the wine, she paused at the mud room to light one of the spare oil lamps before following the boy down the gravel boulevard of the mansion grounds.

A coin, the boy had shown Mr Justinian. A rose with a thorned cross. She recognized the symbol, but its meaning fluttered out of reach.

Instead of taking her outside the walls, the child led her further into the gardens. They hurried past the dry Poseidon fountain with sea-horse hippocampi and once-naked gods sporting their new clothing – a dark mossy verdigris that would one day smother them – through the domed grottoes and overgrown night gardens to where a cast-iron and glass conservatory stood among the shadows of unkempt box hedges and overgrown bougainvillea.

The moonlight sheened off the conservatory glass, made the walls white. The boy gestured to the door.

'In there, Lightmistress.'

Another light source shone inside the leafy bowers. A cold yellow glow, from that new power of electrification.

'Mr Riven wanted to meet me here?'

The child only gave a vacant, angelic smile, made his gesture again.

Her better sense would have told her to leave, but then again, her better sense would have told her not to come to Fiction in the first place. She slowed her racing heart with a deep breath, then with a ginger caution stepped into the fecund warmth.

The Orangery in the night was as gloomy as the day, same smell of moss and dirt, perfume of camellias, and a tart citrus rot from the few runty orange trees that still grew from the planting of nearly a century before.

She winced at the light. Almost as bright as coldfire, the glow came from an unfamiliar pear-shaped tube as round as her head. A yellow arc light too bright to properly look at. Electric light was rare in Lyonne, especially when a few members from the Lumiere *ignis* family could blood-light a whole city with their delicate talents. The charged atoms in the globe made her hands itch.

'The former Baron had the sodium lamp installed to show off to his friends.'

Arden turned at the familiar voice. A figure stepped out from shadows where he had been waiting. Short and slender, a pretty face with the stillness of a wax figurine, gold spectacles as round as marbles, and a gold pocket-watch chain hanging from his waistcoat.

'Do you remember me? Three months can seem like three years in this country.'

She swallowed as the wine threatened to rise in her throat. It was the Guildsman who had given Arden her coins and her instructions to come to Fiction.

'Mr Lindsay? What are you doing here?'

'Working, same as you.'

The small man's beautiful smile was duplicitous, as only a man who has turned up unexpectedly in a different country can be. He wore the same suit as he had in her father's Portside offices, a dull camel woven through with emerald threads. In the orange light, they glittered with a strange enchantment.

Lastly upon his lapel, the same image that had been on the boy's coin. A rose, and black enamel thorns. Arden felt her strength leave her as she realized at last what it meant. The Eugenics Society rose, and the controlling thorns of the Lyonne Order. Symbol of the garden, forever tended and protected from the weeds that might encroach upon it.

Mr Lindsay had come to give her the coin of instruction. This was the thing she had been dreading for months, the truth of her coming here.

It is not for Fire they want you.

'Excuse me.' Mr Lindsay stretched up to the electric tube. 'Let me turn this off. I assume your body can sense the charged atoms in the atmosphere. Electrical fields create quite a physical reaction for the blood-endowed, I am told.'

With a twist, the light was gone. Green afterimages jumped behind Arden's eyes. Her hands still ached. The man's cunning attention never left her.

No, decided Arden. Not a man. Lyonne Order and Nomenclatures. A Lion.

Have the Lions followed you here, Mx Beacon?

'Now then,' Mr Lindsay continued, 'my boy tells me that Mr Justinian is being difficult with endorsing your final degree. Well, if he does not sign the forms, there are other options.'

'You come all this way and through all this covert behaviour just to tell me this?' Arden pressed her still-cramping wrists against her cormorant-feathered hips. 'If you required a private meeting, not a soul would have seen you upon the promontory.'

Mr Lindsay held his hand out towards her oil lantern. 'More light, please. My eyes are not as dark-keen as yours.' Upon receiving the handle, he turned the wick up and gestured towards a marble bench. 'I apologize for being so clandestine. I assure you, there are reasons. Come, sit.'

Though her entire instinct protested, she gathered up kraken-hide and silks, and sat beside him.

'So, what more is required of me?'

'What makes you think more is required?' Mr Lindsay asked, his eyes amiably perplexed past his spectacles.

'You are Lyonne Order and Nomenclatures. My father saw it instantly, the moment you stepped into his offices.'

'A perceptive man, Lucian Beacon. He always had a special *sense*, one might say. His daughter too.'

'All right, sir. Enough banter. I am here, and minding my uncle's light, as I agreed. What is this note about helping Mr Riven?'

'I hear you had some meetings with the man.'

She frowned. What business was her neighbour to the Lion? 'We have had occasion to meet, certainly.'

'And he was *proper* to you?'

The words were loaded. She chose her reply with care. 'I did not intend to come here to fight with my neighbours, and that is exactly what I haven't done.'

'No,' he mused. 'You have not fought with him at all.' He took his spectacles off his face, polished each lens slowly and deliberately with a silk handkerchief. 'How close are you to Riven, Mx Beacon? Close enough to leave a warm house in the middle of the night and flee to his assistance, certainly.'

'I would have run from that disgusting lech in that decayed mansion on the flimsiest excuse. Even to save you, if it were your life in danger.'

'Yet still. You came for an ex-convict with a history of kidnapping and murder, and rape-within-marriage, that most grievous sin?'

'I understand what has been said about him, sir.'

'And you do not believe? Such accusations are not made lightly.'

She took her breath and prepared for a speech. 'Mr Lindsay, all my life I have grown up and worked on the docks as a minor sanguis lanternkeeper. I saw more of human existence by my tenth birthday than many a person at the prime of their life. My senses do not recoil from him as they would . . .' She clenched her teeth. '*You*, perhaps. Or Mr Justinian. I suspect that far too much energy has been spent on cultivating an overt brand of monstrosity in him without him taking on a monstrous charisma in return.'

'Yes, true evil is seductive, and beautiful.'

The Lion rose, went to one of the oranges still on the tree, brought the wrinkled fruit to his nose but did not pluck it.

'I share your suspicion,' he continued. 'Let me tell another story, Mx Beacon, an inverse of the one more familiar to you. It is of a girl named Bellis Harrow, a pretty and outwardly unremarkable girl born in a far-flung fishing village whose only importance is illegal plesiosaur trade and a promontory known for shipwrecks. The lass is testmooted late, as many of her generation are on this coast where talent is faded and the moots may only happen once every five years. Children mature slowly here, the genes are dim, and the tests are limited to those laborious endowments more useful to us in the North.

'Whatever the reason for the delay, she is over sixteen years old when she tests positive for rockblood. Rockblood! *Sanguinem petrae!* A talent as golden as her hair! A goddess of the black liquor! Well, there is a commotion. Regardless of her rough Fictish heritage, such golden talents automatically make her eligible for a full degree and Master's certification in the craft or trade Guild of her choosing – sight-unseen – as you are well aware.'

'But she stayed here, though.'

'Sadly, her father refused to let her go.'

'Hmmm, he seemed like the sort of fellow who would welcome Industrialist money.' Arden pretended with mild interest, even as talk of Bellis made her uneasy. This story was as relevant to her as the ships passing her lighthouse on the sea-road. But a Lion had come north and was pulling her into the lives of these troubled people.

Mr Lindsay shrugged. 'The mother was poorly, and Bellis an only child. She was a good daughter. It was curious, but we don't interfere.'

'That's not like Lions *at all.*'

'Scoff all you like Mx Beacon, but talent can be ruined by too much meddling, and as you know, the Fiction-born sanguinem rarely survive long in Lyonne – the city disorients them, makes them vulnerable to misadventure and accidents.'

Like falling into Portside canals, Arden silently added.

Mr Lindsay made a moue of regret. 'For a while all was at peace. She matured into a sweet young woman, no sanguis psychosis, no nervous conditions. Then all of a sudden, this beautiful, filial child abandons her Baron fiancé and marries Mr Jonah Riven, a criminal convicted of a heinous crime and recently returned to the coast. Marries, if one might say, under extreme duress in the Sainted Isles, where such unions can be coerced. A year later, she disappears, with only this krakenskin coat and a lock of her golden hair recovered.'

In the garden, a Middle Country firecracker went up, burst into the sky. Only a lone ordinance, a star-sparkling omen, and not a good one. It reflected as a smear upon the salt-scored glass.

'Some believed in the forlorn tale of her death, for a while,' Mr Lindsay said. 'Me, I was rather baffled when I heard what came of her. Why all the degradation and despair? Bellis and Jonah were best childhood friends before he was sent away to Harbinger Bay for killing his family. She was a filial daughter to her father, why should she not be equally as devoted a wife to her husband? All extremely odd. Then all of a sudden the affair. Another old friend. A priest, as pious as they come.'

The answer arrived to Arden at once, for hadn't she spent ten years planning and wishing for such a thing herself?

'She *escaped* you!' Arden drew a shuddering breath. Bellis Harrow, golden-talented and clever. Cleverer than the Lions themselves. *Oh*, Arden's envy sharpened. *That clever girl!*

Mr Lindsay threw up his hands in gracious surrender.

'You seem rather thrilled, Mx Beacon.'

'I won't lie to you, sir. There's not a sanguinem alive who hasn't dreamed of escaping the Eugenics Society and the Order, and leading their own lives.'

A nerve in his cheek jumped. One eye at a squint. 'Yes, the three of them, Jonah Riven, Stefan Beacon and Bellis Harrow. Concocted a little ruse of a disastrous and violent marriage, an affair and a death. But let me tell you the truth of foolish, immature girls with golden talent who think they can run away from their own blood. There is no place for them outside of Clay Capital's sanctuary. Fiction folk don't know how to take care of its sanguineous, the attention and delicacy that must be taken. Your uncle Jorgen Beacon found that out in the hardest of ways, immolated by grief and despair. He had the *psychosis*. Became the extinguished flame, just like his talent.'

A starfield of rockets followed the first, and their pink-hued explosions cast garish lights across the Orangery glass. Some cheering in the distance. Arden's hands hurt.

'Mr Lindsay, why share the story of a stranger?'

'Because Bellis Harrow-Riven disappeared and Riven refuses to confirm what happened. He's impenetrable but for his weakness.' Here the Lion smiled, 'Love.'

'It can be, if it seems the more gentle way. However Bellis Harrow-Riven still disappeared and Riven refuses to confirm what happened to her. He's impenetrable. But his weakness is his love for the woman he married. Despite his tricky little theatre of sadism, we quickly found out what Bellis had done. Slipped her collar. Run out with a blood talent she had no training for. She's in hiding, and Riven knows where she is.'

'Oh, Mr Lindsay,' she said, dripping scorn. 'I'm not about to seduce Bellis' whereabouts from him, I barely know the man.'

'We would not ask such a thing of you.'

'Then what will you ask?'

'Your assistance. A different kind of labour, but labour all the same. You are to help Bellis survive this exile she has chosen until she is ready to return. We don't want her back. She will come back when she is ready. A bird will always *orient* itself to home. And eventually she will come to Lyonne. That is a given. But if she has sought refuge among the indigenes of the Sainted Isles, because she is sanguineous and unsupported, then her existence is right now fraught and tenuous, and forever in danger.

'You have always helped your fellow comrades on the wharves. You've had a sense of supportiveness about you, they say, a brace against bad accidents. Every *sanguis pondus, transverto* and *vaporum* who have ever worked under your instruction all tell us they trust you implicitly. They say they trust *themselves* more when their reliable *sanguis ignis* Arden Beacon is around. We need you to use that goodwill. Help *her* now, Mx Beacon. Help Bellis Riven survive, as you have helped those around you survive.'

His words were a cadence, a seductive song. She pressed her burning hands together. Trapped them between her knees. Why were they hurting so? There was no cold-flame lantern needing ignition, and even then her endowments were so dim the sense should have been little more than an itch.

'I earned that trust, over years. I don't know Bellis at all. Why would she be in any danger? She is *sanguis petrae*. She'll be useful to Islanders. They can exploit her labour.'

'The autochthonous Islanders worship strange gods, Mx Beacon, gods that pre-date the prospecting of rockblood. She will be anathema to them. A reminder of Northern conquerors and defeat has no place among those brutal shores. Bellis may be fine now, but at some stage she will require Jonah Riven to show his face, and protect her with his dreadful reputation.'

He made the sign of the circle upon his chest, the sea-serpent, and Arden recognized it at once for the blanket ring back at her lighthouse. *The Deepwater King.* The old religion of the Sainted Isles, and the Riven ancestral home.

He continued, 'We cannot force Mr Riven to join his wife, but perhaps you can *remind* him of what he misses. The trust you engender in your associates? Foster the same in him. He may confide in you, Lightmistress, of his loneliness. From what my advisers tell me, you yourself know what it is to hold a torch for a love, for years and lonely years. Yes, Mx Arden Beacon knows what it is like they say, to grow old waiting while her friends marry, have children of their own. She may consider herself trapped by circumstance, but Mr Jonah Riven is not. Give him the permission of a woman with regrets, Arden my dear. Tell him not to end up lonely, and despairing. Tell him he can go to Bellis, and be blessed.'

Each of Mr Lindsay's words lashed her heart with a switch of thornwood. Yes, she knew those shackles as a sanguinem under the rule of the Order. Yes, these were the freedoms she had wished for, and had them taken away.

Arden spoke through a throat tight with resentment.

'This was your intent all along, for me to abandon my home and my family to come here? This is why you didn't decommission the flame on the day Jorgen died?'

'Is it a bad motive? You're saving a woman's life.'

Arden closed her eyes briefly, and let an old grief wash over her. A sanguinem was always a tool and conduit for greater powers, but this request made her bereft of true meaning. The Guild had not wanted her here as Lightkeeper at all. The Lions had made them use Arden, not for the direction of her blood, but an entity to effect another purpose. Bellis Riven was the objective, and Arden was just a source of labour.

She said wearily, 'I don't feel right, instructing Mr Riven about his wife's peril just so he can be beholden to you. He probably has his reasons to stay behind. I'm sorry. I can't . . . I can't impose myself on a private matter and do what you ask.'

Mr Lindsay rubbed his knees as if preparing to rise. 'Oh, well. It's a shame you are unable to help. That's that, then. I'm sure you'll encourage some other official to sign the Guild-membership form, of course.'

'What?' Arden exclaimed. 'Is this you reneging on my contract?'

'Well, your work contract implicitly stated you are required to carry out your duties as instructed before you can receive a full Guild degree,' Mr Lindsay said with such a smugly genuine apology Arden almost wanted to slap him. He stood up with an old man's effort despite the youth of his face. Offhandedly said, 'Oh, and another thing. I was to advise you about a . . .' He fetched a paper square from his waistcoat and opened it. 'Captain Richard Castile? Yes, the Order tells me he has *suffered* quite a bit after you broke off your illicit relationship with him. Has lived quite the monkish existence since, grieving the woman he left in Lyonne.'

As he spoke he plucked the small orange he'd sniffed earlier, and peeled it with a sympathetic nonchalance. She glared at him, feeling the manipulations tighten furiously.

'There's no harm in delivering our message in the sweet requests of a lady.'

'He'll not listen to the sweet requests of a lady either, you fool!' Arden scolded him. 'If the folk down in that town were to give their opinions, Mr Riven is a lustful fiend more likely to forget his wife *at once* and have *me* take her place in squalor.'

'Ah, rather than making him *forget* Bellis, you would *elevate* that memory, I think. I would posit that a strong woman up against the world would in fact be a powerful reminder of his woman over the waves.'

Mr Lindsay held out the peeled orange, and she slapped his hand away.

'I don't want it.'

'But I know what you do want. Mr Castile waits for you.' He leaned forward. 'Give your service to Lyonne,' he pressed. 'Inform Mr Riven of his wife's jeopardy, get him out to her and you may have the chance to have an independent life. You'll still have partial Guild membership whether you assist us or not. This patriotic act would take you all the way there. Full degree. Permission to marry.'

With that, he popped the orange into his mouth, and chewed.

'I have no reason to visit him,' Arden said, low and muti-
nously. 'We are not likely to share a cup of tea and a
heart-to-heart soon. I *posit* you will be waiting a long time for
our intimate conversation.'

'Such was my thought at first. So we devised a meet, another
message sent by my boy-cub to the Black Rosette tavern a mere
hour ago. A message for a Mr Jonah Riven, who patronizes
the merchants' bar.'

Cold, invisible fingers pressed upon the back of Arden's neck.
'What sort of message?'

'An urgent one, from Mx Arden Beacon, just like the one
you received this evening, pleading that Mr Riven should come
help his neighbour who is trapped in the guest house of the
Manse Justinian.'

She gasped at Mr Lindsay's forwardness and stood up. 'He
would not waste his time coming to rescue me!'

'One would hope not, because the guest house is currently
occupied by Mr Alasdair Harrow's deputies, a pair who will
have no compunction in . . .' He lingered, savouring the
moment. '*Hurting* Mr Riven if he were to stumble upon them.'

Arden ran from the Orangery, and in the dark stumbled towards
the guest wing, a semi-detached building linked by stone colonnade. Mr Riven couldn't be so foolish as to heed the boy's
message. Her dress snagged under her feet as she struggled up
an incline in her ridiculous shoes.

'Devilment!' Frustration stung her eyes with hot, angry tears.
She had fallen into the Lion's den. Once their eyes were upon
prey, there would be no escape.

Midway along a retaining wall, a pair of the Manse's hired
guards waved at her as she passed.

'Hoy!' one cried out.

She skidded to a stop. Beyond them, the leafy walkway
beckoned, the doors of the guest house.

'Gentlemen,' Arden said breathlessly, and gave a high strangled laugh. 'Can't be late for the party!'

Her tardiness did not concern them, and they sauntered up, hands on muskets, their broadcloth uniform as dark as the night.

'What brings you outside, Lightmistress?'

Devilment, they recognized her. A layer of sweat glossed her face and she was certain her carefully applied cosmetics would have now turned her face into a circus-tumbler's mask.

'Oh,' she said with such forced gaiety that her voice came at a screech, 'enjoying private company. You understand.'

With that she gave a suggestive wink. They did not smirk back.

'Your friend, where is he now?'

'A separate way. For the sake of his . . . standing.'

'Best you enjoy such breaches of standing indoors, madam,' the first guard gruffed. 'There is an intruder afoot. The grounds are under alert until he is found.'

Arden had never fainted, but decided if she did, it might begin with a feeling very much like this: her blood rushing from her head, and her fingers tingling hot as if a match had been lit under each one.

'Of course, of course. Best . . . best be getting back.'

With the gait of a wounded soldier she stumbled on to the guest wing, and entered through the side door, which she knew the Dowager Justinian often kept unlocked. Slid her way along the dim foyer and immediately realized she had arrived too late; a gross commotion echoed from deep within the bedroom, and a Middle Country porcelain pot lay strewn in pieces across the parquetry floor. A picture of the elderly patriarch Baron Alexander Justinian lay crossways over a chaise longue, a buffet was over-turned, and the entire contents of the fireplace littered the rug.

A yelp of alarm, more grunting, and then a muffled bang which could only have been a silenced musket.

Terrified for Mr Riven, Arden picked up from the floor the only slightly wieldy thing in sight: a small paperweight bust of Sir Alexander Justinian the Elder. Small it might be, the bust was still a heavy chunk of bronze. She ran into the bedroom only to nearly trip over one fallen body. A deputy. The other one stood with his musket in hand, seemingly aimed at a third heap behind the bed.

She did not wait to see his reaction. With all her strength she swung the bust and caught the oafish fellow by the temple. The contact shock jolted up her elbow, twanging her tendons with electric pain. He collapsed like a felled log.

'I'm sorry,' she cried, 'I'm sorry! Oh, heavens . . .'

A blow to the head could kill a man. What had she been thinking? She should have yelled at him, negotiated surrender. But the sight of Mr Riven, that foolish love-struck imbecile lying dead out of misbegotten heroics, had made her panic.

The deputy's chest rose and fell. Thank all the sea gods, then, she'd merely stunned him. She ran over to Mr Riven, sprawled out across the coverlet of the bed. He appeared as if he had left the hot interior of the Black Rosette in some kind of a rush. Beneath his coat wore only his high-waisted trousers and suspenders.

'Mr Riven?' she ventured.

By his groaning, he was conscious. The musket shot, slowed by the silencing device, had slammed into the krakenskin coat hard but had not penetrated the leather.

She picked up the damaged wing of coat to push it aside. A bullet could still cause a man to bleed into his cavities, perhaps a more dangerous scenario than a penetrating wound. When he tried to slap her away, she seized a tiller-roughened hand.

'I've seen you shirtless, fool,' she hissed. 'Are you hurt?'

'*Oof.* I'm not sure.'

'Do I have your permission to find out?'

He opened the coat, and Arden prodded about at the bruises coming up on the serrations of his abdomen. His skin had rapidly discoloured from the force of the projectile but showed no break or blood. The scars of his Tallwater rescue attempts were flat pink marks across his broad chest, and a sharp want took her, to touch them, and him. Not in desire, not quite. But the need to touch capstones and cairns in places where great battles have been fought, to feel the history beneath and become a part of it somehow.

'Where the hell were you?' he gruffed as his breath returned. 'That message said you were here . . .'

'I never sent a message.'

'Excuse me?' He glared at her as if insulted.

She went to the window. Closed and double-glazed, and the curtains had been drawn. No light or sound to attract the guards. 'I didn't send that message, Mr Riven. It was meant to lure you here.'

'Why?'

'We have become ensnared in things bigger than us.' She put her hands on her hips and looked at him as if he were the aftermath of a disaster that she would have to clean up. 'You've been ensnared in this thing from the beginning, I think.'

Mr Riven sat up with a wince and surveyed the two fallen men. 'I believe you, Lightmistress. As soon as I saw they were Mr Harrow's lads, I knew the message was a lure. They intended this as a convenient killing.'

'They don't want you dead. Not while Bellis is alive.'

His terrible blue stare fell upon her then, questioning.

'Bellis? How did you—'

She shook her head. 'No time to explain. I must get you out of here first. *Damn it*. There's guards all over the Manse tonight.'

'I will go out the way I came.' He nodded towards the window, and the wall beyond.

'You can't do that either. Mr Justinian's security detail saw you come in, you enormous fool. The grounds are lousy with staff and mercenaries.'

One of the deputies let out a groan, fighting his unconsciousness. He would not be indisposed for long.

Mr Riven dragged a hand over his rough head. 'They might not want me dead, but they'll kill me if I stay here.' He tried to stand up and only ended up rattling the bedside bureau, overturning the porcelain toilette bottles and hairbrushes. Somebody so completely out of place among the frills and fripperies of the guest room would be equally incongruous outside it. As far as concealing him beyond these walls, it would be easier to hide an elephant that had wandered into the town square. Mr Riven was no stranger to the people of Vigil.

'Wait now,' Arden said. 'We'll make these goons sleep a little longer.'

The adjoining bathroom was, as she had earlier discovered in previous sorties of the Manse, stocked with all kinds of chemicals and potions. Clearly the deputies had noticed this too. Open bottles and pillboxes lay scattered across the dresser: laudanum, the cocaine drops, the heroin tinctures, the opium tobacco and the ergotine.

Mr Riven must have stumbled in while they were both as mad as hatters. They would not remember much of this night.

She found what she wanted, a bottle of ether, and with a handkerchief and an averted head, managed to roll the pair on their sides and send them into a deeper sleep.

'They'll be asleep for a good few minutes,' she said, and pointed at the scars on Mr Riven's chest with a broken, wry smile. 'I was always better at administering sleep-ether than I was at stitching when I completed my minor surgeon's certificate.'

Mr Riven watched her warily. 'Why treat them with such kindness?'

'These men are addled with pharmaceuticals. If we are fortunate, they may awaken to think they themselves caused this situation. But you, sir. You are my biggest problem.'

'Let me pass, and I will be a problem no longer.'

'No longer?' she retorted. 'Mr Riven, have you heard of Lions?'

He snorted at her question. 'The animals or the Investigatory Order of Lyonne? I have dealt with both.'

'The worst of the two have their eyes on you, sir, and now on me. Our problems are entwined. With Bellis at its centre.'

Under the wiry fur of his face she saw wretched hope and concern spring forth. A familiar envy moved in her heart, to see a man with such naked affection for his beloved. No

Clay detachment. No cool appraisals. This was a man who loved fiercely.

'What has happened with Bellis?' he demanded. 'Why are they circling her now? She's gone. From them, from this country altogether!'

'There's no time to explain. We need to hide your escape.'

Arden quickly took stock of the guest-house room. Even an elephant might be disguised, given enough of a garment. She settled on the patriarch's painting. Take away his finery, and the elder Justinian had a hard and angular Fictish face that his three scions, in their unions with soft Northern women, had not managed to keep.

She went to the wardrobe and threw open the doors. The miasma of cedarwood and camphor swelled into the room. Those garments within, completely the wrong size for Mr Justinian and therefore unworn, showed themselves untouched by moth or beetle, fabric as intact as if they were new.

'Get out of your clothes,' she said to Mr Riven.

'Excuse me?'

'The party. There are hundreds of people here, and nobody can possibly know every guest. We can get out through the Manse. There is transport waiting in the forecourt. I already have my exit strategy from this place taken care of, so to speak.'

She pulled a suit from the closet. Its dull faded colours made it seem conservative in aspect, the sort of thing old money might wear. Fashions did not change much among the rich.

'You call me fool, but this is a foolish idea.'

'Your coming here was a foolish idea, Mr Riven, so that makes two!'

'I came for you, neighbour.' He reached for the suit. She pulled it out of his reach and sighed.

'Thank you for your chivalry, sir. Now get the beard off your face. Make it so you belong among those people.' She frowned. 'Do you even know how to groom?'

'I am *not* fully a barbarian,' Mr Riven countered. He yanked off his shirt and alarmingly was already freeing himself of his trousers as he went into the bathroom. The tattoos on his back dipped into his sacrum and the curve of his buttocks.

He closed the door. She heard the water run. She paced the room, casting worried glances at both the sleeping men and the foyer.

Whatever experience of Mr Riven's past had taught him quick grooming, it worked upon him now. Within ten minutes of the mantel clock, the door opened.

A sorcery, perhaps. She had sent Mr Riven in there, but a much younger man than him stepped out. A stranger, with an unevenly handsome face that still needed another decade to settle into mature nobility, the pale Fictish features softened by a cautious, almost shy expression. He might have turned into a creature shorn of his fearsome mane, but something more interesting lay beneath. A bed sheet about his waist gave him the appearance of a statue from antiquity.

In silence, she handed him the clothes of the patriarch, and he let the sheet drop as he began to dress. She kept her eyes low.

He had seen her entire, so perhaps they no longer required false modesty, she thought, and then stole another glance before she could stop herself. His maleness nestled in russet curls, and he unselfconsciously tucked himself into the mossy green of Sir Alexander Justinian's trousers. Despite the urgency of the moment, her cheeks flamed.

Dressed, he could have passed for any low-bred noble master. The tawny suit fitted him perfectly. The boots still held their shine. The narrow waist accentuated the hard work that had formed the clay of Mr Riven into flesh. Only his hair was shorter than fashionable. Hard to disguise the fisherman's habit of cutting a lock from his scalp every time he wished to bless the catch, giving sacraments, the way the sanguis did with their blood.

'It will do,' Arden said, and wondered why her mouth was dry. 'But quick.' She swept a pomade off the dresser. 'Fix your head.'

He beheld the pomade tin the same way a scholar might, if

faced with a Sumerian tablet written with indecipherable code. Mr Riven may not have been a barbarian, but he was not entirely tamed, either. With a *tsk* of impatience she scooped out a wad of cream and ran it over his hair, tried not to think about the mind that lay beyond the assorted lumps and bumps on the skull beneath her hand. The skull of a life hard-lived. He smelled of kraken oil, far too fresh and deeply luxurious for comfort. The higher-priced dock girls used the essential ingredient in their alluring scents, to woo potential customers from the decks of their ships. The smell always had a sense of illicitness about it.

He pulled away sharply.

'My coat.'

She wiped her hand on a towel, mortified that she had allowed herself such a distraction.

'The coat is the most obvious part of you, sir. If you wish to take it, it must be smuggled.'

Grateful for the diversion, she rummaged in the cedar wardrobe, retrieved a carpet bag that wasn't too shabby, and stuffed Mr Riven's krakenskin coat into the satin-lined depths.

The two deputies started to stir. No choice but to leave now. She took Mr Riven's elbow and dragged him through the litter of the guest-house foyer.

Perhaps the enormous import of what had happened here had struck him insensibly mute. Especially since now he was not fighting for his life. He became passive in his caution, Well, so should he be. Mr Jonah Riven would have to trust a Beacon now, put his safety in her hands.

Out in the cool colonnade that connected the house to the Manse she grasped his elbow to her side, forced him to slow down to saunter, an arm-in-arm-with-a-lady kind of stroll, and not fleeing-the-scene-of-the-crime kind of stroll. Her heart beat far too fast. Ahead of them, another pair of hired guards moved into position. They were not the first she had seen.

'Calm yourself,' she murmured, 'or they'll know something is afoot.'

'I am calm. You're the one shaking.'

Small candles lit each column, put in place by the staff to ensure an atmosphere of romance, but instead it had the air of a prison walk. Mr Riven's arm went about her waist and propped her upright to stop her stumbling. The guardians ignored the two lovebirds as they passed. One pulled out a pipe and spoke to the other in a Low Fictish dialect. Arden held her breath so fiercely, her vision started to tunnel.

Once in the portico, a butler opened the door, and they stepped into the Manse. The dull lights, that previous irritation, were now a blessing. She hurried Mr Riven through the dusky rooms, getting closer and closer to the entry foyer until—

'Mx Beacon?'

Arden froze, then turned about with a fixed rictus of a smile.

The Dowager Justinian stood there, in one of the drawing rooms, a glass of sherry in her hand. She had clearly had one too many, and she came up from the chaise longue on unsteady feet.

'Were you leaving? I thought you would want to stay in the guest house.'

'I have an apartment in town.'

'Nonsense. There are no apartments in town, only hovels and front rooms for the harlots.'

The Dowager turned her attention to Mr Riven. 'You,' the Dowager said faintly. 'You wear a familiar face. The old Baron's face, and yet you are young. How can that be so?'

In all her fussing Arden had not seen what she should have seen from the outset. The old man who graced all the paintings about the Manse had been young once. For a reason unknown, they'd confined the patriarch's youthful image to the drawing room of the women – a delicate floral abode in the daytime, but in the night all the crochets and doilies turned to spider webs and crypt moulder.

That youth, Alexander Justinian. The first Baron who had taken the Rivens from their ancestral home in the Sainted Isles and put them to work in his factory. As she glanced up at Mr Riven it became clear to her that Alexander Justinian had taken more than labour from the family, perhaps. Replaced a genetic line with one of his own.

'My dear Dowager Justinian, this is Mr Castile,' Arden said desperately. 'An old friend from Clay.'

Mr Riven dipped his head, and if Arden had not held his muscular arm close, he would have retreated into the gloom.

The Dowager frowned. 'And what do you do, Mr Castile?'

'I work leather and bone.'

Dowager Justinian darted forward, seized his arm and turned it, revealing the scars of rope-work on the palm and knife-work upon the meat below his thumb. 'It is dangerous to cut there.' She threw the hand down in disgust. 'You are sanguis.'

'Somewhat,' he said, yearning towards the door.

The woman wouldn't let them go. 'Alexander and his son were stormtellers. Common enough round these parts once, but bred out of their line, thank the Lord. My son doesn't have a modicum of that heinous trait. Good memory for figures, and his blood clean. He is human.'

Arden gently patted the woman's arm in an anxious farewell. 'Dowager Justinian, I must leave, my ride is waiting for me.'

The Dowager grabbed Arden's wrist, hard, and peered into her face.

'My son will miss you in his bed tonight. He hasn't quite been the same after he lost Bellis to the monster on the promontory. She was much prettier than you though,' Dowager Justinian slurred, the sherry at last taking hold. 'Fairer of skin and face. Wheaten hair, as straight as a waterfall. *Don't trust Bellis*, I said to my boy. Don't trust anyone who cleaves to the dank emissions of the underworld. These are sinful things, *sin* . . .'

Her hand released. She fell off the precipice of consciousness, slid back against the wall and sank into dark, morphiated sleep.

Mr Riven stared down at the Dowager. Her words had enchanted the will out of him entirely.

'Mr Riven,' Arden said. 'She's had too much to drink.'

'She is more than just drunk,' Mr Riven said. 'She never has more than a sherry-glass on an evening. There is something else going on here tonight.'

'Drugged?'

'Absolutely.'

Arden thought of the Lion, Mr Lindsay, making certain all the pieces were in their place. Making sure they were not disturbed. 'There always has been something going on, Jonah Riven, since your wife went to the Sainted Isles and disappeared.'

He turned his attention to Arden, bewildered and angry. 'You must explain what this has to do with me. With Bellis.'

'I have no idea if what the Lion says is true,' she said, tugging him towards the exit. 'But we must go at once or we could find out in the worst of ways.'

18

Half an hour I waited in this freezing cold

'Half an hour I waited in this freezing cold,' the buggyman grumbled. 'Was told ten o'clock. *Specifically* ten o'clock. I could have had other passengers.'

He huffed and tutted at the two bodies who had climbed in his little coach, expecting them to give him the same drunken noise as his previous customers, perhaps offer him a penny or two extra with a slap on the back and a chortle about needing to attend a bed post-haste.

Instead, a pall of deep disquiet bound them.

The pale Fictish man had the fine, raw bearing that would have garnered the attention of any lady, but the guildswoman barely gave him an inch of her attention. She had the cast of severe and purposeful breeding about her, from her diluted features, jet eyes and indifferent curls pinned upon her head. She wore a krakenskin coat, something he'd only seen the wealthiest office-holders wear. She must be a woman of some standing indeed. She couldn't have been unattractive to her companion, but he sat stiffly in his preoccupation, arms folded, head turned to the coach glass.

Fair enough, the buggyman thought. This night brought quarrels too. He did not continue to debate the mysteries of his passengers long, and *tsk*ed the horses down the pebbled curve of the driveway and out upon the crushed-rock road.

A deep, uncomfortable silence filled the coach. A boundary had been crossed in their relationship. An irrevocable binding between two strangers with nothing in common.

Mr Riven spoke first.

'She lied back there,' Mr Riven said, as they left the gates of the Manse. The lantern swung shadows into the cabin. 'The Dowager.'

'About sanguinity being sinful? Of course, it's just the sherry and the drugs speaking.'

'No. About Bellis being prettier than you.'

Surprised, Arden snorted a short laugh. A quick, wretched feeling akin to embarrassment came over her. She didn't need mollifying with faint praise. She knew Bellis had been extraordinary.

'Anyone can appreciate beauty. It is the most common of denominators.'

'So, Mr Justinian is your lover. I think he suits.'

'Heavens, does everybody conspire for me to have relations with this man? I have no interest in Mr Justinian. I have no interest in anyone! The only thing I need to do is navigate the terrible hand tonight has dealt. The Lyonne Order has me in their employ now, body and blood!'

Mr Riven sat like a wraith in the dark seat, with the look of a cur-dog kicked to the gutter. By the way his arms wrapped about his stomach, the bruise about his midsection troubled him. She breathed and tempered her words. He'd proven himself a gentleman.

'Still, thank you for coming to my rescue, false as it was,' she added ruefully.

'So. Tell me why we are here, together like this.'

'I—' she started, and he interrupted her again.

'If you intend to lie to me, say nothing. Look out the window and hold your tongue. I am not interested in a story.'

She looked into the darkness, not knowing what she should reveal, and what she should keep.

'All right then. The truth. In the early summer the Seamaster's Guild invited me to manage my uncle's lighthouse. Because I was *malorum*, and dim of blood, I'd never ever have such an opportunity. I jumped too quickly at the chance. I didn't think about who else might be involved. Tonight they came to me, and spoke of you.'

Mr Riven's breath fogged up the cabin glass.

'Not about me. They came about Bellis. It's always been about her. The Lions have been watching Bellis since she broke a rockblood glass during a testmoot,' Mr Riven said quietly. '*Sanguis petrae.*'

'They are concerned for her safety in her Island exile. The Lyonne Order even desire her fearsome husband to go back out there and protect her, and I must be the one to relay the instruction. All this, for a girl with *sanguis petrae*! I mean, certainly it's a golden talent, but why all this fuss over rock-blood? We have several *sanguis petrae* members in Lyonne. It's rare, but not exceptional.'

She stopped her rant as she saw his pained expression. 'I'm sorry,' she concluded miserably. 'It's been quite a night. I just found out my true value. I am not a Lightkeeper to them, just *sanguis malorum*. I am a puppet, a pawn in their game. It was not for Fire they wanted me, and I'm a fool for even entertaining that they did.'

He returned to the window, and there was such a deep, infinite sadness in him she wanted to lean across and take him in her arms and say, *I am sorry she left you, Mr Riven. I'm sorry for all this, and what was done.*

'You think me fearsome?'

'You must be to someone.'

'Then they are wrong. Bellis doesn't need me. She thrives out there, she has a strength and a will . . .' He stole a look at Arden, as if it had only just occurred to him. 'As much as you remind me of Stefan, Bellis is like you, Lightmistress. Very much so. Strong and gentle at once. I never thought so much and so often of Bellis since I saw you on the beach that day, in gold sea-silk.'

His words should have been a delightful compliment, yet Arden felt herself wallow further into the pit of despair. Mr Lindsay had said much the same thing.

'I was *meant* to remind you of her. To *elevate* your memory of her. It was my only purpose. Otherwise they'd have let the sanguine coldfire extinguish, and replaced the lighthouse with a common gas.'

He was silent for a little while, before nodding.

'Then thank you. For your honesty.'

'Not much of a point in keeping it secret.' She wrapped the coat tighter about her. 'So are you going to go to her? If the Lions are saying she's in danger, she may very well be.'

A muscle in his jaw popped. 'It would be against her explicit instructions. You see, when she left . . . she told me not to follow her, not until she called for me. It's complicated. Hard to explain, but I'm more use to her hidden.' He grimaced, as if a bad thought crossed his mind. 'My name is shored up by the many men who once held it. Riven, the monster caller. Riven, who walked upon the islands and fought even the Deepwater King for His crown, and His Bride. You are right, about being fearsome. I'm more fear-inspiring as a myth than as a man. It keeps her alive. Keeps her protected. Even though Stefan Beacon, your cousin is with her, he's not much of a fighter I'm afraid.'

'Can I still be honest?'

'Do. Please.'

'Don't go. Even if she is in danger. Stay here. We have deal-ings with the Order all the time in Lyonne. If the Lions are trying to move a minor chess piece on their board, it means they have decided to sacrifice it for the bigger play.'

'You think me a minor chess piece?'

She wondered if he was offended, and she stammered apol-ogies, and he put his hand on hers, silencing her, and his touch seemed to bring a calmness over her all at once. She sought out his eyes in the darkness.

'You are not minor,' she said.

'Coming from you, I believe it.'

'But be careful, please. They dangle me as a bait for your wife's memory, but I am the poison to make you obey, and they haven't told me everything.'

'What bait did they use to move *you* on the board, little rook?'

'Only,' she sighed, 'only my deepest and most impossible dreams.'

'What were they?'

'Guild membership, and the return of a man I'd loved for a long time, who was forbidden to me, because I am sanguine, and he is not.'

'Guild membership,' he repeated. 'Dreams. And love. All the treasures of the world.'

'Yes.'

His hand squeezed once, then withdrew. She felt the acknowledgement of her sacrifice in her words. Understood that he knew she could have stayed silent, and those promised rewards would have been secured.

'Again, thank you, Lightmistress.'

A strangeness stirred inside her, as she beheld his crookedly handsome face in the lantern light. What is this, she thought with alarm. Not affection, of course, she barely knew him. Barely. *Barely*. Her night-time fantasies of the brute who might ravish her against all the Society orders had passed away. Another man, another feeling had taken their place. An enigma and cipher, but no less attractive.

She felt dazed by her epiphany. Chalice had been correct. Arden had been too long without desire in her life, and her body had, in starvation, reached greedily for the first bright and beautiful thing out of her reach. She had seen Mr Riven and his passion for his beloved, talented, troubled wife and now she yearned to have such a thing. *I want that, I want that.*

When he spoke, he held a note of uncertainty. 'Release me at the docks. I should get back to the lodge tonight.'

'The lodge? On the *promontory?*' Arden shook her head. 'If I were the Justinian guardsmen, I'd have already deployed out there. If you trust me now, then you can trust me until morning. There is a bed available at the house of Fionna La Grange, I will be quite happy with a couch.'

'Fionna La Grange?'

'Well, of course. She is my stormbride's friend.' Arden noted then the tone of his question. 'Have . . . have you met?'

'In passing. She is the madam of the Black Rosette, a lady of the night.'

Arden gasped. 'Chalice never told me her profession!'

'Don't fret. It's a good choice. She's handy with bar-fight injuries.' Mr Riven winced as he moved about. 'Better her services than Mr Sage's. His wife has not much time for me, and the man cannot keep his mouth shut.'

After half an hour, the cab stopped at a small townhouse at the rear of the Black Rosette. The cobbles shone in the lamplight from the rank run-off from cesspits. A row of duck-boards kept feet from the worst of the night-soil. A pair of drunks in an alley wrestled each other over the last few fingers in a bottle of potato liquor. Overhead, pigeons cooed in their roosts.

From her own roost in a dimly lit doorway, a lady in shabby dress approached them. Her face had the powdery appearance of a moth, and the kohl around her eyes flaked, leaving black spots about her white cheeks. From her fingers a stiletto cigarette-holder dangled precariously.

'Jonah?' she asked in the breathless craquelure of age and lung disease. 'Jonah, is that you?'

'It is, Betsey.'

She stopped short when he came into the lantern light. 'By the devils, lad, but you are dressed in finery. Has the old man of the Manse relented and brought you home?'

Arden sensed Mr Riven's tension beside her. His origins were a secret he did not wish to share, and yet it seemed more people knew than he let on.

'The night has demanded things of me, that is all.'

Betsey sucked at the stiletto. A sweet smell of cigar smoke rose up in lazy curlicues, a pinch of morningflower with it. A subtle madness coiled about the woman, prophecies and spirits.

'Demanded, as the night demands things of us all. Who is this beside you? Not Bellis. Too tall, too dark, and not a ghost.' She sucked on her stiletto again. 'No plain Fictish daisy. A fragile flower from the North, eh?'

Arden spoke up. 'I am a friend of Fionna's.'

A male voice called from the doorway, a plaintive wheedle, 'Betsey, Betsey, come away, my sweet.'

The woman waved towards an alley and the pink-hued light. 'She's in there. Up the stairs.'

Betsey retreated, and they made their way across the duck-boards.

Arden turned to Mr Riven. Twice this night she had heard his name. 'So, *Jonah* she calls you? The Dowager seems to know you with some intimacy.'

'My mother, Thalie Riven, she worked in the Justinian Manse as one of the domestic staff. Betsey knew me as a child, as the Dowager knew me then too.'

Hard to see him a child. She pondered over the scraps of his life, of the mother who had worked at the Manse, and the aristocratic elder who wore Mr Riven's face. They added up to a great deal of inferred history.

At the doorway to Fionna La Grange's apartments, a red Arabesque lantern dangled high over the lintel as a symbol of her profession. The occupant, roused by Betsey's voice, came out of her doorway clad only in a basque and semi-sheer black peignoir gown, the edges tatty with wilting black feathers. Both garments would have come from far and distant shores. Nothing so beautiful originated in Vigil, or Fiction.

Neither, did it appear, did Miss La Grange. She presented as tall and slim, hair bobbed and as shiny as an oil slick.

'Well then, Jonah Riven, I never thought I'd see you cleaned up and at my door any time soon.' Fionna nodded at Arden. 'About time too. He'd been too long pining over poor dead Bellis who loved the boy but never the man.'

Mr Riven bristled and Arden stepped forward. 'Thank you for taking us in, Miss La Grange.'

The woman gave a knowing wink, as if Bellis' mortal fate were not quite the secret the Lions thought. 'Come forth, my dears. Chalice said you would be unaccompanied, Mx Beacon, but I am always prepared for any eventuality.'

Fionna La Grange's rooms were dressed in sateen and fraying trim, and the perfumes could not hide the musk of Miss La Grange's profession. Sex and male sweat. The parlour had the chaos of a theatrical backstage, with haphazard stacks of gaudy showgirl clothing and room dividers, velvet ottomans, crystal-frilled lampshades.

Mr Riven seemed both unconcerned and familiar with the surroundings. He collapsed into one of the ornate leather chairs with a grunt of exertion.

They had arrived at the tail end of a client's time. By the odd and possibly intentional placement of a mirror over the hearth, Arden's line of sight went directly from the cluttered front room and into the equally busy pink-hued boudoir. A man, hairy as a bear from chest to groin, casually released a rag-paper note from a billfold and gave it to Fionna. They spoke in a friendly manner as he struggled back into his workday clothes, before Fionna kissed him on the cheek and sent him out through the rear door.

'Gracious,' Fionna exclaimed once he had left. 'I thought Albert would never make his exit.' She tossed a stray hair out of her face. 'Now, Jonah, what have you done to yourself?'

'Took a musket blast to my side. Coat stopped it.'

'Yes, that glorious krakenskin coat. You should sell it, buy a ticket to Vinland. Less liable to get shot, there.' As he opened his mouth to protest, she waved him to silence. 'I know, I know. You cannot bear to leave your precious Darkling Sea, and are mourning Bel—'

'Fionna, *please* look at my *injuries*,' Mr Riven interrupted. He took off the jacket and shirt, showed his injury to Fionna, who touched him with a confident hand.

'Ah, breathe in, and out, no ribs broken? May have a bruise in the muscle but you will live. Not the first injury you've had recently, either.'

She thumbed the shiny scar where Arden had stitched him before returning to Arden.

'I know you. You are the Lightmistress who replaced poor Jorgen,' Fionna said at last. 'My lovely Chalice tells me of you out there. Exiled on your promontory with only this gormless fellow for company.'

Buffeted by the hormonal fug in the room, dizzy from her sharpened senses, Arden took a few seconds longer than necessary to reply. 'It is a fine and temporary existence,' she said. 'The isolation strengthens spirits.'

'And whets longings, I would say. People gossip that this poor boy killed his wife—'

'Fionna—' he protested.

'They say it, but it is not true. She was a smart girl, much smarter than you, Jonah Riven, and her boat would not have overturned unless she *told* it to do so, ha!' Miss La Grange gesticulated with a half-full wine glass. 'Personally, Lightmistress, I don't think she's dead at all. Everything in its time and place for Miss Harrow. Even staying in Vigil and marrying Jonah here, when the Eugenics Society quite forbade such a thing. Having a Postmaster for a father would make her stubborn like that.'

Mr Riven shared a glance with Arden, an odd, indecipherable expression. Reminding him of Bellis, she thought.

After Miss La Grange applied upon Mr Riven an unguent meant for both bruises and showgirl-wrinkles, she deposited a carafe of cloudy wild-grape wine with two glasses upon a scrolled lacquer side table.

'Now, you know your way around, Jonah, love. You may show Mx Beacon the facilities. Avail yourself of the wine. I understand you are not much of a drinker, but it may soothe inflamed muscles, help you sleep. I unfortunately must bathe and rest. The Manse and all her visitors have kept me busy this evening!'

She nodded at Arden and gave Mr Riven a sly crimson grin.

'Don't make too much noise when you make love to the girl, dear. No wild howling. You're not on the promontory and the neighbours will talk if she is too vocal in her delight.'

'Um . . .?' Arden started.

'Darling, if you were drooling over your neighbour any more I'd need to get you a bib. I'm sure he will be gentle. Goodnight!'

When she left, Mr Riven dropped his impassiveness and visibly blushed. 'I'm sorry, she makes assumptions.'

'Best be quiet about it, then.'

'Huh.' He huffed good-naturedly. 'She suspects Bellis is still alive and I'm still married.'

Of course Fionna La Grange knew. Love-struck fool.

'Do many people know Bellis' true fate?'

'If they think she fled me with Rector John Stefan's help,' he replied, 'then they keep their mouths shut.'

As Mr Riven struggled with the unfamiliar buttons, Arden tried to put her mind off his proximity by examining the oddities of the parlour. The angled mirror and the position of the seats were clearly set up for seductive purposes, and a collection of garments in black patent leather lay draped across a side table. Over the cluttered mantelpiece, a row of glass phalluses marched like pink soldiers heading for battle.

Arden went to touch the largest one, then caught herself at the last minute, for Mr Riven was watching her again.

'Strange, seeing you wear that coat. Bellis last wore it during our wedding.'

'Oh, I didn't realize,' Arden said, burning with embarrassment for not realizing. She shrugged out of the leather. 'It's so fine I didn't even feel myself getting too hot.' She swallowed and said, 'I suppose it's strange seeing me wear it, and not Bellis.'

Mr Riven gave an unexpected smile. 'Although it was her wedding coat, Bellis never wore it much either. She was so little, she'd swim in it. No, that coat belonged to my mother.' He nodded. 'It did it's duty as evidence of Bellis' *death*, but she was never fond if the texture enough to make it a daily thing.'

'It is an unusual feel,' Arden agreed, quietly experiencing a stab of delight. 'Your mother's coat! Goodness.'

Arden picked up a nearby matchbook instead of letting him see her dizzy grin. *Not Bellis' at all!* She composed herself and returned to him. As a coincidence, a Justinian crest was embossed on the paper fold, and Arden remembered what he'd said about his mother's background.

'Since we are speaking of her, how long did your mother work at the Manse Justinian?'

'A while. When the kraken got harder to hunt, Justinian money kept my family alive until some of us showed up with monstercalling talents.'

Some of you. Until you killed them. The thought came like a contamination in her joy, and she worried at its source. Would they ever be able to talk about it? Looking at Mr Riven now, he could not have been anywhere near an adult when the crime happened. Younger than David Modhi, even. A child, accused of a massacre? It made no sense.

Then she thought of the old Baron Alexander Justinian, whose face was so much like Mr Riven's. 'And your father? Who was he?'

He shook his head. 'My mother never said.'

She did not pry further. It could not have been any more obvious that he was not altogether a deepwater man.

'I never knew my birth mother long,' Arden admitted. 'She died when I could count four years old. Old enough to remember, and not completely forget.'

'Was she a Lightmistress too?'

'No. Had good neutral standing in the Eugenics ledger, good family, but my talent comes from the Beacon, the paternal, side. She was an airship pilot. The best that God could deliver without resorting to endowments, they used to say. Not good enough to survive a Vinland Crossing, though.'

213

'I've been through a Vinland Crossing storm, on a convict ship. They are vicious.'

'As are the pirates who patrol the air.'

'Yes. Them too.'

Arden poured the wine and took a huge gulp from her glass, needing the wine to still her nerves. 'My father tried to keep the unfortunate details from me, but no storm brought down my mother's craft. The crew made contact with a rogue inflatable corsair from the Summerlands. Her ship suffered a pirate seizure and . . . well. They tell me it was quick.'

'Summerlanders are not known for taking prisoners. I met some during my time in bondage. They'd rather kill a man quickly than torment them. If it is any consolation, they have no patience for torture.'

'It is a consolation, in its own strange way.'

They were quiet then. She wanted so much to interrogate Mr Riven about his history, about his time in the prison hulks, about his Lyonne accent and the people who gave him those rounded Northern vowels. About his journey, from child to man. He had travelled while in captivity. What had he come to know? Did he ever love before Bellis? Could there be love after? What did each scar mean, and when had he received each one? What was the taste of his skin, his response to a kiss?

'You'd have liked her.'

'Who?'

But she knew who.

The squeak of a gramophone winding came from Fionna's room, and then the piano tinkle of a song popular twenty years ago slid out from under a gap in the door.

'Mr Riven, *Jonah*.' She lingered, not knowing quite how to put the words, but needed to say them. 'Were you really married, or was it all an act to fool the Lyonne Order? Why did Bellis not take her golden talent and go to Lyonne and live like a Queen?'

He winced, and Arden felt quite suddenly she had opened a wound.

'We are married. It was no pretence.'

Now it was her turn to sigh from disappointment, but he went on, 'When I was released from my imprisonment, I had nowhere to go. I came back here. Stefan was a Rector in Garfish Point at the time, a hundred miles away and yet to take his post here. The only friend I had was Bellis. When I would have been flogged in the town square on my first day back, it was Bellis who stood in front of the crowd and stopped them. My best friend. The talent she had, it was a hard burden to carry. *Sanguis petrae* is a Sainted Isle trait, but she was not a Sainted Islander. Unless you've been there . . . it's hard to explain what the Islands are like to an outsider. The rituals. The superstitions. The deepwater folk worship the monsters as kin, and gods.'

'David told me about the Deepwater King,' Arden said, and wished she had the little iron figurine upon his serpent with her, so then she could really see if David was right, if it did look like Mr Riven. 'That he's still worshipped. Like God.'

'Yes, the one, who takes a wife and no man shall sunder them. His word is law.' He looked down at his hands, and the scars across his knuckles. Sighed, and continued with his story. 'So, four, five years ago, Bellis decides she's going to escape the Order once and for all. Went out unprotected, and on her own. She thought that the deepwater folk might more likely accept her on the night of the King.'

Arden recalled Mr Justinian's tale, of the woman dragged out to the islands and wedded in the terrible, brutal ways. Of her return to Vigil bloodied, bruised . . . and married. Suddenly a piece of the puzzle fell in to place.

'I take it the deepwater folk didn't accept her at all.'

'If I hadn't wedded Bellis, they'd have *killed* her. Fed her to the sea and *maris anguis*, the great serpent. But I meant my vows when I gave Bellis my name. I didn't take them lightly. But though she is protected now, like I said, I cannot be with her. Since my family . . . since they died I am no longer welcome back to my ancestral lands. I am a Riven in name only. It is a strong name, but I wear it in sufferance.'

So something had happened out there beyond the storm and in the islands where the monstrosities were venerated as gods, but of it Mr Riven would not elaborate further. Some horror on the Deepwater Night, when the abyssal King of the Abyss came up and stole away a woman for a wife.

'I'm sorry if the rumours about our marriage were troublesome, Mx Beacon.'

'Oh, I tried not to listen to them.'

'We never consummated our wedding,' he continued hesitantly, as if the reality needed softening, and evidence of him not doing Bellis harm.

Arden stilled again. Jealousy and envy only worked had it the scaffold of a coveted thing. In a blink Mr Riven had changed the rules. 'Not consummated . . . you mean, you and Bellis . . . not ever?'

Mr Riven shook his head. 'Our marriage was so sudden. The time was not right so soon after the ritual – we never discussed making it a union of the flesh and in the end, the time never came for us. She was, she was poorly in spirit. The threat of the Order was a great strain on her.'

'I'm quite . . . I'm quite stunned.'

'Why?'

Arden struggled to reply. How could she articulate loneliness and monkish yearnings, the flesh which burned through her fire-aligned blood, the whisper of flame in her mind? How could she tell this man that he'd provided the face for her ruminations in the bleak and endless nights, and even now if he was to ask, she would say yes, *yes*, and take him into her embrace at once?

'I thought you might have been with her that way. Because you loved her.'

He lay down, adjusted his head on the tassel-fringed cushion, looked up at the ceiling. 'She no longer needs me. Nobody will dare touch her, and that is why I can confidently say I will not do as the Lions ask tonight.'

'I'm still worried, Mr Riven.'

'Of what?'

216

'That I might have stumbled into a bigger theatre than just encouraging the pair of you to sail off to your happy ending. The Eugenics Society never lets any endowed child stay in Fiction. Mr Lindsay spoke words of *care* and *gentleness*, letting her *mature at home*, but I don't believe him, not one inch! The moment her talent was revealed, she'd have been sent to Lyonne, sick mother needing care or Mr Harrow forbidding her or not.'

The wounded look came back, and this time interlaced with fear. 'There are always exceptions.'

'What exceptions? Tell me! I am completely jealous.'

The gramophone stilled. The room grew quiet, and the perfumes stifling.

'You would not want what Bellis had.'

'What do you mean, *sanguis petrae* is a golden – oh!'

In her distraction she'd let the wine glass fall out of her hand. Without waiting, Mr Riven rolled off the couch and picked the goblet from the floor, wiped the rug and the hem of Arden's dress with the old Baron's silk handkerchief – and then stilled as he realized where he was, looking up at her, his hot blue eyes darkening the same way they had when he'd seen her on that pebble beach, clothed in scraps of gold.

With an anxious swallow, he stood up and put the glass away. 'Enough wine for you tonight, perhaps. Now you need not worry about the Lions, Mx Beacon. Bellis certainly would not.'

The room was warm. Arden stood up and examined her skirts. The feathered dress beneath, all silks and softness, remained intact, despite the night they'd spent.

Mr Riven watched her all the while. Another expression came over him now, and this one not so rigid and disciplined. If Bellis was an object of worship, then Arden was some other inarticulable manifestation altogether – something unfamiliar and intriguing.

She blurted, 'You speak pretty words of friendship and duty and risking your life to marry her before she got turned into serpent food . . . but did you ever desire her like a grown man?'

217

'I don't know,' he said hesitantly. 'It would be demeaning to think of her in that way.'

An odd rebellion came over her then, against the Lions who would have her chase the jewel of love and an independent life. She wanted to remove the dress, have Mr Riven behold her naked body, invite him to touch her. This man, who belonged to another, was a man more forbidden than Mr Castile ever had been. Oh, but the room was hot, or maybe she was hot, a furnace banked and under pressure. She fleetingly imagined him aroused, wanting her, and the relief he would bring in all his maleness, his scent, his body tender and coarse at the same time.

If he noticed her mood he made no sign of it, turning over on the chaise. 'If I snore,' Mr Riven gruffed, 'you are welcome to throw a shoe in my direction.'

He grabbed the end of a crocheted throw, rolled over and turned away. Arden, abandoned, watched the coke-flame flicker in the grate, and took far longer to sleep.

19

Vigil in the morning

Vigil in the morning became an exceptionally sorry place, dank and dreary, with the sulphurous smell of coal and the odour of the night-soilman's cart. Mr Riven woke early, at the first ray of light though a tiny window set into the sloping ceiling.

'How are you getting home?' he asked, as she stirred on the bed. Arden squinted into the grey dawn, pulled the coverlet to her chin.

'Heavens. I hadn't thought. I'll need to hire David Modhi to take me back.'

'Don't bother. I'm heading in your direction. I can pull my boat up to the pier if you don't mind the walk.'

'Well, that makes you handy indeed.'

That made him smile, and his face, normally so hard and flinty, softened about his eyes.

Arden dressed behind the room divider and despaired at the stained satin of her formerly pretty blue shoes. She had not slept well. Mr Riven had not snored, but the thought of him nearby had been a terrible distraction. She had hoped to escape and dream of anyone else – if not Richard, then maybe one of her first sweethearts – but Mr Riven had persistently slid into that place.

How disrespectful you should think this way, her heart whispered. *He is both married and a gentleman. A hero even, assisting his wife in escaping from the Lions and the deep-water savages.*

'We should thank Fionna for her hospitality,' Arden said when she emerged from behind the screen. 'I hate taking off without a polite gesture.'

'That guinea you left on the mantelpiece will be the best thanks you can give her, along with the extra hour sleeping in,' Mr Riven said. He opened the door and ushered Arden out onto the landing, before walking down the stairs first so he might help her over the two missing ones at the bottom. At the courtyard he added, 'Better than rag-paper dollars. Anyhow, she won't be up until noon. We'll be back on the promontory before—'

'So, the old bitch Betsey was *right*.'

Mr Riven halted suddenly at the male voice. Trapped behind him, Arden had only the view of his shoulder blades, but previous meetings had made her more than familiar with the voice's owner.

'Well, what do you know, lads? The mongrel had time to stop at the whores to wet his pecker before leaving. Shaved, too.'

'Let me pass, Alasdair,' Mr Riven said. 'I do not wish to argue with you.'

Arden squeezed out from behind Mr Riven. Mr Harrow stood in front of them, grinning broadly. His two deputies, very much the worse for wear. A third deputy lingered nearby, this one newly minted by the shiny pewter star on his shabby coat lapel. Gregor Tallwater, probably trying to earn an honest coin. Altogether, they made a crowd of the little outside yard. The skull-grin on Mr Harrow's face faded as soon as he saw Arden.

'Lightmistress? What are you doing here?'

'I might ask you the same thing, *Post*master.'

'I have come to arrest this reprobate for assaulting my men. Best you step aside now, Guildswoman.'

'No,' Arden said. 'Best you step aside. I do not take kindly to threats upon my person or the people of my acquaintance.'

With that she took Mr Riven's hand in her own.

He resisted for a few seconds, but she squeezed hard with caution until her coin hurt. Flicked out with a little finger so it might touch the heel of his hand. An obscure signal of the docks, but if he'd had any experience in prison hulks and other places of ill-repute, he would know what such a secret sign meant.

Trust me. Follow my lead.

'Why do you come here with false accusations?' she continued. 'Mr Riven was never at the Justinian residence, and has been with me all night.'

'You left the Manse with him. Witnesses saw you leave. Which means he consorted at the Manse with you during the Master's Ball.'

'I certainly did not leave or consort with Mr Riven in the Manse. I left with Mr Castile, a friend and chaperone. Then I came here to the Black Rosette to spend time with my . . . lover.'

Beside her, Mr Riven tensed. Mr Harrow swallowed, affected disgust.

'Lies. My men arrested this fellow in the guest house. He got away. Clearly with your help.'

'You mean, Mr Justinian's pleasure house. A room stocked with all manner of drugs and recreational pharmaceuticals? These men here, still so inebriated they can barely see as much as when I stumbled across them last night, now concoct a story so they may excuse whatever general shambles they may have caused in their carousing? Why, you can ask any of these so-called "whores" to vouch for our presence here all night.'

Mr Harrow bared his teeth like a cremelo highland ape, and his wispy yellow hair crackled with his rage. The sorry deputies cowered.

'You think you can cover for this monster, Lightmistress? You think your succumbing to his depravity without hurt is a privileged game for you blooded folk?'

Mr Riven squeezed Arden's hand so hard she nearly cried out from it. But she knew what Riven meant. The Postmaster's invective was mere talk: Mr Harrow was a man grieving, lashing out. Let him vent, let him direct his anger to her, and then be on his way. If Mr Riven fought them, he would go to prison, and to the hulks and to his death.

In a tempest of bitterness Mr Harrow ranted at Arden, his eyes wild when he saw her silent. 'Does it give you perverted pleasure, when he ploughs your furrows with the same tool he used to rape my daughter and take her maidenhood? Does it excite you to think of how she would cry and try to fight him every devil-damned night? How she came to my house, her undergarments rent, stinking of kraken oil inside her and this creature's sexual odours, begging me to dissolve the marriage? My only joy is that his rotted seed could not infect her with child!'

He continued for a solid minute. Behind him, only Mr Gregor Tallwater had the grace to seem embarrassed by the foulness that emerged from Mr Harrow's mouth. The other two deputies had clearly heard it all before, glad enough that Arden should be the target of Mr Harrow's displeasure instead of them.

Mr Riven lurched close to an anger-induced fit. His neck turned near-purple in his effort to keep calm.

At last Mr Harrow took a breath. He had no more to say.

'Are you done, Mr Harrow?' Arden asked, flatly.

'I am done.'

'Then can we pass?'

He jerked his head sideways. 'Get out of my sight.'

'Gladly.'

She dragged Mr Riven across the courtyard duckboards. Only Gregor shared with her an apologetic glance, and it appeared he would not have argued if Arden had dragged him away from this unholy indictment as well.

As soon as they were in the streets and had made their way in silence across the town square to the salty fog of the harbour, she seized Mr Riven's chin so that he would meet her eyes, not go to dark places in his mind.

'Jonah,' she said, using his first name as if he were a hurt child. 'It's for the best that Mr Harrow exhaust himself on his own illusions. If he had truly loved his daughter, she would never have got into her mess. She'd have gone to Lyonne a golden talent princess and eaten honey sweets and sat on velvet chairs and grown fat among silks for the rest of her life.'

He turned on her, despair making his blue eyes gleam almost incandescent. 'You think me a dupe, for helping her and not getting real love in return?'

'No. I think everyone is a dupe, for putting so much stock in sanguinity. The damned Sainted Isles and their unmanned rockblood wells. This cursed town. Bellis' fool idea of using you to escape the Lions and secure her place in the Islands by putting fear in the hearts of other men. The devil knows there are enough women in the world who live in a marriage of such abjectness for real. They cannot be whisked away to some mysterious islands with a lover when it all becomes too much. Bellis did not need to add her story to theirs, however the end may have been justified in her mind. You may have been the only good thing she had while she was here. She didn't deserve you, Mr Riven.'

He let Arden go. Her hand smarted from where he had held her hard. She rubbed it with a wince.

'I'm sorry,' he said of her aching hand, and perhaps for more. 'I have kept to myself for too many years. I know there are stories. Bellis encouraged them. I suspect she knew it would make her eventual disappearance more legitimate, and send a message to the people over the waves that she was not to be trifled with, and neither was I. But what Mr Harrow said . . . sometimes it's difficult to maintain that image without feeling ashamed of it.'

She huffed a breath. 'She wove her protective deception well. You are quite the scoundrel, as everyone was at pains to tell me in no less detail than Mr Harrow did just now.'

'Yet not knowing the truth, you still came to me as a neighbour, and with dignity.' He briefly touched the end of Arden's coat sleeve. Patterns his mother had made, not Bellis. 'It says much for your character, Mx Beacon.'

'Does it earn me some credit towards being your friend?'

'You have earned every right to be my friend.'

She took off her glove and held out her hand for him to shake. Her left hand. Blood to blood. Would he know?

He did. 'Ooh, and gently,' she said, as his fingers closed around her palm. His hand was callused with work and bloodletting, deliberate, but gentle too. She need not have worried.

He gave a crooked smile, and that same tightness budded in the centre of her chest. In Clay Capital he would not be at all handsome, too angular and Fictish, his nose too thin and his smile too crooked and his skin kissed by shades of sea foam, not sun.

But still. He was not hers to love.

Somewhere over the waves a woman had asked her best friend to *wait*. Asked him to protect her by his unseen presence until she was ready to call him back. Like the lich-ship gears, this love of Bellis and Mr Riven's had been set into place long before Arden had arrived. It would continue upon her departure. She was merely a stowaway upon this journey.

They went to the harbour, where Mx Modhi had already taken her Harbourmistress position in her rocking chair, and her first pipe of the day. She saw them coming, Arden Beacon and a groomed Mr Riven, and did not recognize him at first. Only when he spoke to her did her eyes turn into hard squints.

'People have been seeking you,' she said through a cloud of tobacco smoke. 'Magistrate Harrow especially.'

'I am aware of this.'

'You'd best not be up to nonsense, Jonah Riven. My position here does not allow for illegal activities.'

Arden quickly interjected, sensing tensions rise. 'I assure you, anything that Mr Harrow may have said is all down to mistaken identity. I can vouch for Mr Riven.'

224

Mx Modhi obviously had opinions on Arden's vouching, but chewed on her pipe to stop the words from coming out and costing her the coin of her harbour fee. David Modhi scrambled to prepare Mr Riven's boat ready for departure, and beamed in joy when Mr Riven thanked him for taking such care. The youth's wispy moustache trembled with delight. 'Anything for you, Mr Riven!'

Compared to the pleasure boats of the visiting Masters, Mr Riven's craft was a shadow coated in pitch. The boat's name on the black wood became apparent as Arden came close. *Saudade.*

Now that she could see her without danger of being run down, Arden noted that all her trimmings were the same oily black wood. Mangrove-ebony, a prized timber for shipbuilders if they could ever harvest enough to construct a craft more sizable than a dinghy. The mangrove stands formed floating islands that travelled piecemeal across the Darkling Sea. The largest stands were rumoured to be found in Sainted waters, where the sea monsters sported. It was a monster-hunting ship, down to its bones. *Saudade* had all the solidity of an ocean transport barge.

Other than the high wheelhouse, the bulk of her was mostly below decks, to resist tipping in hard swells. She had side wheels to keep her hunting-craft nimble and enable her to plough through Sargasso fronds without fouling, but given her speed Arden suspected a screw-propeller under the water too.

Propped up by a winch at *Saudade*'s stern was a smaller craft, a tender boat made in the same black wood. The little dinghy had a brass motor of some oil-burning type, perhaps kraken or rock distillate.

Mr Riven helped Arden aboard over a mist-slippery gangway. Arden ran her hand along the rail. Intuited that bloodwork had been used aboard her, powerful sacraments.

Inside the wheelhouse, things both antique and modern. He owned both spyglass and spectrograph, but also a near-new and extremely expensive echo box, technology only the principal signallers had.

He noticed her staring at the box.

'Echo box. Traces shoals, floating pumice, stalker ships. It is a cunning little machine. It uses electric signals, the same as a Sumerian-Congolese wireless device, and traces them upon this paper roll.'

'I never took you for a technological fellow.'

'I prefer *pragmatic*, myself,' he said. 'If I had the time and the necessity I could refit her in all the latest inventions.'

'Mr Riven,' David Modhi called up at that most inopportune time, 'I've taken down the gangway!'

'Good lad,' he said back, throwing him a wave. 'Say thank you to your mother for me.'

'I will, Mr Riven!'

Arden smiled as they cast away. 'I think he has a little crush on you.'

'Poor devil,' Mr Riven said, after the youth had run back to the harbour shed to once more be in thrall to his mother's commands. 'He deserves a better life than this.'

'I've seen his test scars. At least he's tried.'

Mr Riven nodded. 'He's falsified his name and gone to at least six more moots, up and down the Fiction coast. I took him each time, the optimistic whelp.' Mr Riven shrugged. 'Even if he was positive for something, it would be a risk if he tested for the wrong thing.'

'What would be a wrong thing?'

She saw his jaws clench, and realized he'd not meant to speak.

Arden sighed, and nodded. 'Well, he looks like he's nearly of age. A sanguis shadow would have shown up long before now. The best he can hope for is that he is *malorum*, a late bloomer, I suppose. The Society isn't too fussy with *sanguis malorum*.'

'From your voice I'd assume you have familiarity with the condition.'

She nodded. 'I failed my eleventh- and thirteenth-year tests, tested just positive at seventeen. The only reason I was allowed a third test was because of my father, and my name. He is Portmaster for Clay Portside, and he is a Beacon.'

'Then you know what it is, to have a name that precedes you.'

'When did you test?' Arden asked. 'Prior to your, uh, prison term? You obviously have *something*.'

To her alarm Mr Riven gestured for Arden to take the wheel. 'Never tested,' he said. With a yelp, Arden grabbed the paddle wheeler's mechanism. Alarmingly, Mr Riven intended to show her how to drive *Saudade* out of the marina.

'Never . . . never tested?' she stammered, trying to navigate both a powerful steamer and her own tongue at the same time. She had served her assigned duty on slow dockside tugboats, but this craft exceeded anything in her experience.

'Our family has always had endowments,' Mr Riven said as she steered, half-terrified and half-exhilarated. 'Why test for something I already know I have?'

'But you could have left this place. Got away from everyone who wished you and your family harm . . . oh, a buoy, is that a buoy? Did I just run over the signal buoy?'

'Keep going. You're fine.'

'My Lord, she's a powerful craft. You could get all the way to Clay Portside in your boat.'

He walked to the window. '*Saudade* was never my boat. She belonged to my family. And kraken-calling is a fisherman's talent. Specific to a region. It is not a talent of any importance outside of here.' A light rain fell across the glass. 'My blood is tied up with this ocean. The devils that live beneath the waves, the leviathan, the *monstrom mare*. This is what my blood trammels. If I'd left for Clay, what could I do there?'

He turned to Arden, who had committed to a grip on the wheel and relaxed into the engine's power.

'Was the same with Bellis. The Sainted Isles lie east, not north, not in Clay. That's where the rockblood flows. It's where she yearned for. When she needed to go, I let her go.'

'I can't say I've ever experienced any geographical under-pinnings to my sanguinity myself.'

'There's fire everywhere in this world. Everywhere and in

everything. Besides,' he turned back to the rain-lashed glass, 'even if I was not tested for endowments, they came for me in the end. Took me to the prison hulks. Tried to make sure I died. Which I did not.'

'You must have been barely a child.'

'I was fourteen.'

'Fourteen! How could they have pinned a slaughter on a child?'

'Huh, so, Vernon spared no grisly detail about my crime.'

She sighed. 'Some nonsense about you having killed your family in a night. Everyone on the promontory.'

'Then that is what I did.'

'I will not believe you. I know what lies Lions are capable of.'

'Sometimes they don't lie.'

The side wheels ground through the slosh. Arden wondered what she could say. Words of comfort? Too late now, such things were behind him. He stared out beyond the horizon, where the cloudbank grew, undoubtedly thinking of Bellis beyond that straight edge, under that self-same cloud, needing him.

The waves slapped *Saudade*'s bows and sheeted across her forecastle. The forward rock became pronounced as they hit deeper water, making the brass crossbar at her feet a great necessity in keeping her upright.

'See,' he said once they had left Vigil harbour, 'you're a natural skipper.'

'Is she the only boat your family owned?' Arden asked, once she found her balance.

'There were several in my grandfather's time. And my father had two more, *Sonder* and *Sehnsucht*.'

'What happened . . . after . . . after, you know. They died?'

'*Sonder*, I've no idea where it went. *Sehnsucht* I gave to Bellis and your cousin Stefan, to pay for passage to the Sainted Isles. The penny for the Old Guy. Somebody else has her now, or she was long ago made firewood.' Then, unexpectedly he asked, 'Who was Mr Castile?'

She started. 'Excuse me?'

'When you said you had a chaperone. And to the Dowager. Nobody can lie properly when put on the spot. Ergo, there was a Castile of your acquaintance.'

'A man of my social circle when I lived in Clay Portside.' Then, emboldened by their newfound familiarity, 'He was my lover.'

'Your first?'

'My first *important* one.'

'The one the Lion bribed you with.'

'The very one. I'm no fool, Mr Riven, he's probably on the other side of the world by now and living quite high on the hog. I've not spoken to him since the day he left, a year ago.'

Mr Riven frowned, entirely confused. 'Why would a man do something so unfathomably absurd as leave you?'

She let herself smile at his compliment. 'It's so political when endowments and genetics are concerned. Not everyone is as noble as you, Mr Riven. He wouldn't run away with me, and I was quite terrified to do it myself. My cowardice, you see.'

'I cannot see you a coward.'

'You would be surprised.'

She must have telegraphed a need for distraction, for he pointed to a rope on top of a rivet. 'Lash the wheel, slow the engine. Let me show you something.'

Arden did as Mr Riven requested and followed him down to the deck. He pulled off his jacket, rolled up his shirt, held out a tanned and lean arm. With a knife blade from his pocket, he put a nick in the side of his hand, where a coin might be if he were a Lyonnian sanguinem. A callus pinched there, from a hundred cuts. Once he let a few drops fly he withdrew from the railing.

'Come see.'

She held fast to a post, for the wheels were still going at a chop. The intermittent sunlight caught the cloud of water vapour from the wheels, gave the spray a corona of rainbow colour. As she waited, the wheels slowed to a gentle turn.

'What am I looking for?'

He gave a sly smile, and suddenly, she didn't care, only wanted to admire Mr Riven's face. Unsymmetrical, too pale, his hair too dark-dun a shade of brown to mark him as kin to the yellow-crowned longboaters of the Estotilian winterlands. Yet in all ways he was beautiful. As she surveyed him, she had a sense of coolness, for the flume of the waves had risen from the stilled wheels and surrounded her, the light refracting as in the very path of a rainbow. Down below . . .

Arden's breath stilled. The water turned to moving glass.

No, not glass. A thousand moving, twisting shapes of luminescent transparency, for the colours had turned to life.

'Are they cuttlefish?' she shouted over the threshing waves.

'Krakenspawn,' Mr Riven shouted back with unconcealed delight. 'A hen has managed to lay before dying. It's a good sign.'

The kraken had taken up the propulsion that the wheels had abandoned, and *Saudade* picked up speed, moving with the slightest side-to-side yaw until they came in sight of the dark rocks of the Riven Promontory. The churning bodies of the new-hatched little monsters threw off flashes of electric brilliance. She could not tell if it were them or the running tide that caused such speed.

With a dismissive gesture, Mr Riven flung out his hand and with a rainbow flash, the krakenspawn were gone. The boat coasted on the residual momentum.

Arden stayed on the deck while he returned to the tower, to reverse the wheels and gently drift in to the pier.

The morning had taken on a delicious strangeness now, shiny-new with possibilities and responsibilities.

'What happens from here?' she asked when Mr Riven came down out of the cabin. 'Because I'm obliged to report to the Lions if you decide to go anywhere.'

'You'll be waiting a long time to make that report.'

It was not her place to opine on his decision. But she could not help her feelings. Found herself sneaking looks in his direction, and finding herself gladdened by his sight.

'You're still not going back to Bellis? I know you said it last night, but feared the wine might be talking.'

He shook his head with a half-grin. 'If the Lyonne Order has taken interest in her after all these years, they've left it too late. They have no influence over there. Why do you think she kept heading to the Isles?'

Mr Riven tied the boat off and helped Arden onto land. His work-roughened hand warm in hers. Making her brave. She could easily have broached the gap herself, but she appreciated the concern, and besides, a sense of safety strengthened those hands of his, an impression that he could pluck a person out of the wildest seas.

The wind roused up, and the sun came out a little, and the golden bloom on his cheeks made him seem otherworldly, an ancient idol carved from an occluded marble. She internally debated furiously about how to say goodbye, about how to steal a few more minutes with Mr Riven.

They were disturbed by a feeble *yip* from the pier's landing. A brown and white terrier dog, grey at the muzzle, trotted down the wooden jetty.

'Ah, Lightmistress, the boss has arrived. Come and meet Chief.'

'Hello, Chief,' Arden said to the little dog. She squatted down to scratch him under his salty jaw and patted his wiry back. 'Hello, old pup.'

The dog gazed up at her with eyes blued from cataracts, then put his paw on her knee. Mr Riven's critical attention was upon her. The dog's opinion was a great test.

'Dogs are keen judges of human character,' Arden said, standing up with bony, scruffy Chief in her arms. He licked her under her chin, tasting krakensalt from their journey.

'They are indeed.' Mr Riven stroked Chief's head. 'I'd only owned him a year when my family was . . . when I was . . .' He stopped. 'Did you know Jorgen Beacon looked after him when I was gone? Took care of the two boats as well. *Saudade* and *Sehnsucht*.'

'Mr Harris never told me. I thought you were at odds, because of Stefan.'

'No, it was not Stefan that made us distant. Well, maybe a little. My uncle Zachariah had quite a friendship with Jorgen. They were stuck on the same promontory, like us.'

He turned to walk away, before stopping to say, 'Well, are you coming? I can't have you stumbling back in those heeled slippers. If you fall off a cliff, Mr Harrow will accuse me of having given you a shove.'

'We can't have that.'

'There should be some boots that might fit you.'

Arden put Chief down and followed Mr Riven up the pier path to the factory sheds.

A selection of wind chimes, some bright, and some ancient with salt-rust, made a symphony as they entered the small quadrangle afforded by the building shells. A cormorant on a roof watched them, one of the compound's constant birds. Mr Riven disappeared inside the first of the warehouses, came out dragging a shipping trunk banded in iron. The locks were broken, and the hinges almost rusted solid. Inside, under old portside uniforms and shipbuilder's diagrams, the trunk was filled to the brim with boots, some of them barely worn. From the variation of sizes, more than one person had owned the contents.

Arden picked out a pair of general-purpose low heels, brushed off the dust and knocked them out for spiders.

An odd smell wafted out of another open barn door, hot metal and salt water.

'It is the hen,' Mr Riven said at Arden's unspoken question. 'Mother of the spawn you saw earlier.'

'You caught her?'

'Yes.'

'Can I see?'

He nodded. 'But say a prayer on entry, Lightmistress. She has made a hard sacrifice and deserves respect.'

The factory hunkered down low and dim, with a row of lanterns set about a long, broad table that was more a giant chapel altar than a butcher's block. At first, the creature seemed entirely *eye*, a golden disc wider than the reach of Arden's arms, shining in the lamplight. The pupil gleamed wise and cold, having beheld all the mysteries of the devil's abyss with a form beloved only by God. A luminescence was inside her sizable cranium, which Arden figured roomy enough to hold three Clydesdales in an embrace. Yet the kraken turned out smaller than Arden had previously thought. This was not to say the creature was *not* massive, but of a conservative heft that might destroy only the *Breeze* or *Saudade*. Certainly not to tangle up an entire clipper ship as in the woodblock paintings of her old books, or an armada as the old stories suggested.

The hen's long legs were pale, and in the low light had the softness of a child's arms. The chain and canvas harness Mr Riven had used to haul her onto the sacrificial altar from his boat still cradled the head the way fingers might hold a giant egg.

Reverence here, no violence. A lying-in-state, not a slaughter.

Mr Riven watched Arden examine the kraken hen in silence until she had finished her worship.

'I took her yesterday,' he said at last. 'She had laid the last of her eggs. A *monstrom mare* in its natural habitat will prefer to die upon a pontoon of black mangroves, part of the ecology of the creature's natural environment. My boat was the nearest vessel to achieve that end, so she came to me in consent.' He reached out and touched the hen's rubbery flesh. 'Now we wait for her to die so she can be harvested. For the oil in her head, the fabric of her skin.'

'It sounds quite a process.'

'Yes, and there is not much of a window to do either. After she breathes her last, the decay is quick. They bleed ichor, not blood. The mortification is absolute. If she is not prepared, there will be nothing left of her except seawater tomorrow morning.'

Suddenly the creature's siphon, big enough for Arden to have wedged herself in up to her waist, let out a miserable puff of air with a seawater plume. Arden yelped, caught the misty brunt of that last exhale.

'Oh! She's still alive,' Arden said, wiping her face and arms. 'And now I smell of salt-rust.'

Mr Riven grinned and pulled a pony-plant chamois off a rail, held it out. 'I'm sorry, I should have warned you not to get too close.'

'Getting too close is the ultimate warning for all things,' she replied, meaning to say it in grudging humour, but as she took the fine vegetable leather, her hand met Mr Riven's own, and a shock of longing went through her, a feeling beyond desire, for the ground had opened beneath her and all she could do was flail and fall.

He dropped the towel and Arden reached up for him as a vine in darkness might reach for sun. On tip-toes she pressed her mouth to his chapped lips and thought for a moment he would resist her, that she had made a terrible mistake, that she only intended to crash and burn this nascent friendship with an unwanted kiss.

Then he let out a moan so soft it could have been a sigh and wrapped his arms about her, a grip both tight and trembling, and crushed his mouth against her own with such untaught carelessness it could have been the kiss of a child.

What was this? Was it love, or anger, or exultation at stealing this wretched left-behind lover who had been made monstrous to protect a golden queen?

Or was it her own obsession grown beyond its bounds? His entire body stood rigid and humming in her arms, a human tuning fork struck and held, and the raw newness of him when she'd spent so long without made the furious stabs of desire in her belly as painful as glass shards. She kissed him greedy as a thief. He was an illicit feast she'd stumbled on when all her life she'd been content with scraps, wanted to taste the dark mysteries of his mouth, the salt of him, hear his gasp of pleasure when he—

Without warning he pulled away, leaving Arden gasping.

'Bellis,' he said through a tight, hoarse throat. His breath came fast and shallow.

Bellis. Bellis, her shadow, the Woman Who Fled and Lived.

'Jonah.' Arden stepped to him again, not yet ready to relinquish him. He took her shoulders and held her away. His expression was more akin to grieving than passion.

'It's too risky for her, Arden. Her safety depends on our marriage being true.'

'A safety *imposed* upon you by a marriage you had no choice but to comply with! She should never have gone out there if she knew the deepwater people would be so upset.'

He backed off as if she was spitting poison instead of truth, and Arden pursued him no more. Only sat by the table as he shook his head.

'She is still my responsibility.'

'What if she were no longer your responsibility? It's been years, Jonah. She is an adult.'

'And do what? Be with you instead?' he said, and it felt so blunt and emotionless that a frightful thought made her blood run cold as the salt upon her skin.

'Maybe . . . you could. I would not say no,' she stammered. 'I'd like to try.'

'Try. Like an experiment?'

'Not . . .'

He shook his head. 'No further now. Arden, you are beautiful and so wonderful but I could be no more than an amusement to you, something indulgent to pass the time before you go back to Clay Portside and leave me with as much thought as you would discard scrap and spoil.'

'I didn't kiss you for my own *amusement*, Jonah.' Arden's tears prickled her eyes and she hated that he made her feel this way, run headlong into her fears of mistakes and abandonment. The Order saw her desires as dangerous and unwanted. But it hurt so much more when a lone man should come to the same conclusion.

'We are lonely, you and I, and I thought . . .' Her cheeks

were so hot they would burn if she touched them. Humiliation crisped her breath to ash. Where was the lightning to strike her? Where was the ground beneath her feet to open and swallow her into a peaceful oblivion?

He ran his hands through his hair, leaving runnels in the dyed pomade of the night before. An absent, impatient gesture.

'I am not some brief occupation for your spare time. I am not an object for you to use when it suits, or a rag for wounded hearts.'

'Jonah, I didn't mean it that way. I'm completely adrift. Just now it seemed that you were the only real thing that I could be certain of. Jonah Riven. Not even my blood belongs to me!'

And now she was reduced to begging, as if she could not descend any lower. A look of infinite tenderness softened his eyes, as brief as a whisper. He made to move towards her, as if about to hug, and comfort.

The sympathy ended almost as soon as it began, and he caught himself, his expression twisted with anguish.

'I made a promise.'

The spell was broken. She was bested by Bellis. Mr Riven's first and only love. He lived only to provide her protection. She was once again *malorum*, a lightless failure. She could not bear the shame any longer. Ran from him as he stood in the darkened warehouse with his dying beast, fled into the grey, cold day. The seabirds cried above her. The waves fretted against the shorelines. The ache of desire that had come so suddenly to her now twisted into a miserable thud.

As she crested the hill she rolled her ankle upon a loose rock while running in the unfamiliar shoes, and coupled with her exhaustion, she slowed down to a limping walk along the trail.

'Stupid, stupid,' she said to herself, while her smarting ankle brought tears to her eyes.

Her ankle, and the other things. Self-pity was an easy cloak to wrap herself up in.

How awful she was. How greedy.

I will cease to think of him. Let him do what he wishes. I shall tell the Lions he is angry with me, and by the end of the month I shall be far from here. I will not have my Guild Degree, or employment. I shall wear a commonblood *coat.*

But no sooner had she come about the corner bluff than she saw Chalice standing outside the lighthouse with a stack of pigeon crates, each one bearing the seal of the Lyonne Investigatory Order.

20

Arden had expected
that she would break

Arden had expected that she would break to Chalice the news of her recruitment into the Order with some delicacy, perhaps over the last of their fig-brandy, because Chalice in her cups was infinitely more agreeable than Chalice in her normal day-to-day. Instead, the admission came with a box of messenger pigeons dumped outside her door.

Each bird was banded about the leg with a metal ring. Engraved on each, a tangle of thorns entangling an open rose.

Now Chalice knew Arden's shameful secret.

'Not every day one is gifted Clay Tipplers owned by Lions,' Chalice said peevishly as Arden approached. She stuck her finger in through the wire, and a yellow beak pecked her. 'Bad-tempered as the bloody delivery driver who dropped them off.' She withdrew her finger. 'I must wonder when I was to be included in this little complication of yours. Lions. Here's me thinking you were just another Seamaster's Guild ingenue.'

'Please understand, I didn't want you to worry, Chalice. You'd have been in a state if I told you what was really going on.'

'What was going *on*?' She turned to Arden, eyes narrowed,

judging every mud-splattered, salt-encrusted, kiss-abraded inch of her. 'What the devil have you been up to, Lightmistress? Don't think I didn't see you coming in on Mr Riven's black boat either.'

Without the gentle preamble she would have preferred, Arden was forced to tell Chalice about her father's suspicions, the work instruction she should never have had, and the constant fear that one day her true function would be revealed.

The admission of Mr Lindsay's appearance as a Lyonne Order agent and her subsequent instruction to befriend Mr Riven raised only an eyebrow. Chalice was truly unflappable, and for that Arden loved her.

The kiss, however, Arden left out.

Chalice, she suspected, already deduced that such a thing had happened between her and Mr Riven. Maybe more. The storm-bride went to place a teapot on the fire pit, dropped in handfuls of pennyroyal and raspberry leaf along with the tea leaves.

'So, you rescued our intimidating neighbour on the words of your Order handler,' Chalice said, stirring the concoction. 'Had a deep and meaningful talk on the duties of a husband. Well then. The puppet master gathers his strings.'

'The Lion made me think I had a choice. A mendacious choice. Either I left Mr Riven to his fate, in which case he might have died, or I went and rescued him and established some sort of connection.'

'And did you establish a connection?' Chalice asked, stirring her witches' brew so hard it sloshed into the fire.'

'Of course I did,' Arden sighed. 'They knew my weaknesses, that I wouldn't let Mr Riven come to harm. They'd have lost their only tenuous link with Bellis Harr . . . *Riven*, I mean. Their runaway sanguinem, taunting them from across the waves.'

Chalice gave her a sideways eye, as if to say: *come on now. You dropped her marriage name on purpose.*

'That's not the kind of connection I'm talking about. Arden, talk to me. How close did you come to that man?'

Arden looked at Chalice's angry face and down at the minty brew so astringent it made her throat sting. 'Chalice why are you making a pennyroyal tea?'

'Did you and him . . .?'

'No, goodness gracious. No! He's married, and he loves his wife. I am merely his neighbour.'

Chalice stopped stirring the tea and gave a relieved exhale at the abortifacient mixture. 'Indeed. At least it hasn't been a night of entirely bad choices. One wouldn't want the daughter of Alasdair Harrow getting upset at you. If she's anything like him, she would be a terror.'

A mutiny stirred in Arden, a resentment towards that loved and perfect woman. 'If Bellis cared about Jonah, she'd not have sailed away without him,' Arden sniped. 'She's given up her vows, as far as I'm concerned.'

The stormbride jutted out her chin in preparation for some harsh truths. The words that came were more measured than Chalice probably wanted them to be. 'Darling, when I said you should think of getting yourself *companionship*, I in no way considered *him*. If you've ever listened to me in our brief time together, keep your wits about you and your emotions cool.'

'Are you telling me to stay away, *Headmistress* Quarry?'

'I'm saying, be convivial and neighbourly all you like, but if Lions are involved, you leave Mr Riven deal with his wife *alone*, do you hear?'

'Goodness. If it's such an importance that I should promise you, then all right. I shan't involve myself in his personal matters. He's really not interested in me . . . that way.'

Mollified somewhat, Chalice left the tea to brew. Arden later drank some, for the menstrual cramps were due in a few days, and the concoction helped women's pains.

In the yellowing light, Chalice prepared the lighthouse's winding mechanism for Arden's shift, but did not, as part of her afternoon ritual, go immediately to bed. Instead Chalice began loading her dry-sack with a change of clothes and her travelling coat.

'I forgot to tell you, in all this morning's strangeness. I have business in town. Mr Sage is harvesting one of his night-flowering herbs for me, and if I'm not around to watch him, he'll do it all wrong.'

'You're leaving?'

'Only a night. I'll take your *Fine Breeze* across to Vigil and return in the morning, if you can cover the first three hours of my shift.' She nodded to the empty earthenware cup in Arden's hands. 'You are not the only one who gets the noonday demons around here. Perhaps some nightflower will be just the cure.'

Arden didn't know why she pained at hearing Chalice would not be around. Chalice always spent the nightshift asleep – it wasn't as if she would miss the stormbride's company. The instruments foretold calm weather, no need for the woman to stay.

And yet, Arden did not want to spend the night-time staring between the Riven compound and the horizon where the Sainted Isles lay. She feared him leaving, and what that meant. Like he'd said, he had not thought much of Bellis until seeing Arden. Now with the memory of a kiss burning his lips, would the night bring urges and pining for the love he'd never consummated? The what might-have-been would crowd his memories. He would board his boat, sail towards the horizon to his woman beyond the waves.

We cannot force Mr Riven to join his wife, but perhaps you can remind him of what he misses.

Jealousy was a sin, a terrible sin. Tonight of all nights she needed company and a friendly ear. Even if it was Chalice.

Fleetingly, Arden debated on telling Chalice to stay, then decided it a mean-spirited request. Was obviously not for the plant-harvesting Arden's stormbride was spending a night in Vigil. She gave Chalice as benevolent a smile as she could. 'Enjoy your night hunting mandrakes and night-blooming things.'

For all her ill timing, Chalice was not ignorant of her Lightmistress' sorrows. 'Now are you sure you will be all right? Last night was a trial for you.'

241

'I will manage well enough. Oh, and I saw Gregor Tallwater doing Harrow muscle work, behind the Black Rosette. Doing it, but not enjoying it. If you cross his path tell him I don't feel badly towards him for this morning's unfortunate altercation. It can't be the best life, working for Mr Harrow.'

'Not much money in grunt enslavement, if it is a Harrow doing the paying,' Chalice said impishly. 'At least we can put aside our previous concerns of our shipwrecked foundlings making an illegal run to the Sainted Isles. They'd need more than pittance wages to pay for a boat out past the permanent storm.'

'His children have a better chance of surviving here than they would over there.'

Chalice darted forward and kissed Arden on the cheek. She smelled of pennyroyal mints and a herbal liquorice: comfort and authority at once. 'There will be yet a few weeks before the first of the Deepwater festivals, and winter. The ashes and leaves augur well for a fair season, then you can go home to Lyonne. I know this place has been a trial.'

'Made better with you.'

Arden hugged her stormbride back and let her go.

Approaching dusk made her maudlin sometimes, and tonight more than most. As she had told Mr Riven, Arden's mother had been an airship pilot before her death at the sword-hands of Summerland pirates. Arden's understanding of the climes might not have been a blood talent, but her inherited instincts were strong all the same.

There was a storm coming. Arden grumbled to herself and tapped the recalcitrant barometric tubes, which had spuriously committed themselves to fine weather right until the entire sky became overcast. Once they begrudgingly gave correct measurements, she went up upon the lamp-room gantry and checked the glass.

For the first time in years Arden recalled the woman she remembered only in fleeting, sightless moments. A smell of jasmine, a visceral memory of being embraced. Pale blonde hair as soft and billowy as a dandelion flower against her cheek, hair so different from her own. The blurred mother murmured promise of her return, soon, soon.

And the thick scent that came with her mother's departure. *It's only a little rain, my darling, only a few little days. Will you be good and wait for me to come back from Vinland? I'll bring a rubber dolly and diamond ring for my favourite girl.*

It had fallen to Jorgen Beacon to tell Arden, when Lucian was too bound in grief to speak. Her father's visiting younger brother, with his thin, smudged face, moustache so spiky and severe.

Your mother has gone, girl. She will never come home.

The high sea licked over the wooden pier as Arden watched *Fine Breeze* sail away into the aged day. Her instincts for trouble were not Beacon-born. They flitted in and out of her awareness, never quite real, but never completely absent. The cold wind chased her skirts, pressed against her bones like a great friendly animal.

'Calm yourself, Arden Beacon,' Arden said to herself. 'It is only the weather, and the changing seasons.'

She retired inside the lighthouse and prepared her first watch of the evening. Her spyglass showed no flags upon the Vigil message pole, or messages telegraphed in light from the Harbourmistress. There were no flotillas of prospectors, just the lone grey silhouette of a lich-ship, that automatic coffin-vessel forever winding back and forth from the rockblood wells of the Sainted Isles to the refineries of Dead Man's Bay.

By sundown a gale came up, and properly so. The fishing boats did not return to harbour, for they would sail north to miss the worst of the storm cell.

There was, however, *Fine Breeze*, bobbing gamely through the sleety bluster.

'Chalice,' she scolded under her breath. 'It's nearly dark. What are you coming back for in this wind?'

Her stormbride would be cold and wet when she got in.

Arden went to load up the fire, and put a kettle to boil for tea, muttering her practice rant. How could Chalice be so foolish? If she'd had an argument with Mr Sage on the correct way to pull up a weed by lamplight, then she should have stayed in one of the guest rooms at the tavern. No need for Chalice to make her way back here.

'By the graces of all the devils,' she called down the tower as the door opened to let the wet occupant in. 'Chalice, I thought you were more sensible than this.'

She ran down the stairs with a blanket in one hand, a cold-fire lantern in the other. Nearly got to the bottom before a great loom of trouble came over her. She stopped, one foot hovering above the final shadowy landing, watching the light and dark flicker below.

Deep senses, lantern keeper's senses, the ones that told of the shift in a current, or the shape in the fog, now told her that it wasn't Chalice downstairs. Too many people. The lantern-light skipped and swam over the concave walls.

She turned to run, but too late, for the intruders who had come into the lighthouse had secured a head start. In the snuffling twilight where the lit lamps and the dark warred between each other, she did not see them until one seized her about her legs and pulled her down onto a landing. She fell, mere inches from splitting her head open on the iron stair-rise behind her.

She thought, *I will leap up to my feet, I will kick him,* but the caustic smell of ether and the awful nothingness that rose up to greet her were stronger than her will and Arden fell into a whirling, punch-drunken night.

21

I just wish you didn't have to kill them

'. . . I just wish you didn't have to kill them. The boy and the woman.'

'Shut up, Sean. Hold the tube steady.'

'Still. Bad luck taints such a sin, even if the Magistrate himself permitted it . . .'

'Helena, stop that cripple's tattling, or so help me—'

Hushed murmurs, imploring. 'Sean, little brother, it's fine. We'll be long gone, oh my babies will forget us and our evil . . .'

'It's a sin . . .'

A scuffle followed, the sound of a landed punch and a cry in pain.

Then snuffled sobs, a woman's careful soothing.

Arden groaned, and the breath required to make such a sound hurt her. A pain throughout her body, her mouth cottoned, her head whirling still. She tested her arms, and they would not give. The tower was cold, the fire had gone out.

The woman's voice again. 'Leyland . . . She's waking up.'

'Hold her arm, it's hard enough getting the vein.'

A pain jagged sharp and centred now, in the crook of her

arm, which hung over the armrest of Jorgen's rocking chair. And a face in the centre of her rapidly tunnelling vision, cragged and pale. Leyland Tallwater. He smelled bad, the vinegar sweat of a man in high crisis. She recognized the tight bun and Hillsider features of Helena. The linen bandages that must have been taken from Arden's kit now bound her tight to the chair. Her heart beat fast in her chest. *Blood loss*, she thought with an odd clarity. *I'm losing too much blood.*

Through the veil of her lashes she saw the needle in her arm, almost black with clots, the metal lying hot and heavy upon her skin as the snake in the Garden of Eden might do, after feasting on the blood of . . .

. . . *no, wait, wrong story, why can I not think straight*, she thought. *Speak to him, Arden. Make him stop.*

'Leyland,' the woman pleaded, 'this isn't right. Magistrate Harrow was too insistent. It's a bad idea. I don't trust him.'

He ignored her, and strange again, Arden did not much care, for a lassitude had filled her, a warmth rising and rising, her eyesight almost vignetted in black clouds, a beautiful way to die.

Lucian Beacon appeared from the gloom of her past, comforting his young daughter when she first saw a horse put to sleep on the Cotton Wharf after a crane had snapped and broken the poor creature's legs. Her father had let Arden press her face into his chest, smell of clove-spice and lantern oil while she heard the pitiful whinnying turn to snuffles and silence.

She is not in pain, my darling. The most humane way to kill an animal is by bleeding them out, her father in her mind told her.

Her heart had not the blood to pump, went into a fluttery tachycardia, and she imagined herself back in the moot of her third trial, the rebuilt royal Wharf and the test cubes all lined up with the thickest glass, each cube as thick as three encyclopedias bound together . . .

She forced herself back into the present, scared of drowning in the bituminous murk of time. If she disappeared, she would be gone forever.

Convince them, Arden. Convince them not to take this path . . .

If the patriarch would not speak, then maybe the woman who lingered nearby would.

'Helena,' Arden implored breathlessly, 'tell him to stop.'

Helena, or the blurry shape that was most probably the Tallwater wife, waited for her expressionless father-in-law's approval before saying apologetically, 'We need to buy our way onto the Islands, Lightmistress. It is imperative we do this. A penny for the Old Guy. Your blood . . . They say a pint of incendiary *ignis* blood is worth its weight in gold. The Magistrate said so.'

'But it won't work. My blood . . . I'm *malorum*, not strong . . .'

Leyland did not pause in his work. 'Helena,' he warned. 'Stop talking to her.'

Helena withdrew out of sight. 'She's dying, Leyland. It's wrong to kill, even one of *them*.'

'Do you think I care, woman?' He tightened a belt at Arden's bicep. 'Here. It's full. Put it with the others.'

Arden heard the scratch of a metal lid on a glass thread, saw in the vision-tunnel Helena Tallwater slide the mason jar into a crate of similarly filled containers. In a quirk of reasoning she counted a full crate. Three jars were already dark with congealing blood.

Arden gathered enough spit to say with all the corrosive effort she could muster, 'Were your grandchildren's bodies not enough for coin, Leyland Tallwater?'

Leyland glanced away. Oh, he had tried it, tried it! Had offered all three most probably, and in the Black Rosette they'd have cursed him, and kicked him out.

Then Mr Harrow would have come, pickled with revenge and grieving. *'I have a solution for your problems. Take a boat to the lighthouse. A pint of sanguis blood will get you passage to the rockblood isles.'*

'You people with your contaminated blood, your sin, your

cheap labour,' Leyland Tallwater growled. 'The sins of the world are upon you. It is a good thing, to allow you to die.'

He released the tourniquet. Her blood leapt into the jar.

No

No

No

She might as well have said no to death. The vision-tunnel closed. The pain left her. She was floating now, with the old devil, with death.

Death who smelled of salt and kraken oil, death who said her name through a cave of utter darkness, *Arden, Arden, oh God.*

No.

22

I saw him passing

death

Death, who scooped her up in his arms and took her into the storm.

death

Death, who took her to the water's edge, yelling her name, telling her to wake, to wake, to stay awake by the devil and the deep blue sea.

death

This was not a watery hell, but a tempest surrounding her, this was the water come alive from the monstrous call of blood, this was the story they told of the Rivens on the promontory who were half-kraken, half-man, spawned in unholy congress with the monsters of the deep.

Save her, a voice screamed into the storm. *Save her.*

Mr Justinian saying, *I've seen him take the corpses from the beach. Caught him in the act.*

Her bloodied dress torn off by the ocean. A venom flowing into her, replacing what the Tallwaters had taken, filling her with a brutal vigour, not blood, but something else. She jerked and shuddered in the arms of Jonah Riven.

She gave herself over to wildness, was beset by a hunger that burned through her, and in the tempest of the storm she clawed open Mr Riven's shirt, went to kiss him upon the sparse rough hair of his pale broad chest, the straining cords of his neck, the hollow of his throat, she wanted him with an urgency she had never wanted anything before.

'Arden, it is the storm,' he protested, but could he not feel it, could he not be a part of this terrible ritual that had yanked her back from the precipice of —

death?

And he could not contain himself for they were both awash in the surge and with a cry of despair he gave in to the moment. He returned Arden's kisses with hard, angry, inexperienced kisses of his own, tore away the silk that bound her breasts and sucked electrical sparks of pleasure from her skin and nipples with a mouth that knew nothing of a woman's body except what instinct gave him. They fell against the stony shore in a desperate embrace, riven by inhuman passions, raw ichor, blood and all the combined essence of the ungodly creatures summoned from the benthic horrors below.

Arden tore at the last of her undergarments before pushing down the kraken leather strides of Jonah Riven, clutched him close, ground her quim against the curled hair of him, dizzy with savagery. He was hot and proud, the thing that would bring her such relief, he slid reflexively along the channel of her thighs before pushing inside her with such a rush of sensation she cried out from it and he froze, said her name, his face with desolate surrender.

'*Gods, if you wish for me to stop, I will, I will . . .*'

But she couldn't stop. She wanted to speak. A small horrified part of her wanted to say, Jonah, you are right, this is not us, this is not me. But the monster he had summoned only wanted satiety, wanted the one who had called it from darkness, and he smelled so good and he smelled of blood and salt and skin, and she embraced him among the stones of the beach and each time he plunged into her body the storm-sea heaved about them in turn. He clung to her as a drowning man might fight an ocean for driftwood, thrust clumsily upwards again and again, following an instinct as old as time but no less terrible. His belly slapped against hers as his rhythm increased in urgency. She accepted him in all ways, inside her body, his chest rasping against her own, the heat of his exposed throat. Spent himself, hot, hot, into her cold body. The phosphorescence of the water around them became clear and he beheld her with such a vaulting, desperate emotion.

The moment passed in fits and starts. His strength left him he shuddered and fell away, still gasping for breath. She reached for his hand and he grasped hers.

They lay there in the cold lip of the shore as the rain fell upon their naked bodies and the monster, the old devil himself, withdrew, having done the thing the blood-bound man had asked of him and saved the woman he . . .

Book Three: Blood

23

Sing to me

Sing to me, love
Of all that was
When once we walked upon golden fields
Sing the sky, love
Sing down the stars
My virtue will be your reward.

Silly old song. Arden had never cared for it. The gramophone scratched as the record ended. She could hear it in the next room. A hand wound it up again, and another record of much the same kind of music began playing again.

But maybe Mr Riven considered the song a favourite. In which case, she did not mind. She hadn't considered him romantic before. It didn't quite fit with the brutish idea she had formed of him in those months separated. In a way, she rather welcomed this new material in her patchwork image of the man.

Shadows dabbled across Arden's eyelids, sunlight hitting the surface of water. Through her closed eyelids she sensed dawn light, with all the colour of fire. She could smell kraken oil and aromatic ashes, a pleasant ambergris perfume not so far away, a more utilitarian soap, old wood, and her own body, a crust of blood and organic matter over smouldering embers.

Her senses were more alive then than they had ever been. Her legs slipped in a nightdress of silk, her feet in between cotton sheets. She rolled over and the hedonistic warmth gave way to her injuries. Arden touched herself carefully, explored the abrasions between her legs and the tenderness between her thighs.

Well then, no fever-dream, what had happened the night before. The insides of her thighs smarted terribly, but not as much as the crook of her—

Arm

'Devilment!'

Arden sat up with a gasp, clawing at her memory of tubing and touched nothing except the ghost of a bruise.

She had been deposited into the chintzy surrounds of an unfamiliar room. A feminine room, bedecked in creature comforts and faded pastel colours, patterns that were nearly white where the morning sunlight hit them day in and day out.

Bellis, Arden thought. She had stayed here once. Before that, another woman's room, maybe generations of women, who had knitted the bed covers and crocheted the curtains, had embroidered a tapestry on the wall, where krakens and plesiosaur frolicked about an archipelago of islands.

The Sainted Isles. The birthplace of the Rivens.

The bed was narrow, befitting a girl and not a wife. A single bed, with a *Stella Maris* star above the plain bedhead. Upon the yellowing crochet of the side table, a Fiction Vulgate Bible bound in fish-skin. Her goose-down pillow still felt damp from the towel that must have bound up her salted hair. The simple nightdress clothed her inside out and back-to-front.

Wincing from her bruises she climbed out of bed and moved for the door.

The music came from behind it, and suddenly it made Arden nervous. She had shared something miraculous and dangerous with Jonah Riven. Had known him intimately.

256

'Jo—'

The door opened, and the Harbourmistress' son, David, stood there with a porcelain water-jug and a string bag full of clothes.

'Oh . . . David,' she corrected herself. 'Mr Modhi. I thought Mr Riven would be the one to greet me.'

'Goodness, Mx Beacon, Lightmistress,' the Harbourmistress' boy stammered, trying to avert his gaze, for the raw silk nightdress was threadbare and tight. 'I didn't mean to wake you up, Mr Riven said you would sleep more and that I should bring you some clothes and a jug of hot water to, *um*. To wash.'

'Give it here,' she said, her early-morning fancies dashed into reality.

'Be careful of the jug, the water's hot. I boiled it only a few minutes ago.'

'I will be careful.'

'There's a bath, but Mr Riven says it takes a long time to stoke the boiler. You'll need to make do with this for now. Call if you need more . . .'

Arden flashed him an impatient smile and closed the door.

She retreated into the room. Sure enough, a small, simple bathroom adjoined the bedroom. It had a claw-footed bath that – from the maker's mark on the enamel – had long been appropriated from a much fancier Clay hotel. To top off the small luxuries there was even a halfway-modern water closet that actually flushed. Arden wanted to weep with the joy of facilities that were not in essence holes in the ground.

All this was here, and she had imagined Mr Riven living in a ruin!

She washed herself as best she could, the salt from under her arms, her throat and hair, between her breasts and legs, tried not to think of Jonah Riven there, his hands his mouth, his yearning body, and found no true pleasure in the thought, for his act wove a coarse thread through the warp and weft of the Tallwaters' attack.

It is the remains of the night, she told herself. *Whatever poison had brought me back from near death, it still courses through me.*

Clean as she could possibly be in the circumstances, Arden emptied out the string bag on her bed.

A never-worn lady's bloomers and chemise, slippery with salmon-coloured silk, still with faded Clay Capital shop-tags tied with string. Not her size, of course, they would fit tight rather than loose as intended. She wondered who they'd been bought for in the beginning? Maybe not Bellis, they seemed last century's fashion. Another woman perhaps, one who had died.

The dress, though, belonged to Arden. The best blue one from her signal-keeper's graduation, torn away by the sea on that day she had come to find Mr Riven with the plesiosaur child. She rubbed the broadcloth against her cheek, before sliding the dress over her head, fastening the release-panels back into their origami of folded fabric, and pulling on her borrowed shoes.

The rest of the lodge was constructed from the same basalt stone as the church ruins, and simple in its layout, so it took Arden very little time to locate Mr Riven in the stone kitchen, shirtless, back to her, trying to sew together a split eyebrow in a slice of morning sun. The piece of silvered mirror before him reflected his face back to her, but was too tarnished for him to see where he should go with the needle. His hands shook with exhaustion.

She considered the mottled skin of his half-tattooed back, the chevrons following his spine. Whatever healing had been done to her, it had taken a toll on him.

'Do you want some help?'

He turned to Arden. Bruise popping in the hollow of his eye, one cheek hard and white.

Arden ran her hands nervously though her thick dark curls, suddenly aware how different she must be to Bellis Harrow, the dissonance she must present to Jonah Riven, and then hated that she should care.

'I'm not being vain with such a tiny injury,' he said, holding the offending needle in front of him. 'I've decided I'd rather not be quite as fearsome as I'm made out.'

'It would take more than a cut to make you fearsome, I'm afraid.'

He poked at his eye with the needle once again, and she sighed.

'Oh, give it here. You'll make yourself blind. I might be rubbish with a needle but at least I can see what I'm doing. Come, sit.'

He did so, and she laid her hand on his warm shoulder, and the night came back to her in flashes of lightning and breath. He trembled beneath her touch, the terror of a wild thing cornered.

'Head back,' she said. 'Careful now, the iodine will sting.'

The crown of his head against her belly, and like it had been when she had tended the wounds at his chest, he did not wince at the needle's entry. Older scars pocked his brow. His lost expression reminded her of a child, a pale craggy child, asleep to fever dreams. She would have caressed the bad thoughts away had their relationship followed such warm currents, but the union had been consummated in violence, and they were in the cool frost now.

A pair of neat stitches in his brow, and ends clipped with a small knife. A daub of antiseptic honey and brown paper.

'There,' she quipped with pathetic humour. 'You are beautiful again.'

'And you've recovered.'

'David is alive too. It's been a busy night for all of us.'

'He's tougher than he seems. From what he said the Tallwaters took both him and your stormbride from the harbour in your boat.'

'Oh! Mr Riven, I didn't realize. He never said . . .'

'The lad's modest, I'll give him that. Escaped them and made his way onto shore to raise the alarm. He might not have blood talent, but he's an excellent swimmer.'

'And Chalice Quarry? They took her too?'

Mr Riven shook his head. 'David says she jumped from the boat first. She was bound, hand and foot, and sunk like a stone. I'm sorry.'

Arden twined her fingers together and fought down a wave of anxious illness. Without Chalice she would be utterly alone. 'Oh. Chalice. Oh.'

Upright, he pulled a bubbling kettle from the stove and poured tea into enamel cups. She smelled ginger and coast-sedge, the aroma of the saltwood shavings in the fireplace, and Mr Riven's warm skin. Pleasant smells, yet with the probability of Chalice's death they were perfumes of despair.

'If it helps, when the tide turns *Saudade* will be free of the kraken dock. I can take you to Mx Modhi. I must return her son, anyway. If by chance your stormbride made . . .' he drifted off, not wanting to give her false hope. 'Whatever happened, we will find out for certain.'

'Thank you.' She heaved a breath, to calm herself so she might think usefully rather than all a-jangle. She took the offered cup of tea. 'There's a full story in last night, Mr Riven. They were stealing my blood.'

'*Penny for the Old Guy*. Passage onto one of the islands.'

'I don't remember all of what they said, but it sounded . . . it sounded as if *Mr Harrow* had suggested it.'

Mr Riven would not meet her gaze. 'Then it was not personal. He was trying to hurt me through you. The Tallwaters were merely an opportunity. Incendiary blood is worth more than kraken oil in some places.'

'Not *my* dim blood. They'll find that out soon enough.' She paused. Gathered her thoughts and said shyly, 'Then you put me in the water with the kraken. Or some . . . thing? I felt it. I felt myself dead, and coming back.'

A movement outside the bay window captured his attention more than anything in this kitchen. The delicate light made him fragile, fine-boned. His skin was pale as a cuttlefish skeleton, his body dreadfully vulnerable despite Mr Riven's Fictish vigour and the terrifying ink. The memory of the night wrapped around them in Sargasso strands, strangling them, pulling them into dark, sunless places.

'*Aequor profundum*. My mother called it *the trick*. She used it once, on my uncle when a bar fight nearly killed him, and I heard it rumoured . . . she brought my cousin Jeremiah back from the dead when he was attacked by a *maris anguis* on his initiation day. A sea-serpent bit him almost in half. Many a time I wished it had finished the job.'

Arden pondered on what he's told her. 'Healing someone from that bad an injury . . . it's a sanguinity, Jonah!'

'It's a shadow sanguinity,' he corrected her. 'Monstercalling is our talent.'

'Yes, but an endowment like that on top of what you already have . . . why, something like that would have the Eugenics Society all over it. They'd either collect everyone up to Lyonne or . . .'

She trailed off.

Or.

She did not want to say it, because it was impossible. The *or* that had suddenly come to her was *death*. The *or* was an entire family killed in a night and the blame placed on a child meant to die in a Harbinger Bay hulk prison.

But even that conclusion made no sense to her. A healing talent was harmless. Shadows and permutations were unwanted, but never engendered more than sterilization, at the most. Certainly, shadows spoiled the ledgers, interrupted the inheritance line, but the Eugenics Society were pragmatic about the necessity of evolution. If something new and useful were to appear in the sanguineous lineages, it would come first as a shadow. If it were dangerous in the way most useful talents were, then they'd find ways to manage the risk.

She could think of nothing so hazardous that an entire bloodline should be wiped out.

Mr Riven studied her. 'You're trying to find an excuse.'

'Excuse me?'

'An excuse, for what I did to them. When I killed my family. Hoping the blame is elsewhere, on Lyonne. But it's not, Arden.

261

The blame is mine. I was young, I had no control over my talent, and they all died. That is what I live with.'

'I wasn't . . .' she started, then took a breath. 'How often have you used this *aequor profundum*?'

He frowned. 'Not often. I never had a skill at it like Thalie did. The biggest thing was the plesiosaur pup.'

'Yes, the pup! I saw it that day, on the beach when I had almost drowned.'

A blush appeared on his neck and cheeks, as he remembered her in her gold silks. 'I'm sorry, what I did last night. It was a violation. But it never felt so strong as last night, when I used it on you.'

'Are you ashamed of saving my life?'

'No. Of course not.'

'Then why speak of it as sin and not miracle? What you did was miraculous, was epic and wonderful and incredible and can I not just thank you for that? Why must it be so difficult?' She laid her hand on his. 'Jonah, I want to thank you.'

He took her hand and gently placed it away.

'You are alive. I need no gratitude. But we cannot deceive ourselves by thinking there was any emotional truth in what happened when I brought you back.'

The moment had passed. Mr Riven had thrown up a wall about himself, and busied himself with his shirt and his boots.

Arden needed to get away. 'I will wait at the dock for the tide to come up. It's too stuffy in here.'

'All right.'

She pretended to leave casually, but once out in the quadrangle had to sit and gulp deep breaths. Was not love or desire that had moved Mr Riven to take her upon the beach, only an urge in his blood like Bellis towards her petrolactose islands, a deceptive instinct. He felt nothing towards Arden at all.

The morning sun had been but a fleeting apparition of a pleasant day. Outside, the clouds returned in slabby formations, grey and formless as the rock of the promontory, and the wind blustered about with an old crone's natter.

Chief waddled up to her on arthritic legs, snuffling his grey snout at her skirt hem.

'I have nothing for you, pup,' she said. 'If I had known, I'd have waited until your master cooked his breakfast before leaving.'

'Ah, he's already had a feed, the little reprobate.'

She had not noticed David Modhi nearby. The youth wore some cast-off Riven clothes that dangled off his thin shoulders. Behind him, upon a washing line, the dress from last night hung on a recycled line of telegraph cable.

'Earning your keep with the laundry, I see?'

He gave a self-conscious gasp. 'Oh Mx Beacon, I didn't see you naked . . . in any disgraceful way. After Mr Riven took you off the beach he, *um*, tended you with the door shut.'

'It is no concern. It really is not.' She re-tied her belt, and gathered her strength for her conversation ahead. 'So tell me. How did the Tallwaters come to have my boat?'

'Yesterday afternoon,' he said. 'I saw them in the harbour. Just hanging about. I should have known some nefariousness was afoot earlier. I sometimes talk to Sean Ironcup on the eventide, and normally he is a fine conversationalist, but yesterday . . .' David sighed and shrugged. 'Sean seemed distracted. I would even say ashamed almost, as if he did not wish to be seen with me.

'I could not find Mother anywhere, and at the time I was glad of it. She doesn't trust the Tallwaters, and doesn't like me talking to Sean.'

'But she still must have impressed some suspicion on you, David.'

'Yes. I saw the senior Tallwater and Captain Cormack speaking with each other. Deviously. Making a deal. I heard your name. I suspected they were up to no good.' He dipped his head, blushed again. 'I meddled with Captain Cormack's ship. They were going to hire it and I scuppered the engine before anyone could be the wiser.'

'Quick thinking, Mr Modhi.'

'It didn't work. I hadn't thought it through. They saw Miss Quarry come into harbour and decided to take *Fine Breeze* instead. I can't remember much of the rest, only waking in the bilge well of *Fine Breeze,* a prisoner, with Chalice. Sean made apologies, but he is in thrall to Leyland Tallwater. They all do what he says.'

'And Chalice? What happened to her?'

'Um.' He frowned. 'We listened to them talk for a while. They intended to exchange us for some payment in the Isles.' David's eyes shone. 'Blood or enslavement, one or the other. Devils. Miss Quarry jumped into the water fully bound rather than contemplate such a thing as slavery. I was not brave enough at first. Afterwards Sean Ironcup retied my bonds loose enough to slip. I waited until we got close to the promontory shore before I bailed.'

'You were still brave, lad. It is just as brave to wait and get a better sense of the situation. You are alive and Chalice is—'

A ferocious clanging from the waterfront interrupted their talk, and Arden winced. Whatever could have made such an inopportune noise?

A dark shape loomed through the sea-fog. The wrong shape for a boat, and yet familiar all the same.

'What is that coming in to the pier, David Modhi? Even I can't work it out.'

David didn't wait. He took off in a run. The fog congealed and shivered as Arden followed him down the rocky path to the promontory dock. The clanging grew louder, and now Arden could discern the distinct shape of a gable roof and a large whitewashed sign.

A sign bearing the words *VIGIL HARBOUR.*

David reached the dock first. He did not show the same surprise as Arden did, and watched with weary defeat as the entire harbourside of Vigil carved through the water towards the promontory shore.

'Why, Master Modhi, is that your mother's houseboat adrift with half the harbour with it?'

A chorus of signal buoys clanged piteously, having been swept up along the unstoppable force of a hundred feet of pontoons, while decking and glass floaters and at least a dozen skiffs and dinghies dragged along behind in an ignominious bridal train.

His upper lip and baby moustache trembled. 'Mother has come.'

'And she brought her responsibilities with her!' Arden seized up a coil of rope. 'Quick, David, help the juggernaut dock or it'll overshoot us and head into the cliff.'

David ran down the long length of the jetty, stopping only to make certain Arden could keep up, before sprinting off again. The fog came with them, turning the world white. The houseboat bell rang through the pea soup. Arden took the coil from David, tossing it out to the dark-hooded figure leaning out of the window of the houseboat.

'Got it!' a familiar voice barked. 'We're pulling her in.'

Suddenly Arden saw the figure in the window, the red hair, the stout shoulders.

'Chalice!' Arden held out her hand, gasping, and the hood reappeared, with Chalice's dear freckled face beneath it. Their fingers met and clasped.

'You're alive, Arden?' Chalice could not have been more startled if a spectre had made an appearance on the dock. 'Alive and not a ghost? Oh my, I feared the worst!'

'Mr Riven saved me!'

'Ah now, that is good,' she said somewhat uncertainly.

Once David secured the houseboat, Mx Modhi came out of the wheelhouse in a flurry of denim, waxcloth and a sou'wester upon her frowsy grey hair. She grabbed her tall son's head, clutched him down to her massive bosom to rub his back and murmur affectionate things, and David swooned in his mother's love.

'I didn't know our house could move, Mama,' he muffled into Mx Modhi's breast.

'Kraken oil will get anything moving,' the Harbourmistress replied. 'And those reprobates that kidnapped you would have experienced the full extent of my ire had I caught them! After all the liniment I wasted on that brother? Why, they even left their children behind in their rush to get to the Islands. Three little orphans now.'

'I'm so sorry about losing your boat, Arden,' Chalice said as she climbed onto the pier. 'I was rather outnumbered, so fell back on my one useful skill of slipping knots.'

'Boats can be replaced. The priority is that we are all safe and well. And you, Chalice! I am pleased to see you, so very much!'

'Darling, you are whole and untouched! I nearly had conniptions, hearing them talk,' Chalice said. 'How they intended to take your blood. *All of it.*' Chalice took Arden's shoulders and gazed upon her with such fiercely relieved emotion, in any other circumstances Arden would have thought Chalice in love. 'I believed I would come here to find you dead and drained, and my heart was breaking. I didn't know what to do. But look, not a scratch!'

'Chalice, you find me more alive than ever.'

'I've never been so happy to be wrong. By the devils, I hope the Tallwaters meet their maker with an eternal debt.'

Arden shrugged. 'Seems a Tallwater trait. Making bad decisions without thinking it through. Six pints they might have taken from me, but all they'll get is some dim *malorum* blood that will barely feed a flame. The Old Guy won't get a penny.'

Chalice dropped her hands.

'What?'

Arden blinked. 'Six pints . . . Or four. I can't quite remember. It seems a lot, it does! But as I said, Mr Riven rescued me. Some . . . ah, local folk medicine.' She declined to say more, as a protective feeling encouraged her to silence. 'As much as it's uncharitable to wish harm on those wretched fools, the Islanders will punish them well enough when they discover the rotten deal they've made.'

Arden expected Chalice to nod with the same agreement and joy. In fact, she would have expected any other reaction except for Chalice to turn an odd shade of green, open then close her mouth speechlessly. When at last words came out she croaked, 'Devils, did you say they took six *pints*?'

'Chalice, whatever is the matter?'

Chalice gave a grimace, too shocked to be entirely coherent. She grabbed Arden's wrist, hard enough to hurt, and thrust up the sleeves on her dress. The needle marks were still there, faint from her impromptu miracle.

'Oh no . . .'

Arden yanked her arm away from the stormbride's manhandling. 'Stop it! This is most unpleasant.'

Mx Modhi let out a rumble of disapproval. 'The thieves bled her. Well, here is an unmitigated disaster.'

'Why is it a disaster?' Arden snapped. 'It's only *malorum* blood. It's of no danger to anyone except the fools who want to trade it.'

Chalice clutched the hair at her temples, shook out her hands, looked about as if the solution to her crisis could only come in the form of a miracle. 'By God. By *God*. We should *never* have sent you here.'

A familiar loom of disaster came upon Arden. All of a sudden she didn't want to ask what it was that afflicted Chalice so. Her deep familial sense for trouble weighted like stones in her belly.

Mx Modhi dug her pipe out of her dress pocket, packed the bowl with tobacco with the insouciant submission of a deckhand having been told that the ship is about to founder after he has spent the day being ignored about the leak.

'Go on then, Quarry,' the Harbourmistress drawled. 'You might as well tell the woman. Mr Lindsay will tell her himself soon before he has to put his own head on the disciplinary chopping block.'

'Tell me *what*? And how do *you* know Mr Lindsay, either of you?'

Cornered now, Chalice reluctantly pulled the pewter Guild

triangle from around her neck. The metal moved on a hinge. Her coin began as triangular locket, the symbol of her assistant profession.

Once flipped about, the triangle became a rose crucified upon thorns.

A rose on thorns, just like the pin Mr Lindsay wore. Just like the bands on the messenger pigeons in the roost. Symbol of the Lyonne Order and Nomenclatures, forever pruning, forever gardening.

Arden recoiled from Chalice as if she'd been knocked sideways.

'Chalice . . . you're a Lion?'

24

Do they know

Do they know how he healed me? was her first thought. *Have I just said too much about him?*

'All right. I am a Lion. Mx Modhi is a local agent,' Chalice said faintly, not that Arden was in a mood to appreciate the differences. 'She's been here a long time, keeping an eye on things for us.'

'Oh, really now.'

'And well,' Chalice said, distraught and awkward at her sudden unveiling, 'and well, this thing that has happened to you, this blood-theft, it's quite unexpected. It wasn't supposed to happen. We will handle it, of course. It can't be helped. But your placement here is ended, I'm sorry.'

'Excuse me, did you say *ended*?'

'Yes, Mx Modi can take you back to Garfish Point. You can be on a train back to Clay tonight.'

Arden reeled back, stunned from Chalice's unveiling, and the urgency of her. 'I'm not leaving, Chalice. The flame still needs me—'

'It wasn't for flame you were here! You completed your duty, but the blood . . . the missing blood is a complication we must deal with ourselves. It is safer for you to be home while we fix it up.'

'Why?'

'You just are. Safer. Please darling, the more questions you ask, the more at risk you will be.'

Arden's chest squeezed painfully as if enclosed by a mighty fist, and her breath came out in a wheeze. Was this her own leash being tightened? She would not have it.

'I'm not leaving just because you say so, Order Coin or not. The Order doesn't control my lighthouse. It's the Seamaster's Guild who do that, and I see no Guild*master* here.'

Harbourmistress Modhi chewed upon the goat-horn stem of her pipe as if in a pendulum swing between extremely bored and frightfully annoyed. 'Huh, I knew this would happen, Quarry.'

'What?' Arden snapped at her.

'Postmaster Harrow was in a state all day,' the Harbourmistress said. 'You must have riled him up good and proper with your lustful gallivanting with Mr Riven, for him to suggest that the Tallwaters do what they did. The worst possible scenario.'

'Then have the Order send *Mr Harrow* away in punishment!' Arden snapped at them. 'Or does he control the Lions when it comes to murder just like he controlled them when it came to his daughter?'

She pretended to brush a loose strand of hair from her face. Was in reality the tears of frustration and anger. She had probably just condemned Mr Riven to the Lions, all but confirming his shadow sympathies. They'd have him sent for a castration, have him returned to this coast neutered, like a show-dog born with a confirmation defect.

She turned around and stomped away, unable to bear looking at her deceitful stormbride.

Who was not a stormbride at all.

Chalice ran after Arden, her Order medallion clinking around its hinge. 'Arden! Please, darling, listen to me. I meant what I said. It's all gone wrong, we should never have sent you here. But you were the only one who could perhaps break through Mr Riven's defences around Bellis. Others have tried and failed, you were our final chance!'

'You should have sent a *whore*!' Arden shouted back. She tore off the krakenskin coat, threw it on the ground so the eyes winked up at her in the dull day. 'Then Mr Justinian could gloat about *two* murdered whores!'

Chalice stumbled behind in a punch-drunken trot. Arden moved too quickly up the slope to the lighthouse for Chalice to catch up. She remained outside while Arden made a deliberately slow and thorough check on the measuring instruments and the flame of her misbegotten tower, and shed angry tears all over the ledger paper, making the ink run where they fell.

'Please, let me fully explain what is happening here,' Chalice pleaded up the column from the doorway, her voice echoing off the walls.

'You just wait your turn!' Arden yelled back. 'The Lyonne Order can just wait before they prostitute me out for another trick.'

'They are not—'

'Lies! Lies, Chalice, why the Order brought me here like bait-meat for my neighbour's memory. It was worse that you lied about it yourself, for I *trusted* you!'

'I didn't know about that, darling! I didn't know!'

When Arden finished her duties and left her lighthouse, Chalice was not there.

The tattered semaphore flags snapped in the wind. A chain rattled against the flagpole. Arden found her stormbride sitting miserably on the cement base, head in her hands, rocking in her ballooning waxed canvas skirts. Arden's krakenskin lay across Chalice's knees. Against her chalky-white face, Chalice's hair had darkened with sea mist and sweat.

She had cried enough. Only a slow exhaustion upon her, and the cold.

Chalice held out the jacket. Arden put it back on.

'I thought you'd go back to your Lion business,' Arden grumped.

'Go back to what? My heart is broken. I care for you very much.'

'I wonder if you people really care, or just fret over the outcome of your conspiracy.'

'My love, I honestly didn't know what Mr Lindsay planned for you. All my orders were, look after the Lightmistress while she completes her task. You were at the gates of hell and harm here, and I was meant to keep you safe.'

'Well, you didn't do that very well, did you? I was attacked in my own lighthouse by people completely *not* Mr Riven, while you were entertaining Mr Sage and plucking herbs!'

'Was not Mr Riven I was meant to protect you from!' Chalice wailed back. 'I was to protect you from bloody *Bellis Riven*!'

After Chalice followed her unexpected disclosure with a little sob that was less sadness and more relief that she didn't have to pretend any more, the stormbride collected herself. Despite the seeming ridiculousness of her statement Arden felt pity enough towards her contrite traitor that she returned to the outdoor fireplaces and put the kettle on the stove. She bid that Chalice sit near the fire.

'So, if I have a cat-fight and roll around in the dirt with Jonah's wife you're to jump in and rescue me, then? She going to return and gossip about me to Mrs Sage in the market place, hmm?'

Chalice did not take kindly to mockery. 'It is no laughing matter. Bellis is not to be trifled with.'

'Ah, so she can manage herself. Mr Riven is not needed for her protection at all. For a moment Mr Lindsey almost had me fooled.'

Wearily, Chalice shrugged. 'I was not privy to such detail. Mr Lindsay gave me my duties and I did them as he asked,' Arden said bitterly. 'Humiliated myself. Forced by loneliness into love with a man who cannot love me back. But Mr Riven's wife is oblivious to my existence and I am as much concern to her as a butterfly flapping its wings on the other side of the world. So elucidate me on your cry of *protection*.'

Chalice swallowed, and spoke. 'You asked me once why the Eugenics Society allowed Bellis to stay in Vigil after she was tested *sanguis petrae*.'

'I did. Some guff about this being Fiction, and not Lyonne. And Mr Lindsay spun me a tale of gentle nurturing. But that wasn't the reason, was it?' She sucked a breath and recalled the words from Mr Riven's mouth. *There are exceptions.*

'No. It wasn't the reason. The Society didn't know what they wanted to do with Bellis once they realized what talent she *really* had.'

'So. Your golden princess had a good old Fiction shadow.'

'*Sanguis petrae was* the shadow. By her main talent, she trammelled something else.'

Though Arden had been told so much already, a fresh chill came upon her. *Something else.* The thing that made Bellis different. That kept her from going to Lyonne. That made her dangerous to Arden somehow, that she needed a Lion chaperone. 'Spit it out then. What did she have?'

'A thing so awful, that even the Society fears it, but wants very much as well. There have been many mutterings behind closed doors that I am not privy to.'

'A thing so awful,' Arden repeated dryly. She recalled her last witnessed dock accident with the *sanguis inertiae* and the careless worker who had walked into the halo of blood-forced air. Died so suddenly there had been no blood when the *inertia* tore him to pieces a second later. She'd spent an hour chasing off the stray dogs attempting to run off with body parts, while at the same time trying to calm the stunned young man who'd had his first fatality but not his last. 'A thing so awful to keep her here.'

'You think of death, Arden, but there are things that are worse. A thousand times worse! The Society were content for a while to leave her in the Sainted Isles. But a year ago a message came from our deepest agents. Something's happened to her. Something bad. They needed Mr Riven's assistance desperately. That's all I know.'

'Why not send the Lyonne Navy and protect Bellis Riven with a thousand guns and cannons if she's so bloody vulnerable?'

'Because she doesn't *need* protection. She needs *control*.

Because Jonah Riven was able to bring her back under sufferance before, he could do it again. It's not her safety he brings at all, it's her *compliance*.'

Arden breathed in a huge angry lungful of salt air. 'On. *Oh*. So there it is. Bellis is too independent for the puppet master's strings.'

'We will all be puppets, if by chance Bellis gets your blood. Because those jars are heading towards her now, with a bunch of Clay City Hillsiders with not an ounce of sense to call their own.'

Arden waved her off. 'Dim *ignis* blood is of no value to anyone. Why would it be of value to Bellis?'

'You are *sanguis malorum*,' Chalice said flatly.

'Well yes, but—'

'You are *sanguis malorum* in a family who have never, not once, bred without strong sanguine endowments, not even your priestly cousin for all he tried to hide it. Instead, your flame is scant. How does that happen? Whoever heard of a dim Beacon?'

'Stop.' Arden's voice was cold as her fire. 'Hush now, Chalice. I saw your face when you realized my blood had gone away with the Tallwaters. Even pure *ignis* serum would not inspire such terror.'

Chalice's cheeks were almost as red as her hair, and she cast a guilty glance in Arden's direction. 'Am I not allowed to speak?'

'I know what you are going to say. You will suggest to me that I too have a shadow, and this concerns you, as I am now in danger of whatever lies over that horizon. And I will reply, if I did have another endowment, it would have shown up in testing long ago and the Eugenics Society would certainly have put it to laborious use. But they didn't, because what I have is useless.'

Chalice looked at her, bleak. 'Would you like to know what it is you have?'

Arden snatched up a cloth and put the whistling kettle aside. Its strident cry faded to splutters. A heaviness in her. Grief, almost. She had suffered muchly being *sanguis malorum*, dim of light, but at least the little fire she had was a Beacon expression, a pure talent in an honourable ancestral line measured in centuries. She had been content, with her small blue flame, her skerrick of *sanguinem ignis*, she could call it her own.

Now even that confidence was muddied by the threat of a shadow, power cut in half, less than the sum of her parts. Her future dreams of work and meaning were corroding before her eyes. *She* was corroding.

'No, Chalice,' Arden said. 'I don't think I want to know. Because you are saying that my shadow endowment was never of any value to me or the Society, but of great use to another person more cherished than me, more loved and more free. To think my blood will give her freedom, but only commit me further into servitude . . . it hurts beyond meaning.'

'Darling you have . . .'

'No, don't say a single word.'

Chalice's translucent skin crimsoned. 'If Bellis receives your blood, she will want to know its source Arden.'

'The Sainted Islands cover an area as large as Fiction. There would be tens, hundreds of thousands of prospectors and indigenes there right this minute. How in all the wide expanse of ocean is my blood going to land in one missing woman's lap?'

'Postmaster Harrow knows his daughter is out there.'

'Excuse me? Postmaster Harrow yesterday spent ten minutes cursing Jonah for harming her!'

'But not for murdering her, am I right? That man steams open every letter and correspondence that comes in or out of this town. He listens on the telegraph every night. I don't care if Gertrude Modhi says she wrote to the Lyonne Offices in code for twenty years, a child could crack those missives. Everything we know, he knows!'

Chalice stood up, and pointed an accusing finger across the waves towards Vigil. 'Mr Harrow labours under the belief of the dutiful, battered daughter, fleeing from her cruel husband. He will trust that Bellis does not yet dwell in the abyssal court of the Deepwater King. He would have told the Tallwaters how to take your blood and how to find her.'

25

No

'No,' said a third voice.

They'd been so wrapped up in their private exchange, they had not heard Mr Riven's arrival at the lighthouse. By his face, he had heard everything. Arden saw his panic. She tried to head him off as he bore down on Chalice, fists balled.

'Jonah, wait.' Arden dashed between him and Chalice. 'She hasn't said she's going to do anything.'

'She's Lyonne Order,' Mr Riven rasped. 'They've experimented and assassinated and ruined lives for centuries. They will not make a sinner of Bellis. I will not allow it.'

'That's not what—'

'Arden,' Chalice said. 'Go back to the lighthouse. Let me deal with him.'

'You don't know Bellis, *Lion*.' Mr Riven's voice dropped to a growl. 'You treat her as a mad thing needing control but you don't know her.'

'Oh, but we *do* know her, Jonah Riven. *We do!*' Chalice shrieked back. 'Jonah Riven, do not imagine for one second we believed Bellis' sweet innocent face, her delicate lies, her mental fortitude against the endowment God cursed her with! From the very beginning we saw her true sympathies and *you* enabled that, you supported her through the flowering of her abominations. *You!*'

'Chalice!' Arden shouted, too late to stop the words coming out of the woman's mouth, but Chalice, once started, could not be stopped.

'Your monstrous wife will not be much longer happy out there shuffling around some deserted island like a castaway!' Chalice continued at a wail. 'She'll not be content forever on the dregs of her power! She will turn her eyes towards Fiction, or Lyonne, and what will happen then? How deeply will her sin go? How deeply will it be your fault? More deaths upon your head, Mr Riven? More slaughter to your name?'

Mr Riven raised his fist, the whites of his eyes rolling in his face gone near-purple with rage.

'I would not strike a woman,' he said quietly, and if not for the cords straining at his neck he could have been giving confession at a church. 'Or a man less my size. But you, Madame Lion, I will say it again. You do not know Bellis. Nobody did. She was a good person and you people treated her like *shit*.'

'She would not have ever been in control of it, Mr Riven. Not ever, not even if she were a *saint*. Even you and your little healing tricks could not ever cure that wound festering in her mind. We kept her safe. We even let you out of prison so you would do your duty, and you still let her go!'

'I want you gone from this promontory, Lion,' Mr Riven said with such abyssal coldness Arden feared for his soul. No man could speak such banked-down fury without immolating on the spot. 'And gone from Vigil. All of you. You have forced this evil upon Bellis.'

'We will go only if you return to your wife and tighten the noose, Mr Riven,' Chalice said. 'Oh, don't whine that you've made a promise to stay here and leave her to her mendacities. Search your heart. You have felt it this last month, haven't you? Felt your longings sharpen, your desire for healing focus. Ever since we brought Arden Beacon here, and have you for once wondered why?'

Mr Riven's harsh gaze landed on Arden. He'd acknowledged much the same to her in Miss La Grange's boudoir.

'I never said anything,' Arden protested. 'I don't know what is going on!'

Mr Riven winced as if she'd betrayed his secret. He was a man in despair. Arden wanted to wrap her arms around him and take him down from that terrible precipice. *I did not mean for this to happen, whatever this is.*

She saw the decision in his face, the making up of his mind.

'No,' she said. 'Jonah, no. Don't go to Bellis, please.'

'I need to warn her. That blood of yours is a poison.'

Bleak and cold, he turned to leave. His strides outmatched hers. It took a while before she could catch up.

'Jonah. It's what the Lions want. To use you.' Her breaths came in short gasps. 'They would make a *slave master* of you.'

'Or will you be the master? You've *influenced* me. Somehow. I heard Miss Quarry say it. A wicked influence in your blood that Bellis must not get. Well, then. Go. Go find your safety. You've done enough damage.'

His rejection struck her as a blow. She wanted to protest her innocence, but he moved too fast to catch up, and she had to stop to catch her breath.

She barely noticed Chalice sliding alongside, speaking low and insistent.

'Arden, it is time. Mx Modhi has a boat ready.'

'No, Chalice. Don't speak to me.'

But the woman spoke despite Arden's insistence. 'Your watch here is ended, darling. We played with the fire of your shadow endowment, but we underestimated the risks of your presence when Bellis Riven was so close. Let us deal with the remains. Go on back to Vigil with Mx Modhi now, and back to Clay. You'll get your Guild degree, I promise. You'll get your airshipman lover, or any other thing you want.'

The words broke the spell. Arden turned to Chalice. 'You knew what was offered?'

'Yes.'

Arden held up a fist, clenched, daring her to come closer.

'Am I so easily manipulated, you Lion *witch*? Are these my strings? Well, I cut them now! They are cut!'

'I—'

'I'm not going home. And her name is Bellis-damn-*Harrow*. She is not a Riven. The marriage was a sham all along, and Jonah's just too damn honourable to realize it.'

Arden broke away and began to run. Chalice struggled to keep up. 'Wait, Arden, where are you going?'

Arden whirled, snarling. 'To stop him from doing something stupid. Whatever mendaciousness is going on here, he doesn't deserve that infliction.'

Arden didn't wait to hear Chalice's blessing. She hefted up her skirt hem and ran after Mr Riven.

'Jonah,' she yelled. 'Jonah, wait.'

The urgency of her footsteps made him slow down.

'What is it now?'

She gasped cold air, her lungs burning. 'Yes, there is something wicked in my blood. It was kept from me too. But we can still get the blood-jars back before they get anywhere close for any Islander to pick up. Whatever is in them, we won't endanger Bellis by letting them near her.'

'The Tallwaters already have an advantage of a day. It's almost enough.'

'If they're trying to get out to the Sainted Isles in *Fine Breeze*, they'll take nearly two days to do a trip that *Saudade* could make in less than one. You can get to them before anyone else does.'

'You'd wager ten hours on your uncle's boat?'

'*Fine Breeze* handles like a bathtub. Lyonne Hillsiders cannot sail from one side of a canal to the other without getting lost. I checked the currents earlier, they'll be pulled around the southern route, the long route along *Tempestas*. We have time.'

'The southern route?' His thoughts were so ferociously deep, even the air stilled around him.

'Check my instruments if you must. They are never wrong.'

He released a breath. 'All right. All right then. I trust your instruments.' He ran his hand through his shortened hair. 'We'll bring David Modhi,' he said. 'I need another experienced engineman if I'm going to run *Saudade* at full speed.' He turned and caught Chalice trying to make as unobtrusive an exit as possible. 'And you have a few martial tricks up your sleeve I would wager, Madame Lion. Willing enough to use them on me, before.'

Cornered, she protested vehemently. 'What, I'm not trained for that kind of fighting . . .!'

'I don't want that traitor coming with us,' Arden said.

He was not finished. 'Perhaps it would be best if you stayed behind instead, Mx Beacon.'

Even more untenable. Arden shook her head stubbornly. 'No, three people against four adults is too much. You need my help. I will not stay behind. I'm coming with you.'

Saudade was already stocked from days of kraken fishing, and ready for a good week more. Mr Riven's choice of crew, however, would prove harder to assemble.

Mx Modhi had words to say when she discovered her son had been given an offer to crew on board the black ship. Though most of her argument occurred behind the closed door of her now-floating harbour office, her disagreements rang loudly over the pier.

'I'll not have it, David. You're not going to go with him.'

'You've always hated him, Mother.'

'I'm no fool. Disaster stalks that man the same way it took his family. He'll be the end of you, David. The end!'

Arden swayed from one foot to the other, uncomfortable at hearing a private conversation so openly. Would have felt better if she could have met someone's eye and shared the awkwardness, but she could not bear to look at Chalice, and Mr Riven was in a world of his own, so all she had was the old dog, Chief, gazing expectantly up at her with his milky cataracts.

The rickety door flung open, and David escaped, wound up and fuming.

'Get back here!' Mx Modhi bellowed. 'I'm not done with you.'

The boy turned to Mr Riven, hoping for a word of support. He only shrugged, midway between thrusting a brace of harpoons into a leather quiver. 'You are eighteen years old, and a man. Your family discussion belongs to you, and the conclusion belongs to you.'

'David,' Mx Modhi warned from her doorway.

David turned about to her, panting with exultation. 'I'm eighteen. I'm a man.'

'You'll be a dead man!'

She slammed the door shut.

Chalice rubbed her hands together. 'Well then, now that that is agreed upon, I'll, ah, leave Gertrude Modhi with some instructions on what to tell Mr Lindsay and we can be off.'

'And get her to feed my dog,' Mr Riven added. 'If anything happens to me, her boy gets the boat. I have a will with the Black Rosette tavern keeper.'

Chills in her bones, and Arden tried not to linger on his words. Surely their journey would not come to that.

Once on *Saudade*, Chalice paced the foredeck, twisting her Order medal in her hands so it became a storm-spouse triangle, untwisting it to become the rose of the Order. David remained joyously active with his newfound liberty, running to secure the ship and lay the mooring ropes into neat coils.

After some barked commands to the youth, Mr Riven climbed into the wheelhouse to ignite the kraken oil engine. Blue sparkles coughed from the funnel. The side wheels churned through the water before the screw-propeller foamed up the water beneath. With the same dark, imposing grace of the creatures it hunted, the boat moved away from the dock, and at last they were in pursuit.

Although, thought Arden, it did not feel much like a pursuit. More like a tilt towards the Sainted Isles, and an inexorable slide towards doom.

26

I have come

'I have come to broach the ogre's tower.' She stood at the door to the wheelhouse and held a tin box of biscuits liberated from her own stores. 'And I bring food. It's not much, but better than dried meat and coast-limes.'

Mr Riven stood at his wheel, his attention focused on the late afternoon sea. Long golden rays of sunlight came from behind them, casing the wheelhouse shadow over *Saudade*'s bow. Despite the kicking wind, there was not such a swell on the water when the currents veered south, and *Saudade* was large enough to swallow all but the deepest troughs.

'Set it aside next to there. We'll have them with supper.' He pointed at a shelf below the wheelhouse port window, and a polished ironwood crate that held the echo box. The crate was open.

Arden peered in to watch the carbonized copper drum with its constantly oscillating needle. The needle scrawled a scratchy little line through the carbon upon the drum. At each revolution the line was re-carbonized, and the needle drew again.

'I take it Miss Quarry is not being an adequate conversationalist if you have to come to me,' he said gruffly, yet with enough welcome that Arden knew he harboured no ill will towards her.

Arden adjusted her fingerless gloves. 'I'm not really in the mood to deal with a treasonous assistant right now. I'm feeling a little adrift.' She gestured to her hands. 'These. What are they even for?'

'You didn't know you had a shadow symmetry before today, did you?'

'It seems so unlikely to be true.' Arden shook her head. 'I'm cautious about accepting anything Chalice says. The Order are well-versed in the expedient lie.'

'I did not mean to make a dishonest woman of you, Arden.'

Ah, so he'd heard as well her accusations of harlotry. Arden felt the imps of shame poking her with their tridents. 'I said things out of emotion. I was angry with Chalice. I regret not one second with you, Jonah.'

'Hmm.' Mr Riven pretended to be casual, but she could tell he was both shy and curious, and not altogether comfortable with the questions that now must be asked. 'Has Miss Quarry said what it is you trammel?'

'No. I won't give her the satisfaction. They'll find some way to exploit it! I refuse to be a tool for the Lions to use.' She stopped, and sighed. 'Oh, say it. I'm being irrational and stubborn.'

Mr Riven gave a questioning shrug, easy for him, who had admitted to two sanguinities but probably held more in his wild Fictish blood.

'You're not irrational. And don't pay any attention to anyone on Bellis and her monstrousness. She was no fool. We all made certain to find her sanctuary, and she lives there now. She is safe. You are safe, and God willing we catch up with the Tallwaters by tonight or tomorrow and put this to rest.'

'Jonah,' she started. 'What . . . what other talent did Bellis have? What made the Order so scared that they couldn't bring her to Lyonne?'

'Something very old, I think. Not seen for a long time.' He adjusted the wheel. A muscle popped in his cheek. 'Stefan knew first, before she did. Our Rector learned a lot sneaking around those libraries of prohibited books in Clays Church's catacombs. Learning about the sanguinities the Society had erased from the bloodlines. I only wish he hadn't told her what he suspected. Things only got bad after Bellis found out. Your decision to remain innocent is the right one, Arden Beacon.'

A small, shy warmth bloomed in her chest. 'Thank you. I needed to hear your blessing.'

At the sound of the scratching beside her, Arden glanced at the drum again. The needle continued to scrawl shapes on the enamelled copper. Apart from one or two shadows that might have been whales or megalodons, there was nothing of any size that could be considered her yacht. Her worries mounted. What if they didn't catch up with the Tallwaters? What if they were too late and Bellis was delivered six pints of *sanguis* blood that could . . .

That could do what? A small part of her regretted not asking Chalice for specifics, but at the time it had all been too much.

'Are you still very upset with me? For my poison blood? For my putting Bellis' mortal soul in danger?'

He glanced down, and something about her expression must have stirred his pity. Mr Riven pointed towards the horizon. 'We're still a way out from the main current. You should catch some sleep in the cabins.'

'I couldn't. Not really. It's like a wire is plucked in my mind and keeps humming, and will only get more insistent. Until all this is over. I'm scared if we don't find the Tallwaters, that something terrible will happen.'

'I won't allow it to happen.'

She wanted to kiss his rough mouth and hold him close, and have him tell her that no matter what, everything would be all right. Out there, and between them.

'Come,' he said. 'I need to show you something.'

He set the wheel to due east, then called David up into the wheelhouse from the engine room. When the young man arrived a minute later, Mr Riven gave him brief instructions.

'Keep heading in that direction, lad. Keep the sun at your

back and follow the compass east until you hit fast water, then let it take you south. Lightmistress, follow me.'

Although she'd been introduced to the wheelhouse on the morning after the Guild Ball, she hadn't been down below in *Saudade*'s cabins before. They were decked out in the same dark wood as the hull, so that it took her eyes a while to adjust to the compact, decorative surroundings. Polished brass in an angular rococo style. Lanterns set into the walls with sconces of frosted glass.

Mr Riven gestured towards a great desk, where a huge map printed on silk was rolled out from end to end, with a great thick pane of lead crystal over it. The map looked very old.

'Look,' he invited her.

Not as soon as she would have expected, given her familiarity with the area, she recognized the lands on the western edge, Fiction and Lyonne. Most ocean-current maps had the Sainted Isles well off the chart, among the sporting sea-serpents and the warnings: *Here be dragons.*

In this map of Mr Riven's, the two landmasses of Lyonne and Fiction only skirted the eastern edges. It was the three islands of the Sainted Isles that provided the map's focus, with the whirling *Tempestas* at its centre.

One island had the outline of an animal's head, the other was a system of archipelagos scattered like the pages falling from a book, and the third, the smallest and most southern, was like a woman's face in profile. *Equus, Libro, Maris.*

Equus was the largest and closest of the islands, north of *Tempestas*, with permanent storms. Arden knew Equus, for the island was where the prospectors went, drawn by the siren-song of work and wealth. It was where Bellis would have gone when she first fled, and where the Tallwaters intended to go now.

'I've never seen it in such *detail*. All the maps in Lyonne are drawn second-hand.'

'They've changed since then, with the rockblood drilling.' Mr Riven straightened it out. 'This map came with my great-great-grandfather, in the days before the automata took over Equus.'

Arden nodded. 'Every Hillfolk and street-rat in Clay knows the way into Equus. They talk about the path in taverns and in bedrooms. It's their magical land, the sunset country. The Tallwaters will be expecting the northern passage.'

'Yes, but like you said, the currents favour south this time of year. Alasdair Harrow might have found out about your blood somehow, but the land-bound fool didn't consider the *currents*. They'll flank the *Tempestas* storm wall the entire distance, and come south under it. Arden, now you tell me where it leads.'

She inspected the silk with a dome of optical glass.

'It leads to . . . Maris Proper. The southern island.' Arden read aloud: *volcanic, deserted, uninhabitable.* Grey crosshatches in the water. *Barren. Poisoned water. No Fishing.*

She looked up at Mr Riven, and met his eyes. 'It's a desert. A sea-desert! The Tallwaters won't come across anybody down there.'

Mr Riven leaned back, a sense of calm about him, as if the worry had drained away. 'I trust you now, with Bellis' whereabouts. When we knew she had to hide, Stefan and Bellis didn't go to Equus, as one would assume. They went to one of the Libro refuge islands to the north-east. Up here. There is a secret church he'd seen on his old liturgical maps.'

'That's almost three hundred miles away!'

'Three hundred miles, and safe. She lives in seclusion and solitude at an abandoned religious priory. The Lions can't find her there, and neither can her dammed father.' He nodded. 'And thank the gods, no murderous Hillsiders with six pints of sanguis blood.'

'A secret island,' Arden said. 'But why there instead of Equus?'

Mr Riven pushed the protective crystal and wrinkled the silk a little. 'She burned those bridges the first time she fled. Ran into a lot of trouble with the deepwater folk on the northern shores of Equus. She could never return after our marriage, and neither could I.'

A strange little silence came up between them. A portent of

deeper questions. 'Have you thought about what we'll do once we've got through this, and gone back to Vigil?'

'You told me. You have dreams you've dreamt all your life, Arden. If I stay with you, I fear I might stop them from coming true.'

'I don't know what my dreams are, Jonah. They changed when you put me into the ocean.'

He shook his head. 'I need to explain why I didn't want you to come along on this journey. My motives were utterly selfish. *Aequor profundum* – sometimes it doesn't work and I nearly lost you to it. I lost my family to the evil that's inside me, I . . . I thought I could manage it, and then you nearly died in my arms . . .' Another pause. 'It terrifies me, Arden, these feelings I have come to experience towards you. This loss of myself. This terror. This way that I forget all but you, even Bellis becomes like a faded memory. Would be best if I let you go.'

She took his hand then, intending to tell him to quiet himself and calm down, but as soon as he slid his rope-roughened palm into hers a visceral tremor went through her, unforgiving as a hot desert wind, and Mr Riven's blue eyes darkened in the kraken-lights.

'Arden . . .'

'Yes,' she said, and he fell upon her raised mouth to kiss her then, a moan of effort and surrender escaping him at doing so. She accepted him with a love born of desire and sadness, marvelling how lips so hard upon his face were so soft and hot upon her own, the way his tongue met her own nervously, unsure of intimacy even now, but wanting, wanting.

She wanted him. Arden fumbled for the hem of his knitted top, pulled it up and his pale chest was flushed with this startled rush of sexual quickening. She moved her hands on, over shoulders indented with muscle, a back hard with work, the ghosts of scars upon his skin, a living map of the journey he'd taken to get back to his ocean and his monsters. There was a slight ridge to his tattoos, their patterns under her fingers suggesting a sea-snake's scales.

She took his hands, those forearms rope-burned from salt scour and harpoon cable, stroked him into compliance and guided his hands to the waxed cotton covering her breasts. He felt her with silent wonderment, bent to nuzzle sparks of sensation through the cloth, panting with effort and surprise at the way his body had responded so powerfully without permission from his mind. With his busy thoughts preoccupied, she could leave him to unhook the button-eyes at her flanks, let the dress panels fall, the sleeves detach. At her encouragement, his hands slid inside her chemise, outlined her body with his slaughterman's hands, pausing only to bite soft at her lips, her jaw, attend to his own heated desires with his eyes half-shut, for the taste of her skin transported him to other worlds.

Still distracted, his thumbs brushed over Arden's nipples, causing her to murmur at the unruly shocks through her pelvis, between her legs. He pinched harder, she bit his bottom lip. She was wet. On shaking limbs they fell upon the worn carpet.

The seawater sloshed and rocked through the hull outside, growled through the black mangrove wood with the rhythm of blood through an artery. Mr Riven collected Arden up in his powerful arms and his clumsy kisses grew harder now, more confident, his ragged breath increased as the chains of his necessity pulled him so taut that his body quivered the way metal hummed in high wind.

Beyond her rush of insensate wonder, the demons in her mind still whispered. *Will he change his mind and stay?*

Too late to fret, not when her own need was a hunger that could not be slaked by mere gestures of affection alone. She unbuckled the belt at his breeches, tugged the leather tongue and let it fall away. He was already hard.

As she handled him, Mr Riven panted deep in his throat, before gasping aloud, '*By the gods, by the gods.*' Wanted to thrust into her hand, gain a portion of the pleasure denied him as a husband in a convenient marriage. The urgency was up, no time for long meanders.

She pulled aside her undergarments so that the hot length of him might slide inside her.

No gentle explorations now, no murmurs of fealty and of love. Had she not been so ready his hurried, rough entry might have been uncomfortable. She gasped as he took her, as he dug his fingers into her shoulders for support, seeking relief. He was beholden to darker spirits, the ones beneath them, all around them. He surged inside Arden with the passion of his own tide, gasping each time he moved, and each time she dug her fingers into the resisting slabs of his buttocks he cried out. His crisis became too much for him to carry and his body stiffened, the contortion of a man under the lash. He spent himself with a strangled sound, then collapsed upon Arden with a sob.

With a guilty, drunken rush of pleasure Arden climaxed in joy.

The waves whispered and muttered their secret language. The side wheels beat the water. The beams creaked. The last shudders of her own culmination left Arden in fits and starts. She put her nose into the short fuzz of Mr Riven's skull, breathing in the scent of him, sea and spice. His body still shook. Where could she put her emotions? He had not wanted to stay with her, and the devil knew how many men had been content with a roll in the hay before moving on to other lovers.

He softened inside Arden's body and his breath lost its panting rhythm, but otherwise Mr Riven made no movement to detach himself from their embrace. His weight upon her had a comfort she did not expect. By now she'd have tipped her previous lovers off and would be stepping into her dress, one eye firmly upon the exit. Jonah Riven she could not bear to let go.

'So, lost your bones, monster caller?' A little levity she tried, to cover her pinching, nervous heart. She dared not move, lest he slip out entirely, and she lose this tenuous, intimate connection. The lights slipped over the sweat of his pale, flushed skin, and the moment took on a deep gravity.

He did not reply, only rose on his elbows, and his gaze scraped over Arden's face, trying to read her for deceptions, work out why he'd been so easily compromised, why Bellis had been supplanted in his affection by Arden's presence. If she satisfied him, he gave no sense of it.

'What's wrong, Jonah?' she asked.

'*Saudade*,' he said, 'is a word in Old Fictish. There is no equivalent in Lyonne for the feeling of *saudade*. To miss something, to yearn, to remember a moment that might not have existed.'

'I have felt this, though my language could not name it.'

Mr Riven nodded. His thumb caressed her shoulder, her arm, placed a small kiss after it, the kind one might lay upon the body of a saint. She trembled at the juxtaposition there, his rough chin with two days' growth, his lips swollen from kissing and so soft. She envisioned those lips in other places, saying words that she longed to hear.

'If my family had not died, if I had not been sent to prison, perhaps I could have made a little fortune on the coast. Perhaps I might have gone to Clay Portside as a young man, and met the lighthouse keeper there. I hope she might have allowed me to court her.'

Arden touched his face with tenderness, wanting to wipe away the sorrow lines so deep-set within. The people of Fiction always aged beyond their years. There was a coarseness to them, the way a leather might bleach in the sun and become hard. Was that Jonah's fate, if he survived this journey?

'There are many lighthouse keepers in Portside, and I was only good for signals before my uncle died. But I would have gladly allowed the mysterious and handsome man from Fiction to court me.'

Her words only drove him into a deeper despair. Arden reached to kiss him again, and this time there was a bittersweet taste to his kiss-abraded lips, a regret for what they could have shared if the world had not ridden roughshod between all the chances that might have allowed them to meet in earlier, more hopeful times.

He grew hard again within the embrace of her body, and

moved with the aching tenderness of a farewell. Arden held on to him in the silent terror of their eventual parting, but she could not stay motionless, and she jerked and quivered with her second climax. He grasped her hips, her thighs, finished with a final half-dozen grunting, ragged strokes. Oh, Mr Riven, still too inexperienced to maintain those rhythms of love into that moment when desire collapses with all the force of a mountain on the Day of Judgment. He slipped out of her in his zeal and with the clumsy gaucherie of a raw youth, spent his essence in the hollow between Arden's centre and thigh. The sudden expression of abject shame that came over him as he suffered the throes of a too-quick orgasm needed kissing away.

'By the sea, Arden,' he said, his breath hot and hoarse against her cheek. 'If only . . .'

He never got to finish. The engines, previously a background grumble, suddenly screamed. *Saudade* lurched sideways.

Outside, one wheel was beating air. The hull below them screeched in metallic pain.

'Devils!' Mr Riven exclaimed. 'That was a collision!'

Arden fumbled for her dress, still punch-drunk from love-making and her limbs decidedly uncooperative. 'Go. I'll be all right. You check the below deck, I'll check what's going on upstairs.'

He nodded, and as he was halfway into his breeches he dived forward and kissed her. Kissed her twice and had he done so a third time she would have damned the boat and the inrushing sea to tangle once more with Mr Riven on the carpet, would have committed desperate adultery with him as they sank into the deepest oceans.

'Later,' he said, and ran barefoot out into the corridor, heaved open the trapdoor, and descended below.

Arden took longer getting into her own dress. How complicated could it be, wearing women's clothes? But within a matter of seconds she was outside, in the wind, and seeing exactly what they had collided with.

27

A hull, upside down

A hull, upside down, floating in the water. A hull, with a bulbous, broken keel painted as red as lacquer. Chalice Quarry looked down at the wreck as if flummoxed by its sudden appearance.

'*Fine Breeze*.' Chalice Quarry nodded at Arden guardedly as she approached. 'Was already like that when David steered into it.'

Her poor capsized vessel yawed and bobbed in her death-throes. Arden panged with gladness. A terrible accident had occurred, and lives might very well have been lost, but it meant that their troubles were at an end.

Still, it presented a mystery.

'What could tip over a perfectly good boat in flat sea?' Chalice asked. 'We haven't reached *Tempestas* or Sainted waters.'

The large cloud wall of the Tempest boundary was a good ten miles away. Even hopeless Lyonne Hillsiders would have known better than to chance a little vessel like *Fine Breeze* against the storm.

'I'm willing to leave the secret to the Old Guy and never find out,' Arden said, happy enough that she did not want to curse too harshly the sea-devils who'd given her such a gift. 'She was built to come out of a capsize. This was fated.'

David stuck his head out of the wheelhouse window. 'I'm sorry, Lightmistress! I tried to avoid the boat, but she was so low down I didn't catch her until the last minute.'

Arden waved back. 'Nobody could have seen her and there's no damage, David. Don't fret.'

Mr Riven exited the forecastle trapdoor, slimed with kraken oil and pitch. He went to the balustrade to survey the water, and the capsized *Fine Breeze*. Without a word, he cleared the edge of the deck and dived into the water, disappearing beneath the opaque surface.

'What was that in aid of?' Chalice asked. She tilted out over the deck rail, but nothing remained other than whitecaps and *Fine Breeze*'s water-faded hull. 'They'd be dead for hours,' she shouted into the water.

Whatever their fate, Mr Riven had to make sure. The moralities of life upon the sea required such efforts.

Arden called for David to throw down the boarding gear, and David reappeared with a yellow canvas bag. It made a solid thump as it landed on the deck. The crossbars and knots of a rope ladder spilled out of the waxed mouth. Arden tugged on the leading end and motioned Chalice over. 'Help me get it secured to the rail.'

'I doubt there's an air pocket,' Chalice said between puffing, for the wood slats and lengths of sisal made it heavy indeed. Arden ran to help, and they jostled the boarding bag to the edge of the deck. 'We had quite a solid collision.'

They made fast the rope ladder and waited. The ship knocked up against *Fine Breeze*'s wreck.

'Surely Mr Riven should have found what he wanted by now,' Chalice said after several minutes of their watching the impenetrable water.

Chalice was right. He should have. Jorgen's boat contained only one cabin, no *Saudade* rabbit warren. The reconnaissance should have taken seconds. Not this long.

'You go in,' Arden said to David urgently. 'Something's not right.'

The young man nodded and pulled off his boots.

Just as he had set one bare foot on the ladder, Mr Riven cleared the surface with a gasp.

He had not risen empty-handed. He hauled up a body into his arms, a man limp and pale.

'Grab him,' Mr Riven shouted. 'I'm going back in.'

'Jonah—' Arden started, but he was once more gone under the water, and David was struggling with a corpse.

The woven straps that Mr Riven used to pull kraken hens onto his boat still coiled neatly upon the forecastle deck. The thick webbing barely fitted under the corpse's arms, and Arden half-expected the shoulders to detach completely with the slightest force. Dead men rarely lasted in the ocean. The hungry things consumed the flesh of the dying even before they drew their last breath.

To Arden's relieved surprise, the body held together, and with Chalice's assistance, they managed by sheer effort to haul it up onto the black wood. Arms and wrists bounced limply upon the deck. Strands of violet kelp fronded the face and shoulder in a manner more befitting a pagan burial.

She saw at once who Mr Riven had rescued.

'Sean Ironcup,' she said. 'Helena's brother.' A stabbing whirl of disgust and enmity directed towards the dead man. If she didn't have witnesses she might even have kicked him.

Chalice took Arden's arm and pulled her back. 'Easy, sister. He's more than paid for his trespasses towards yourself and God now.'

David loitered about in concern. 'Can we not resuscitate him? I've seen my mother bring back a few.' He mimed pressing down on bellows.

'Be my guest.'

With a dulled impassion she watched David kneel and put several enthusiastic puffs of air into the corpse's lungs. After a minute of compressions upon the blue sternum, the hopelessness became obvious. David sat back, panting from his exertions.

'You've done your moral duty, Mr Modhi. Go help Mr Riven,'

Arden said brusquely, as David attempted a second round of resuscitation.

'I've heard of it taking an hour.'

'He doesn't deserve a minute. Go.'

When David retreated, she knelt to formally acknowledge the thing they had plucked out of the sea. How small he seemed, now that the kick of life had gone from him, how wasted his frame, how young his face. She could almost pity him. 'I suppose we will be charged to give you a sea burial, Sean Ironcup.'

The sound of Mr Riven's voice commanding something of David brought her back to the present. If there was anything more found in her boat, she did not particularly want to discuss it with Chalice around.

'Get some cloth to wrap him,' Arden said to Chalice. 'Like you say, we have to respect the dead, especially if they don't deserve it.'

Chalice, unimpressed about being sent off the deck, returned into the dim interior of *Saudade*. Once the Madame Lion was safely ensconced and out of hearing, Arden ran to the edge of the deck, only to have David throw a glass jar at her.

Arden nearly dropped the slippery object, before clutching the blood-filled mason jar to her chest.

'Devils, David, I'd rather not be sweeping this muck off the deck.'

'Can't climb with one hand, Lightmistress.'

He pulled himself off the ladder, and Mr Riven came after. He'd turned nearly as blue with chill as the dead man. Arden snatched up one of the rough blankets used to protect the wood from rope wear and threw it over Mr Riven's shoulders. He wiped the seawater from his face and head, nodded at the mason jar.

'The Ironcup boy was trying to hide it. Fell out of his grip when I moved his body.'

'Only one jar?'

'Last one. Five broken jars in the crate, blood in the water.'

'I take it the other Tallwaters aren't down there.'

Mr Riven made a sign to the negative, ran the canvas over his torso to dry off. 'Like I said, a lot of blood. These are plesiosaur waters. A pod could easily finish off three adults in a matter of minutes.'

Arden held the jar close to her chest. The blood had jellied since last it flowed through her veins. Soon she would let it fall into the ocean. She knew that she should say a quick prayer for the dead Tallwaters now, but ended up saying one of quiet blessing to herself. It was over. It was over.

On the deck, David still fussed over the dead man. A little sense of guilt wormed into her heart. Had it been Sean Ironcup who had broken the jars? Or had he only condemned his family's share to give himself better options of survival?

They would never know, she thought. They would cast him overboard and go back to Vigil, and she would map out a new life that included Jonah Riven . . .

Mr Riven had not moved from the deck.

'Jonah,' Arden asked gently. 'Aren't you cold?'

'We have a problem.' Mr Riven tilted his chin towards the Tempest boundary. 'There's a ship in there, just beyond the Wall.'

'A boat? Prospectors gone off course maybe? We're too far south for Equus, and Maris is uninhabitable.'

'I don't know. I've not seen a Lyonne-built ship to withstand such weather. Your blood might not have been going north to Bellis, but it was definitely going to someone. Someone still waiting to collect.'

Arden nodded. She did not doubt his hunter's instincts. 'All right. We'll leave *Fine Breeze* for salvage and go. I'll tell Chalice.'

'Tell me what?' Chalice exited the door, closing it solemnly, laid some linens next to Sean Ironcup's body. She sagged with knock-kneed relief when she saw what Arden carried. 'You got the blood! Oh! You got the blood back! Excellent!'

Chalice stopped speaking. Her joy was not shared.

'What?'

Arden grabbed Chalice's arm, offered her excuses to Mr Riven and dragged her away.

'Madame Lion,' Arden hissed once they reached the opposite deck. 'Who else knows . . . about my shadow endowment, about Bellis? Do any of the Islanders know? Would they manipulate Mr Harrow, make him think he was helping his damn golden daughter?'

Chalice's lips pressed together. A wave passed over the boat, drenching them in a spray.

'Not more than ten officials within the Order were allowed that information. It . . . was too sensitive a matter to speak of.'

Arden pointed at *Fine Breeze*'s hull. 'Then pray to the gods and devils this was an accident. Jonah says there is a boat beyond the storm wall and it has not moved. He thinks it might be the ones who intended to rendezvous for my blood.'

A thin blush of pink spread under Chalice's freckles. 'If it was, why would they stay?'

'Let's hope they're just waiting for us to leave.'

'Yes. We've got your blood back now. The last of it. We can toss it over the side and go home.'

'This won't end by throwing away this jar! If someone got Mr Harrow to send the Tallwaters out here, someone, somewhere *knew* there was something more than just *ignis* about me. And if he knew, then others would know.' She pointed accusingly at the storm wall. 'Even *them*. What chance of others knowing our secrets, Chalice? Can you even trust your own people?'

'The Order would never . . .'

Their conversation was punctuated by Mr Riven clearing his throat. 'Ladies,' he said. 'Whatever business demands this privacy needs to wrap up damned quickly. Our guests are coming.'

The sea-fog had slunk upon the ocean. A thin, distant sound headed up the darkening of the sun. Carried through the moist air and still ocean, a threshing of bows against waves.

Arden did not need the spyglass Mr Riven offered her. It would have made no difference. The fog was too think, and even she could not see anything beyond the Wall, but she had her own signal keeper's instincts too. A boat *was* out there. Not by chance, not here where the volcanic island of Maris poisoned the water. The boat lingered there on purpose.

She hefted the jar in her hand. A solid, jellied weight. A sudden panic for what it represented. The shadow that had complicated her life. She needed to be rid of it, and she readied her arm to throw . . .

Only to have Mr Riven's hand firmly placed on top of her own. He nodded at the corpse bound in sheet. 'If worst comes to worst, we will need something to bargain with.'

'You can't possibly consider such a thing, Mr Riven,' Chalice scolded. 'That blood isn't worth anything to anyone except your wife.'

'I can consider bargaining for our lives,' Mr Riven continued. 'The current's pulling us into the Tempest. We might hide there until that ship passes, but if she's any bigger than a fishing boat, we're in no condition to get boarded by pirates.'

'Pirates?' Chalice asked. 'Here?'

'We're in a desert, Madam Lion. There's no living to be had but theft.' He took the jar from Arden, and nestled it inside the lifejacket box, before closing the lid. 'Rather it, than you.'

Arden nodded, and would have kissed him had the situation not been so charged.

David had by then reluctantly abandoned Sean's body, and was halfway through the retrieval of the rope ladder when he paused, head cocked like a sparrow that hears the worm. 'What is that sound?'

He shoved the heel of his hands into his ears as the whistle picked up. A constant harmonic of agony, the cry of atmospheres caught in a perpetual collision.

'Storm wall,' Mr Riven barked. 'It's closing in faster than I thought. Get inside, all of you.'

Mr Riven ran for the wheelhouse ladder and seized the riser. A simple action, enraging the gods, and no sooner had he boosted himself to the first rung than a wave with all the power of a massive fist backhanded *Saudade*, six ways to Sunday.

With a whirl of vertigo Arden was boosted up by the rising deck and tossed into the side of the cabin with such an impact, every tooth in her skull rattled.

Chalice and David went sliding past her in a startled jumble of soaking limbs and open mouths, and if they had been screaming, the roar of the Wall took the sound away.

Another wave, *Saudade* lurched to starboard. This time Arden took off down the end of the deck with the speed of a bottle rocket. In a single, time-frozen moment, the wreckage of *Fine Breeze* tossed up into the air, suspended in spume and wave-wash, before descending towards *Saudade*. The little yacht dropped upon the forecastle deck with an unholy chorus of splintering wood before smashing into the railing, opening a gap on one side like broken teeth in a jaw.

Arden slid towards the edge, and slipped. Unable to arrest her long fall, she saw herself as though from above, as if through the longest of spyglass lenses, a small figure in waxen broadcloth sliding across the oil-slicked wood to where the balustrade was broken, to plunge over the side . . .

28

. . . and stopped.

Her skirt caught on a hook that jerked her from neck to knee, and Arden spun on an axis of wet broadcloth to discover the corpse, blue with cyanosis, now holding the hem of her dress in the grip of death.

His staring eyes had the shade of granite set in pearl.

The fist tightened harder on her skirt. The stitches crackled. Sean Ironcup, yanking her away from the seething wreckage of *Fine Breeze* as the wood battered and chewed upon the side of *Saudade*.

'Sean,' she shouted. 'Hold on!'

Then just as suddenly Chalice joined him in trying to haul Arden up from the brink, three souls locked against the storm of the Tempest Wall. All the while behind them a man shouted in strangulated harmonics, shouted Arden's name.

The boat pitched forward again and now the three were all in the sea, no air, no breath, no purchase in the roil and thunder. Arden could only dream of fire as she clung to the submerged edge of the boat, her head under the waves and her ears filled with seafoam and water.

Just as suddenly the boat bow flipped upwards once more, propelling them all high into the air with a seabird's vertigo.

Arden snatched at a railing, only to have it tear out of her hands from the inertia of the boat's fall . . .

And then they plunged again.

The storm no longer roiled or roared. Only silence here, and her battering heart in the cavern of her chest, and her dragged down to lightless depths. Fingers clasped and scrabbled. Was that a foot upon her shoulder? A wisp of hair at her hand? All three of them, caught in the wreckage of a floundering ship?

Arms as cold as death reaching about her.

Arms muscular and alien all at once.

Long arms, and bright cobalt rings.

29

Was the dumping that woke her

Was the dumping that woke her, flat on her back on the hard wood of the deck, her head shooting stars. A boneless hand flopped in her face, and she could not be certain if her own or somebody else's. Whatever had happened, wherever afterlife she had ended up in, it was an infinitely less soggy, choppy and very much calmer one than her life of two minutes previously. The Tempest still roared, but at a remove, a distance long passed.

Arden coughed seawater from her lungs and sat up.

'I'm never getting used to—' she started to say, then stopped.

Through the haze of rain, a single golden eye beheld her.

One giant golden eye, staring from over *Saudade*'s transom, wider than the full stretch of her arms. Up and up, it loomed overhead, so round it filled the world in concentric circles huge enough to fall into. The double pupil, blacker than the oldest and deepest wisdom, stared down at her with the detachment of kings.

' . . . devils,' she finished.

With equal languid nonchalance, the long arm that had seized them from the water moved about the deck in the manner of a drunken person searching for a door key in the dark. The kraken's limb spanned wider than Arden's own torso and shone with a bright metal iridescence, even in the dwindling storm.

Arden could only bear mute witness as the entire scolex of the monster rose in majesty above the deckline, same as every woodcut and eyewitness account of kraken attack she had ever seen or heard. The blue phosphorescence of a living *kraken crucifix* left afterimages in her vision, so bright was it, putting the colours in her coat to shame.

Oh, she thought. Oh, he was the devil and God as one.

Seven more arms rose up to join the lone limb, lashed at the storm and writhed luminous against a lightless sky, before slipping away into the fog and plume.

Arden clung to the deck in a wreckage of terror and exhaustion, and a pair of arms – a man's arms, not monster's this time – picked her up with infinite tenderness and against the rocking boat helped her below decks. She collapsed upon warm leather, as her lungs expelled an ocean.

He could not stay long. His rope-callused hand caressed her cheek once, making certain she was not mortally injured, before he was gone back into the storm. The snapping doors belonged to the passage of Chalice, limping down the stairs in an overhand shuffle with the formerly dead Sean Ironcup.

'So we have an unsinkable,' Arden said with some effort. She sat up and peered at the Hillsider. 'You've survived your second capsizing.'

'No thanks to you,' Sean replied, still feisty despite his partially maundered state.

Chalice dumped their revenant in one of the upholstered chairs, then put her hands on her hips, glowered down at him. 'No nonsense, young man. You've caused us a fair bit of trouble. Attempted murder of a Guildswoman, and a sanguinem at that? Stealing a boat? Consider yourself formally under arrest by the authority of the Lyonne Investigatory Order and Nomenclatures.'

'What's that mean?'

'It means you're stuck with us until we can take you to a

decent Magistrate who isn't leading you into iniquity like Mr Harrow. You have a right to be kept alive, but that is quite about the limit of it, I'm afraid.'

'I won't try to run away,' he said, both wretched and defiant at the same time. The chill and sudden dunking had aggravated his palsy. Both sides of him curled up with spasms. 'I know what I did was wrong.'

Chalice clicked her tongue and fetched Arden a blanket from the camphorwood chest. Arden shook her head at the offering. 'I'll change into a dry dress. Give it to the lad before he ties himself into a knot. Maybe get one for yourself too, Chalice.'

'I'm quite all right,' Chalice said, and with a gentleness that belied her mood, she tucked the blanket around Sean's thin shoulders. He watched them both warily through swollen, red-rimmed eyes, but did not complain.

Behind a brass divider all rococo with weed-fronds and clam shells, Arden slid out of her sopping blue uniform and into her spare dress, a dark linseed and wax wet-work garment hardened from the cold. The kraken eye still played behind the curtain of her mind. Jonah had summoned it, that creature. Had given a monster instructions, compelled the thing to save her. Was for a moment, the monster's master.

The *aequor profundum* in her blood moved hot through the chambers of her heart. Every moment that passed, every event that confronted her with her own mortality, she was becoming more tied to Jonah Riven. She had not yet the time to think of it before now, but in this dark panelled room with its moving shadows and winking brass, a future began to congeal. A possible future, with her half-Islander lover, and her coins gone, and the city of her birth forgotten.

I want that.

The thought filled her with triumph and panic. The Lyonne Order would not let her go so easily, but if Bellis had achieved it, then she could too. Maybe there would be room on the secret island for all of them.

'What a performance!' Chalice continued on the other side

of the room divider. 'The menfolk are up in the wheelhouse effecting emergency repairs. We're lucky our hull is intact. The side wheels are completely shot to smithereens, but the screw is still working.'

As she spoke, thunder grumbled outside, and the boat lifted on a great wave before sinking again.

Arden shook her head, dismayed Chalice could court fate so blatantly. One did not count lucky stars until broad daylight, and they were still in the night-time of their crisis.

'Don't thank any deity just yet. We're still not past the Wall, I assume.'

'No.' Chalice steadied herself against a support beam and snorted. 'Anyway, what's the chances of our captain keeping at least a whiskey in this office, hmm? A dram of spirit to ease our conditions, and then we could go about drying our clothes.'

While Chalice went on a hunt for liquor, Arden returned to Sean Ironcup.

'Some gratitude is in order on my behalf,' Arden said to him. 'You grabbed me as I was sliding off the deck.'

'I wasn't much help, my stronger side doesn't feel much different from my leeward. We still fell in.' He gasped then, remembering. 'What manner of monster seized us?'

'Blood-called kraken bull.'

'He was big.'

'He was big. Angry too. Same I was angry when you bound me and bled me, no more than an *animal*. What moral *failing* had you think hurting another fellow human was worth profit?'

Sean's face crumbled. He was not so guilty, she decided, had been dragged on this malarkey out of sheer familial duty, but if he considered himself a man, then he had to take a man's responsibility, whether he was nineteen or ninety.

'I'm sorry! I'm so sorry! Leyland said that there was no way onto the Islands without payment. He wanted to sell the girl, my sister's child! Tried to auction her off to the highest bidder in the Black Rosette when a man arrived.' He made motions of his hands. 'The Magistrate, Gregor's employer. Approached Gregor's father and said he would give all three children a home if he were to do a task on his behalf . . .' Sean heaved a breath, close to tears.

'And your sister did not protest?'

Whatever bulwarks the boy had put up against his family's disintegration, they were swept away on Helena's mention. Sean began to weep. Blubbered some things. Arden caught the gist of his crisis. After the transaction in the Black Rosette turned ugly, Helena had closed down, gradually, like a great house might do for the night. She still had a modicum of function about her when they had come to steal Arden's blood, but that was the last time she had spoken. The children were gone. Her work was ended. Best she die in fractions.

'Leyland, I think, would have been happier for her to die as well. She had the blue fever last year, can bear no more children. Her family had no money and her blood . . .'

'She carries sanguine traits?'

'No traits. Not in the Ironcup line. Leyland never liked her, or me. If Gregor had married well there could have been the chance of sanguinity. It might have meant a reversal in our fortunes, and we would never have needed to come out here.'

The strength sapped from Sean, he fumbled for the blanket's end, curled up in speechless horror at what had been done in the name of Leyland Tallwater's ambition.

The ship lurched again. The sound of shouting, footsteps. A heavy piece of equipment lost balance, slammed into a supporting structure above. Someone cried out in pain. Mr Riven, at battle with the weather.

'Hold on,' Chalice called from the rear of the ship. 'We're back in heavy water again.'

Arden fell onto the floor and clutched the carpet, suffering *Saudade*'s sway on all her axes.

Then, the way a curtain can fall upon a stage play of destruction, the storm abruptly subsided into a desultory scatter of wind and did not resume. The ship's sways eased into a rhythmic bob. Arden waited for another minute before chancing an upright position.

Chalice let go the brass post she'd been clinging to and regarded the black wood ceiling beams as if she could see the sky through them. 'Looks like we are fully out of the wall-storm at last,' she said, with no small measure of relief.

'Yes, but on what side?'

The deckside door slammed again.

Mr Riven was a mess. The tattered remains of his shirt had turned pink from the alarming wound that ran diagonally across his chest, bigger than the ones he'd opened to save Arden with *aequor profundum*. The wound still bled. But his face was alight with indignation, his mouth a grimace, his pupils dilated in rage.

'You,' he said, pointing to Sean Ironcup. 'Explain yourself.'

Sean Ironcup stared at Mr Riven, his eyes bulging with terror. 'I was dead, now I am alive, and the Redeemer provided me with a breath so I can walk the world.'

Sean pulled his knees up. His palsy wrapped him in painful iron bands, for the entire situation had wounded him. Ah, thought Arden, he's going to lose himself.

Swallowing her antipathy towards Sean Ironcup, Arden sat down next to the young man and tried to remember how her father talked to people in distress. Lucian Beacon had been gifted with words as well as fire. He could rouse a fellow to great achievements, talk down an angry fighter, console a grieving widower.

The latter Lucian did best, having been one himself, once.

'Mr Ironcup, breathe in and out, there's a dear. Take that air in like it's a *fine* liquor. And when you exhale . . . yes. Now, begin at the moment you realized the current was taking you south, and not north of the permanent storm.'

Mr Riven remained silent and glaring as Sean did as Arden commanded. His jaw trembled, then steadied.

Shakily, he began to speak.

'We . . . we knew the current would take us south, not north. Mr Harrow said it would. He said someone needed *ignis* blood and they would be prepared to pay passage.'

Arden exchanged a concerned glance with Mr Riven. There was a sense of too much planning going on here, more than the opportunity of some Hillside folks about to be killed in a tavern.

'Why would the Magistrate send you south of the storm? There's nothing here, not even people.'

Not even Bellis, Arden heard him add silently.

'I don't know. It was a different route than the ones they sing of back home. I didn't want to go that way but Leyland said it was what Mr Harrow wanted. We went south until full morning. Leyland let off a signal as he approached the Tempest. A craft approached to meet us.'

'What sort of craft?' Mr Riven pressed. 'Describe it.'

Sean Ironcup blinked. 'Why, it would have been like this one, sir. Ghostwood, though, not black mangrove. It burned rock-blood. I remember the smell, it is on my fingers and in my head. As noxious as ash and a trillion dead things turned to rot and slurry.'

A cold finger of warning traced Arden's spine. Mr Riven had asked such a specific question, knowing what the answer would be.

'Did it have a name? Across the bow, carved in red like a wound?'

Sean shook his head. 'I remember only a difficult word. Not in Lyonnese. *Sen . . .* something.'

'*Sehnsucht.*'

'Yes, that was it.'

Before Arden could stop him, Mr Riven grabbed Sean and hauled him up. 'Who were the people on that boat? Was there a woman there?'

'I don't know, sir,' Sean cried. 'I don't know! They took Leyland off, Helena and Gregor. Beat them up a bit, sir, this I recall. I thought I would be next. Then a man, he boarded first and he broke the jars. He told me . . . *play dead,* he said to me. *Pretend you are dead.* So dark . . . I couldn't see him, but he spoke with a Lyonne accent. Shoved me into the rope box with the last jar and then . . . and then . . . and there was crashing and yelling I don't remember what happened after that. Not until I woke up here.'

'What did this man look like?'

'I cannot say. It was dark, the salt water was everywhere, it blinded me.' A gasp. Stared at Chalice. 'The man had a coin about his neck, like yours. Made me look at it. Told me it was his coin of instruction.'

Chalice clasped her medallion tight. 'There was a Lion aboard?'

No sooner had she spoken, Chalice gasped, as if having spoken out of turn.

Mr Riven dropped Sean Ironcup back on the chair, where he once again folded up in a rumple of limbs and anxious terror. Turned on Chalice 'A Lion there as *well*? Where are you people *not*?'

Chalice effected a stubborn look. 'He couldn't have been one of ours. If he was, he was under deep cover. Despite our efforts, we have next to no influence in the Sainted Isles.'

'Please Chalice . . .' Arden warned. 'Tell him the truth. We're all on our own out here.'

The duplicitous stormbride could have been a criminal in a courtroom under questioning, for all her eyes were wide with truth and horror.

'Mr Ironcup must have misread this coin-wielding fellow's intentions. Lots of people wear coin pendants. It could have been a mutiny, an argument that had him hide you in the closet. Nothing to do with us.'

Mr Riven huffed a breath, went pale. 'The lad told the truth. If there was an Order man on board that ship, then he was there because of Bellis.'

30

So it's true

'So it's true? You really gave her *Sehnsucht*, Jonah Riven?' Chalice scolded.

'Only to get to safety. Only to get away from you. She was meant to get rid of it after reaching sanctuary . . .'

He staggered. Arden went to catch him but it was a blank-faced stranger who shrugged her off.

'I can't think. My mind . . . If I don't get rest, I will pass out on the floor and be useless to anyone. Fix this, Lightmistress. You and David Modhi. Get us away from that boat and out of this storm.'

He blood-drunkenly made his way to the private berth. The door slammed. If it had had a lock, he would have slid it shut.

'What happened?' Sean asked in the blistering silence that followed. 'Um, are we going home now?'

'Shut up,' Chalice shot back. 'You've caused nothing but trouble, boy.'

'But how can the Captain sleep? Right in the hour of our need!'

'Because he sliced himself open to call that kraken bull to save our lives.' Arden squeezed the last of seawater from her braid, feeling herself as exhausted as Jonah had been. 'You give blood to the sea like that, it pulls strength out of you. Do they not teach the conservation of energy and mass in Hillsider schools? When he wakes up, then he can help, but at this minute we are on our own.'

Sean wisely did not reply. Still irritated, Arden bound up the damp locks of hair that had escaped her hairpins and readied herself to go outside again. If they were on the wrong side of the storm wall and floating about in the Tempest's eye, the combined experience of David and herself would not make the crossing without Mr Riven behind the wheel.

They'd barely managed it the first time.

'What was that last little exchange about?' Chalice asked. 'Who did she give the boat to?'

Arden shrugged, felt the bite of anger. 'Not the slightest clue.'

Chalice's eyes narrowed. 'Did he actually think anyone would purposefully give away a damned monster-hunting boat? God and devils, I once saw daguerreotypes of *Sehnsucht* in Mr Lindsay's briefing notes. It's grotesque. More than twice the size of this one.'

'You should be the one to answer who owns *Sehnsucht* now, Miss Quarry. Your being a Lion and all, and your man aboard her.'

Arden's tartness made Chalice huff. 'I told you, if Sean's benefactor was Lyonne Order, he was under the deepest cover.'

'And he will remain that way, Chalice. When Jonah wakes up, we're going back to Vigil.'

Chalice put her palm on the map glass, stroked the *Libro* island archipelago with her thumb. One of those the secret islands, where Bellis and Stefan had taken refuge. Telling Arden without words that she knew more than she was letting on.

'But will *he* want to go back, Arden? Mr Riven might be curious to know what became of his first love, and of the people who still bear his name.'

A quick stab of covetous jealousy went through Arden. A jealousy tinged with guilt, for she was indirectly the cause of his troubles, and he would not love her for that.

'He is not at all curious. His work for you is *done*, Chalice Quarry. And so is mine.'

31

The Harbourmistress' boy yelped at her

The Harbourmistress' boy yelped at her when Arden turned up unannounced at the wheelhouse.

'Lightmistress, you took me by surprise.'

'Sorry. I was taking advantage of the reprieve with a nap. How long before the current turns?'

'By the map, the daylight should have us turning west and back to Fiction,' David said with a nod of certainty.

She didn't have the words to express her relief, but hugged his shoulders. 'I will be happy to see even Fiction again.'

This was followed by a yawn, for Arden had only managed a brief but unsatisfying doze in the cabin earlier, but the aches and pains and anxieties of their return made her restless, and she finally surrendered to waking.

The moon shone through the clouds. A small kraken-oil lantern cast a cold blue glow over the instruments.

'Where's Mr Riven?'

'Still sleeping off a blood-hangover, as they would say in my home country. It will keep him unavailable for a while.'

'Is that all? He didn't look well before, and I worried.'

She patted his arm gently. The boy was hopelessly in love with Mr Riven, and in that respect she and David were kin;

both bound to the wrong man by troubled emotions and unable to effect any true response from him one way or the other.

'I'm sure he will come out of this syncope by the current's turn, and we can go home, and forget this day like a bad dream.'

'And yourself, Lightmistress?'

'Only a few bruises and scrapes, nothing to measure a casket over,' she said. 'I have tangled with a *monstrom mare* and lived to tell the tale.'

At first he smiled, and then the smile faded, and he slipped back behind the wheel.

'What's wrong, Mr Modhi?'

He pointed ahead of them, over the damaged bow. She tried to peer out of the wheelhouse and failed, for the night and fog were so absolute. 'It's back.'

'The boat's back? I thought it moved on after the monster came.'

Relying on her Beacon-born darksight, Arden scanned the gloom. Through the marbled wisps of fog and sea-plume, there was an outcropping of rock that to call an *island* would be far too generous. Almost as a mere optical illusion, such was the faintness, a column of boiler-lit smoke seemingly rose from one corner.

'Devils!' Arden took the wheel from David. 'Very sneaky of them. Top observation, Mr Modhi.'

'I can see well in the dark.'

'Indeed. Keep those eyes of yours peeled, for I've a feeling you'll see more shortly.'

Once the rudder was under her control, she shoved the engine-order telegraph to stop. *Saudade* was mechanical, and instantly she moved perpendicular to the current. The propeller slowed. The boat began to drift side on, but with much less speed.

The dull, distant roaring of the Tempest Wall continued.

'All right. The storm is loud,' Arden said, counting her blessings. 'It's good. They might not have heard us.'

She went to the crate, and opened it up, inspected the

313

revolving drum. A shape had taken form on the carbon. The rock, jagged and huge. Behind, a rectangle tapered at one end.

'What are those lines here?' Arden asked, pointing at a riffle of linework between the boat and the rock.

'Thresh-waves.' David said. 'She's not powered down. The island is floating, and they are using it as either pier or cover.'

'We are all drifting at the same speed. No doubt they have an echo box of their own. Waiting to see who will make the first move.'

Down on the deck, Chalice Quarry emerged from the cabin with her hair mussed from sleep, and a wet-battery flashlight in her hands. She frowned up at the wheelhouse. Arden held a finger to her lips, bade her turn off the light, then beckoned her inside.

'They're back,' she said quietly as Chalice entered. 'Our monster didn't scare them off at all.'

Chalice swallowed nervously. 'Oh, I was wondering why the engine stopped.'

'More for your concern, where is Sean Ironcup, Chalice? You're charged with looking after him tonight.'

'Mr Ironcup consented to getting locked in one of the storage rooms. He's worked out it might be safer for him all round if he not appear to take sides if things take a wrong turn.'

'Are they going to take a wrong turn?'

Chalice gestured towards the night before examining the echo-image of the rocky island. '*Sehnsucht*, I presume?'

'We haven't yet seen, but your presumption is likely correct.'

'Darling, if Bellis is on that ship, you need to get Mr Riven awake.'

'No. After blood loss, rousing him is just going to hurt. And if we don't change angles soon, we're going to run into that boat or she'll try and run into us. The current takes us right past that rock. We need to turn *Saudade* off this fast water.'

David suffered a look of pure despair. 'It's too early. If we turn off now we'll hit the storm wall. Besides, we won't outrun *Sehnsucht* against the current,' he said. 'I remember stories about *Sehnsucht*, Mx Beacon. She's a bigger, more powerful craft than *Saudade* ever was. She's made for fighting monsters.'

Arden took a breath. This ship. *Sehnsucht*. This ghost which haunted Mr Riven in blood and love, and now in the childhood he had lost. He would want answers, about what had happened to Bellis after she sailed away. He would not be content with watching her go by like a *memento mori* afloat on the water.

'David,' she said, 'get down below and open all the engine throttles.'

'Mx Beacon?'

'We can't outrun her cross-current, you say? But if we keep going and with a head start, I think *Saudade* can do just that. We are unencumbered, half as small again as that white behemoth.'

'But the water just gets harder to escape the closer we get to Maris!'

'Let me worry about that. Go. Go!'

Chalice waited until the boy had left the wheelhouse to express her complete dissatisfaction. 'He's right, Arden. We'll hit fast, hot water soon. Once that happens we might not be able to turn out so easily.'

'We don't have a choice. That ship is in hunting mode, and she's not waiting for plesiosaur.'

From down below there came a screech and growl as auxiliary boilers filled with kraken oil. The gears started to turn with the slow, massive torque of lower-deck screws, and then they moved, slow at first, then faster still. The propeller grumbled up white water, the remaining vanes fell off her damaged side wheels, but it mattered not. Manoeuvrability was not the issue here.

Saudade thrust forward until the bow wave curved up nearly as high as the deck. The needle on the echo box juddered with such frantic oscillation, it was almost impossible to make out each new picture.

Then the fog parted and the moon cast its cold light. Arden saw Bellis' ship for the first time.

Sean had not been at all creative when he called *Sehnsucht* a ghost ship. The craft could have been constructed out of fog and ice, for all that it stood out from the Tempest mist. Arden ran to the wheelhouse window, watched on with horrified wonder as *Saudade* thundered past that white shadow. She was like *Saudade* in design, but so overwhelmingly larger.

'She's turning,' Chalice yelped. She grabbed Arden's elbow. 'Arden, she's turning.'

'I *know*, Chalice. I'm trying to concentrate.'

'This isn't right. We should be chasing *them*! They tried to steal classified Order secrets!'

Arden debated shouting down the speaking tube for David to give her more oil, but without Mr Riven's intimate knowledge of his boat, she was unsure how much to push.

Chalice pressed herself against the door frame while Arden hugged the wheel with hands and knees. They were on the current, a dun-coloured sluice through the canyon of fog. The *Saudade*'s wheel became capricious and unsettled. The craft failed to aim true, and any moment now it would snicker out of her hands and spin. Had she not the lantern-turner's strength, she would have lost her grip.

A smaller paddle wheeler would have found no purchase in the disturbed water, or kept up with *Saudade*'s screw. They'd have escaped scot-free. From what little she'd seen of *Sehnsucht*, the vessel had vanes that bit deep, so she still kept behind, even if she could not gain without a screw propeller to give her speed.

Behind them, the ghost ship slid into the wash *Saudade* left behind. With each passing minute it receded in their view.

'You know, we could probably lose them completely if we went faster,' Chalice complained. The dawn stained the clouds in sickly yellow, and now there was light enough for even Chalice so see. Every few seconds she would hazard a peek out of the wheelhouse windows to make a disapproving noise.

Though most of the night had gone by without seeing their

pursuer, the echo box told the story of the big threshing ship, slow but inexorable, following them along the dun current. If she lost ground, it was not enough to lose *Saudade* completely. If the white boat had won races against *Saudade*, it must have been in a time before Mr Riven had upgraded her engine to accommodate a propeller.

'Can't you pick up the speed a little?' Chalice asked for at least the fifth time that night.

'This is not my boat to make go faster or to risk,' Arden said. 'We can keep going this speed indefinitely, but if we don't do something drastic, she'll stay on our tail until this ship starts falling apart.'

'Which is how long?'

Arden tapped one of the brass indicators. 'She could run like this for another hour or two maybe. Eventually we're going to overheat the valves.'

'Then do something drastic.'

'What?'

'I needn't be making suggestions to you, darling.'

Arden had words she could have said, but held them all the same. Chalice was not wrong. When she spoke at last to David, she could hear the defeat in her voice.

'Get up here, Mr Modhi. You take the wheel. I need to wake Mr Riven.'

Chalice Quarry tutted. 'Huh. You said he couldn't be woken.'

'I did not say waking was an impossibility, only that it was highly unpleasant.'

Mx Modhi had trained her son well. He did not dally on a command, and was out of the engine room within seconds, taking the wheel so she might do the most solemn of duties.

She went below decks, into the dark halls.

Arden lingered at the cabin door with a vial of ammoniac hartshorn from the surgeon's box, uncertain of what to say to him when he woke. She rested her head upon the wood, breathed deep, and pushed it open.

He lay upon the old night-silk sheets of the bed, shirtless and unconscious in a half-state of undress: he had clearly been trying to undo his waistband buttons when he had succumbed to the malaise of a kraken-calling comedown. Prior to then, he had made some effort to tape up his wounds. Plasters and bandages ran along the length of a crusted blade-track that had been roughly stitched, so he resembled nothing so much as a discarded doll, ill-treated and mended and treated ill again, so many times over that he was no longer fit for anyone except for the one who had loved him first.

Images and memories not hers came unbidden: child Bellis, whispering promises to love him through the storms of life, even though hers would be the worst of them. Child Bellis and child Jonah curling little baby fingers about and making promises to cross their hearts and hope to die, die, die. And elsewhere a small Arden Beacon, a squib of blood that was either useless or mysteriously disastrous with no appreciable in-between.

She would never kiss him properly again, she feared, never experience what it was to kiss him in love, and not ambiguity, or ambivalence, or stolen. Like her coat, second-hand his feelings for her were ill-fitting, made for another.

'Goodbye, Jonah.'

She bent to his lips and kissed him there. He stirred, murmured words in Old Fictish.

Then she broke the hartshorn vial beneath his nose.

The scent of the smelling salts hit her just as they hit him, a urinous punch of searing stench, and Mr Riven inhaled with the gasp of a fist darted into his diaphragm. He sat up, coughing, and frowned, instantly aware of the ship's engines. 'Why are we at full speed?'

'*Sehnsucht*,' Arden said. 'Bellis' ship. It's definitely following us. We've been having a merry slow chase for most of the night.'

She stood back, waited for him to gasp and run to his wife. And for a moment it seemed certain. A leaping agitation in his eyes, then the familiar curtain closed. The chances of Bellis being on the same ship that she and Stefan had sailed to their Island sanctuary, they were slim to none. Two people on their own could not have fought off pirates with a view to a ghostwood vessel. They'd have been like castaways in plesiosaur waters.

'How long away is she?'

'Maybe half a mile. *Saudade* got a head start on propellers. Though *Sehnsucht* is not catching up, she's not slowing down either.'

He shook his head to clear his mind. Tried to stand. Thought otherwise. The blood-hangover making his body tremble. Fell back down with his hand over his eyes.

'Why do you wake me to tell me this, Arden? Could you have not given me another hour asleep?'

'Whether it's your wife or pirates, it's better if you're awake. We need you ready.'

'Just give me a minute.'

Arden shifted uncomfortably, her envy making her speak. 'Do you think Bellis is on that ship?'

'I thought about it. Searched my heart. I don't think she's on board.'

'You don't?'

'Stefan promised me, Arden. Before they left. Whatever happened, Bellis would stay with him. She knew full well how important that was, how her life depended on it.'

'Then why did those people go after my blood, Jonah? Why did they destroy *Fine Breeze*?'

Mr Riven propped himself up on his elbow. 'Is it not obvious now what is happening?'

'No! Explain it to me!'

'The Lyonne Order own *Sehnsucht* now,' he said wearily. 'Probably from the moment Stefan let it go. That's why there is a Lion on board. If your blood is so important, would they have chanced its safety to Madame Quarry alone? Would the all-powerful Lyonne Order not have prepared for something like this to happen, had their agents standing by?'

'I . . . I guess so.'

'*Sehnsucht* could catch up to us easily if they wanted her to. It's an escort. We'll make it past the Wall, head back to Vigil with Mr Ironcup.'

'And you? Will you come back with me, to Vigil?'

He sat up. 'Isn't that the plan?'

'I don't know what the plan is. What is the plan, Jonah?'

He looked as if he were thinking, and she held her breath, terrified of what might come after. Then his eyes crinkled, and when he smiled she had never seen something so beautiful, or that filled her heart with such gladness.

'To run away with the Lightmistress, if she would allow me.'

The days and months of her solitude had done their part in reducing her to a raw nerve, and even his humour could not stop her blurring tears and half-formed syllables.

And Mr Riven swept her up in arms and kissed her with those lips and held her close to his poor wounded body.

Arden pushed him away. 'I am not a thing to mollycoddle. You turn hot and cold, and it is unconscionable to me. Are you staying, or going? What are your intentions?'

He released her, his gaze went to the floor. His voice had a strange thoughtfulness to it. 'It hurts me, the reality of you.'

'Then it's my fault now?'

'Always!' he said. 'You are everything. You filled my head with thoughts of you every day. Every *day*. When I first saw you on the beach in your golden threads I thought you were more beautiful than . . . than any dr*eam*. Even when I look at you I am torn. How could I be anything else for Arden Beacon of Clay Portside but a savage from Fiction? I learned enough from Stefan to know what your posting means. I fear you one day returning to Clay and forgetting the simple creature you dallied with, and I will be twice broken.' His bloodshot eyes were rimed with suffering. 'Twice broken, for I *loved* you.'

'Love? You speak of love when you would not let anyone love you back? You are so infuriating, Mr Riven,' she said between gasping sobs. 'The most infuriating man I have ever met. I don't take lightly my affections. I'm no coquette.'

Her pronouncements confused him so, and he seemed so stricken that she had to kiss him again, and he whimpered at the pain in his chest and when Arden went to pull away he only darted in again, his clumsy, uncouth mouth rough and greedy on her lips.

'Ah,' he said, and his eyes became dark with desire and his lips red and swollen from kissing, and she had to sigh to herself, for how often had she read in her penny presses about women swooning from kisses? Tough, incorrigible Mr Riven, weak and pliant before her. His excitement was evident in the soft leather of his breeches.

He took her hand, a silent query in him, regret and shame and longing at once. Her touch had merely started a cascade. Was perhaps not fully aware of his body's response, only that it came with so many others he could not distinguish.

'Oh, come now? In your condition? We have no time.'

'We must be quick, then,' he said, already unbuttoning himself.

'You are love mad,' she laughed, only the words came out hoarse with her own rapid quickening, and they were fools together, scraping out these hollow minutes from the uncertainty beyond them. She scooped him free of the leather strides and stroked the thick, silken length of Mr Jonah Riven, wanting to own him for the moment when he was so unquestionably certain of his love for her, when he spoke from lust and sexual hunger and yes, maybe yes, the thought of Bellis forever between them.

If her body wanted Mr Riven then, her mind was merely a startled passenger. Desire had the same landscape as pain, and its map – though detailed in familiar places – had lines hastily scrawled where they did not intersect with true trust and true love.

This was one of those places. She went into his lap, and his mouth again claimed hers in insatiable gulps. He wanted to devour her with kisses. His trembling hands moved under her skirts, over her thighs, through the still-damp lace, and was there he touched the centre of her in newfound intimacy, took startled delight in the folds of warmth he'd only experienced so briefly before.

Had they the time Arden would have guided Mr Riven's fingers to where they pleased her most, the creamy folds between her labia, the hard arousal of her clitoris, but the creaking juddering reminder of their rapidly gaining pursuers made her take matters to their conclusion. She mounted his lap, guided his penis into the hot centre of her, and he jerked up with forceful, inelegant thrusts into Arden with the same determined expression of a man committed to a fight.

Once more they heaved together, moved on by the thrum of the levers and their own breaths in the dark room, and their lovemaking was the engine that drove on the ship, an engine bruised and battered in both body and soul. Two people who had been tested and failed in all their dreams and perhaps had little else but one another, and even in that they weren't sure; for to what others had they promised themselves first?

Lost to his crisis, Mr Riven growled Fictish words, and his thrusts shortened and quickened. His arms tightened about her waist, the strength in them elating and terrifying at once. He lingered at the precipice of a terrible, violent act, and although she had consented to his bed, the fear remained that were his mind to change she could not stop him.

Arden was too wrung out and sore to climax again, too overwhelmed by this man's demands upon her body. So she held Mr Riven carefully as he breathed through his final peak. He came inside her, and she let him grow soft within the heated embrace of her.

They held each other with the closeness that only comes with uncertainty. Aftershocks of pleasure still coursed through him. Arden laid her cheek on Mr Riven's sweat-damp shoulder, doubtful if she should stay in this illusion of love or wake up to her place in his affections. Time had stood still in this room. Perhaps only five minutes had passed beyond the doors.

There was magic here, the same as those stories of children who walked through glowing doors into other worlds and remained in timeless stasis as all outside grew old and faded away.

But such stories rarely ended well. They always had to return to the cold, real world to die.

'We need to go,' she murmured. 'We are almost at the Maris waters.'

He pressed a soft kiss to both her eyelids, her mouth. 'Ah, devils, you are lovely, Arden. I wish I could do it again.'

Hard not to smile, so she hid it in his shoulder, then nodded, serious again. 'For the best, we really have to get up top.'

He pulled on his damp clothes and submitted to Arden sticking some more dressings upon his cut. They would have been better served with stitches, but he was flighty under her hands, like a captured animal that could not sit still.

'Right,' he said with a breath as he slid back into his coat. 'Let's evade my father's boat and it will be finished once and for all.'

'About time,' Chalice said to them when they made it to the wheelhouse. 'Ghostie's been gaining on us. What took you so long, anyway?'

Arden murmured non-committal words about trying to patch up wounds which needed a second pair of hands, but Mr Riven ignored Chalice's criticism and moved out onto the balcony with a pair of range-finding binoculars, for calculation, and a telescope, for a closer view.

'She can't be gaining, not while I'm running kraken oil under screw.'

'I'm not guessing,' Chalice said. 'I'm very good at distances.'

'Teach you that at Lion School do they?' Mr Riven jibed. He did not wait for Chalice to respond, only put the glass to his eye. 'Now, lets see who's running this old girl. Maybe old friends of yours Miss Quarry.'

'Well I—'

He was barely looking five seconds before something made him startle, and put the binoculars down. His confidence had whisked away, as if with the wind.

'Jonah?' Arden asked, concerned at the sudden departure of colour from his face. 'What do you see?'

He did not reply, not at first, only to say to David, 'Lad, ease back on the oil.'

Chalice murmured in protest, but for all that, she had read the situation fast and knew when it was time to fuss, and time to commit to silence and caution. 'She'll *definitely* catch up.'

Mr Riven turned to Arden, and whatever was on his lips, it could not be spoken of. He seized her hand.

In the silence she felt the heartbeat in him, his palm gone slick with sweat.

'Jonah?'

'Arden,' he said urgently. 'Get Sean Ironcup. Have David help you all with unhitching the tender dinghy at the back of this ship, lower it quietly and bring the Lion with you.'

'The dinghy? You said we could evade her.'

'Yes, I said that.' He pointed at a fog bank. 'You're all going to float as far back as you can to disappear. Then I'm going to tow you on a spider-web line, an invisible leash. Arden, listen to me. You cannot be here when they board.'

'What do you mean, *board*? Jonah, what's going on?'

A thump sounded overhead.

Mr Riven's hand tightened upon Arden's. His head tilted up. Said in the most grave voice, 'They had a trebuchet on the deck and—'

A voice said, 'Excuse me, I hate to interrupt.'

Chalice squeaked. However it had happened, a man was on the roof of the wheelhouse and his ruddy nose was in the open window, staring upside down at them.

The man was squash-faced and blond, with prison tattoos on each cheek. He looked at them with a pleasant if crooked smile. 'I'm sorry for interrupting your discussion, friends, but there are more important things you must contend with.'

The man's accent was strange, as if he spoke with a stone in his mouth. At his hands a small gas-powered crossbow.

Mr Riven lunged in front of Arden, and in the scuffle all Arden could see were limbs, and Chalice's head striking the wall, and a bronze coat snapping back as the bowman shouted, released a bolt from his crossbow.

It struck Mr Riven in the shoulder with the sound of a mallet to wet meat. With a scream of fury Mr Riven was smashed against the opposite wall, pinned by the five inches of black dart protruding from his collarbone.

He grabbed the bolt with both hands and pulled, and might as well have tried to draw a lance of iron from a rock.

The wail of pain from below came from the bowman, back-broken from having been torn off the roof from the recoil.

Arden ran to Mr Riven, afraid to touch the bolt, but in fear if she stayed. She gingerly placed her hands on the thin shaft and found no purchase there. 'Where's the tool box? I can pull it out.'

'Run,' Mr Riven gasped.

'I can't leave you.'

'He said *run*,' Chalice shouted, yanking Arden up by her collar. 'They have a catapult and glider-men! We must get in the lifeboat before another one lands!'

'But Mr Riven . . .'

Chalice shoved Arden through the wheelhouse door and buffaloed her onto the ladder. 'Move you, fool,' Chalice wailed. 'He's holding them off. You're the prize they . . .'

Chalice never got to finish. With a sickening crunch, the armoured prow of a ship rammed into *Saudade*'s side, nearly throwing Arden from the rungs.

A ship as ghostly as a fog, white as boiled bone, except for the glossy black square of her elaborate nameplate and the letters red as blood.

Sehnsucht.

32

Mr Riven made a sound

Mr Riven made a sound only once, and that was when the smartly dressed man, the first to board, finally snapped off the bolt that had fastened him to his wheelhouse wall. The barbs had proved difficult to prise from the black mangrove panels. Armed with a fearsome hinged tool, the man sweated through his silk shirt, his damask waistcoat and a medic's shawl with several false starts before untying his mustard-coloured cravat and rolling up his sleeves.

Arden, still kneeling in the corner where she had been shoved quite roughly before, watched the removal of Mr Riven's dart with bewildered dread. The man was Lyonnian. His accent did not belong to a Fiction pirate. He was not the only one with such confusing origins. Among the several pirates who had invaded their ship, fully half of them chattered like Claysiders.

The man put the bolt-cutter aside and nodded at the more utilitarian-dressed Sainted Island sailor who had accompanied him. 'All yours, Mr Taufik.'

'Thank you, Mr Absalom,' said the one called Mr Taufik good-humouredly. Opposite to the generous physicality of Mr Absalom, Mr Taufik had the spare, proletarian bearing of a Hillsider with a Pasifica-man's sea-severe face. 'There was a moment where I thought I might have to present our captive to the Queen with half the wall attached.'

'One mustn't upset the Queen.'

'No, one must not.'

'Carry on.'

Now that Mr Riven was free, Arden tried to scoot towards his prone body, only to have Mr Taufik slide himself between them.

'Oh no, your friend is in no condition for touchy-feelies.'

'Sir, he is hurt.'

'Mistress, we are all hurt in one way or another. And if he doesn't survive a bolt to the shoulder, what good is he, as a man, or a Riven?'

He bent down to touch the shiny end of the bolt as it protruded from Mr Riven's shoulder. 'My broken-backed scout downstairs tells me you can be clever when it comes to your freedom. And my Queen wishes to talk to you, sir.' He turned back to Arden. 'Therefore I'm not taking any chances on an upset. You understand. We are all of us beholden to our vows and orders.'

Mr Taufik called a pair of sailors up to the wheelhouse. He pointed at Mr Riven, said some words in a tradesman's cant that Arden vaguely found familiar – the rhythms were as familiar as a dockworker's dialect though the consonants were all wrong – and they hauled him up to his feet.

'Careful,' she pleaded.

Mr Taufik gave a gallant sort of bow. 'They will be careful. The Captain does not wish him harmed. You can stand up now, girl.'

In the midst of it all, Arden rankled. She had not been a girl for nearly a decade, and Mr Taufik was easily her age, but she was hardly in a place to quibble. She stood up on unsteady feet, feeling the weight of the shackles bear down upon her wrists.

'So, you are the lighthouse keeper of Vigil.' Mr Taufik touched the brim of his seaman's cap to nod respectfully. 'The navigational coldfires of Lyonne are legendary all around the world. It is a respect that you have earned well, Guildswoman.'

On the splintered deck, Chalice had not been granted the trial of an innocent. They'd bound her arms securely behind her back and gagged her into the bargain. Clearly these pirates had seen immediately in Chalice what had taken Arden weeks.

Chalice kept flicking her attention to *Sehnsucht*'s deck, willing Arden to focus on the ghost ship.

There was nothing on that high deck, not a person. David and Sean were missing.

One of the crewmen approached Mr Taufik, wearing impatience on his salt-burned face. 'Tauf,' he said. 'There's nobody else on this boat.'

'Have you checked everywhere?'

'The head, the engine rooms, the cabin. There's nobody.'

Mr Taufik frowned. 'There should have been five souls aboard.'

'Aye, if the craft is properly stocked, but there's a tender boat winch at the back of this boat. Whatever was on it, is missing.'

'Hmm, *she* won't like that.' Mr Taufik considered the fog and what it meant. The day was here now, and the sunrise on a distant Island shore gave the permanent storm a jaundiced murk. 'Hard to survive out on these waters with only a small craft. We'll call the other two lost at sea and be done with them. We have what we came for.'

A wretched tingle of hope made Arden perk up. The boys had escaped, though if Mr Riven heard the good news, he gave no notice of it. He looked the part of a man familiar with detention and chains. An excoriated distance overwhelmed his expression, his pale skin gone a driftwood grey. They had taken no chances with their prisoner, bonding him to a yoke-contraption that fixed his wrists on either side of his head, must have caused considerable agony to his wounded shoulder.

She felt his pain. Felt the wound as if it were upon her own flesh.

'Jonah,' Arden whispered when Mr Taufik's attention was averted. 'Are you all right? What do we do?'

Whatever fugue had caught him now slipped. He wobbled his fingers, only just realizing they had bound him in a most specific method, a position that would not allow him to draw his own blood. A way they should not have known, unless . . .

His waxen face turned to her. 'Don't get close to me. Whatever happens, you and I, there is nothing between us . . .'

Mr Taufik returned, and snatched Arden away. 'Ah now, no talking to the merchandise. We must all get on *Sehnsucht*. I fear *Saudade* is taking on water. If anyone is hiding on her, well then. I hope they can swim.'

Shock-numbed, Arden allowed a sailor to help her across the gangway and onto *Sehnsucht*.

The moment she set foot on that bone-white wooden deck, a kick of cold jolted through Arden's body. Dark *Saudade* always had an aura of warmth and intimacy about her, her rich mangrove wood echoing a holy relic. This bleached giant of a sister-ship had the smell of slaughterhouses and desecrated tombs, along with a fungal sediment of decay.

Like criminals they were led onto *Sehnsucht*'s broad open forward deck, an area that could accommodate fifty people if needed be, a hundred at a crush.

Only twelve stood here in the wind apart from them, waiting, along with Mr Absalom, insouciant upon the bow, as if an interesting stage play had come to be acted out in his presence.

The pirates set Arden and Chalice aside, leaned them against the bridge. Mr Riven was placed upon the foredeck to stand bloodied and on display. Arden yearned towards him. If she could have taken his pain upon herself she'd have done so, twice over.

The sound of a door opening made the entourage shuffle to attention. Someone else was on the ship who did not slot so easily into the role of Sainted Island bandit.

A woman.

The Pirate Queen?

She was a girl, younger than Arden, her dark hair bound up in an abalone fork. She wore a flowing yellow sea-silk robe embroidered in black pearls that would have better befitted some royal court than the deck of a ship.

Or at least the dress had been yellow, until the stains of dirt and blood had streaked it orange in places. Many of the pearls had fallen off in the way such decorations will do if they are worn for a very long time and not carefully maintained.

She shared a look with Arden, distress and mortification combined, before concealing her face under a silk shawl of faded yellow.

'I am Persephone Libro, the Queen's lady-in-waiting and spoil of war. You are guests upon *Sehnsucht* of the Maris Island Cluster,' the girl continued, her thin reedy voice fluting in the empty air. 'These are the Marians from Maris Proper who have welcomed you.'

Arden frowned. The girl spoke by rote and a harassed familiarity, but what had she seen and done to make her so desperately dishevelled?

Spoil of war, she had said. Persephone Libro, a Sainted Isle girl and spoil of war. What political upheavals was she referring to? How in danger were they?

Mr Riven, unable to hold himself upright, fell on his knees. The bolt was not bleeding badly, however it did something to him that made him hunch over in ashen pain.

'Listen,' Arden said urgently to the gathered men. 'There is a code among sailors and pirates alike. You cannot leave him like that.'

Mr Taufik winced, then hissed at a pair of bandits. 'Get him to his feet.'

'Captain on deck,' a male voice shouted. 'Her Majesty on deck! Queen of the Islands is present, you louts, you wretches. Bow to your damned Queen!'

The sailor holding Mr Riven quickly snapped to attention again, and the others followed. Released, Mr Riven fell back into a kneeling crouch.

No false alarm this time. Everyone had frozen in place.

Then the twelve men fell to their knees. Arden shared a glance with Chalice, and at the stormbride's nod, they both carefully bobbed.

The dress came first, ruffles and layers of discoloured white. Stained satin slippers stepping across the white wood. Tiny hands in fingerless cream gloves, entwined piously about a wedding ring of black iron worn over the cloth. The ring was too large for her finger, and stained the glove-satin green.

The face, sharp and Fiction-pale, was so deteriorated by an internal, seething rage it was as if she were a porcelain doll left to crackle into decay. Frayed yellow hair touched her thin, bony shoulders. The crown she wore was ship-hull nails dipped in gold. A livery collar of plesiosaur teeth bound up in wire obscured most of the tattered lace of her bodice. A train of fishing net, tangled and worn, followed her along with a brace of glass floats.

Arden found she'd been holding her breath. Who was this woman? Not Bellis, the beautiful girl who Jonah loved.

This had to be someone else.

Two men swept the floor before their Queen with brooms of a bitterbush. The acrid fragrance of the brushes overwhelmed the salt in the air.

Mr Taufik stepped forward. 'We recovered them,' he said. 'One man, two women.'

The husk Queen ignored Mr Taufik and her prisoners to gaze down at Mr Riven's crumpled form. She shook her head. 'Jonah,' she said. 'My God, husband. You shouldn't have come.'

33

When he didn't immediately reply

When he didn't immediately reply, Bellis grabbed the bolt-end in Mr Riven's shoulder and twisted it terribly, forcing Mr Riven out of his daze.

'I said you *promised* me you wouldn't *come*, Jonah.'

He groaned, said her name with a breathless wheeze. 'Bellis, you were in danger . . .'

She cut him off with an impatient gesture. 'When am I always not in danger, in this boat of venomous snakes? I'm told Mr Absalom had to take you off the wall. Well, then. Was a time you would have torn your arm off at the root rather than remain imprisoned so.' A sadness in her soft, fragile voice, as if she had lost something important. 'And now you kneel in submission to pain. The years have diluted you, husband.'

'Wife, this is different. The Lions know where you are, they want to control you, and use you now.'

'Use me? Why would you hold me in such low regard? The Lyonnians and their Order have wanted my labour forever.' She looked around her, smiled benevolently at her gathered silent crew. 'I was doing quite fine, and now you came back to me like this, ruined, by these devils, *ruined.*' She grabbed the bolt again, and she was weeping as she did so, fat milky tears upon her broken-doll face, oblivious to Mr Riven's suffering as she revelled in her own.

'The man I married would have held himself above pain! What stranger wearing my beloved's face are you? These witnesses of mine cannot be fooled by such a despicable disguise!'

Mr Riven was transcendent with agony. A sound of strangulated surrender came from him. Beside his head, his trapped hands balled into fists. Old injuries opened, sending blood pouring down his exposed forearms.

Arden could stand it no longer. 'Stop it, damn you. He's hurt, and he came on your behalf!'

Bellis stopped testing her husband and glared at Arden for the first time.

Mr Riven swallowed deep huffing, shuddering breaths, began urgently trying to capture her attention back.

'The women have nothing to do with this . . .'

Bellis waved the voices away. She was done with him. One of the Islanders shoved a bight of coir between Mr Riven's teeth. Her attention was on Arden now.

Chalice Quarry made murmuring sounds that could have been plea or prayer. The girl in saffron yellow wrapped her arms around her body, brought one fist to her mouth.

Bellis was smaller, up close. A twig would have more strength. The acrid-bush smell was about her, a petrochemical aroma of heated stone and rockblood.

'I know that coat of yours,' she said to Arden.

'Your wedding coat,' Arden replied as steadily as she could. She knew she should have diplomatically added, *and you may have it back*, but could not, for the coat had the importance of a contested trade region. Even now, Arden was not about to give it up.

Bellis wrinkled her nose, drawing sharp lines across her face, highlighting the deep shadows beneath her eyes. 'The hell that ugly thing was my wedding coat.' Tugged at the collar. 'Was forced on me by necessity, but never mine. The Deepwater Queen does not wear the coat of her enemy.'

She circled Arden, inspecting every inch of her. 'So, you're the one the angels talk of, when they sing their songs from the Lion's den.' Bellis pushed up the krakenskin sleeve and touched the inside of Arden's arm. Her thin white finger looked like a chicken bone laid against Arden's skin. 'They sing so sweetly, of something in these veins that entangles and endows. A strange chemistry, bred out of our genetic lines, but still commanding fear, the way mine does.'

Arden wanted to recoil from that dry, hard finger. 'I don't know what—'

'So very, very Lyonne to lose sight of the gold from over-gilding,' Bellis said, sharper now. 'Well, we here in Fiction might not have thousand-year ancestral ledgers, but we know good breeding, and who to *fuck*.'

Bellis' pinched Fictish features turned mean, and she grabbed Arden's arm hard with her fingerless gloves, dug in her bony fingers. Had Bellis still retained fingernails, she'd have broken skin. Instead those tiny fingers were knobs, like the joints at the end of bird bones.

'You have no right to destroy my life's work! Jonah Riven, my *Jonah*, was carved in suffering and restraint, a creature conceived only to inspire terror and protection and one day be a leader to challenge even the dirty *anguis* worshippers on the fucking northern shore, and somehow he ends up back in my lap like this, like *this*, snivelling with a little hurt, for *everyone* to *fucking see*!'

Behind Bellis, Mr Riven tried to stand up. One of the crewmen shoved him by his wounded shoulder, forced him into kneeling again.

No, Jonah, Arden prayed through her terror. *Don't make it worse.*

Chalice moaned. This time she wiggled her fingers, and an outsider would have seen only a woman trying to make comfort of their bonds. But she kept making the same finger sign, over and over again, and Arden recognized the signs she saw on the Clay Portside docks among men who had been imprisoned for crimes or just bad luck, the secret language of captives, made with their hands.

Fire, she was saying, but with emphasis. *Fire.*

Bellis turned on her gathered crew and berated them with a spitting rant that was as familiar to them as breakfast gruel, given their resigned expressions. 'Which one of you will be running back to Miah Anguis, huh? Scurrying back to the slaughterman of Equus with little tales of this evening, of my once-terrifying husband so toothless, so lame? Oh, he'll come to my castle and murder me with a laugh . . . and then I'll fucking kill the lot of you!'

A dozen pairs of eyes turned to their feet in terror, except for Mr Absalom, who viewed them all with the odd benevolent humour of a person secure in his position.

Fire, Chalice repeated hurriedly. *Sacrifice. More. More.*

Bellis spun to Arden, leaned in, her breath a miasma of petrolactose fumes. 'So how did you do it?' she wheedled. 'How did you take what was fierce and brilliant and important to me and soften it to rottenness? Did you fornicate with him like a fine Lyonne *whore?*'

Mr Riven jerked upright on his knees, his body trembling, eyes wide as a hunt-spooked animal that senses danger but cannot articulate its edges. 'Bellis, nothing happened between us,' he started to say through the rope bight, before Mr Taufik tugged the end and silenced him.

'We are all puppets,' Arden protested. 'All of us. You might think you are free now, but Lyonne controls us with words, spreads rumours to make us dance. They wanted you to dance right back into their arms.'

'There was a special dance around you too, was there not?' Bellis mused, tapping her lip with her finger. 'Some odd symmetry, some strange shadow, and they exiled you to Fiction, an experiment. See, I am exiled here too. An experiment. I know. Safe and sound and so very far away from Clay City so I can't cause any trouble.' Bellis simpered and giggled. 'Oh, every once in a while the Order sends a spy or three, but nobody has got me talking yet. It is I who make them talk. And sing. And they sing such a strange song of you, I am very curious, Arden Beacon.'

'If you and I were truly twinned in any kind of special blood chemistry, we would be meeting in the Lyonne Towers as honoured guests, not on this ship,' Arden said urgently. 'All I can do is make *ignis* fire, and that not very well.'

'A fire,' Bellis echoed emptily.

Arden implored her. 'You must believe me. I've no wish to hurt you.'

'Oh, you wouldn't hurt me. Not in the slightest. The songs all alleviated that worry.'

Behind Bellis, Mr Absalom smiled, and even from across the room, Arden could see one tooth was Djenne gold. He reminded her of Uncle Nicolai Beacon, the confidence in him, the way the moving parts of the world operated around him yet affected him not at all.

'We will discover the truth of that music soon enough, Your Majesty,' he promised.

A clatter of activity distracted Arden from her interrogation. The sailors were hauling up tin water buckets from over the side of *Sehnsucht*, placing them in concentric circles about Mr Riven as he knelt in his supplication to those gods of pain. The water sloshed on the deck.

'Now I have an opportunity, see,' Bellis continued. 'Certainly, I have been delivered back something broken, but what is broken can be mended. I can purge the softness and the rot from him. Not enough to kill and maim. But enough pain to remark and remember, and to do it before witnesses.'

One of the *Sehnsucht* sailors ran up to Bellis from outside the door. 'We found the blood our messenger said she'd be carrying. Hidden in the lifejacket crate,' he said breathlessly. He held aloft the mason jar. Beside Arden, Chalice stopped murmuring and became still.

'Your blood?' Bellis asked Arden with a beatific smile. 'In a jar? Well, that will save us the problem of cutting you.'

336

'Bellis . . .' Arden implored.

'Of course, it wouldn't be unlike the Lyonne Order to try and trick me. This could be poison blood, and if I were to daub it on myself – well then. Would I not be the fool?' She caressed the glass. 'Can I tell you of my experience with fire?'

Arden did not reply. Saw the horror coming.

'I saw a terrible accident once, in an automatic refinery fire on Equus.' Bellis' white fingers fluttered in the air before her. 'A long time ago, in the days before I was married. A man burned alive because they were stealing the rockblood from the mechanica, and forgot the mechanica cannot abide being stolen from. Such a screaming fit he made of it, up in flame, eyes popping in his skull, *pop-pop*. And the heat, like the surface of the sun.

'Oh, I was full of sorrow for him at first, for I was young and did not appreciate that his test was necessary and holy. How someone could survive such an immolation – it is only a question for God and His devils, but afterwards, this previously weak, cowardly man, this man who had not a single quality of leadership, was *transformed* by his pain. Made *anew*. A prophet he became, blind and hideous but powerful, oh yes. People now set themselves alight for him, and I, with my own secret flame burning within my breast and in my heart, know that this is how I will save my Jonah from his own weakness.'

Arden would have risen to her feet were she not held down. 'He can't be saved if he's dead!'

Bellis poked her finger into Arden's cheek. 'You aren't dead. Because I can smell the *aequor profundum* on your skin. He *healed* you. That secret Riven talent. Let's see if he can heal himself.'

Chalice made noises into her gag that sounded like *no no no*.

Gasping, Arden strained against the ropes. 'Bellis Harrow, your soul will be damned forever if you hurt him.'

'*Harrow*, you call me? Harrow, when I was wedded to a Riven before witnesses?' She came close to Arden, tilted her chin in Mr Riven's direction. Bitterbush stench all about her.

Petroleum on her breath. Her teeth blackened with coal. 'Bellis *Riven* I am, protected only by my name. Only two things are feared on our Islands, the threat of fire and the name of *Riven*. I will be both threat and Riven, after today.'

With that, Bellis stood and in a whirl took the mason jar of Arden's blood from the subordinate and up-ended it over Mr Riven's head. The blood had congealed down to gelatinous lumps and smeared him in gore. He shook his head to whip the muck from his eyes. He growled furiously through the rope bight, trapped but not surrendered.

'Oh, look. Nothing happened. That is a shame. You did say your cold flame was weak, so I cannot fault your honesty.'

Bellis smiled down at her husband. Her expression softened to him for the first time and Arden glimpsed what she may have once looked like, as a child. He was suddenly beautiful to her like this. She caressed his bloodied, whiskered face, his shoulders, then ducked down into a squat, caressed his leather-clad thigh as if teasing him, pressed a thin, hard hand between his legs. Whispered something into his blood-smeared ear as she did so.

When he did not react quite so enthusiastically to this, their long-awaited reunion, she slipped her hand past the waistband of his strides, clasped what she found there, stroked him.

Bellis meant to humiliate Jonah further, reduce him to nothing before her men, show him in sexual thrall to the Queen of this death-white ship. And Arden understood with a dreadful clarity what it meant. Maybe . . . maybe if he responded to her gross ministrations, Bellis would spare him. Maybe if he showed Bellis proper deference, this would all be a threat and never carried out.

Arden wanted Mr Riven to look at her, to silently give him courage in this abject act. *Grow hard at her touch*, she implored. *Spend yourself into that hand of bones and skin. Make Bellis believe she is that upon which all your desires hinge, even when there is nothing left outside of promised pain and endless despair. This might save you.*

But his gaze had turned blank and distant, and he shrank in upon himself, encased in a cocoon of his own flesh. Bellis continued to stroke him and whisper her fascinations. Nobody moved, except Mr Absalom, who watched them all with his knowing basilisk gaze.

The fact that Mr Riven didn't – or couldn't – respond clearly vexed Bellis. She gave him one last malicious squeeze and stood up suddenly. 'What's wrong with you? You have lost your vigour. *Impotent*. Neutered. Like a dog.'

She turned back to Arden. Bared her teeth. 'Now we find out what the Lions were talking about. Persephone!'

The yellow-dressed girl fished in the folds of her dress, and pulled out a pint-jar that might have once been a milk-bottle. Bellis discarded the lid. Aromatic fumes washed over them. Distilled petroleum, and flammable as the sun. A man nearby lit a flare, a crimson, phosphorous eye, almost too bright to look at. Laid it between Jonah's knees.

'*Ignis* fire is cold, more's the pity. But my fire is strong.'

Arden saw Mr Riven swallow a breath. The phosphor flare turned his skin an unholy colour. The sailors readied their buckets nervously, ever fearful of a fire upon a wooden ship.

'Healer,' Bellis said. 'Cure this.'

Jonah, Arden breathed.

The liquid fell upon him and the fire ignited.

34

A whump of hot flame

A *whump* of hot flame and a roil of smoke and char that filled the air with embers. Arden might have screamed, if not for the rattle and bang of people falling upon the decks and a lone body stumbling out of the smoke into Bellis' arms.

'*Save me, Holy Maria*,' the burned sailor groaned.

'Get off me, you brute!' Bellis shoved him away into the acrid mist. 'Where is he? Where is my husband?'

The smoke was thicker than the fog, a grey murk swirling with trails of white. A fire had taken hold of the forecastle, flames licking as high as the wheelhouse.

The smoke swallowed Bellis from Arden's view, and in the melee Arden dived for Chalice, tearing off her gag.

'Quick Chalice, move!'

Arden dragged Chalice sideways, down the length of the deck. Anyone would have been blinded by the smoke if they'd not worked all their lives in pea-soupers, could tell by the echo of a footfall where to go.

She got her stormbride about and twisted off the shackle catch, freeing her arms. 'Did you see Jonah, is he dead?'

Without waiting for the obvious answer Arden turned about so Chalice could do the same.

Once Chalice had her bit out, she spat coir and said, 'No, he healed himself, your blood can—'

A man loomed out of the clouds, still in stocks. Mr Riven, his shirt blackened and in tatters, emerged slightly singed but otherwise unharmed. His eyes bright. Arden sobbed in relief. She wrapped him up in her arms, wanted to take the weight of him if she could.

'How? I saw you consumed!'

'I need . . . to get help. To call up . . .' he gasped, and began to cough, each spasm wracking his injured chest. He'd used sanguinity from the blood in his wound, but too much, too much . . .

'Jonah, *dammit*.' Arden seized one bound hand. 'Let me get the stocks off.'

'No time,' he croaked. 'We have to get to the back of the ship before they put the petroleum fire out and regroup.'

Chalice took the other side of Mr Riven and they stumbled through the clearing air.

'These people are mendicants of the highest order!' she protested, as they came across the dinghy lashed to *Sehnsucht*'s side. 'You too, Chalice Quarry.'

Mr Riven shook himself free of their hands. 'You must lower the lifeboat, quickly.'

A throat cleared with a cough. Arden's shoulders wrenched tight. They were too late.

'Ah, I *thought* you would make it back here,' said the deep Lyonne voice. 'My instincts for sensing benightedness are still keen despite repeated exposure.'

Mr Absalom stood on the deck with a harpoon spear in his hand, one long enough to spike a leviathan if he had to. His eyes streamed red from the smoke. His waistcoat was singed from escaping the fire upon the deck.

He nodded at Mr Riven. 'So it's true. The woman is a cata-lyst. That blood of hers turned your little healing trick into something powerful. You survived immolation.'

Mr Riven made to lunge at him, but Mr Absalom did not

have the clumsiness of a brute fighter from a dock pit, nor was there a chance of Mr Riven defeating him while bound up and close to collapsing. Arden stepped in front of Mr Riven before he could move, caught him about his waist, could feel his heart in his chest, the dread in him.

'Wait, Jonah.'

'Arden,' he said. 'Don't trust this man.'

'Sir,' Arden said to Mr Absalom, 'let us go. We did not deserve this inhumane treatment from your *Queen*. I can see you are different from the others, but there is no help you can give other than letting us go.'

Mr Absalom shook his head. 'At present the others scramble about their Maiden Queen and try to stop *Sehnsucht* from springing a burning leak, but not for much longer. If a lifeboat is to disappear, then they will blame me.'

'Then make up something, damn you! If you consider yourself noble Djenne, or Karakorum or whatever you are! If you wear the embellishments of great people, then live up to them! Just say we struck you from behind or you passed out. Have you no pride?'

Mr Riven sagged behind Arden. She caught his body, and he had seemed so much more solid when she had held him in joy. Now he was a wraith.

'Jonah, I need you awake. Don't falter now . . .'

'Arden, you can't be here.'

Behind them, Chalice struggled with the rearward lifeboat rope.

'The damn thing has an Athenian knot! I can't budge it.' She stared hopelessly out towards the horizon. '*Saudade*'s drifting. We'll never catch her.'

Mr Absalom stood above them, watching with all the pitilessness of a desert. 'They will make a vivisection of you, Lightmistress. Bled and torn limb from limb until you are meat. Your blood has proven itself worth a little parlour trick, but the Queen will want to see it work on herself. She has many shadows that, were they to be increased, well . . . she would be a very powerful creature indeed.'

Shouts echoed from the end of the ship. Angry shouts. They had been spotted. Mr Absalom's eyes widened.

To Chalice he said, '*Is there no help for the Widow's Son?*'

The words meant nothing to Arden, but Chalice stopped yanking on the knots. A strange, almost blank acknowledgement appeared on her face. 'What do you need, brother?'

He pulled a small tablet of polished brass from his waistcoat pocket and shoved it into Chalice's hands. '*Hide it.*'

Arden had only a moment to look upon the rose and thorn crest of the Lyonne Investigatory Order as her stormbride snatched up the shining locket and shoved it in between her bosoms.

'Take Mx Beacon off this ship,' Mr Absalom urged Chalice. 'Now. But the man must stay here.'

He had given an order. Chalice grabbed Arden's hand. 'Arden, we have to jump.'

She pulled herself away. 'No! What has gotten into you, Chalice Quarry? We don't leave without Jonah.'

The footsteps peppered the deck through the smoke. She stood firm, ready to protect him. Mr Riven made a last despairing sound. His chin fell against her face and the words came out raw.

'Go. Go but remember me. Remember your poor fisherman from Vigil. Give him the Deepwater prayer in midwinter and remember him.'

'I don't know the Deepwater prayer.'

'Nor do I, but I will serve the King soon. He will teach it to me in the court of my ancestors.'

'You cannot die. You cannot.'

Jonah Riven kissed her once upon her forehead, something more tender than passion, more marbled with regret.

From the centre deck, Bellis Harrow screamed.

'Don't you dare move!'

Arden looked at Jonah one last time, then she met the woman's eyes in defiance. Glassy as cataracts, with only evil behind them. With a gasp of a desperately committed breath, Arden tipped backwards over *Sehnsucht*'s stern.

The wake of the water swallowed her in a roar of bubbles, and the cold wash penetrated her with the agony of a thousand needles. When her head cleared the surface, Chalice was already floundering alongside, agitating her skirts to make them buoyant.

'By the Cross of the Redeemer we survived the fall,' Chalice gasped. 'If not for that paddle-foam the drop would have killed us.'

'What the devils did you do?' Arden shouted back, spitting salt. Her krakenskin coat ballooned with air, making her bob on the surface of the water. 'And who was that man you just gave up Jonah for?'

'I saved our lives,' Chalice huffed, dog-paddling towards her within a ring of inflated fabric. Her face had taken on a fish-belly shade from the cold water. 'They have a spy from the Order on board. He knows them, so if he says they'll kill us if we stay, they *will*.'

'This *water* will kill us! We'll not last ten minutes!'

A shriek from the boat interrupted them, so high-pitched and commanding that it could only have come from Bellis: *Get her out. Get them out!*

The paddlewheels ceased turning. The ship listed. A rope ladder flung over *Sehnsucht*'s side. Mr Riven did his best to run interference, but from her water-vantage Arden knew he was hopelessly outmatched. A fist from one of Bellis' sailors struck him once, twice. Hauled him halfway over the port railing, where his bound hands grasped open air on either side of his head.

His eyes met Arden's, and she had never seen such a look on a living thing.

Jonah . . .

Little more than a whisper, an entreaty, a farewell.

Mr Riven bit down hard upon his lip and spat blood into the water.

Bellis let out a horrific piercing scream. *'Get him the FUCK devil AWAY from the WATER!'*

The sailors dragged him back and Arden saw him no more.

Bellis ran to the edge of the boat, pointed at Arden, warning and accusing. Nothing she said, for such demons needed to say nothing.

By now the men charged to bring Arden back had descended the ladder and commenced swimming out to meet their two wretched prisoners.

. . . or they would have done if the surface of the water had not turned to glass and rainbows, a thousand translucent bodies writhing around them, and the ocean falling away, preparing their ascent into heaven.

35

Where are they taking us

'Where are they taking us?' Chalice yelled over the slosh and roar of the waves.

'I don't know,' Arden replied breathlessly, her mind whirring as fast as the water that carried her. Magic? Magic was fragile, a phenomenon that could be explained by science eventually. Her dress clung to her but it was not unpleasant. Like a liquid carriage. Arden forced sense on what she could see: from the corner of her eye she could discern the vague shape of an eye, perhaps a hoof on the end of a long leg, forming from the white wash of the waves that lifted them away. They should have frozen in such water, but the water-horses warmed the water to the temperature of blood. Electric flashes darted about them, they were carried aloft on a tide of light. Hard bodies, threshing tails, manes of wet kelp. Arden grabbed one hippocamp mane to find it fall away in her hands and turn to jelly.

Then almost as suddenly as it had come the phenomenon was gone and the two castaway women were floating in empty sea once more.

'Well, that's a fat lot of help,' Chalice gasped once the last of the horse-waves had receded. She rolled about on the puffs of her inflated skirt. The becalmed sea sloshed lazily about them as the night fell and darkness closed in. 'If he was going to summon a herd of hippocampi he could have at least taken us all the way.'

'He might not be conscious any more, Chalice.'

'Oh. All right.'

Arden tested the waters with her hand. With the fading light, another source of illumination came, this time from deep below, faint red, like the afterimage of a bright light on an eye.

'Water's warm.'

'Hot water current. Sea-vent, or an underwater volcano,' Chalice said. 'Ah, to die of exhaustion and thirst rather than chill. That makes all the difference.'

'Wasn't it your idea to jump?'

'It was a spur-of-the-moment decision,' Chalice protested in between spitting out salt water. 'Jumping felt better than being dragged off for Queen Harrow's entertainment.'

Arden paddled vigorously even though the krakenskin coat would not let her sink. 'What happened on the boat, anyway, Chalice?' she gasped, kept aloft by anger more than anything. 'I can put a fire out, is that my damn shadow?'

'No,' Chalice panted in return. 'Not the fire. You only made stronger what Jonah could do. Water is his element. You *increased* that.'

'But still, a fire like that . . . nobody could heal from it.'

'You're not a very strong *sanguis ignis*, but of that other thing . . . you are strong indeed.'

Arden paddled about. 'I think,' she started, raising her chin away from the water, 'I think I know what Bellis has. What shadow made the Society so cautious and you Lions so interested.'

Chalice tilted her head, frowned, swallowed water and coughed. 'Oh?'

'I saw a broken doll of a woman, yet I saw her issue instructions to those frightening men, on a ship that was once slower than *Saudade*, yet which caught us easily.'

A look of guilt passed over Chalice's face. Yet one more thing to hold against her former friend in the short time they probably had left.

'These old talents overlap, Arden. They were never bred to be specific. Nobody can say for certain what Bellis has, or had, or what she may yet develop . . .'

'*Sanguis orientis*,' Arden said. 'Why not? A Sainted Isle trait for a girl in such close proximity? I saw how she made those men jump at her word. She could command legions if she could work it properly. Sure, it's a scrappy bunch of toothless pirates she compels now, but think her with an army.'

'I don't want to think of it,' Chalice said.

'No. I suppose nobody does. It would be awful, wouldn't it. Her, Queen of Lyonne and Fiction. The Society and the Order would have to work to her command. No wonder they wouldn't let her go to Lyonne!' Her exhaustion made her slightly hysterical, and she giggled and wept at once.

Dark things flitted below them. Arden was certain she saw the long neck of a plesiosaur, the bulbous head of an ichthyic whale. Were Jonah unhurt, these creatures would be in his control. But he was, and they were not.

So Bellis was sanguis orientis. The bloodworked command upon the lich-ships that ran between Equus and Vigil, objects that did what they were told, forever.

'There was a chance she could be . . . amenable though,' Chalice said.

'Oh yes, because Mr Lindsay hoped Jonah would tighten her leash!'

'Well, we thought he would! He did it once! How was anyone to know how much of a ruse of hers that idea was!' Chalice wallowed in her inflated dress. 'Damn it, I'm sinking.'

The night, when it came, was so dark. The fog hid the stars. Away from the warm-water upswell, the cold began to seep in, promising pain. They were neither of them brave enough to enter the cold water and freeze, so they remained paddling around in their little thermocline. Arden prayed for one of the monsters to come up, to eat them or save them. But they did neither, oblivious to the pitiful little lives above them, and she felt for the first time the tenuous link between herself and Jonah Riven sever, like a thread pulled tight until it snapped.

'Arden,' Chalice said, and the harsh tone brought her back from her despair.

'What is it?'

'We don't have to do this. This waiting to end in agony, by thirst or frost.' Chalice took Arden's hand with her water-wrinkled own. 'I have a vial,' she said urgently. 'A poison given to all Lions. It is placed under my skin, in my arm here. If you could dig it out, we could share it.'

'I don't . . . I don't know. Let us think a while.'

'All right. A little while.'

The two women clung to each other for comfort, aware of the only path forward left to them.

The water was getting colder. The current was moving them on.

'Chalice,' Arden said after a long silence.

'Yes, darling?'

'You said my blood could *increase* an endowment. Make someone else's stronger?'

'Or your own. You've been riding on a *sanguis ignis* talent that was just about latent anyway. You were never *ignis*, or *malorum*. Just increased the tiny correspondence with fire you naturally had.'

Had she not been so cold, Arden might have mourned such a revelation. Now they were identities stripped away by water.

'You've been tested, Chalice. What did you say you had?'

'Only the slightest symmetry for salts and minerals. Sodium, some lower metals.' She shrugged as best she could with her shoulders half-submerged in the water.

'Sodium is an atomic component of salt . . .' Arden murmured, as if her mouth spoke a memory she could not.

'See. Nothing useful, I'm afraid. Unless you wanted *more* salt.' Chalice said, her teeth now chattering. 'Curse! It could be rock candy and saltwater taffy I trammel, for all I know.'

349

Arden pulled off her glove, let it float away.

'What are you doing, darling?'

'I saw Mr Lindsay with a sodium light in the Justinian orangery,' Arden said. 'I can't make enough light with *ignis malorum*, but if you helped me . . . if you could control that element, maybe I could increase your interaction with it.'

'To do what?' A note of panic twanged in Chalice's voice.

'Whatever it can do.'

Chalice stared, terrified. For a long moment Arden feared Chalice would refuse. Then she nodded. Pulled her locket out. *A rose upon thorns.* She used the thorn of the Rose Order to dig into the coin in Arden's hand. Arden could not help but hiss at the pain.

Then Chalice inflicted the sharp locket upon her own hand. She had calluses there, from years of work, and Arden wanted to tell her that it was not important, the place.

But Chalice wanted to cut herself in the same place she had cut Arden. It was important to her.

'Ugh, almost, almost.'

Arden senses the blood in the water with a sick lurch, both for the meaning of it, and for the realization that it was her shadow endowment making her so sensitive to sanguinity. She'd always carried that shadow with her, not knowing, oblivious.

Now only if it would work.

The stormbride let the rose locket go. Let it float to the bottom of the ocean. They wrapped their hands together. Arden felt the blood in her grommets prickle and ache. A deep weariness overcame her. *Please*, she thought. *Let something happen, anything, that is not dying on an empty sea.*

Their buoyancy was increasing. They wallowed on the surface of the becalmed water.

'Maybe it is salt. Oh, I could imagine an island of salt,' Chalice murmured, her shivering chin knocking into Arden's ear. Arden's mind was becoming fog. Chalice's voice drifted through it. 'A salt crystal palace.' Their hands squeezed tighter.

'A Kingdom of Salt and we will be Queens upon it.'

'Is anything else happening?' Arden asked. Her hands had gone into a rictus. She was having trouble moving.

'Nothing,' Chalice said. 'Nothing. Is it morning though? It's so light.'

'It's not the sky,' Arden said. 'It's us.' She kicked with all her remaining strength, and the sea might have been a shimmer of yellow light. 'It's you, Chalice, it's you!'

Light all around them, orange as a sunset.

Chalice Quarry's cracked lips split into a grin. She spun around and shrieked into the fog. 'Hey! Hey! Over *here*.'

Through the illuminated yellow mist came the chatter of a small kraken-oil engine, and the prow of a longboat loomed. Same black dinghy the pirates had reported missing from *Saudade*'s stern, with a roof of black canvas. Over the bow, two familiar faces, both incandescent with sodium light and relief.

David Modhi and Sean Ironcup. Still alive.

36

Are you awake

Are you awake, dear? Truly awake?
  I have been awakened to something.
  Then best get up now. You have been asleep long enough.
  Arden sat up suddenly in a bed of soft cotton sheets. She immediately saw the portrait of the senior Justinian staring down at her from the foot of the bed. The Dowager had called him a stormcaller, from old Northern bloodlines. The old baron, Alexander Justinian. He wore shades of Mr Riven's face.
  Next to the portrait, the very real figure of a nurse, who gasped and dropped her tray of potions, before running out of the room. Within seconds she was back with the Dowager Justinian and Mr Sage.
  'Where . . .' Arden croaked with a voice that sounded as if her throat were lined with sand. 'I need to get up.'
  The light through the small, high window seemed altogether too bright. She winced, and the Dowager went to draw the curtains.
  'You're safe in our Manse,' she said. 'The Coastmaster decided it would be better for you to recover here than in Mr Sage's hospice. He sent out a search party, you see. Saved your life.'
  After all that had happened, the simple thought of being

in such a debt to Mr Justinian was the thing to turn her stomach. A more pressing need took her. 'Bathroom.'

Mr Sage came forward. 'Ah, take your steps easy, then, Mx Beacon. You haven't been on your legs for nearly three days.'

She frowned. 'Three days? But I was halfway to the Sainted Isles a minute ago.'

'Dear, whatever you and your stormbride were doing on the open ocean so close to winter I cannot begin to opine, but you caught yourself a dreadful case of *ichor meritis*.' When Arden remained bewildered the Dowager added, 'It's a disease of the water around here. The creatures from the depths have a wicked venom.'

'Chalice, oh, how is she?'

'Hale as anything. Some people have a natural resistance. Some however, not. Up you get.'

The Dowager Justinian helped her into the bathroom, and afterwards waited with a bowl of lukewarm soup for Arden to teeter back, as weak as a foal taking its first steps.

'If you're up to visitors, there's the young lady here for you.'

Arden nodded. 'Give her permission.'

Chalice ran in before Dowager Justinian had a chance to advise her of Arden's decision, and kissed her messily on both cheeks before seizing up her hands.

'Ah, Arden, you're quite alive! Mr Sage came by twice a day and said all you needed was rest. I snuck David Modhi past the nurse at the door. He was so worried. *Ichor meritis!* It's a death sentence in these parts. I would have sent for a proper doctor but . . .'

'Your work is appreciated,' Arden said, and smiled though every muscle in her face hurt and her heart hurt twice more.

When the Dowager left them alone, Chalice closed the door and came close. The rigours of their castaway journey were still on her peeling skin and sunburned face.

'Mr Lindsay interviewed me,' she said quietly. 'I gave him the locket Mr Absalom gave me.' Arden frowned and Chalice waved her hand in dismissal – for a moment resembling the no-nonsense friend she'd known before.

'Don't fret, a copy was made before I handed it over. It contained a map printed on a square of silk, an up-to-date map of the Islands and their cities more detailed than we had ever yet seen.'

'What else did you tell him?'

'Not about Mr Riven, or that you know of your shadow endowment now, or that you made me stronger, if only for a little while.'

'I can't remember what we did. It's all rather muddy.'

'You increased me, made me *sanguinem*. Only long enough to make a little sodium arc in seawater. I can't say it was the most brilliant talent ever to show itself, but it certainly helped the boys find us. Oh, and I brought you a present.'

Then Chalice took a pair of new leather gloves from her pocket and unwrapped the bandages from Arden's hands. The grommets had been sealed with an antibiotic honey-wax.

'To replace the ones you lost.'

'Thank you, Chalice.'

'The Eugenics Society would use you terribly, if they had real proof of what they suspect you capable of, this *sanguinem evalescendi*.' She pushed the gloves forward, urged Arden to take them.

'Doesn't this silent assistance go beyond your Order vows?'

'Oh, I am loyal to the Lyonne Order. But the Order is made up of mere men, and they will make all the same wrong decisions if they try to use you the same way they tried to use Bellis. You deserve to make your own decisions about your body and your blood.'

Arden turned to face the window, where the salt-stumped gardens of the Manse struggled against the climate.

'You appear to be in the minority,' Arden said. 'For holding that belief.'

Fortunately, Mr Justinian's lechery was not sufficient to induce him to intrude upon a convalescent, and for a long time Arden did not have to contend with him. Besides, according to the whispering gossip of the house staff, sickness and disablement were conditions quite distasteful to the young lord of this salt-water estate.

He did not approach to claim his gratitude from Arden until she took her first steps in the delicate winter sun a few days later. She was in an empire line dress of urchin-blue cream, with her beloved krakenskin coat over the top of it, and her wobbly gait had eased enough to stand upright, unaided. One of the walled gardens provided a natural shelter from the elements, caught rays of the morning sun in that brief period before the afternoon fog came in.

She sat among the moss-covered statuary. Her strength returned in small moments. She would rub her grommets through her new gloves, and her thoughts had no purchase, turning to fog and forgotten memories, losing themselves to the chill air. A true endowment she now had, one that was powerful, but only expressed through the terms and skills of others. She herself was a cypher, without purpose of her own.

She was gifted and depleted at once. Jonah was gone. Her body was numb to his passing. He had been torn out of her, and she was hollow without him.

Time passed both slowly and fast. She'd taken some of the brighter days in the walled garden by herself. Today Mr Justinian intruded on her without apology.

'I rescued you,' he said once he had been given grudging allowance to sit beside her on the wrought-iron garden chair. 'That tugboat of Mr Riven's was floating out past the edge of the world and would have kept going had I not sent out a flotilla to search when it was discovered.'

'You have my appreciation,' she said, suspecting Mx Gertrude Modhi had actually gathered the party together not long after they'd left Vigil. A mother would not give up on her son.

'Your stormbride, your Madame Quarry. She said Mr Riven is dead?'

The rush of grief startled Arden at hearing his name aloud,

after keeping it at bay for so long. The air sucked out of her lungs. She could not take a breath. Mr Justinian took her silence as agreement.

'A shame. I know you pitied him and dallied with him. It behoves you well to lean tenderly towards the lesser among us. It is a virtue after all.'

Emboldened, he continued. 'We the nobility have our right as patriarchs of these folk to take whatever minor pleasures they can give us, but one must move on from fripperies and think seriously about the unions that will benefit us.' He sidled close. 'I have made overtures to the Eugenics Society to make an honest woman of you, so your mark of genetic shame is removed.'

His words cut through the numbness with breathless horror. 'You mean marry *you*, Vernon?'

'I have received a letter back from the Council today. An enthusiastic permission.'

Without warning, Mr Justinian was on his knees in front of her, and had snapped the top off a velvet box so she might see a big, antique diamond ring with a band scratched and thinned from all the women who had worn it before.

Arden fumed. There was audacity, and then there was just ambushed rudeness. Behind Mr Justinian's head a thin-faced statue peered out from the bushes. The stone and shadows were familiar. Alexander Justinian, the old baron. There were ghosts all around.

'Was Jonah Riven your brother, Mr Justinian?'

Mr Justinian paled. He stepped back. 'Whatever makes you think that?'

'No. Not a brother,' Arden said. 'A half-uncle, or a half-great-uncle? His mother worked in this house for your great-grandfather, Alexander Justinian, while the old man was still alive, did she not? It's not uncommon, for the lords of such estates to assault and demean those in their employ. I don't suppose there are many civilizing laws here in Fiction to protect a simple serving woman.'

Mr Justinian's eyes popped, and he made weak, mewling noises. 'My great-grandfather Alexander would nev . . .' He stopped. Started again. 'We don't entertain bastard claims here.'

Arden shook her head. 'In Clay Capital, it is genetics and the laws of eugenics, not marriage, that outline the terms of inheritance. Would be an interesting claim for a Riven to make, that the Manse is his.'

'Riven is dead!'

'Allegedly.'

Mr Justinian grabbed her arm, squeezed hard, and spittle flecked his lips. 'Don't think I can't tell that you have let the brute despoil you utterly, Arden Beacon. I know he spilled his seed inside you and that you may now carry his child.'

He was wrong, of course. She knew her own body and her monthlies had come while she lay recovering Arden tried to pull away, but he hung on with grim determination, intent on having her confess.

The moment became fraught with all the bad luck and poor decisions possible for a man to make. She was weakened from her illness. He could make it so that she never screamed again, and claim that *ichor meritis* had taken her life. Anything could happen.

Then he let her go, blushing furiously.

'I know what the Lions are capable of.'

'Yes, and they will test whatever issue comes from me. Landed titles are granted by Lyonne laws, not Fictish ones, and Lyonne inheritance is through genetics alone. If there's any dispute in ownership the legal vultures will come calling, and your title claim as Lord of the Justinian manse will become very, very weak.'

He backed away. A sneer on his lips. 'You think you have won both child and Lordship, Arden Beacon? Then I'll tell you what that thing in my father's glass jar really was. The cryptid in the study, the bell-jar you were so very much drawn to? That *thing* in the jar was the twin that exited from the Riven woman first, when she birthed your lover. Was the eight-legged monster, the snake-coils in her belly that first tumbled out of her and into the world. A monster twin coiled in the womb. That mutancy lies coiled up in your dear dead Mr. Riven, and who knows if it yet sets root and grows within *you*. Perhaps this is the real thing the Lions wished to have come about.'

Arden viewed Mr Justinian with pity, and no tenderness. Perhaps he did or did not tell the truth about the creature in the jar.

So what, if Mr Riven had been birthed with a poor, sea-creature twin? The Eugenicists of Clay Capital would have considered that a fair sacrifice for the endowment of blood. Mr Justinian had been away from Clay too long. Otherwise he'd have known that—just as the Order had decided with Bellis Harrow—it was considered better to be birthed monstrous than birthed without talent at all.

She squared her shoulders. Faced him with a gaze both limpid in its nonchalance and loathing.

'You do not scare me, Vernon. Give your mother my thanks for her hospitality, but when her duty is done to the Seamaster's Guild I will be on my way.'

37

Mr Justinian had the last word

Mr Justinian had the last word. He would not give her permission to return to her lighthouse on the edge of the Darkling Sea. Another girl took her place at the lighthouse now, a bride from the South, someone who could run a lighthouse on her until the Guild decommissioned the flame.

But Arden, of course, had not yet been given orders to leave. For now, she was effectively homeless, and without employment. Since their last conversation, Chalice had been sent back to Lyonne in disgrace in the dead of night. Without the chance to say goodbye.

In the face of her loss, the loss of Jonah, those blows were inconsequential.

A day later, the Dowager arrived in the guest house foyer as Arden was packing to leave, her hands bound up in an agitated tangle.

'A visitor for you,' she said, a thin note of fear in her announcement. This was not the same disapproving voice that she had used when Chalice had come to visit. The caller's importance was not lost upon the Lady of the Manse. 'He says it is most urgent.'

Mr Lindsay stood behind the Dowager's black-crêpe shadow,

bowler hat in one hand, briefcase in the other. His face was guileless as a child's. Arden nodded her permission. He waited until the mistress of the house was gone and the doors firmly shut before speaking.

'Such a shame you did not find her son worthy of a match,' he said. 'We could have used you in domesticating our young Coastmaster. His family name is still starred in our ledger through his great-grandfather. It was a great loss that we could not keep the bloodline strong.'

'I have no emotion for him one way or another.'

'Of course. But I'm certain he'll work on that for as long as Mx Arden Beacon lives in this house, won't he?'

'What do you want, Mr Lindsay?' Arden asked, and did not bother to hide her annoyance.

He sat upon the edge of the daybed, fingered the crochet throw as if admiring the stitch work. He found the small bust of Baron Justinian, picked it up, studied the bronze handiwork. Perhaps he mused upon the likeness between the bust and the man who had lived upon the promontory.

'Miss Quarry also tells me there was an . . . ah . . . interesting electrical phenomenon that led to your being found. The search party saw the glow in the water and naturally came to your assistance.'

'That is correct.' Arden pressed her lips together firmly before speaking. 'A glow. A sea monster glow.'

'Not something else?' He looked at her, sly and knowing. 'Not something that the Order has long hypothesized but has never seen replicated in any individual?'

She took the bust out of his hands and placed it back on the marble side table. 'Tell me why I am entertaining your presence, sir?'

A smile split his thin cheeks. 'Well, you see, after his dereliction of Magistrate duties, Mr Alasdair Harrow has been escorted to Clay City. I thought you would like to be informed.'

'You're going to kill him?'

Mr Lindsay shook his head, as if puzzled. 'For questioning,

no more. If you are wanting someone punished, that other criminal, that Sean Ironcup, will find himself collected by the Constables at the end of the month. It was him that bled you.'

'Was Mr Harrow's idea.'

'Yes it was, and we can't have Order assets be flung about to the wolves without proper advice now, can we? As much as it would have been amusing to see what his fully empowered daughter could do, I fear she would not have shown the correct restraint at finding herself so *potent*.'

'Not without Jonah strong enough to tighten the leash on your behalf.'

'We'd hoped you could have assisted in that regard.'

Arden gave him a long, venomous silence before closing the shipping trunk. 'Well, I couldn't assist. So this little exercise in deception has turned out to be a complete waste of our time.'

'On the contrary. You brought back precious information our spy had so carefully curated for years. Riven may not be able to fully leash his wife, but he can certainly keep her attention focused. With those two in union, the balance of power in that rebellious region will change. Bellis Riven will soon rule the Isles. And though she doesn't know it, Lyonne rules her. Your assistance will not be forgotten.'

She did not trust herself to speak, otherwise she would shout at him to leave. Bellis and Jonah were not in *union*, no more than a broken horse was in union to the brutal owner who wielded the whip.

She will kill him, you little fool, Mr Lindsay. Jonah has no influence over Bellis. Nobody controls a sanguis orientis, *and one day you'll find this out the worst of ways.*

She could not say it. And not saying it made her dizzy with vexation. Mr Lindsay only saw her reeling from her fierce, unspoken emotion, thought it her illness.

'My dear, you are faint. Sit, sit.'

Mr Lindsay fetched Arden a chair. She wanted to recoil from his unctuous touch.

When at last she could govern her tongue, Arden spoke through a strangled throat. 'What happens to me now?'

He made a gesture of surrender. 'Mx Beacon, I know it must have been painful to strike up a friendship with such a dreadfully lonely, long-suffering creature as Jonah Riven. To perhaps . . . come to care for him? And we are not oblivious to what sort of woman Bellis has become. How it must have affected you, to meet her. I can only offer apologies that we could not supply you all the reasons, and give this humble restitution.'

He clipped open the brass hinges of the business satchel, and brought out an oxblood leather diploma roll. A golden tassel swung on the end.

He held the diploma roll out to her.

'Take it.'

She frowned. She had seen such a thing in her father's study, behind glass. The most precious thing he owned. All his status and his professional standing, bound up in whale vellum and a Guild seal stamped in wax.

'What is that?'

'Sanguine Order, Fourth Degree,' he continued. 'Master of Light. Higher than Portmaster, even. Higher than your father could ever hope to attain. You can return to Lyonne, join a lodge and after initiation receive the colours of your Guild Order. You will be Maria of the Unquenched Flame.'

The tassel swung, the golden glints catching the sunlight through the high windows. She shook her head, appalled at the offer. 'Mr Lindsay, a false membership to the associate order is one thing, but if I took that, it would make a *lie* of what the degree represented. I am not so powerful.'

Mr Lindsay came close. With his short stature, he was eye to eye with her as she sat in the chair. His voice was little more than a whisper.

'You and I both know that it is no *lie*, Arden Beacon. You are to return to the city with full honours. No cramped night train for our newest Guildmistress. You will put this time behind you. You shall live in Clay Capital in luxury for the rest of your life and your family's honour will be restored. Your father may regain his status in the Eugenics ledger, the very thing he lost when your *ignis* talent presented so . . . poorly.'

Mr Lindsay's eyes glittered like the tassel. He knew what she was capable of. No stories of quenching fires or sudden salty sanguinities for him. She had been brought to Vigil for a reason, and that reason was bordered on all four sides by Bellis Harrow.

Arden instinctively wrapped her hands over her grommets as he spoke, his words tying her up in chains of honour and filial piety.

'The Coastmaster Justinian still holds *my* leash,' she said. 'Despite your Lion friends and all the laws of Lyonne, that office is still his and he won't let me go so easily. There is no Master of Blood to replace a lighthouse keeper.'

'Perhaps there will be. No doubt you have heard of the test-moot slated for Garfish Point at this month's end, ten days from now. Those charged with tracing the genetics of Fiction say that a *sanguis ignis* is long overdue.'

'You cannot be certain.'

'Mx Beacon, when it comes to sanguinities, we are *always* certain.'

He paused, and smiled, as louche and conniving as ever. 'Oh, and before I forget. Something else for you.'

Mr Lindsay took from his pocket a thin rice paper envelope. Arden's name on the front, in a hand whose familiarity stabbed her with a hot spike of surprise. The wax seal was of the Airshipman's Guild. The postmark was Frieslandish.

'Since you are a guildswoman in full, you may make your own decisions about with whom you may consort. Perhaps even a certain Richard Castile. In fact, he was advised of your new position a week ago, and immediately made his way to Clay Capital.'

'Richard's in Clay?'

Mr Lindsay nodded. 'He composed a letter to you, which I now have pride in delivering. Take it.' He shook his offering as one might try to convince a shy bird to the snare. 'Go on.'

Arden took the envelope. It felt dry and brittle under her fingertips, the way of a newspaper left too long in the sun.

'He misses you, and seeks a reconnection,' Mr Lindsay said with affectionate magnanimity. 'You can reunite with your first love, now. Come. You have *earned* this.'

When it became clear that she would not open the letter in front of him and satisfy his curiosity about the letter's contents – contents he perhaps had a hand in dictating himself – Mr Lindsay shrugged, and touched the brim of his hat.

'Whenever you are ready, then. We will meet again, one week from now, Guildswoman. Remember me on your wedding day.'

The document roll might as well have been dipped in blood. The envelope mocked her with deceit. Richard Castile had not written to her since his departure of the last winter. Would not be writing letters to her *now* unless he'd been forced to do so.

As soon as Mr Lindsay was gone she screwed both desecrated objects up in her hands and shoved them into the deepest recesses of her coat pocket.

38

She could not bear to stay

She could not bear to stay in the guest house. Arden rented some rooms above Mr and Mrs Sage's shop, an apartment that was small but clean. Word had crept out, as all gossip did, that Arden Beacon had suffered trauma at the hands of Mr Riven. Something that had rendered her close to mute and perhaps had put to rest any chances of matrimonial happiness with the handsome young Baron who had once courted her.

Tall tales whispered lasciviously, just as they had done with Bellis.

Mrs Sage, her warnings vindicated, spent the first day fussing about Arden. She was charitable in her pity. Was not Arden's fault she had been harmed so, merely that of the men that had put her upon a rocky promontory with a fiend so close by. Besides, Mr Riven was gone now, no chance of him returning to wreak more damage. She took Arden's silence both as an after-effect of her ordeal and shame that she had not listened to Mrs Sage when they had met all those weeks before.

Arden could not be bothered changing the Vigil woman's mind. What a far more delightful story for a Fictioner to tell, of the ignorant Lyonne guildswoman who had wandered into a monster's lair.

Her life had begun to throw up its walls. The lid was about to close upon her freedom. Mr Lindsay inquired with her every afternoon. If she had dallied with the idea of staying in Vigil, waiting in case Jonah managed to get away from Bellis' clutches and return.

Each day was one more where he did not.

But *Saudade* did return.

She was battered by abandonment and weeks in the Tempest, her central axle broken beyond repair. A fisherman towed her in for the price of a whiskey fifth. As Harbourmistress, Mx Modhi had jurisdiction over who managed the promontory assets while Mr Riven was absent. Some previous instruction of Mr Riven's had granted the craft to David on his death, but since Mr Riven was not confirmed dead, she gave the boat to Arden.

'The salvage is yours to deal with, for now,' Mx Modhi said bitterly on the morning she passed the boat along. 'I don't want my child anywhere near that cursed vessel.'

'It *belongs* to your son, though.'

'Oh? Only upon Riven's confirmed death, and who knows in what form that monster might come back.'

They both knew. There would be nothing left of Mr Riven left to come back, nothing save what Bellis wanted to preserve. If anything, the petrochemical Queen would keep Jonah alive to punish Arden, so that even over the greatest distance she would remember.

Someone suffers in your stead.

Arden walked through the black mangrove boat with her heart in her mouth, bleeding memories. Jonah had had a soldier-prisoner's neatness and austerity about him, all items of necessity stacked and stored with rigid military precision. Being alone in the ship had an intimacy she doubted he would have been comfortable with, were he still here.

Apart from the external damage, Mr Riven had secured

366

everything well from the storm. Perhaps some glassware fallen across the map-room floor, doors flung open. There was little evidence of heavy seas.

Then she came to his cabin.

She only meant to glance inside, but the pull was too much. She stumbled inside and lay face-down upon his narrow bed, still rumpled from their lovemaking and blotted with the blood spots from the injuries he took to save her life. She did not cry, only allowed herself the fall into a deep, terrible abyss.

The lightless reality of Jonah's loss bore upon her with all the horror of being smothered, and when her third and fourth breaths did not come, she had to tear herself from the room and run to the deck, and dry-retch. *Someone suffers in your stead. Forever, until the end of your days.*

She had no life to go back to, only deceptions, only Mr Richard Castile compelled by Lions – by blackmail no doubt – to be the prize for their new *sanguis evalescendi*. The brief hope she'd shared with Jonah – to be free, to love without chains – had risen and died within the span of a day. Now she was wounded and could not heal.

The crisis only passed when she caught herself, for David and Sean Ironcup were on the newly restored harbour with a third man she did not know.

'Excuse me, Mx Beacon. I hope we weren't interrupting.' The man spoke up, taking off his fisherman's hat and wringing it in his big hands. He wore a huge felted coat of black wool, with epaulets winking silver, and a waistcoat of old Lyonne fashion. Across his chest he wore a sash of a minor craft Guild.

Arden wiped her mouth with the back of her sleeve and resumed her composure. 'I'm sorry. You had me in a moment of weakness.' She stood up tall and took deep breaths before joining them on the floating dock. 'It's been a great trial, you see, to lose a friend.'

'We could return later,' the stranger said politely. 'If that would best enable our conversation.'

'No, get on with it,' Arden replied. 'State your business.'

He stepped forward and shook her hand. 'I am Mr Zander Fulsome. I understand you have both a boat in need of repair and cryptozoological trophies. I was hoping we could come to an arrangement in terms of sale and trade.'

Would not have just been Arden to notice the kraken oil containers were all mostly full, and the cured krakenskin segments, as sweet-smelling as crocus stems, were laid out ready for the sale that Mr Riven had planned. David Modhi had seen them with a trader's eye, and known exactly where to procure a buyer.

'David Modhi, your mother was quite adamant,' she said to him warily. 'You can't have this boat.'

David stood tall. 'My mother might have forbidden *me* to do anything with *Saudade*, but that caveat does not extend to you.'

Mr Fulsome continued, 'For the krakenskin I could install a new axle upon your craft. I am the best boat merchant in all of Morningvale, and I can supply addresses of commendation, here and in the entire Fiction region.'

David was practically hopping out of his skin by Mr Fulsom's side. Arden did not have the heart to deny him.

'Sounds like it's a fair trade,' she said, wrapping herself back up with her Lyonne sanguine aloofness. It was not at all a fair trade. She could have purchased another boat for the hide. Two boats even, sleek and fast. Maybe a small balloon-craft. She added, if only for her guilty benefit, 'Mr Riven would wish *Saudade* fixed.'

A date was agreed upon. Two full days, and a team of men who could do in those hours what would take a regular ship-wright a month. Pleased, the boat-builder Zander Fulsome went on his way.

At a nod from David, Sean followed Mr Fulsome to complete the terms of business.

Arden prepared to walk back to her apartment, and found the young man following her at a close distance.

'So then,' Arden said. 'Out with it. I know you have a vested interest in seeing *Saudade* fixed soon and made the worst bargain in doing it.'

'There is a Eugenics Society testmoot in Garfish Point coming.'

Arden nodded, and remembered Mr Lindsay's confident words. He knew the sanguinem that would replace her.

'There is. Though if you had the slightest sense, David, you would keep your distance from anything to do with them.'

Her advice might have been stolen away by the wind. He pulled out some Fiction coins from a fish-bladder purse.

'Please take me there. In *Saudade*.'

'Oh, put them away, David. My employers won't let me leave this town until they come calling. Besides, would you not want to stay with Sean in these last days? He has not long yet before the Lyonne Constables come calling for him too. I can see you've formed quite a friendship.'

'He can come with us. Mx Beacon, I studied Lyonne law. If he stays on a Vigil-registered boat, he is still in Vigil. On a technicality.'

'Technicalities are not law, David.'

'You could technically still be in Vigil, too.'

She met his hopeful eyes and felt a small rebellion stir in her heart.

'Then I suppose . . . Well. I suppose I could make it up and back to Garfish Point. A newly repaired boat does need settling in.'

39

So, to the testmoot

So, to the testmoot, one last trip on *Saudade*.

Along with David Modhi and Sean, *Saudade* beat a fast course along the inner transit stream to Garfish Point, that busy promontory at Fiction's almost-civilized northern shore. From there, it would be less than six hours to Morningvale, and south Lyonne.

And home.

So strange to think of Lyonne as home, Arden thought, as she looked out over the choppy waters beyond the black boat's bow. She had changed so much. Would her friends even recognize her, after their long lazy summers on cool alpine meadows, a woman carved raw by the sea?

Every time Arden was in danger of feeling gladness at her upcoming return, the undertow of regret and guilt would come to pull her back in. She would go home having left pain and destruction in her wake. Not even the sight of small silver porpoises for much of the journey, and the wheeling gulls, drawn by the stirring of fish shoals, could lighten her mood. There was a Deepwater winter coming, she could smell the strange chill in the air.

Mr Castile's letter stayed in her pocket like a killer's confession. Try as she might, the thought of reading the contents only made her tip into a greater despair. She feared the effect the words would have on her. Feared falling in love again, a diminished, rotten kind of love, decayed by betrayal and time. A love belittled by what she'd felt with Jonah.

She did not want to see Mr Castile. She knew that now. Anything she'd felt for him was gone, leaving only an ugly lesion of experience.

Devilments, she fretted. *There is nothing I want less than to be loved under instruction.*

Garfish Point lay ahead of them, Fiction's largest town. The sails and shadows of a thousand crafts chequered the port waters.

'Is that the Order's boat out there?' David called from the wheelhouse, holding out the spyglass. 'It has a rose upon its sails.'

She needed no instrument. She had already caught the unmistakable silhouette of a Clay-class clipper against the orange of the sinking sun. 'Yes. They will have seen me leave. Doubtless the Order will collect me as I reach the shore, and take me to Lyonne. Hang on, David, I'll have the wheel now.'

He offered to stay on the wheel, having more experience at navigating the Point's demanding harbour. She shook her head.

'I'd rather make them come aboard and take me. One must strike a certain difficult tone of rebellion for the rest of my golden incarceration.'

But David Modhi, normally so tractable, made a face and would not relinquish his position. He appeared to have aged in these last few weeks. A man's face was upon him, not a boy's.

'I want to take the wheel,' he said again.

She let it go, and peered at him. 'What's wrong?'

'I've been talking with Sean Ironcup.'

'Yes, among the other things you two have been doing,' she said with a regretful exhale. She knew a burgeoning romance when she saw one. With Jonah gone, his grieving eye had settled on the next best thing. 'He's a good lad after all. He has a great affection for you, I can see that much. It will be difficult when he must leave. Perhaps the Order will be lenient in his sentencing. Mr Harrow was the true sinner.'

Her words didn't make David nod in agreement. Instead, he jutted out his lower jaw with an odd stubbornness.

'Lightmistress, if I were to test positive this time around—'

'It's very unlikely, David. This final test is merely ceremonial. They already know who their sanguinem is.'

'But if I was, I would have to leave Sean and go to Clay Capital. I will go into seclusion. We might lose each other.'

She shrugged. 'Let's cross that bridge when we come to it. This time tomorrow, the pair of you will be steaming back to Vigil.'

And I will be locked in a cabin with iron on my wrists.

So preoccupied was she with her fate, it took her several seconds before she became aware of the light in the wheelhouse. 'Devils, David, cover that lantern—'

She stopped. That was no light from one of the oil lamps. David Modhi clutched a coldfire lantern, one of the little storm-lights Jorgen had kept in the lighthouse – a miniature version of the lighthouse flame, kept for emergencies. The flame burned without heat. David's face was split by tear tracks in the bright yellow glow. His hand was bleeding.

With a gasp she struck the light out of his grip. The lantern smashed. They were plunged back into a colourless dusk.

'You tested *yourself*?'

'Yes, I know it's forbidden,' he said. 'No need to scold me. But I wanted to see for myself because I *knew*. I knew what I was. And last year, this happened.' He picked up the lantern. 'Mr Riven said I'd probably expressed the trait earlier. I don't know why I wasn't told.'

'The Eugenics Society is careful with Fiction bloodlines,' Arden said, feeling a cold sense of purpose growing in her. 'They know what might come out of such wild genes.'

Bellis. Jonah.

'I didn't come for the test,' David said. 'I came to get us away.'

In the harbour beyond, the clipper unfurled its sails. The Order boat had seen them. The mainsail was the last to hoist itself up. There would be an engine on board the ship as well, something fast, maybe.

She pressed her hands against the wheel spokes. 'David, this is not a choice. You have to go to the test and on to Lyonne. You can't have wild *ignis* endowments. The Order wouldn't let you.' Her breath escaped her as she saw the ship prepare to give chase. 'They won't let you live.'

Arden thought of Bellis, allowed to stay. *Unless they want to use you.*

'I don't want to lose Sean. I want to choose who I love. So drop us in the ocean here. It cannot be more than a mile to shore. We'll find our own way. Find somewhere to go. Just . . . don't tell the Order.'

Their conversation wasn't unwatched. Sean Ironcup stood on the deck with the replacement crutches David had painstakingly carved for him, his face marbled in hope and dread. She understood how David and Sean must have discussed a life on the run. Understood that they had already made up their minds what they were going to do.

All this had happened while she had been too busy with her own preoccupations to notice.

'Once upon a time,' she said, 'I dreamt of such a thing. Running away.'

'What happened?' David asked, knowing instinctively that her answer was wrapped up in her decision from this point forward.

She cut the throttle to the engines. A cloud of blue-sparkling kraken-oil smoke wafted over the forecastle. She pulled out Mr Castile's letter. Brandished it like a warrant of judgment.

'The one I loved was too scared to go through with it. That's what happened. And so our love withered like a flame unfed. But I shall not hold him to an old promise. His life is his own, just the same as mine.'

With a flourish she ripped up the envelope and tossed it out of the side window. *Goodbye, Richard Castile*, she thought. You were a young girl's fleeting lesson, but now lessons are over.

David blinked, as it dawned on him what Arden intended to do. She throttled forward on one wheel. *Saudade* started to turn.

'You're not letting us off here?'

'I'm taking you somewhere the Order can't touch you,' Arden said. 'And I'm going to set things right. I'm either going to rescue a man, or pay homage to a dead one, but whatever I do, the decision is mine. Are you coming with me?'

A huge grin spread across David's face. 'Certainly am, Lightmistress!'

The clipper was in full sail now, but against the current, the waters were far too quick for the large ceremonial ship to reach full speed. Within minutes of turning, *Saudade* had lost their three-mast pursuer. The kraken oil bloomed blue from the smokestacks, and Arden's coat shone in the half-light of the wheelhouse. One could fancy she had taken on the luminescence of the beast herself.

David Modhi went to tell Sean the development, and they embraced upon the forecastle in between bobs and heaves. Well then, she thought. The Order had certainly chosen her well. Wasn't she primed by experience to help lovers find one another? To increase a flame, a fire, a rebellion?

And now she was on her own journey, something not proscribed or ordered or necessary. Nobody pulled her invisible strings.

I'll find you, Jonah.

Maybe she would. Maybe she would not. Maybe Bellis had eviscerated him and replaced him with cogs and machine parts, like they did with the lich-ships on their eternal sea-road. Maybe he believed Arden had forgotten her fisherman from Vigil, thought her returned home with her old lover. But still. She would look. If he was alive she would find him, and if Bellis had transformed him into either corpse or monster, she would remember him in the Deepwater midwinter, and say a prayer so he might enter the cathedral of the King.

I'll find you.

The sun set upon the eastern horizon and the indigo sky spilled with stars. She still felt him: in her blood, and in the hide of the monster's skin she wore, and in the vast, lightless depths of the sea.

Fin

Acknowledgements

A million thank-yous to the usual suspects: my agent Sam Morgan, my editor Vicky Leech, to my family for putting up with all this, particularly Mum and Dad, Linda and Kerry and especially Eric and Xavier. Thanks to all those patient coffee-shop and café staff who kept me hydrated during the entire process.

Shout-out to my friends online, at work and in real life, both the Liminal and Clarion South crews, Axe Creekers, assorted drongos, my Nemesis, the Good Locust and Papa Bear.

And to Paul Haines, never forgotten.